DEADFALL

DEADFALL

Kate Sawyer Medical Thriller Book Two

DEBORAH COONTS

Published by Chestnut Street Press

eBook ISBN: 978-1-944831-08-0
Paperback ISBN: 978-1-944831-09-7
Hardcover ISBN: 978-1-944831-10-3

Cover design by Streetlight Graphics
(www.streetlightgraphics.com)

Formatting by Kate Tilton's Author Services, LLC
(www.katetilton.com)

CHAPTER ONE

I KILLED IT.

Dr. Rita Davenport tilted her head and opened her mouth to catch the raindrops. Spring had hit London with a lion's roar. Twirling in circles, she laughed at the weather gods—just like them to rain on her parade. Well, not her parade alone—the whole team back in Oregon deserved the credit.

What a day!

A bit dizzy, she stopped. Pressing a hand to her temple, she bent over slightly and waited for her world to steady. Joy burbled through her, welling from an emotional hot spring.

But underneath, there was something else, *someone* else, dark and...hungry.

She could hear it, whispering, calling to her.

A flush of fear. She bolted upright, her gaze lasered into the shadows.

Nobody there.

There's nobody there, Rita. Get hold of yourself. You've had a long day.

Little food, even less sleep, amped on adrenaline, riding a high, Rita told herself. The hotel first, then the airport, then the luxury of a business-class ride home. A glass or three of Champagne, a Xanax and she'd be fine.

But worry niggled at her. She clutched her umbrella to her chest, then adjusted her briefcase, which hung on a strap across her back. She didn't think to open the umbrella against the rain. She was cold, so very cold. A shiver racked through her rattling her teeth.

A sinister whisper, louder now. *"Run."*

She whirled around, scanning the darkness. Danger lurked in the shadows.

A familiar fear, it oozed through the web of her mind jumbling thoughts, fracturing logic. Panic seized her, stealing breath.

Think, Rita. Think!

Swallowing hard, she still clutched her umbrella—a tether to the real, a defense against the unreal. A game she'd used in the past —hold something tangible...something of this world, of life.

She pushed at the wet strands of hair sticking to her cheeks and forced herself away from the fear. Another shiver. Her teeth chattered. What had she done with her overcoat?

Where was she? Struggling to regain her focus, she shielded her eyes against the rain and cataloged her surroundings. A wet street. Streetlamps. Tudor buildings, most not more than two stories, lined both sides of the road. On the ground floor, the shops stood dark, the light having moved to the apartments above. Darkness surrounded her with dread.

Headlights coming at her on the wrong side of the street. A klaxon horn. She leaped back, stumbling on the curb, then catching herself.

Light streamed through the windows of the pub down the street. Distant voices, happy, raised in a struggle to be heard over the music. A guitar and a plaintive horn, then a lovely, fresh voice, strong, alive...real.

Had she come from there? She couldn't remember. Squinting into the night, she struggled to read the sign under the weak bulb above it.

The Whistle and Goose? Yes, that's where she'd been, where Logan and her colleagues celebrated. The light called her back.

The voices didn't speak when she was in the light. And it would be warm there.

She took a few halting steps in that direction when a voice stopped her, this one louder than the voices that followed her and hid from the light.

"Rita! There you are. Wait up." A warm baritone that agitated her.

She worked to pull up a name. Dr. Evans Hunt. That was it. He hurried to join her, the tails of his open tweed jacket flapping behind him. His stomach strained against his shirt. Spots of rain peppered his khakis.

Arriving red-faced in front of her, a smile splitting his face, he seemed unmindful of the weather, the darkness pressing close, the voices calling. "How's the party?" He lifted his chin toward the pub. He towered above her.

She followed his gaze. The light no longer beckoned, its brightness suffocated by fingers of fog, poking, prodding, searching, enveloping.

"I...I don't know." She chewed on a lip and fought the urge to run.

"That good, huh?" Dr. Hunt raised an eyebrow, and his smile widened as he self-consciously ran a hand through his thick shock of still-brown hair, making the tangle worse. "I must look like..."

"A man running through the rain and the darkness." Like the tendrils of fog, fear slipped through her defenses. Rita felt the falseness of her attempt at a smile. She rubbed her arms against the cold, but it had burrowed deep.

Dr. Hunt didn't seem to notice. "I'm sorry I'm late. A couple of our colleagues from New Zealand cornered me in the bar. You know David Thorne?" He didn't wait for her nod. "A brilliant geneticist, but he has a fondness for the grape if you know what I mean. And an awe-inspiring tolerance. I couldn't keep up, knew that going in—the wisdom and limitations of age—so I didn't even try."

Evans's enthusiasm would've been infectious if Rita hadn't been so cold. So scared. Something hunted in the darkness pressing in around her, blocking the light. Its hot breath brushed the back of her neck and she shivered. "What do you want?"

"*You,*" the voices whispered.

"What?" Evans's face swam back into view. "Want?" he repeated as he shrugged, never losing his smile. "Nothing more than normal." He brayed a self-deprecating laugh. "You already gave me most of it. The conference! You were brilliant. Well done."

A hint of light rode in on his laughter, pushing back the darkness. The voices muttered then retreated.

The conference. Our paper! Of course!

"Say, why aren't you using your umbrella?" Evans's words tumbled on a wave of enthusiasm as he covered her under the protection of his, not that it was much defense from the looks of him. "You're soaked. And you're freezing." He shrugged out of his jacket and wrapped it around her shoulders.

She stood straight, letting her arms fall to her sides, still gripping the handle of the umbrella as if keeping a sword at the ready. "It went well? The conference?"

In his excitement, Evans ran past the hint of a question in her voice. "You had them hanging on every word, my dear. No discord! No argument. Unheard of in the annals of Alzheimer's research. Especially for a first paper and a novel approach that might put most of them out of business. We trod on a few toes today, but they couldn't deny our work. A huge win, Rita—you should be ecstatic. Now the last phase of funding should be assured. We can move forward. We have a chance to offer very real hope where there is none."

"They know?" Rita's voice was a hoarse whisper.

"*Of course they know.*" *The voices echoed her fear.* "*Run, Rita. Run before they take it all.*"

Dr. Hunt's smile went limp; confusion clouded the joy. "Of course they know. That's the point. We depend on our network of specialists. You told them! Boy did you ever!"

Rita felt her control unraveling. *They'd take it all.* "The more they know, the more they can do to stop us."

Evans pursed his lips as he finally sobered. "Why would you think that?"

She knew what they wanted, what the voices told her. They wanted to take her research, to shut down the project. "They're pretending to want to help."

"Do you have proof of that?" Evans's voice turned serious. The world of pharmaceutical research was dog-eat-dog, staying ahead of the pack, outsmarting them if need be, the only path to survival. And sometimes putting your work out there was the only way to claim it.

"We're talking about huge sums of money, Evans. Money ruins everything."

"He wants the money, then he'll take it all."

"Money as the root of all evil, is that it?" Evans' happiness fled, anger replacing it. This was old territory for the two of them. "Let it go, Rita."

"If you're going to quote the bible at least get it right," Rita snapped. For a moment she felt like her old self again. The familiar argument galvanized her. She peeled off his jacket and thrust it back at him.

"The love of money, I know." His smile faded; the look in his eyes hardened. He took the jacket without argument. "Rita, you're brilliant, but you're a pain in the ass. This is how it works. Results cost money."

"Ah, the great altruist worrying over money. Is that all I am to you, Evans? Money?"

"Of course. Without money we can't find a cure."

Although she expected it, she staggered back as if slapped.

"He's using you," the voices whispered. *"He's one of them. He'll take it all."*

"What about the funding?" He seemed oblivious to the dagger he'd buried.

"Money. You see. Everything comes down to money."

The argument surrounded her with the familiarity and comfort of an old sweatshirt, bringing her back to herself, to this man—her boss, her nemesis, sadly nothing more. "Evans, you know they'll try. They have to. Their economic lives are at stake. We may have this round of funding in place; I'm not sure. It hinges on how well our paper was received."

"It couldn't have gone better. That's what I've been trying to tell you. Your money people will be thrilled." Evans' smile broke through again.

To be so focused. Rita struggled to hold on as her thoughts threatened to scatter. The voices grew louder now.

"Run. Now!"

She pressed the heel of her hand to her temple as she glanced back at the light from the pub, barely a glow now, shrouded and white-cold.

"They're waiting for you there. They know what you have."

She shook her head. "Quiet!"

"I didn't say anything." Evans's voice held a hint of concern. "Rita, what's the matter?"

She shrugged away from his outstretched hand. "Nothing. It's nothing." She pushed back at the fear and the voices. "My money people want an interest in future profits. This is the last round of philanthropic investment they will do." Rita released her temple and held up her hand, silencing the rebuttal. "Evans, you know this." Darkness feathered the fringes of her reality, the aperture of light closing. Her hand shook, and she examined it with the same cool objectivity that she would a foreign object.

"They get a tax benefit." Exasperation crumpled Evans and he looked like the Ph.D. he was—although he did have an Indiana Jones side to him. But Evans Hunt searched the world for botanical cures rather than holy relics.

"It's not enough." She stuffed the offending hand in a pocket. The mumble of voices grew louder, buzzing in her ears.

"It'll have to be." Evans bit down on the snap in his voice. "We're doctors. We are not looking to make a financial killing off human suffering." With a pocket square, he dabbed at his nose, then gave up and blew. "Damned cold. Came on all of a sudden." He tilted the umbrella so he could see from under it and raised his gaze to the heavens. "This weather. April in London. It's a wonder we don't all have walking pneumonia." He sneezed, then wiped his nose on the damp rag he'd tugged from a pocket. After stuffing it back, he reached for her elbow. "Come, let's get inside. We should join the party."

She shrugged away from him. "Don't be stupid; it's always about money. The money to fund the research, to get things done, to cure them, to save them, to buy a private jet and a house in the Hamptons. Suffering is quantified every day. No one will do it without a profit."

Evans gave a mirthless laugh. An angry red claimed his cheeks. "Jesus, Rita, you're even more cynical than usual. What's the matter with you?"

She shivered as a chill raced through her. The rain increased. The pop of the raindrops off the taut fabric of the umbrella sounded like distant gunfire. Evans had never liked her. She saw that now. His contempt lurked in the sly, tight grin, the hint of superiority in the tilt of his jaw.

Money. It gave life and, in return, exacted a slow death.

The chant of the voices grew louder. *Run, Rita. Run. Bad men.* She backed away from Evans. With the rain pelting her, she raised her face and asked him, "Do you hear them?"

Finally, he focused, his brows snapping into a frown. "Hear who?" He reached for her. "Say, are you okay?"

"You don't hear them?"

Run! Now!

She backed away. Hurried little steps.

Evans followed. "Rita. What's the matter?"

She turned and ran.

Evans' voice trailed after her. "Rita! Stop!"

"They want it all. They'll destroy you. Run!"

A wild fear surged through her. She was powerless against it. The voices, the fear consumed her.

Putting her head down, she raced through the rain. Her ankle turned on an uneven cobblestone. She yelped, then kicked off her heels and ran.

Finally, gasping for breath, she slowed. Drenched, wild with worry, she fought for air in ragged gasps. Darkness smothered her. And something evil lurked inside—a hand reaching up to pull her into the darkness.

Light, she needed light.

She pulled her briefcase around to cover her chest like a shield. They couldn't take her work...the team's work.... Nobody wanted it, not really, not in the way all the others thought. It was too simple, too easy. Too inexpensive. No, they didn't want it; they just didn't want the world to have it.

He would protect it. He'd promised.

The sound of her heart pounding drowned out the voices and calm leaked in between the beating rush of blood.

It was late. The streets foreign and unfamiliar, almost empty. The stores closed. The homes above hidden. Light from within an eerie glow that framed the shutters holding it in.

Safety there. An odd thought, Rita shook it off.

Where am I?

The rain wormed inside her collar like a snake seeking warmth.

She could hear a voice calling for her.

A man, head down, hurried toward her. Rita took an involuntary step to the side, hoping the darkness would hide her.

The man looked up, startled to find her standing there.

"Are you one of them?" Rita whispered. She held the collar of her raincoat together at her throat.

Taking in her bedraggled state, he paused. "No." He gave her another look, taking in her nice clothes, her computer bag, the expensive purse.

"You're not one of them?" Rita glared into the darkness over the man's shoulder. "I can hear them."

"Who?" He followed her gaze. "There's no one there." The man took her arm. "We both need to get out of the rain. Let me help you."

Rita jerked her elbow free. "Here." She thrust her unopened umbrella into his chest like a weapon. "I need to go."

Another quick glance over his shoulder. "There's no one there."

Rita gave a weak smile, but the voices grew louder.

"Don't trust him."

She staggered a little bit. "Can you hear that?"

"What?"

"Never mind."

"Run. You can't trust him."

Rita rubbed her arms. She was cold, so very cold. The fog of darkness blotted out her light. Something evil. No...*someone* evil. The man in front of her—his face blurred, his features shifting, cruelty twisting his mouth.

She gasped, raising her arms, a flesh-and-bone shield, as she backed away.

As quickly as his face had shifted, it returned to normal.

Rita blinked and staggered again—her world tilting, then righting like the dizziness after a carnival ride. Pulling in a deep breath, she marshaled strength and shook away the haunting. *What's the matter with you?*

"I've got to go." She turned and ran, seeking the cover of darkness.

When she glanced back, he was gone. And she was alone. But the feeling, the cold, the worry, wouldn't leave her. *There's no one there.*

Voices whispered in the dark, taunting her.

The breeze had picked up, a herald rushing in front of the intensifying storm. Rita laughed at her fears. *It's only the wind.*

But the voices shouted her down.

She twirled again, her briefcase in one hand clearing an arc around her. The rain trickled into her eyes, filming her vision—she didn't care. She couldn't see them, but she knew they were there.

They were after her. Like wolves circling a lone fawn, they remained hidden, waiting.

Home. Portland. I want to go home.

Rita worked for her thoughts, but they skittered into the darkness, rats running from the light. Dark thoughts nipped at the edges.

They'll try to take this away.

Fear choked her gasp. Shivering now, the cold serpent of fear curled in the pit of her stomach.

Enemies. They'd do anything to stop her.

Footsteps behind her. She gasped as her heart leaped.

A glance as she ran.

No one.

Only darkness.

The welcoming sign for the Underground shone like a beacon, calling her. She'd be safe there in the light, away from the darkness.

She batted at ghostly hands squeezing her throat.

Tugging at the scarf wound around her neck, she pulled it loose, then let it trail through her fingers onto the wet pavement as she ran.

Another glance behind. No one.

But she knew they were there. She could feel them. Hear them.

She fled, her briefcase a shield clutched tight.

Down the stairs. Over the turnstile.

When she saw the light, she leaped toward it.

CHAPTER TWO

Closing my eyes, I worked through my mental exercises, if only to prove to myself I was still here. *Who are you? Kate Sawyer. Where do you live? Portland, Oregon. What did you do? Cop. What do you do now? Survive.*

Satisfied, after a deep breath, I opened my eyes to orient myself in today's reality. Each morning, I never knew what would be there and what would be gone.

My place. My bedroom. My man. I recognized it all. Today was a good day.

Beck had slept over. It wasn't the first time for us, but it was still new enough to feel...I reached for the words but couldn't find them.

Words weren't my best thing—they got lost in the tangles and plaques in my head. At least that's what Logan told me. The whole exercise pissed me off, and then the anger made the memory loss worse.

The vicious cycle of my life.

Of course, it had to be the words I lost and not the anger.

Anger. The gun. The shot. The blood.

The memory came out of nowhere to sucker punch me.

Without thought, acting in blind anger, I'd grabbed the gun, lifted it, and squeezed the trigger. He'd been my rock. He'd died. He'd deserved to die. But why had life picked me to deliver the fatal shot?

That memory, seared into the tattered flesh of my brain, tormented me daily.

I'd been right. But I'd also been wrong.

No more guns. Not ever.

Suddenly, I was so cold.

With my back to Beck, I moved until I pressed up against him, absorbing his warmth. Summer temps hadn't yet pegged seventy and a numbing chill hung in the fog still thick in the weak early morning light. I'd left the balcony door open, not sure why.

Maybe I needed a way out.

Of course, being twenty floors up would make escape a bit complicated. Funny the things a mind processed and the things it forgot.

Escape.

My life was complicated enough without Beck in it. But he felt good...right. I wasn't sure it was good for either of us. He disagreed.

Most days, Alzheimer's was all the challenge I could handle.

The stem cells helped. My brother had donated them.

A memory ripped through me. Not one of mine. My brother's...Hank's. I could feel his pain; the cold as death closed in. He hadn't been afraid.

Having Hank in my head was a downside to the therapy—his memories had ridden in on his stem cells. I'd learned to control the memories...most of the time. Controlling the disease proved more elusive.

At least for today, I was still me. That was something.

Beck spooned around me, curling an arm to hold me tight against him. "What are you thinking?" His voice was hoarse with sleep.

"Not me. Hank..." I trailed off. His death still haunted me, probably always would.

I'd killed him, too...in a way.

Beck disagreed, but my opinion was the only one that mattered.

I'd learned to live with Hank in my head; I'd learn to live with the guilt.

"Don't." Beck's voice held an edge. He couldn't fix this, and as a cop and as a man, he didn't like problems he couldn't fix.

"Hank's last thought was of me," I whispered, giving voice to the horror I would always hear. What he felt when he died, that was the worst.

They'd harvested more stem cells after he'd died. Logan hadn't told me, even though he knew the memories would come with the cells. It had been that or quit the therapy, and to Logan, that wasn't a choice—so he hadn't given me one.

I was still pissed. Forgiveness wasn't one of my better qualities.

Beck pulled me tighter. "You only hear him when you're afraid."

I shifted away from the truth and ran into the iron band of his arm.

"The clinical trial? It's bothering you?" Concern graveled his voice.

"How did you know I was awake?"

"Your breathing changes." He twirled a finger in one of my wayward curls.

I hadn't cut my hair since Hank died. Not sure why. I was used to the blonde, but the curls were new.

And a man playing with them, newer still. I liked the smell of him, something masculine and musky, safe. "You listen to me while I'm asleep?" That sounded like an invasion. I knew he didn't sleep often or well, haunted by memories of past actions he couldn't erase or fix and a daughter who was lost. I knew the drill...sometimes. Other times, when the memories were as thin as gossamer, I welcomed the not remembering and the sweet anesthesia of sleep.

Bad things hid in my past.

"You watch me when you can't sleep," he countered.

And we made desperate, angry love when we both couldn't sleep.

"Don't avoid my question." He looked like he knew what I was thinking.

"I don't like questions." Most likely because I feared not having the answer. He knew that, or I thought he did, so I didn't give power to the fear by voicing it. "Questions make a conversation feel like an interrogation."

"Interrogation? One question and you think you're being grilled." A soft laugh gurgled from deep in his chest.

I snuggled back until soft flesh met hard. "This time, I know what's coming."

His struggle for control, to not indulge his physical need, vibrated through him. Guess he really did want to talk. "This is serious, Kate. I want to be here for you, help you. You're not so great at letting me in."

"Trust issues run in my family." I tensed at a memory, a pain. *Hank?* But no, not his. This one was mine. Beck's arm pulled me tighter.

I didn't like being held. But knowing he liked to do the holding, I let him. "Detective, you do know my being with you is a charity thing, right?" Beck was short for Detective Hudson Beck of the Portland Police Department and, truth be told, him being with me was the charity thing, not the other way around.

Beck nuzzled my neck. "I love being the beneficiary of your philanthropic largesse."

I struggled for the definition of *largesse*. Not there. Didn't matter. Not now, but it would irritate me later...if I remembered. And I remembered more and more each day.

"The next phase of the trial starts today." Beck floated that thought out there, testing to find the beginning of my memory today. A game we played

"I know." Did I? I wasn't sure. It sounded familiar. Sometimes I had trouble remembering hopeful things. The hurtful, the horrible, those infiltrated my memory like smoke, the stench lingering long after the fire.

Beck pushed back the quilt, exposing my arm. "Read it. You wrote it all down."

Block letters marched in meticulous rows down my forearm like an ancient proverb tattooed for permanence and clarity. A proverb, maybe. But not ancient. And only for me.

Memories. I wrote the important stuff on my skin with a black fine-point Sharpie. As the ink faded, I half believed the words permeated into my soul, or at least my brain. In the meantime, when I fell into a hole in my memory, the words served as a reminder. I yanked my arm back and thrust it under the covers. "I know."

"Are you scared?"

"Scared?" I coughed to cover the hitch in my voice. Logan had been struggling to keep up with the plaque formation. Despite the stem cell therapy, the plaques continued forming at an alarming pace—the glory of my genetic anomaly. The trial held the hope of stopping the formation and restoring the synapses I'd been told were still there, just blocked.

"What of?"

"Failure." Beck laid out the word gently like an offering to appease the gods or incite a war.

And there it was.

"WHAT DO YOU MEAN, Dr. Davenport is dead?" Dr. Logan Faricy didn't understand. Rita dead? He stared into the receiver as if seeking wisdom, then pressed it back to his ear. The call had caught him totally ragged out and in mid-dive for the couch in his office for a quick nap. He'd caught the red-eye from Heathrow, waited in the interminable customs line at SeaTac, then had driven over two hours straight to the office in Portland. Riding a serious post-celebration buzz, he was too excited to sleep on the plane, and now he was paying the price. "Who are you again?"

"Detective Inspector Potts with the City of London Police Force." A clipped voice and measured emotion. "I'm sorry, sir. Took us a bit to identify Dr. Davenport. The train was going at quite a clip. It was late; the night schedule for the Tube was running. The train was at full throttle, I'm afraid."

Logan ran a shaking hand over his eyes, brushing away the tired and swiping the hair that had fallen across his forehead. *Rita dead?* "The Tube?"

"Yes, sir. The subway, I think you Yanks call it. The doctor jumped you see." The detective inspector sounded tired and removed. "Preliminary report ruled her death a suicide."

"But I was with her last night."

"Really?" The detective inspector's voice piqued with curiosity. "Last night, you say? Where were you and Dr. Davenport?"

Logan figured detachment came with the job. "Some pub around the block from our conference facilities. Half the world was there with me. Should be easy to establish on your end." Logan swung his feet to the floor and pushed himself upright. "And no, Detective Inspector, I don't see. Rita wouldn't jump in front of a train. We'd had such a success, you see." He gave the detective a quick summary. "You'll have to excuse me, Detective Inspector, I only just got back home myself."

"From London?"

Logan clung to his last shred of patience. "Yes."

"I see."

The simple sentence was laden with accusation. Logan rushed into his fear. "We're scientists. Researchers. Of course, we have enemies. Billions are at stake, not to mention tens of millions of lives. She must've been pushed." He leaped to his feet, swaying a little. "Yes, that's it. Someone must've pushed her."

"The platform was empty, sir. We've checked the tapes. There was no one else."

"There had to be someone else."

"If there was, then he was a ghost."

"Someone must've followed her."

"We've only just identified her. And retracing her steps is difficult. We put out her photo, and a man came forward. He encountered her on the street. It was pouring rain, but he said she gave him her umbrella. That would lend credence, albeit thin, to the theory she meant to do herself harm."

Logan ignored the theory. "It must've been him. You must find him."

"We've talked with him. He has an alibi. He did say one thing of interest, though. He said Dr. Davenport acted a bit buggy."

"Buggy?"

"Odd, like she was seeing things, had the DTs, that sort of thing. Said she heard voices. He had the impression she was quite inebriated."

"Not possible. Rita didn't drink more than a glass of wine ever. An alcoholic father, I think. What else did the man say?"

"She kept looking around like someone was after her. He seemed concerned she was not herself."

"Buggy." Logan tried to imagine a world without Rita in it. *His life* without Rita in it. She'd never looked his way—she'd set her hooks for a larger fish. But she'd never extinguished his hope.

"Right. I've been told this was not her normal state."

"Absolutely not."

"Would she have any enemies, sir?"

"Enemies?" This was like a bad movie. "Like enemies who would want to kill her?"

"Yes, sir." The limit of the detective inspector's patience sighed through the line. "Dr. Davenport was your colleague, you say."

He implied a level of familiarity Rita Davenport would never have allowed. No way the detective inspector could know that, of course, but Logan had felt her frost many times. "That's why you're calling, isn't it?" In the detective inspector's hesitation, Logan could hear the hollow whisper of shared pain.

"No, sir. She listed you as next of kin."

"Oh." A sense of horrible loss pressed Logan back into the couch. Work was all Rita Davenport had lived for, and now it looked like it had killed her.

"Can you tell me what you and Dr. Davenport do exactly?"

"No, not exactly—the information is closely guarded." That was a bit of a stretch since he and Rita had shared their findings with what amounted to the extent of their world at the colloquium in London. But Logan wasn't in the mood to explain the esoterica of misfolded proteins to the detective inspector. "Have you recovered her briefcase? Her laptop?"

"Her briefcase was recovered at the scene. No computer. We're searching the neighborhood and her hotel room. We'll let you know what we find."

Logan doubted the detective inspector would tell him anything but thought it unhelpful to say so. Rita's laptop was password-protected, but he knew that wouldn't stop anyone who was determined to get in.

"What would be in her computer you would worry about?"

"We're geneticists. Our patents alone are worth a staggering sum."

"What kind of patents?"

Logan rose and began pacing. "Testing protocols and other various things. We've discovered a bit of a breakthrough in the tangle diseases—ALS, Parkinson's and Alzheimer's, mainly. We play outside the box. We're a nonprofit and raise our own money for research. That's one of the things Rita was doing in London. Our path to clinical trials takes a fraction of the funding the others need."

"Others?"

"Traditional pharmaceutical companies. Researchers."

"And they wouldn't like that?"

"No. We've come up with something revolutionary. If it pans out, we'll put them out of business, in this arena anyway. The money Rita was raising would complete the funding for our Phase Three Clinical Trial. We've already started it."

"I see. So pharmaceutical companies would be potential enemies. Anyone else?"

"Sure, anyone who lives on grant money and has no viable drug to show for it. Less than two percent of the Alzheimer's drugs developed show even a slight improvement for the patients. And ALS is largely ignored—the patients are too few in number and die too quickly after diagnosis."

"That's appalling." Even someone removed from the suffering found it impossible to remain unmoved.

"For so many more reasons than you can imagine." He thought of all the people currently suffering, the people who cared for them. By the age of eighty-five over a third of the population would struggle with some form of dementia. Staggering numbers, staggering cost...just plain staggering in every way. "Millions upon millions of reasons, Detective Inspector."

"So all these companies, these grant recipients. This would make for a lot of enemies?"

Logan sagged back into the comfort of the couch. "Too many to count."

He expected a curse, but the detective inspector remained remarkably contained and irritatingly British. Just the thought of the helplessness of the medical community so far against the brain diseases ravaging humanity sent emotion surging through Logan. A fight response with no enemy to pummel. Defeated, he waited for the next question.

"Am I right then, yesterday, Dr. Davenport presented a paper at the colloquium which was well-received?"

"Yes."

"Then what? You went to the pub for a bit of celebration?"

"Yes, the Whistle and Goose, I think."

"Who was there?"

Logan snorted. The question was preposterous. "Everyone. The place was jammed. You Brits enjoy your pints."

"Quite right, but were any of your colleagues there? Anyone who looked out of place?"

"We're all lab rats, Detective Inspector. We look out of place anytime we are out in public." Logan closed his eyes and tried to imagine the pub, the crush of people all elbowing for space and a lukewarm beer. Harried bartenders, rumpled scientists, officious doctors. But no one immediately struck him as looking like a killer.

Then again, what did a killer look like?

Logan analyzed the flashes of faces—some familiar, others total strangers. There'd been music, snatches of laughter, lots of smiles, a soccer game on the television above the bar in the corner, the sound muted. Not a sour note he could remember. "I didn't pay all that much attention, mind you. I wasn't looking for killers, just enjoying our moment. Most of the conference attendees had packed in. Rita and I sat at the bar—I'd left the talk a bit early before the rush, while people were still saying their goodbyes and all of that, to snag a couple of seats. Rita hurried in soon after. She didn't stay long. Drinking isn't her thing."

"Was she acting odd?"

"You asked me that before. No, not odd, riding a wave for sure, we all were. Our discovery could change the world."

"And apparently threaten someone else's." The detective inspector's tone turned brusque. "Would you make a list of all who you remember at the pub? I have a list of the conference attendees and I have the video of Dr. Davenport's talk. I'm hoping there's a panorama of the crowd."

Logan reached over to his desk and tugged at the corner of a notepad sticking out from under a pile of research journals and articles. Tilting precariously, the tower threatened to fall and engulf him, but so far, it withstood gravity and all logic.

Wading through all the research being done around the globe was a losing battle, but Logan hoarded it all as if the Holy Grail lay buried in one of the reports. Most of the information was available online, but somehow that seemed like sacrilege to Logan. Something about holding the tangible rendition made it real. Dust swirled in the shaft of light angling in from the half-blocked window behind his desk as if he'd disturbed an ancient crypt.

Kate had told him he risked death working among the paper towers. The thought of her brought a smile. Then reality swept it away, the riptide after a tsunami that scoured the beaches clean.

Kate. What would she do if they had to cancel the trial?

Leaning back, he crossed one leg over the other and balanced the pad on his knee. "I'll do what I can, Detective Inspector." Turning conscious thought off and tapping into his photographic memory, Logan scribbled names.

"Very well then, I'll be in touch."

Then the spear of reality hit him. "Detective Inspector?"

"Yes."

"Whoever killed Rita, and I'm sure she didn't die by her own hand, well, that person may have killed our clinical trial. I'd start looking at who would most benefit from that if I were you."

"Thank you, *Doctor.*" His tone indicated he was anything but grateful.

Logan gave the cop a pass—he wouldn't take kindly to a cop offering advice in his lab, and he figured he'd earned the tone.

But it was Rita they were talking about.

And Kate. The thought of her sucker punched him again.

Only in her mid-thirties, Kate had a genetic time bomb that had exploded in her head. Plaques bloomed in her brain like weeds in the spring. And they'd continue to form. Stem-cell therapy kept almost apace, but they were losing the battle, only slowing the inevitable.

The trial was her last hope.

CHAPTER THREE

Breakfast had been two mugs of coffee so strong Beck had warned it would eat a hole in my stomach. So, I blamed the caffeine for the jittery feeling as I parked my BMW F-800 GS in the parking lot at the base of the tram that would carry me up Pill Hill to the hospital. I'd made this trip more times than I could remember—not that that was surprising. But each ride up was difficult as hope flared. I used to fight the hope. I didn't anymore. Life without hope wasn't worth the pain to live it.

Of course, with hope came the specter of disappointment.

Not much scared me anymore. But disappointment terrified me.

With my Sharpie, I scribbled the parking space number on the tag attached to my bike key, then pocketed them both and ran for the tram—a hitching gait with my bum leg that refused to heal fully. My knee had been ripped apart, shot, ripped again, and now refused to buy into the speedy recovery everybody hoped for. My body had joined forces with my brain, the mutiny almost complete.

Some days, when fear reigned, I could add my heart to that list.

The tram agent waved me on as the doors began to slide shut. The car was full, but no one nodded as they averted their gaze. I was used to it. With translucent skin draped over the peaks and valleys of a frame carrying too little weight and too much pain, I looked near dead. Scary for folks walking their own healthcare tightrope. The block letters sneaking from under the sleeves of my old NYPD sweatshirt didn't help. Self-consciously, I tugged at the fabric and tried to make myself small.

This wasn't my normal day to see Stella. In fact, I no longer had a normal day. It'd been a while since she'd wanted to peer into my brain. I wondered, why now?

The four-minute ride encased in the tram car dangling from the wire left me gasping for air and desperate to escape. Before the car stopped swaying, as the doors started to open, I flung myself through the small opening. The guard at the desk smiled and rose from his chair. "Can I help you?"

I waved him off. "I got it. Thanks."

He didn't look surprised—he knew me well. After I'd staggered into the ER, gun in hand, a bullet in my knee, and the Watchman going crazy, everyone knew my story. Now I was a fucking celebrity. Used to hiding in the shadows, needing to hide in the shadows, I didn't like it.

The medical office building adjacent to the hospital boasted brighter colors and a bit of forced happiness, but they did little to hide the fear that stalked the hallways. Everybody came here hoping for the best but fearing the worst. I was no exception.

Stella was waiting for me, her door open. As I hurried through the vestibule into her office, I tried not to think about what had happened here.

My fault.

The blood was gone; the horror remained. I'd made many visits since the man had managed to bash in her head before I buried a knife in his chest, but the shadow of that scene remained like a set piece on a stage that the audience could see through—something that defined the action but didn't hide it.

As I jammed my hands in my pockets, I pasted on a frown and tried not to look too closely at her office. Everything looked the same. The big desk. The same knickknacks. The new letter opener with the malachite handle I'd given her for Christmas rested near her right hand. I'd buried the previous one in the chest of the guy who almost killed her, so I'd owed her a new one.

The same before-and-after photo of Mt. St. Helens hung on the wall behind her desk. "When are you going to get rid of that?" I asked, pointing. As an icebreaker, it sucked, but it was all I could muster.

"What's your beef with the mountain?" Stella lifted an eyebrow as she read my face. Today, she sported her tribal colors, a fancy headdress, and a wrap dress sort of thing. With her facial structure, mocha skin, black eyes, regal bearing, and self-contained attitude, she could pull off any look...and did. She also took me in stride.

"Half of its gone. It's deformed."

"No." She gave me a knowing look. "The mountain survived. And it's regenerating, growing, reclaiming itself."

The parental look she bestowed was bad enough. If she'd said, "Be the mountain," I wouldn't have been responsible for what happened next. "So, what's this about?" I sounded angry. I wasn't.

"Sit."

With both hands on the arms of the chair, I lowered myself. And I waited, my heart in my throat. I rubbed my knee, a poor effort to ease the throbbing reminder.

She opened my file and pretended to read. We both knew she'd memorized every word. When she looked up, she was all business with a hint of pain in her pinched expression. "You've got to clear my psychological assessment before you can join the trial."

"Pass an assessment?" I leaned back, trying for casual. "That's a joke, right?"

Stella bit down on her smile, but a hint leaked through. "Honey, you are a one-woman wrecking machine, but that doesn't mean you're psychologically impaired or fragile. In fact, I'd say the opposite."

The fire of hope lit in my chest. Hope—the setup to disappointment. "So you'll clear me?"

"Of course."

I hid my relief. "Then why am I here?"

"Relax. You're as nervous as a deer in late November. I thought maybe it might be good to talk about how life is going." Stella, with her arms crossed and her mouth a thin line of no-nonsense, presented a wall. The look in her eyes told me this one I couldn't go over or through.

I blinked at her a few times then pressed myself against the back of the chair, finding comfort in its solidness. Almost more than the not remembering, I hated the talking. "Okay, what do you want to know?"

I'm pretty sure she heard my give-up, but I didn't look at her. I couldn't anymore. Not today... Not when I did all I saw was her bloody body lying on the floor, two men rifling through her desk. Then I killed one. Couldn't remember about the other. Didn't want to. Most of all, I remembered the warm blood oozing from his chest and over my hand. Driven by some Macbethian compunction, I rubbed my hands together as if soaping them under a faucet.

Through the half-wall of windows on the far side of Stella's office, the day had brightened with the green promise of spring. A bit misleading. I was still rubbing off the chill left from the ride over.

"What month is it?" Stella asked.

"April," I snapped, daggering her with a look.

"Ah, now I have your attention." She leaned forward, her hands overlapping on her desk. "It's been six months."

"Four." I wanted to duck my head, but I didn't. Running from the past did me no good. Hell, I already had the past on the run—I needed to capture it, hold it, burn it into the gray matter when I could.

"You remember it all?"

"That's like asking someone if they're a sociopath."

She raised one eyebrow. "Not quite. I'll take that as a yes."

"Take it however you like."

Her face softened. "Kate."

I shifted in my seat. "Sorry. Nervous, that's all."

"What if the trial doesn't work?" Stella cut to the chase. "How will you handle that?"

"Man, you and Beck. That's how he started my morning." Well, that and a wasted hard-on. I ran the zipper of my jacket up and down.

For once, Stella didn't bark at me to stop. "We love you, honey." She waited a beat, probably letting me process that.

I didn't know how, so I shelved it.

"Can you handle the drug not working?"

"Stell, I don't even know if I'm in the half who'll get the real thing and not some sugar pill." Unable to sit any longer, I jumped up and started pacing. "All this could be for nothing, right?" I whirled on her. "Even Logan doesn't know. That's what you told me, yes?"

"It's part of the double-blind thing."

"Empirical efficacy." I hiked up my sleeve, exposing my self-inflicted hieroglyphics. "I wrote it down. Makes great bedtime reading if sleep isn't a goal." I resumed pacing. "To answer your question, no, I'm not all right. Would you be? All of this and I could still end up needing someone to wipe my ass and remind me how to eat. My reality, Stella, and I have no control over any of it, other than putting a gun to my head."

"You thought of that?"

I paused mid-stride, hefting the weight of the truth. "Sure. But not yet. Only when hope is gone, and by then, I probably won't remember how to pull the trigger." I threw myself back into the chair, hunching my shoulders, then giving in to the urge to cross my arms tightly across my chest. "I've said too much."

"I'd be worried if you weren't thinking about those things. The fact that you can talk about them? Well, it's a good sign. Healthy."

She picked up a pen and scratched across the bottom of the form, then handed it to me. "Hell of a thing, I know."

"What's this?"

"Your clearance."

"You think I'm psychologically stable?" I felt one corner of my mouth tick up into a sardonic grin.

"Stable?" She gave a small laugh. "Let's not push it. But you've got a handle on reality. More so than most."

THE PARTICIPANTS HAD BEEN TOLD to gather in an auditorium down the hall from Logan Faricy's office. As I passed by, on the off chance he'd be there, I stuck my head in. He sat with his back to me, staring at a pile of paper that leaned like that Italian tower. The name was there—I could feel it teasing me, but it remained just out of reach. "You got a death wish?"

He whirled around at my voice.

I recoiled. "Whoa. What's eating you?"

His mop of brown hair was dirty and unkempt. One cheek still bore the imprint of something he must've slept on. Although if the dark half-moons hanging under his eyes were any indication, he and sleep hadn't been on speaking terms.

A smile flickered but didn't light. "Kate," he sighed.

If he was happy to see me, he hid it well. Normally, he could at least pretend some enthusiasm, not that it mattered. How he felt about me didn't even hit my radar as long as he fixed the Swiss cheese between my ears. I parked a butt cheek on the arm of one of the chairs, angling it so I could look at him on the couch he'd pushed up against the right-hand wall. "Give it up. What's eating you?"

"We've got a problem."

My heart hitched. "That much I could tell. I used to be a brilliant detective, don't you know? At least that's what they tell me."

Not even a whisper of a smile this time. His eyes met mine.

They were bloodshot, worried, a faded hint of his normal vibrant, dark brown.

Bad news.

If history was any indication, bad news came when it was ready, not necessarily when *I* was, which left me straddling the fence between wanting to get it over with and wanting not to hear it at all.

He glanced at his watch, then rose and stepped toward me. "Now's not the time, though. We're late." With two fingers, he slipped the button of his lab coat through the buttonhole as if securing armor.

"Logan?" I pressed into my feet, gluing them to the floor.

"Not now, Kate. I'm still trying to make order out of it. Let's meet the others. They're waiting."

He helped me up, then secured my elbow as if to prevent me from sitting back down in protest. He held tight as we joined the flow of white-coated, scrubbed-up folks surging down the hallway. Logan nodded to a couple of colleagues. He ignored one who gave him a pointed glare. Corpulent, with a ruddy face, he trundled toward Logan, shifting into a shoulder block as he passed. Logan took the contact and the other man's ire in stride. In the crowded hallway, the contact could've been accidental. The look he threw at Logan's back told me it wasn't.

Something shouted at me to follow him. But Logan pulled me in the opposite direction. I twisted my arm to get away.

Logan tightened his grip. "Not everybody is an enemy, Kate."

True, but life had taught me circumstances could shift friend to foe without warning. "Who was that?"

"Dr. Ward, one of the researchers. He's been living off grants for drugs that have no hope of working. Been doing it for decades."

I turned back around, catching only his retreating back. "He's stealing hope from someone else."

"Alzheimer's is our least formidable enemy." Logan's lips thinned to a line. "I've said too much." He tried for a side-smile.

"And you with your conspiracy theories will start seeing guerrilla warriors in every part of the hospital."

Paranoia. Part of my own unique kind of crazy. The part that kept me alive.

Following the tunnel of white walls, gray floors, and white ceilings, I felt my hope recede. "Whoever designed this place makes me not want to be here."

"So, a hospital is a place you normally want to be?"

I caught his eye. "I'm sick." He didn't need to be reminded—or maybe he did. After a point, I guessed patients became lab rats. I was here to remind him otherwise. "Now, tell me what's going down."

His shoulders dropped. "Rita died." The words leaked out of him like a confession.

"Dead?" I stopped. "How?"

His grip like a vise on my arm, he had to stop, too. Keeping his focus in front of him, he urged me forward. "I don't have the details."

I anchored myself to the linoleum. "Did she have any family?" I should know, but I couldn't remember.

"Just us." He lowered his head and finally looked at me. "Aren't you going to ask me where that leaves the trial?"

"No."

"Why not?"

"Rita *died.*"

That did get a smile, a weak one, but it was there. "Remember I told you, when you found yourself again, you'd like what you found?"

"Not really."

"Well, I do, and for what it's worth, I like the Kate you've found. You should, too." He saw my look. "It's a victory, Kate."

Unsure of the response and unwilling to make the wrong one, I dodged. Memories returned, but social skills lagged a bit—not that I had many to begin with. "How'd she die?"

"They say she jumped in front of a subway train."

We stood there, face-to-face in the middle of the hallway as a sea of medical staff dodged around us. "She wouldn't do that."

"No, she wouldn't." Logan set his jaw as a tick worked in his cheek—the only signs of his anger and pain.

The conclusion hung between us. "Why?" I whispered. "Why would someone kill her?"

The cop in me wanted answers. The human in me wanted revenge.

"So many possibilities."

An unexpected answer. "I thought we were trying to do good," I whispered.

A body shouldered in beside me. I gave ground unwillingly until I saw who it was. Dr. Evans Hunt, the head of the study. He sneezed into his handkerchief, then wiped his nose, which was red and irritated—his eyes, too. He looked like he hadn't slept in days. He reeked of smoke and menthol and yesterday's Scotch.

"Bless you," I said, a perfunctory response.

"It'll take more than that, I'm afraid but thank you." Dr. Hunt looked like death had paid him a visit. His normally full and ruddy cheeks were now deflated and wan. Worry stretched his mouth into a grimace. He sneezed again. Stoop-shouldered against his height, today, his burden weighed heavier.

"I guess you've heard?" His gaze swept over Logan, then me, not lingering long, then coming to rest over my shoulder. I felt a chill.

"About Rita, yeah," Logan said. I nodded my complicity even though he wasn't looking.

Dr. Hunt shifted, then leaned into us. I stepped back—last thing I needed was a cold.

He lowered his head looking at Logan from under the shelf of his brows. "You were one of the last to see her alive."

"At the pub with everyone else." Logan's voice turned still and cold. "I don't like your implication. Surely you saw her as well?"

Dr. Hunt pursed his lips. His eyes flicked away for a moment.

"No. Our paths didn't cross. She'd left the pub by the time I arrived."

"I spoke with the detective inspector." The way Logan said it sounded like an accusation. "She didn't stay at the party long. She left to catch her plane. Apparently, she wandered away from her hotel, got lost. A man tried to help her. The police found him."

Dr. Hunt leveled his gaze. "She'd just left you at the pub, right?"

Logan took the accusation out of his voice, but he didn't apologize. "She didn't stay long. Accepted a few congratulatory slaps on the back. The usual. She turned down offers to buy her a drink. Like you said, she had a plane to catch."

"She seemed okay to you?"

"It was loud. We were all focused on celebrating." Logan cocked his head. "Why?"

"People with it all together don't normally jump in front of a speeding train." Dr. Hunt paused, adding weight to his words, then continued. "But she seemed okay at the pub, is that what you're saying?" Dr. Hunt pressed.

Logan pursed his lips; his focus drifted back. "Tired. A little shaky, but we all were. And you know Rita; she never was comfortable in a crowd."

"Poor Rita." Dr. Hunt pressed his handkerchief to his nose. Squeezing his eyes shut, he captured the sneeze. "Damn cold. And damn London weather. Came on all of a sudden." He stuffed the wad of cloth back in his pocket.

"Where does this leave the study?" Logan asked. "I don't mean to sound callous, but we have a roomful of people whose lives hang in the balance."

"Rita told me before the colloquium broke up the funding was in place." Dr. Hunt flipped to business mode. A veil of practicality masked the emotion I'd seen as he stepped away from the pain. "But to be honest, I haven't checked. Rita was the interface; she was the key."

"Rita wouldn't jump." Logan circled back to what was most

important to him—heart over brain, even in a man who lived in his head.

A curious fact about Logan—one I felt I'd newly learned. I wanted to scribble it on my arm—I had a feeling it would be important later—but I had only so much epidermal real estate. But trusting my brain was as difficult as trusting someone who had lied to me.

"She wouldn't take her own life." Logan sounded sure. "Not when the finish line was in sight, especially not then." He turned to me, grabbing my arm. "I need your help, Katie. *We* need it." He looked to Dr. Hunt for confirmation.

Dr. Hunt took the cue. "Find her killer, Kate. Make her work worth it. Give her a legacy."

I felt the searing heat of their attention. "You're overselling. You had me at 'find her killer.'" I turned to Logan. "You got contact info for the cop handling Rita's death?"

Logan rooted in his pockets before coming up with a crumpled bit of paper. Just a name and number he'd written on a blank script. Probably against some doctor's code of ethics, but I didn't point it out—the guy looked haunted enough.

"Detective Inspector Potts." I caught Logan's gaze with mine. "Homicide?"

He nodded.

"At least we have the right guys looking."

"He's not convinced it wasn't suicide, but he appeared open-minded."

"What did he tell you?"

Logan brought us both up to speed with whispered words.

"If she was alone on the platform the obvious conclusion is she jumped. But why?" I looked to Logan for the answer. "Was she prone to Depression? Anxiety? Paranoia?"

Logan shook his head vigorously at first, then trailed off as he got a faraway look in his eyes.

"What?"

"An idea" He held up a hand. "Don't get excited. I need to do some research. Don't need to go charging down a dark alley without a flashlight."

Dr. Hunt sneezed again.

Logan eyed him but said nothing. "We have to go. The study participants need our attention."

With Dr. Hunt following us, Logan stretched his features into his competent-doctor face and ushered me inside the room. A small auditorium, rows of seats arced from one side of the room to the other and terraced upward from the lab table down front. Two hundred participants. Two hundred or more worried family members or friends. Well, one hundred and ninety-nine—I was the lone wolf in this crowd.

Huge whiteboards covered the front wall. A projector hung from the ceiling—a slick system of computer-driven writing that I still marveled at. The lecturer had a stylus; the computer did the rest, making the writing mimic a marker in whatever color the writer chose by tapping a small keyboard at the bottom of the center screen. As an artist, I could play with it for hours—and had.

As we entered, heads turned. Conversation stopped. To say I was the youngest by decades would be close to the truth. Alzheimer's afflicted the old and the unlucky. And occasionally, someone like me with a DNA time bomb playing Russian roulette with plaques and tangles in my brain.

Logan stepped to the front of the room. I took my usual spot at the top in the back—up the stairs, punishing myself. Before Logan had gotten set up, one angry man up front, his hand resting on the grip of a wheelchair, spoke up. "You guys better be hitting the ground running today. My wife doesn't have much time left."

I could barely see the back of the woman's head as she slumped in the chair. Her gray hair had been mashed at the crown, leaving a halo that exposed gray skin. Gray. Was that the color of death? If not death, then maybe dormant life? Or lack of life? I looked at my own skin.

Gray.

Where was the line between dormant and no going back?

Had I crossed it?

Terrifying questions with no answers.

I knew I was alive, though. My leg ached with a sharpness that demanded attention. My knee would never be the same—at least all my body parts were consistent.

Desperation radiated off the man who had seized the floor. "My wife. You must help her now!"

Logan tried to placate the man, insisting they were doing all they could. Hollow words, but they were all he had at this point. We all wanted a miracle but wishing it wouldn't make it so.

It never had.

Unable to shoulder the man's pain along with my own, I zoned out. Distracting myself, I watched the sea of people who didn't know they were being watched.

A cop's game.

My gaze wandered over the group, looking for something out of place. Most of the participants sat in their misery and fear awaiting their sentence. Would the Governor of Life call at midnight to grant them a reprieve?

One man caught my eye. I'd almost passed over him, but something made me pause.

Dressed as one of the staff in scrubs and a look of distant care, he slipped through the crowd. Pasty skin as if florescent was the only light he saw. A buzz cut, gray maybe. Trim but broad shoulders. A slightly off-center nose and eyes that were too small under a broad brow. In one hand, he held a wad of plastic bags. He sifted through the crowd, shimmying down one row, then starting on the next. After a whisper to the nearest person, he gathered cups and cans. Part of the cleanup crew. One of the unnoticed who made life happen.

I was about to dismiss him when I saw him pull out a marker, tug off the cap with his teeth, and scribble something on one of the cans before he deposited it in a new bag, segregating it from the others. He continued through the rows. A whisper. A pass.

Most cans in one bag. But after another whispered answer, a scrawl, then that can earned a bag of its own.

Up front, Logan droned on about the program. His gaze flicked over the can collector. He didn't pause, didn't glitch.

Pushing myself off the wall, I eased toward the man collecting the cans, intending to cut him off as he reached the end of his current row. I'd made it halfway down when, like a wary animal, he sensed my presence. Over the heads of those seated, he looked at me with dead eyes.

And then he ran.

Without thinking I bolted after him.

<hr>

CHAPTER FOUR

<hr>

With a ten-second head start, he banged through the double doors next to Logan's platform. I ignored Logan's surprise, which quickly turned to displeasure. I ignored that too as I caught the doors on the backswing, knocking them aside with a lowered shoulder. They banged off the stops as I burst through into the hallway. My head on a swivel, I cleaved into the stream of white coats as I skidded to a stop.

Which way did he go?

The sea of people surging toward me from my left parted upstream, wrenching their heads around to look behind them. Between the bodies I could make out the back of the man as he dodged through the crowd.

He glanced over his shoulder. Our eyes met. A quick grin, then he ran. Pretty fast for a tall, broad dude who looked like he had a football past.

Ducking my head, I forced my legs to move. My knee screamed. Too much, too soon. The doctor's words shimmered through the haze of pain.

We won't be able to fix it again.

I pushed the words aside. The pain slowed me. As if being a

mental cripple wasn't enough. Anger flared. The anger took care of the pain, but it wouldn't last...it never did.

A human machete, the man cut a swath through the forest of people.

I surged into the trail he cleared. With each step, I gained on him. My knee screamed then buckled. I howled as it took my weight. A man reached out and grabbed my arm, steadying me. I took his help, then shrugged him off. Focusing on the runner, on closing the distance, I ignored my body's protest, ignored the pain, ignored the warning.

As I flew past, a different person grabbed my arm. They didn't jerk me to a stop. Instead, they moved with me, using their weight as an anchor. I couldn't shake the viselike grip. "Let me go!" My voice sounded harsh, a cold demand.

The person held on. "Katie, you can't." A whisper filled with concern, but insistent.

Beck.

"I have to." I twisted and pulled. "Let me go."

"No. Your knee."

Like a wild fish on the line, the hook firmly set, I fought. "I need to go. Now!"

"Katie. Calm down."

My eyes on the man, my anger a fuel I couldn't control, I clawed at Beck's fingers. "You've no right." Blind with fury, I kicked at his shins. I felt eyes on me. People had stopped. Why didn't they help me?

My feet found only air as he dodged and held tight. "Katie. Breathe."

Squirming, fighting, I swiveled to watch as the man disappeared. The sea of people closed behind him, drowning my hope.

Panting with the effort to escape and to control the rage, I put a hand on Beck's chest. "Go get him." I stopped resisting. "That man. You need to get him," I gasped.

"Why?" Beck glanced over my head.

"He was taking Coke cans." I fought for breath. While my

health was recovering, my strength and fitness weren't. "Goddamn it, Beck. Get him. Now!"

He didn't move. He'd made his choice. Beck looked at me, a smug look as if I'd lived down to his expectations.

I hated my weakness. I hated being sick. I hated having to prove myself again and again. I hated people thinking I was still crazy.

And right now, I hated Beck.

"Why don't you go?" Leaning around Beck, I checked again. Nothing.

The chase was over.

Rage seethed through me, a beast I couldn't control. "Why did you stop me?"

"Your knee."

Maybe he believed that. I didn't. And worse, his words held pity.

My vision swam. Leaning over, I put my hands on my knees as I fought for breath and clarity. "Why didn't you go after him?" My voice vibrated with anger.

"Katie." Beck adopted a calm, patronizing tone. "Stealing aluminum cans is hardly an offense worth prosecuting, much less one to blow out your knee over. And you can't go tackling people in the hallway."

I'd done it before. *Hank.* A hallway just like this one. Memories flooded through me with the cold flush of a drug. Another chase. A bad ending.

Death.

I shivered. Hank's loss, his fear, weighed heavy.

The memories come only when you're scared.

Was I scared? Only a fool wouldn't be.

"Rita's dead." My voice sounded distant, removed...like someone else's. "That guy was taking cans, talking to people. Then writing on the cans, putting them in individual plastic bags." I cocked an eyebrow at him. "Sound odd to you?"

A moment to process, then Beck cast a hurried look down the hall.

"Don't bother."

His gaze came back to mine—his blue eyes held sorry.

My blue ones held pissed—I saw their reflection in his. "You didn't believe me. You didn't trust my instincts." I still gasped against all of it. "I'm a cop, damn it. Been a cop all my life." An undercover cop who had worked a life of lies—at least the part I could remember. My instincts came from the parts I couldn't remember.

And my instincts kept me alive.

Beck let out a sigh, and his shoulders slumped as if the air had held them up.

Even though my knee screamed, I refused the show of weakness in rubbing it. "If it had been somebody else. Another cop. Not me." I let the thought hang, the conclusion obvious. "*You* wanted me to join the force. To help, you said. How can I help if you, of all people, don't believe me?" I yanked my arm from his grasp.

"Your knee."

"Is an excuse. Had you trusted me, you would've stopped me, then taken up the chase yourself." I could tell he was sorry. It didn't matter. "Will I always be broken to you?" Not waiting for an answer, I turned from my anger I saw reflected in his eyes. I had every right to be furious. So why didn't it feel good? I'd stalked a few strides then stopped. I didn't want to hurt him. But kill him? Maybe. "Why are you here?" I turned around to face his disappointment. This time, I had a feeling he was disappointed in himself, not in me.

He shrugged into my question. "It's a big day for you. I didn't want you to be alone."

The fog of my anger evaporated. "You came for me?" My voice thinned to a whisper. Accustomed to being on my own, I found his caring both liberating and confining.

"Of course." He raised his hands. "If I come closer you won't kill me or bust my balls or anything, will you?"

"I'm not sure." Quite frankly, I wasn't. Anger still seethed, a coiled snake poised to strike.

Anger. One of the reasons I didn't carry a weapon…not that one had been offered. But with me, control was elusive. The cops were still learning my limits. Hell, so was I. But, of all of them, Beck should be the one to trust me. He knew me best. The fact that he hadn't pierced me with the sharp stab of betrayal.

He stepped into my space. Even still, I wasn't used to that, to his nearness.

"Rita's dead?" He had a moment to ask the question before a commotion sounded behind us.

"Kate? Kate?" Logan shouted, his voice fringed with worry.

"Somebody else to call me a nut case," I muttered.

"I didn't…"

"But you did." Even though I wanted to reach up and push the hair off Beck's forehead and wipe away the worry lines, I silenced him with a glare, then raised my voice. "Over here."

Shouldering through the last of the crowd that had gathered, Logan stopped in front of us. "Detective," he acknowledged Beck. "What was that about?" he asked me.

I told him.

He strained to see over my shoulder. "Did you get him?"

"No." I threw a side look at Beck. "My knee." I could lie—a sure sign my brain was regaining function. "Did you know the guy?"

"I didn't get a good look. From the front it's hard to see past the lights, but he looked like a janitor I've seen around."

"A janitor?" I hadn't expected that. "Why would a janitor collect cups and cans, annotating them? You think his job would be to just pitch the trash."

Logan blew out some air that lifted the hair that had fallen across his forehead. He looked between Beck and me. "His behavior certainly seems odd. I'd sure like to hear what exactly he was after."

"If I'd been allowed to catch him, perhaps I'd have an answer to that." Needing distance, I stepped away from Beck.

I was best on my own—I knew it, but I didn't have the courage to live it. In fact, life had made sure I couldn't. A reality I fought every day and probably always would.

Logan missed the accusation in my voice, or maybe he ignored it. "Let's get back to the others." He herded us toward the auditorium. "I left them in good hands, but we're waiting on Dr. Hunt. This is his baby." Logan scanned the hallway. "I wonder where he is?"

"Wasn't he with us earlier?" I remembered but didn't trust it.

"Yeah, but he got a call right before I started."

As if on cue, Dr. Hunt, with another man I didn't recognize in tow, met us at the auditorium door. "Glad to catch you all together," he said.

I couldn't read his look.

He nodded toward the man beside him. "This is Benton Myles."

Short and broad, Mr. Myles had the aura of a man used to getting his way. Handsome to the point of distraction with his blond hair perfectly trimmed, his face freshly shaved, he oozed confidence like a birthright. He wore a well-tailored wool jacket, jeans pressed to a knife edge and probably costing more than my weekly paycheck, loafers no socks, a black T-shirt, and a get-out-of-my-way attitude. The Patek Philippe on his left wrist was in keeping with the stepping-off-a-yacht-in-Monte-Carlo presentation. His wide gold wedding band was not.

Mr. Myles screamed money, but only to those who noticed the details.

The name meant nothing to me. From the look on his face, Beck didn't know him either.

Apparently, Logan did. He grabbed the man's hand and began pumping it. "Mr. Myles, it's a pleasure." He swept his arm toward the door to the auditorium. "We're just getting started. Would you like to see the impact your dollars are making?"

"Not now, Logan," Dr. Hunt barked. "We have a very large problem."

"More than one, then?" I asked, unwilling to let the men gloss over Rita's death. I never knew whether the men passed us over because we were women or because the research was more important than all of us. I preferred to believe the latter, but I suspected the former.

The new guy gave me the once-over. I was used to it, not that I liked it. What was his name? Myles something-or-other? I resisted the urge to pull out my Sharpie and make a note on a patch of exposed skin.

"Who is this?" He lifted his chin toward me and asked as if I wasn't capable of answering.

Before one of the men replied, I jumped in. "I'm perfectly able to introduce myself. I may be...afflicted...but I'm not impaired." A small lie. Okay, maybe a bit larger, but small was all I'd give it. "I'm Detective Kate Sawyer." I didn't offer my hand as I emphasized the detective part. Like everyone, I needed a place to belong, something that reminded me to fight. And being a cop was the tribe I identified with.

Being a cop was all I had.

And they wanted to take it away. I was a liability. I could see it in their eyes.

"I'm a member of the trial." He looked surprised, then his expression closed.

For the second time today, I saw pity, and my anger burned.

Beck put a hand on my arm—he knew my buttons, even if he pushed them from time to time, or maybe because he did.

"What's all this about?" Logan asked.

Evans scanned the hallway around us. "Come with me. All of you. You need to hear what Benton has to say."

He sequestered us in a small office across the hall. When he closed the door, I realized the office had belonged to Rita Davenport. Cool and chic, every choice reflected her persona from the clean desk in a burnished wood—clearly an antique—to the stylish credenza nestled under the window that took up the top half of the far wall. Gold-tasseled rope gathered drapes in a heavy cloth dyed the color of a deep burgundy. A kilim rug in cool blues and purples hid the laminated flooring. Her journals, each bound and notated, filled the shelves of a glass-fronted shelving unit next to the door. Two Queen Anne chairs angled in front of the desk.

Very refined. Very coolly aloof. Very Rita.

Not that I'd known her well. As someone who likes to remain removed, I recognized the trait in others, and I respected it. "What did Rita do here?" I asked as I scanned her journals looking for a clue.

I felt Rita close. The whispers of a ghost.

"Synthetic biology," Logan said as if I had a clue what that meant.

I searched for snippets of past conversations—those would be all that remained. "Like a human-machine interface?"

"No. Like individualized medicines." Distracted, he didn't give me his full attention, clipping his words. "Curing genetic disorders, that kind of thing. Understand?"

"No clue." But I was wise enough to save it for later. To remember, I discreetly tapped a note-to-self into my phone. My phone served as an alternative to marking up my skin. The most important stuff I tattooed; the rest went in the phone.

With the door closed and Logan not feeling chatty, we stood in awkward silence. Maybe everyone else felt as I did—like a trespasser.

Evans nodded to the new guy.

What was his name?

"Benton, tell them what you told me."

Benton, that was it. Benton Myles. I didn't care what other people thought. With my Sharpie I made a note of his name on a sliver of translucent skin on the underside of my left forearm where it met my wrist. For some reason his name struck me as important.

He watched me; his head cocked to read what I wrote. "It's a 'y' not an 'i'," he corrected, then he pointed at one line all in caps. "What's that say?"

As I printed, I looked where his finger pointed. "No guns."

For some reason, I didn't like him. Maybe it was the studied hints and subtle one-upmanship. Maybe it was the wary tiger way he had of watching us all—removed, hungry. Maybe it was the fact I really didn't like anyone. No matter, he still smelled good. While I was losing my sense, my primal senses clearly were trying to pick up the slack.

I turned the 'i' into a 'y' and then kept my Sharpie ready. From the looks on both his face and Dr. Hunt's, notes would be a good idea.

"You saw Rita in London?" Logan asked Mr. Myles but he sounded like he knew the answer.

"Yes. We spoke about the success and the future funding."

The light dawned. "You're her money guy, right?" I asked.

The others winced. Guess I'd stepped a toe over the acceptable question line. Like I could care.

"Yes." Mr. Myles met the question head-on. "Rita and I had dinner. My wife..." His voice hitched. "She died recently."

"I'm sorry."

He gave me the flicker of a tight smile. "ALS. It wasn't unexpected. Still..." His expression closed. "It was too late to get her into your trial. Right, Evans? That's what you said."

"Yes." Dr. Hunt had the decency to look uncomfortable.

I tapped some notes into my phone. Mr. Myles could be an angry man or just a broken one. Either way he hit my radar.

"Tell them, Benton," Evans urged again.

"I received an ultimatum today," Benton started in, not wasting any time. "A note. The police in the UK are analyzing it." He pulled out his phone and punched up a photo which he passed around.

The note was elegant in its simplicity. Crayons on white paper. Block letters.

She didn't have to die. Another will. You can stop it. But you must hurry. Time is running, the clock ticking.

"And your interpretation?" I asked, raising my eyes to meet his. Green. Unexpected.

Hank. My brother had green eyes. Like our father? That memory had faded.

"The clinical trial, of course. Whoever this jackass is, he wants me to pull the funding for the trial." He looked around the group. "Someone wants to shut you down."

"Why?" Logan said. "We're looking for a cure, not developing a weapon of mass destruction."

Anger with nowhere to go flushed Dr. Hunt's face. He focused on Logan. "We have lots of enemies. You know that. When news of our success reaches the highest levels, money will be stripped from other programs." Then he took in the rest of us with a glance. "And I, for one, can't imagine being able to find a killer among them."

"I think we can help there." Instinctively, the cop in me, the side that knew no fear and was unhampered by hope, took over. "Do you have any more information regarding Rita's death?"

Dr. Hunt pulled out his handkerchief and sneezed. "Sorry." He tucked the cloth away. "Benton?"

"She had no drugs in her system. Nothing seemed out of order. An elevated white blood cell count, nothing more."

"No drugs to cause the paranoia?" Logan asked.

"None they could find."

"How did you get the tox results back so quickly?" Beck asked. "Normally those panels take weeks."

"When you don't care how much money you throw at a problem, you'd be surprised what you can accomplish."

"How?" Beck honed in.

"I went outside normal channels. Rules don't interest me. Results do."

I liked the comment and feared the man who lived it.

That observation went into my phone with the others.

Logan stepped to the window, keeping his back to us. We'd spent enough intimate time together as he poked holes in my brain and pumped in drugs for me to have learned at least some of his nuances. He was onto something.

I stepped in beside him. "What is it?"

He waved me to silence. "Give me a minute."

Both of us stared out at the courtyard.

A slab of concrete trapped on all sides by an institutional building. The metal seams joining concrete panels leaked tears of orange rust, streaking the off-white. A cell for the few flowering plants clinging to life in the scattered planters. Even though they had enough rain, the sun only carved an arc on the south-facing wall—none of it reaching the ground. Yet the plants and flowers all yearned skyward, desperate for the light. No matter the odds stacked against them, everything fought for life.

I didn't like courtyards. Nor rooms with closed doors. The air hung still and stagnant, tepid with our body heat. Beck, Dr. Hunt, and Benton or Myles or what's-his-name clustered close. Dr. Hunt did the hushed talking. Beck took notes with his ever-present pencil and tattered notebook. I'd teased him before about taking so many notes it looked like he was the one with memory issues. Reflexively, I tugged my sleeves, covering my personal Sanskrit.

"I'm trying to figure out how they killed Rita." Logan's comment saved me.

Too much introspection was a bad thing. Panic, then anger—I was a two-stroke engine unless someone switched my gears. "You have an idea?" If he didn't, between us, we'd be batting zero.

"Several, only two really viable. But," he turned to look at me, "your aluminum can guy got me thinking. He might narrow the possibilities to one."

"Do tell," Dr. Hunt said as the others gathered around us. He eased in beside me, then he grabbed his handkerchief and sneezed again. "Sorry."

I wanted to open his mouth and ram that wad of cloth in as far as I could. As a doctor he should appreciate the germs he spread.

Beck closed in on my other side, separating me from Logan. I caught our reflection in the window: four men and a pixie. Beck was as tall as the others, but not as broad. And he had the same shaggy-haired, awe-gee-shucks look of the boy next door that Logan sported. I liked the type.

Surrounded by the men, I almost disappeared. Not a bad thing. I liked working in the shadows.

Logan turned slowly back to the group. "How long have you had that cold, Evans?" Logan daggered his boss with a narrow-eyed look.

"My cold?" Dr. Hunt gave a small laugh. "My cold means nothing."

"How long?" Logan's voice was hard, demanding.

Dr. Hunt got the hint when it hit him between the eyes. "It came on quickly. During the second or third day of the conference, I think. Why?"

"Tell me what you did that day."

Dr. Hunt took a deep breath. "Okay. Things started at noon that day. Just kicking off the colloquium and all. I had lunch with some of our South African colleagues."

"Where?"

"A restaurant down the street from the hotel."

"Okay, then what?" Logan waved his unspoken protestation to silence. "Let's narrow this down. Did you have any meetings in an enclosed room?"

Dr. Hunt pulled out his phone. I assumed he was checking his calendar. "Yes, two. The first one with the medical ethics group. The second was at Cooper Livingston's invite. He asked me to sit in on a data discussion."

"Was Rita at either?"

"Yes, the data discussion. Mapping the genome is a huge data issue. And epigenetics multiplies that exponentially. All that plays into the individualized medicine Rita was so keen on."

"How was she acting?"

Evans blew his nose again. "Fine. I said she was acting fine." He dismissed the question with an airy wave, his irritation showing in a slight flush to his cheeks. "She did ask us to turn up the heat. We were all roasting, but she was chilled."

"Okay. Get on the phone with a couple of them from each meeting." From the intense look on Logan's face, it was clear he meant right now. "I want to know if any of the others have colds."

Evans stepped away from the group and we waited. No one said a word. What was there to say?

When he returned, Evans was shaking his head. "I reached several from each group. Some weren't happy at the hour. Only two of them came down with colds."

"Did they each attend both meetings with you?"

Dr. Hunt rolled his eyes toward the ceiling as he paused. After a moment, he returned to stare at Logan. "No, only Carter Livingston's."

"Where was it? Organized beforehand or impromptu?"

"Totally on the fly. You know Carter. It was at some head shop around the corner—a room in the back. Apparently, Carter was well known to the proprietor."

Logan blinked rapidly as if to keep the thoughts racing in his head from escaping. "Are you taking any medications?"

Dr. Hunt swallowed hard as he looked around the group, pausing to make eye contact with each of us, stopping on Logan. "You're onto something? This is important?"

"Very."

"This doesn't go outside of this group, okay?" Evans waited for us each to nod, then took a deep breath, letting it out slowly. "I have a rare form of cancer, genetically driven. I'm taking an individualized medicine. Rita put me onto it."

"I need to see that medicine," Logan insisted.

Evans pulled an aerosol spray from the pocket of his jacket. "If this gets out..."

"Your funding could be in jeopardy," Benton said. He was the money man; he would know. "You're the driving force behind this trial. It's your research."

"Yes, but others can take it from here." Evans sounded like he doubted his own words.

"Not the same."

"Are these made here?" Logan turned the spray bottle. "There's no manufacturer on the label."

"No, an outfit in Nevada. They overnight them to me just before I run out. Last shipment was short though."

"This didn't come through legitimate channels, did it?" Logan asked, a dog with a bone.

"No. I didn't have decades for researchers to jump through FDA hoops. I'm a dead man walking anyway, so what's to lose?"

Logan had that look.

"What is it?" I asked.

"If I'm right, this is how Rita was killed."

CHAPTER FIVE

"WHAT?" I THINK WE ALL SAID IT IN UNISON. ALL EXCEPT Logan who held the bottle aloft.

"Hell, Logan, you look like you found the fucking golden ticket." Clearly, Evans wasn't pleased, but he was also worried. He kept glancing at the money guy who ignored him.

"I couldn't understand her apparent paranoia the night she died."

"Paranoia?" Evans scoffed. "Aren't you jumping to conclusions?"

"You have a better reason for her suicide?" Evans scowled but remained silent.

"Rita had a genetic anomaly," Logan continued. "Her father died of Parkinson's. She carried the gene. And her gene had a particular nuance to it, an anomaly that, when switched on, will trigger psychosis."

"What does my drug have to with that?" Evans wasn't handling this well.

I wasn't sure which part was getting to him: Rita's death and the fact he may have played a part, or the money man looking ready to bolt.

"Mind you, I'm wandering way out on the limb of speculation. I won't know whether I'm right or wrong until I test that drug of yours, Evans. Mr. Myles, I'll need some of Rita's blood, and quickly. All this has a short shelf life. And the blood will need to be transported properly. Is that a problem?"

"Shouldn't be. Longest it will take me is a round trip to London in a G-5, but that's the worst-case scenario." As he pressed his phone to his ear, he turned on his heel, pushed through the office door, and disappeared into the hall. Before the door shut behind him, I heard him say, "Wally, we have a problem."

Beck must've heard the same thing. He caught my eye. I nodded, and he disappeared after what's-his-name.

Why did short-term stuff not stick unless it involved bloodshed or death? As a cop, the goal was to intervene a bit before that happened.

The red in Dr. Hunt's face now wasn't quite as intense.

"Logan, explain." I hadn't understood a word so far, or not much of them anyway. "You think someone used Dr. Hunt's meds to trigger a psychotic episode in Rita which caused her to jump in front of the train?"

Logan's eyes widened. Despite the worry in them, he smiled. "Kate! That's great!"

"What?" His change in demeanor forced me off the mainline to a sidetrack.

"You remembered."

"Oh, for God's sake, Logan. Your treatment is working, or at least keeping up with the disease. Stop being that kind of parent who praises a child for something mundane."

"Mundane?" He included me in his smile. We both remembered a not-too-distant past when what I'd just done had been out of reach. He had saved part of me, then I saved the rest. My knee had been collateral damage.

So had Hank. The knee I could live with...

"Give it to me in layman's terms. What are we dealing with, if you're right?" I'd probably asked a really hard question, although I had no way of determining that.

"It's cheap and quick to map DNA now. So, for instance, I can take a sample of yours, map it, and start searching for things that can cause you harm, which is a much larger data-crunching issue. If I'm one of the good guys, like Rita, I search for health problems to fix."

"Like my cancer," Evans added.

"Precisely." The two men warmed to my edification, Logan still taking the lead. "But, were I of a different mind, I could look for things that could hurt you. Triggering a disease, those sorts of things."

"Or Rita's psychosis." I connected the dots he'd laid very carefully for me to follow.

"Yes."

"How did the killer use Dr. Hunt?"

Dr. Hunt looked like he knew, but he let Logan explain. "We can edit DNA now. The process is complicated and not pertinent, except the part where we cut out the offending sections of DNA and replace them with DNA we build. We introduce the new DNA into the system with a virus."

Dr. Hunt sneezed.

"Voilà," Logan said, tilting his head toward his boss. "The virus used could give the recipient a cold—in fact, using a virus that way is a stroke of genius. Each virus that replicates in his system will carry the new DNA strands. They won't trigger psychosis in him. He doesn't have the genetic anomaly that bit of DNA was designed to trigger."

"And when I saw Rita at Carter Livingston's group meeting, I was throwing off viruses by the billions," Dr. Hunt said, finishing the buildup but leaving out the *fait accompli*.

Rita had died.

"A weapon with no signature," I said, at a loss as to where we would start.

"Not exactly." One side of Logan's mouth ticked up. I knew that look—he was on the chase. "I can analyze this and then get confirmation from Rita's blood. Then we work backward through the manufacturer." He looked at Dr. Hunt. "We need to get Thea involved. This is her purview."

"Who is Thea?" I asked.

"Thea Janeway. Rita's assistant."

Logan, Dr. Hunt, and I found Thea in her lab, staring out the window at the same drab courtyard. Along the way I'd looked for Beck, but he and the money guy had disappeared.

Thea turned at our approach. Blonde hair pulled back into a bun and netted. A trim figure underneath a white lab coat. Jeans. Birkenstocks. Probably still looking forward to her thirtieth birthday. Tears streaked her face. Her brown eyes held her pain. "I just heard." Pulling the sleeve of her lab coat over the heel of her hand, she swiped at her eyes. "What happened?" She speared Logan and Hunt with a look. "You two were *there*."

The hint of an accusation.

Perhaps feeling his guilt, Dr. Hunt said nothing.

Logan ignored her question; instead, he gave her the short and sweet of his theory.

As she listened, interest pinched her face. Her pain evaporated—a look of revenge replaced it. "The bastards. I'd love to cut off their balls."

The men squirmed. I liked her already.

"Could've been a woman," I said, testing.

She tossed me a murderous look. "And you are?"

Dr. Hunt rushed to make the introductions.

"I see." She eyed me coolly.

"Could it work?" Logan asked.

"Totally."

"How would they get her DNA?" I asked.

"Bodily fluids. Cells, except red blood cells."

"Saliva?" I thought about the guy collecting aluminum cans.

"Sure."

Logan's gaze met mine. *Bingo.*

"What?" Thea asked, catching the look between Logan and me.

After he explained, she no longer eyed me as a disgrace to my gender. I wasn't sure I cared.

"They didn't have to go to those lengths to get Rita's DNA," Logan said, drawing daggered looks from the rest of the group. "Her father died of Parkinson's. She wanted to know if she had the gene. I helped her."

"And that information is where?" Thea asked.

"Our trial database, behind several firewalls and security measures. Everything we do here, everyone we treat, has a genetic profile on file."

"We'll assume our information has not been breached, which seems reasonable since someone is still collecting aluminum cans from the trial participants. Whoever is behind this could've been collecting DNA for a long time. None of us even thinks to protect it. We should. Even the Secret Service takes extraordinary measures to keep the president's DNA from getting into the wrong hands. They can't, of course. We leave the stuff all over the place. The President is no exception, but they try."

The extent of the vulnerability started to leak into my gray matter. "You'll check for a data breach?"

"Of course. We actually check all the time as a matter of security for our patients' records. If it came from outside, we would have detected it." Logan left the other conclusion unspoken...*if it came from inside...*

"But it's not easy to target someone like Rita was targeted?" I continued my thought train despite a short track.

"No, damned difficult, thank God," Thea answered. "But getting easier every day." She pulled the netting off her bun and shook her long hair loose. "Pretty soon mapping our genome will take a couple of days and cost a few bucks. We're not there yet, but almost."

"How long?"

Logan answered my question. "Two billion chromosome pairs to string together still takes a week or so."

"Two billion?" I gave a low whistle. "So, to find a weakness, a target, wouldn't you already have to know what you were looking for?"

Logan kept the stage as tears welled again in Thea's eyes. "Yes, genetic research is in its infancy. We're getting confident in targeting a few diseases that have only one or two genetic switches like Huntington's. But most of the other diseases have hundreds, maybe thousands or more genes involved. Then we have to figure out what might trigger the anomaly, which is equally as complicated. Assuming you know your target and how to trigger it..."

"That would be much simpler." I gave voice to the obvious but hearing it would help burn it into my brain.

"It's a huge data manipulation issue. You need a ton of computing power and you need to design your search right, but with both of those things, you can find it fairly easily."

"Who has access to that kind of computing power?"

Logan deferred to Thea. "What do you think? Legit or underground?"

"Underground." She sounded confident.

"Explain," I said.

"The people like us who use the computing power in this country do so for legit purposes. We apply for access, and it's granted or denied. Fairly tightly controlled as that kind of computational power is still rare and in high demand. It's mainly cloud-based supercomputing. Of course, quantum computing will change all that, but that's not here yet. Another, *thank God*. Someone really needs to wise up and get control of all this, or we're going to find ourselves dealing with an incredibly specific biological weapon." At Logan's look, she gave a tiny smile. "Okay, crawling off the soapbox now. Now the supercomputing for someone who wants to do what they did to Rita is available offshore, and only in a few places."

"But they already knew her weakness and how to trigger it," Logan said.

"Even easier," Thea agreed with a nod.

The cop in me liked the sound of that. "It sounds like we can reverse engineer this whole thing. My partner and I can work back through the manufacturer."

Thea kept her tone arrogant, her words clipped, as if being one of the boys meant you had to be an ass. "The IP address of whoever ordered everything will be spoofed," she said, thinking out loud. "We'll have to go back through the whole lineage of this stuff, starting with the end product and working our way through the food chain from the manufacturer, to blueprinter, to designer, to mapper, to the person who requested the mapping and the design." She pulled over a stool, then sat with a weary slump, her slender body bowing under the weight of a Herculean task multiplied by the terrible burden of loss. At least the tears had dried.

I envied her the tears. I had yet to shed any over Hank. Most nights I fell asleep wondering why.

The rest of us grabbed stools as well, circling them as if lost at sea and trying to keep the sharks at bay.

With his hands on his knees, which pushed his shoulders up around his ears, Logan shook his head. "Hell of a problem."

"It gets worse." Beck's voice sounded from the doorway.

We all turned as he worked his way through the lab to join us.

The new guy trailed behind with a murderous look on his face. He didn't bother with a stool. "The ass has poisoned one of us."

"Are you sure?" Dr. Hunt accepted the possibility without argument.

"Of course I'm not sure," the new guy snapped.

I glanced at my forearm. *Benton Myles.*

"Don't be a fool," Myles finished, endearing himself to no one... not that he seemed to care.

Briefly I hoped the target was Benton. Horrified, I shut the thought down. Sometimes I was a bit more human than I was comfortable with.

Beck stepped in. "It's the note. To paraphrase, it says another will die and we can stop it."

"But the clock is ticking," Dr. Hunt added as if now it all made sense.

"A stretch, but if you're right," I said, picking up the baton, "how do you figure out who?"

Evans turned to Thea. "We need Carter."

She stiffened as if she'd been Tasered. "No!" One word. Firm. Controlled. Absolute.

"Look, I don't know what went down between you two, but we have someone's life on the line here." Evans gestured around the group. "I was just with him in London. He seemed fine. Besides, it was his little soiree Rita's killer chose."

"Speculation." Thea shook her head—a non-verbal expression loosely translated as "Men!"

"Are we sure it's one of your team rather than one of the study participants?" Beck asked the group.

"Does anyone have a copy of the note?" I asked, not trusting my memory.

Benton thrust his phone at me. "I took a photo."

I read the words three times. "It says 'another.' We can assume he meant to use that word."

"Or she." Thea tossed that hand grenade out there to land at my feet. Her tone told me she didn't think a woman could be so heartless.

I knew better. "Or she. You're quite right. I've seen enough bad in the world to know women are as capable as men. And, if you rule out one upfront, you do so at your peril."

"Police work is like science, then."

"More like guilty until proven innocent. We leave the high moral ground to the lawyers."

That didn't get even one chuckle, not that I intended it to. Chasing murderers was a game with no latitude for morality. "This is a sophisticated game. So, I think we can be safe in assuming the word choice was specific. They used the word 'another'. I'd interpret that to mean another like Rita. Someone close. This is personal." I glanced at Beck. He pursed his lips and nodded. I wasn't looking for approval, only agreement, and I took it as such. I had no idea how he offered it. Nor did I care. The walls had gone up. Self-protection elevated to a fine art. I pushed him aside. "And since the guy was collecting aluminum cans that had been used by the study participants, we can assume whoever is behind this is still in the collection mode, maybe for a future death if we don't do as he," I nodded to Thea, "or she, wants us to."

"They could've been collecting our DNA for a long time and we'd be none the wiser," Dr. Hunt said, repeating the fear expressed before, the color once again rising in his cheeks.

"I suggest Beck and I start with the manufacturer, see what we can dig up." Everyone nodded in agreement.

Beck pulled out his pad and pencil. "Dr. Hunt, can you give us the name and contact info of your supplier?" He made it sound like the guy was buying opiates on the black market.

Perhaps that would be easier. The only things I understood about the path ahead were we were chasing a killer, and he or she used a world I hoped would help me hunt the others, but that was the extent of my knowledge and understanding.

Dr. Hunt glanced at Benton Myles, who remained stoic, not acknowledging the look. With a shrug, Hunt palmed the bottle, handing it to Beck. "An outfit out of Nevada. Nitro DNA."

Beck made a note of the name. "And the contact info?"

Dr. Hunt pulled it up on his phone. Beck copied it down. For some reason I got the impression Dr. Hunt wasn't happy about sharing.

"You won't find anything there. It's a shell company. No physical location. The work is done offshore. It's not exactly FDA approved."

"Okay, but they have to have some footprint somewhere," I said. "I'll start digging. What else can be done on your end?" I asked.

Dr. Hunt squared off with Thea. "We need Carter on this. The underground manufacture of this stuff is his purview. He knows the players."

"Who is Carter?" I asked.

"Carter Livingston." Thea spat the name as if ridding herself of accidentally ingested poison. "He's an ass," she said, underscoring her loathing.

"Maybe so." Dr. Hunt was undeterred. "But the killer is operating in Carter's world. None of us here knows how it all works. Carter knows the designers, the mappers, the blue printers. As I recall, that's the straw that broke the camel's back of your relationship."

Thea's lips thinned. "Carter's not one for rules."

"Sounds like a long-shot." Even though right now it was the only one we had, I couldn't help my skepticism. Chasing killers through the Dark Web that was designed to hide them. A more than a long, long shot.

"It's not as impossible as you might think." Thea still looked unhappy, but onboard. "The guys playing outside the lines aren't constricted by all the regulations like we are. You'd be surprised at what they're doing. But they also have a bit of a Don Quixote complex, at least some of them."

"How so?" Her reference confused me. I hoped for clarification in the explanation.

"Little hope of saving the human race but trying. Their theory is if we map everyone's genome and create a database of their genetic weaknesses, then, if they are targeted, we will have the map to find the solution quickly."

"A valid theory," Logan said.

"Impossible," Thea countered.

"Everyone thought mapping the genome was impossible." Evans chose his side.

Thea gave in with a shrug.

"But the not-so-altruistic," I said, thinking out loud. "Giving people designer time bombs triggering psychosis. I'm impressed and horrified. Freak science from a B movie that we'd enjoyed because it wasn't real."

"And it's not just psychosis," Thea said. "It could be cancer, Alzheimer's, maybe even a particular self-destructive behavioral addiction. Anything with a genetic component. We know genetics isn't all of the answer, but it is a part of the puzzle. All of it works together—so many pieces with unknown consequences."

Hunt took charge. "Thea. Go find Carter." He held up his hand, stopping her argument. "Just do it. And patch up whatever is between you."

"Evans," she started, then stopped. "I can't."

"Someone in this group will die if you don't."

"They may even die if I do."

THEA JANEWAY LIVED in a small Craftsman-style home tucked in the woods high on the hills west of Portland. Close enough, but far enough away. From up here she could, if not forget the ugliness, at least hide from it for a while.

As she turned into her drive, her brows bunched into a frown. A gleaming Ferrari, red of course, was parked in front of her garage, blocking her entry. She backed up and pulled in next to the curb.

Shadows crept through the neighborhood while the city below still bathed in the glow of the dying day. As it sank behind the hills, the sun left this side of the mountain early. She gathered her things then kicked shut the car door. A shiver chased through her. Not cold, but dread. Bad things come in threes, she told herself. This one would make two. Carter would make three.

If she survived number two.

Her father huddled in the puff of a down jacket, his hands fisting in the pockets, his face begging for a jab, his eyes missing nothing. Fingers of wind had mussed his gray hair. Women were drawn to him; men feared him; Thea hated him.

She stopped at the bottom of the steps. "What are you doing here?"

"I want to make my peace."

"Bullshit." Thea stalked up the stairs, then shouldered past him.

"Thea, what I did was your mother's only hope." He touched her arm. "You've got to forgive me." At her cold look he let his hand drop. "She would've died anyway."

Thea, her hands balled into fists at her sides, looked up and closed her eyes. She pulled in a deep breath. ALS—a death sentence. They told her she'd have eighteen months with her mother before she was gone. She got three—her father had made certain. "You knew it would kill her." She gave him a hard stare. "You knew your drug was poison. You murdered her. It was wrong." Almost as bad, he hadn't told her he'd been dosing his wife, using her as a guinea pig.

"The district attorney disagreed. It was all legal. I had her permission."

"Legal doesn't make it right." That was where her father's ethics fell apart...if that wasn't an oxymoron altogether. They'd never agree. She understood what he did, at least from his moral low ground, but that didn't mean she'd ever forgive him. "Mother was beyond being able to make an informed decision." She couldn't prove it now that she was gone, but they both knew. "Aren't you cold?" She unhooked her carabiner keychain from the hook on the side of her computer bag, then fingered though the keys, looking for the right one.

"You changed the lock." Her father looked perturbed but not surprised. He needed a shave, which Thea thought odd. And his hair could use a trim. But his jaw was still strong, his eyes an ice-blue. As a child she'd been sure he'd absorbed all the warmth, and if she got too close to him, she would freeze. As an adult, she still half-believed it—danger lurked in his aura, an attitude of expend-ability, as if everyone existed for his use. His eyebrows shelved together in a frown. "Damned inhospitable."

Thea focused on the lock. "Most people wait for an invitation."

"I'm not most people, Thea."

There was so much truth in that statement, truth Flynn Janeway didn't intend, that his daughter almost laughed...almost.

The lock resisted—a bit of rust, Thea didn't normally enter her own home through the front door. And she didn't have many guests. After a couple of tries, she got it to move. She stepped inside, depositing her computer on the bench against the wall. The backpack she was more careful with—it contained one vial of Rita Davenport's blood in a cold container. Benton Myles had told her he could move mountains, then he'd proved it.

The front door hung open—she didn't kick it closed. That was as much of an invitation as her father would get.

Unwrapping her scarf, then shrugging out of her wool pea jacket, Thea tossed them both over the back of the couch as she moved through the living room toward the kitchen. The front door closed behind her.

"When are you going to finish decorating this place?"

"I'm sure you're not here to give me decorating advice." A comfortable couch, a good bed, a 4K television to catch football or baseball, a coffee machine, a bottle or two of stellar Champagne, and a house was a home. The rest was just stuff. She selected two flutes from the glass-fronted cabinet, then took a few moments to choose the bottle before popping the top.

Her father watched as she poured the bubbles. He accepted his flute with a slight bow. "Don't you have any of the good stuff?"

"No. I only have exceptional stuff."

A tired saw, but it was theirs. They clinked glasses.

Thea savored the dry lightness. Great Champagne was tangible happiness. This was almost great Champagne. Or maybe she was just a hard sell after an abysmal day.

"So, I'll ask again. Why are you here?" She took a deep breath and looked at her father. Like Churchill or Grant, Flynn Janeway was a great warrior who was lost without a fight. While his battles raged in the trenches of Big Pharma, it was no less bloody a war. And the warriors who won weren't nice men, just effective in a game most didn't know they were playing.

Intent on carving her own path and making a break with her past, Thea had kept her distance, made her own choices, paid her way even though Flynn had offered to pay for all the education she could stand.

Even at seventeen she had known anything from Flynn Janeway came with a string attached.

When she'd returned with an MIT Ph.D. and a grown-up confidence, she and her father had brokered a delicate peace. A peace shattered by what he'd done.

A huge bear of a man, all bluster and bombast, he lived at the top of his lungs and expected everyone to jump when he said so. Thea had done enough of that. He didn't scare her anymore. But what he was capable of did.

"You could at least hang your diploma on the wall." Her father eyed her over the rim of his flute as he took a sip, the delicate crystal trapped in his large hand.

"I did. Guest bathroom above the toilet, so you can admire it while you do your business."

He grimaced, giving her the point. Accolades were important to Flynn.

Thea knew he'd recognize her specific placement of hers for what it was—a rejection of everything he stood for. A small victory, but that's how wars were won.

"Why are you here?" Thea took two greedy sips then topped off her glass. Chugging the stuff was sacrilege, but some nights called for that kind of sin.

"I heard about Rita."

Her father's opening salvo didn't surprise her. Nor did the missing apology, although she kept waiting for her father to surprise her. He never did. What did Emerson say? Consistency was the hobgoblin of small minds? Flynn Janeway wasn't a big thinker, so his consistent narcissism was a fitting byproduct, at least by Emerson's way of thinking.

Ever the dreamer, Thea held out hope that people could change, not that she'd seen much evidence.

Flynn held up his flute to the light, buying time, remaining distant. "Killed herself, I hear. Guess your study isn't going so well."

Thea shrugged away the hurt, finding protection in pretending not to care. She wasn't her father's daughter. She clung to that lifeline, repeating the mantra over and over until she believed it. "And here I thought you'd come to commiserate. I should've known gloating was more your style."

"Thea." Her father made her name sound like an accusation, one filled with pity at her weakness.

"Our study is fine. I'm sure if you didn't attend her presentation, you have heard about it by now. If she killed herself, then it wasn't over that." Thea stepped back, leaning up against the counter. "You still funding studies for drugs that don't work?"

His mouth pulled into a tight line. "Hard to tell whether they work unless you test them."

"I have. They don't work. But you keep testing, developing, continuing a disproven line of inquiry because the money keeps coming in. Big Pharma. Big government. An incestuous relationship helping the two parties involved at the expense of the ones who really need it. You don't care which team you work for as long as the money's right."

"It's how the medical research world works. You know that better than I do."

Not even a close approximation of the truth, but that was the argument he wanted her to take—the one that would deflect them both from the truth. "It doesn't have to. We're proving that." Thea hesitated before filling her flute again. If she knew Carter Livingston, and she did—far better than made her proud—it'd be a while before she'd have Champagne again.

"I made your Dr. Hunt a huge offer for your testing protocols."

"I know." She didn't, but her father didn't need to know that. Not that she was surprised—making the offer was the natural next move for her father...while he still played by the rules.

"He turned me down."

Thea bit back a smile. Evans Hunt proved her confidence in him, in the program, was not misplaced. "I know."

Her father's face flushed crimson but his voice and manner remained controlled. "You all are fools."

In her father's world, where money was the yardstick by which everyone measured success, Thea was sure he was right. But in her world, she measured success by how many patients she could save. Same game; different goals. And only one of them could win.

Thea sipped her wine and said nothing. She'd lost Rita—nothing to be smug about, only heartbroken. Each loss took a chunk of her soul. When they'd taken all of it, would she be like her father?

"You know anything about some orderly at the hospital collecting Coke cans?" The question sounded odd, even to Thea, but she intended to be oblique.

"What?" For a hint of time, Flynn's expression dropped, but he recovered quickly. "No, why on earth would I? I don't have anything to do with your sainted hospital."

"Just wondering." Thea also wondered whether he was surprised by the oddity of the question or if there was a Shakespearean reason he seemed to protest too much.

"Your drug really works then?" Flynn posed the question to sound like an afterthought.

Ah, the reason he came. Finally.

Flynn's bait-and-switch act didn't work on his flesh and blood—the only upside to being a Janeway Thea had found, at least after her mother had died. And right now, Thea was tiring of his shell game.

"And our testing protocols. Feeling the pinch, are you?" Now Thea was the only family he had left, as far as she'd been told. Flynn was the kind of guy who would spread his seed on the theory that humankind would benefit. Opinions differed on that, and Thea's was one of them. She hid her smile behind her flute as she took a sip. "I mean, what would happen to the Great Flynn Janeway if some upstart outfit of ragtag scientists proved the efficacy of a natural compound in the treatment of the tangle diseases? What if we made a huge step toward solving the puzzle of the immune response with its genetic component?" She lowered her voice, adding a bit of drama. "What if our testing protocols were so refined that we could discredit and eliminate drugs in the pipeline before billions were spent on them? What would happen then? The money spigot would go dry. Billions would disappear from your bottom line." She snapped her fingers and didn't hide her gloat. "Poof."

"Need I remind you that where there's money, there's murder." The whisper of emotion slipped from his voice, leaving it hard and hollow.

Thea went cold. "What do you know about that?"

The black holes of his eyes looked like the barrels of a pair of pistols. "If she didn't kill herself..."

"She didn't."

He set his flute down with precision as if emphasizing the obvious conclusion; then, he hoisted it in a mocking salute.

Thea's hands shook. She wrapped one around the other, holding her flute to keep her father from noticing. Money. Chum to a shark like Flynn Janeway. What did he know that he wasn't saying?

"I'm asking unofficially." An odd comment from her father who didn't normally skirt the issue.

"You know as much as I do."

Even though the room was cold, a sheen of sweat glistened on his brow.

"You've gone all in, haven't you?" The realization left Thea strangely unmoved.

Her father's face melted a bit, his skin sagging into age and the truth that came with it. "The kids these days..."

Thea could only imagine. They ran research programs as profit centers and jacked up the cost of being sick because desperation knew no bounds. There was a special place in Hell for each of them, including her father.

One made their choices and lived or died with the consequences.

Flynn glanced toward the front door. "Where are you going?"

Thea didn't follow his gaze. "To bed." Clipped words. An invitation for him to leave.

"You can't hide, Thea. Not from me." His lips turned up in a half-smile that didn't touch the darkness in his eyes. "I knew you before you met yourself. You've got that look. I remember when you and Carter used to prowl the jungles looking for magical cures."

A shot in the dark that hit home. "Yeah, well, one of us grew up. The other decided there was great truth in hallucinogens. Someone needs to tell him they tried that in the '70s."

"You're justifying."

She gave him a long stare. "Don't we all?"

Her accusation was water to a duck. Flynn grabbed the Champagne bottle by the neck and poured himself another glass.

Every fiber of Thea's being took offense when he threw back the glass, downing it in one gulp.

"Seems to me you're still looking for magical cures." His insult lacked his usual force.

"If you really believed that, you wouldn't be here." He may have met her as a child, but he'd have to deal with her as a woman.

The delicate stem of the glass broke in his hand, drawing blood where the glass punctured his palm. He ignored it.

But it told Thea how much his self-control cost him. "What's that important, Flynn?" Thea tore a square of paper towel from the roll on the counter, then took his hand and pressed the bit of paper to the wound.

With the other hand, Flynn rooted in his pocket then tossed a clear plastic case on the table. Blue and red capsules filled the small box.

Thea didn't want to ask, but her curiosity won. "What's that?"

"The Longevity Consortium's first drug. Still very experimental." He took both of her hands in his. "It works, Thea."

She yanked her hands free, wiping his sweat off on her pants. "You're a long way from knowing if it really works and on whom and without horrid side effects."

"We know more than you think."

She reached for her glass, then dropped her chin to her chest. "You've been testing it, haven't you?"

Flynn was smart enough to not admit such a huge legal transgression, but Thea knew; she could see the truth in his eyes...and a bit of wildness there.

"Who's in that consortium with you besides Dr. Ward?"

"How do you know about Dr. Ward? I'm the public face of the consortium."

The poster boy for bad medicine, criminal, actually. "He came to my office yesterday. He let himself in. I caught him poking around when I returned."

Flynn set down the pieces of his empty flute and raised his hands. "Not on my orders."

Protestations of innocence that fell on deaf ears. "So who are the men involved in your shady, if not totally bogus, fountain of youth boondoggle?"

"Just a bunch of money guys who'd rather their participation not be known."

"Probably the same group as usual: Jasper Clarkson, Benton Myles, for starters. I thought you hated Clarkson. Didn't you two actually come to blows or something?" The thought of grown men fighting intrigued her. Now, if she could just find someone who could beat the crap out of her father.

"That was personal. This is business."

"That reeks of desperation, if not felony fraud." She tossed back the rest of the Champagne, ignoring the sacrilege. "I need to hit the head. Would be nice to find you gone when I return."

Thea took a bit of time to rearrange herself. Winning at Flynn Janeway's games took control and cunning. At least she could work herself back to control. Cunning wasn't a tool in her toolbox. Thea preferred the full-barrel approach.

Flynn was still in her kitchen. Worse, he'd opened a bottle of the good stuff.

"You brought your work computer home and your journals. I saw them in the hall. You're going to find him, aren't you?"

"Who?"

"Don't play me." Although he said it lightly, Thea heard the warning. "Do you know where Carter is?"

"Last I heard, he was in London." Thea poured herself a glass of the good stuff—Laurent-Perrier Rosé.

Flynn also helped himself. This time he chose a stemless flute. "At the conference. We just missed each other."

So, her father *had* been there.

He seemed a bit overeager, trying to hide it by focusing on holding his glass aloft and gazing at it in the light rather than looking her in the eye. "Since when are you interested in Carter Livingston's whereabouts?"

"Last time you mentioned his name I believe it was followed by a string of epithets that ended with a threat to kill him the next time you saw him."

"He deserved it." Thea still felt the pain...and the intense need to inflict pain on Carter Livingston. Serious pain.

"I'm sure he did."

She waited for him to formulate an answer to her question. What did her father want with Carter Livingston? And if he wanted him so badly, why hadn't he taken it up with Carter in London?

Flynn clearly struggled with his answer. The truth was easy; lies took time. And with Flynn Janeway, lies were his go-to. That didn't mean he was casual in his half-truths—on the contrary, he was very calculated, sorting through the possibilities like a Tarot reader turning over cards, choosing the one that would yield the most payoff.

The little boy who cried wolf all grown up.

"What he did to you..."

"Is my business." Thea slammed the door on that line of

conversation. The hurt still burned through her. When she found Carter, she wasn't sure that she wouldn't kill him. With time the wound had only festered. "What do you want with him?"

"Who said I do?"

Thea rolled her eyes, finished her Champagne, then stalked off toward her bedroom.

"We have a data project that we could use his expertise on." Her father followed her.

"If I hear from him, I'll tell him."

"You used to be a better game player than that." He grabbed her arm, pulling her around, forcing her to if not look at him, at least to listen. "You're too close to this one. Let it go."

She pressed a hand to his chest, insisting on some distance. "Go away. If you send someone after me, he won't be able to keep up, so don't bother."

Her father didn't argue. "Be careful, Thea. There's more at stake here than you realize. They've already killed once. They won't stop at killing you."

For a moment, Thea wondered what it would be like if he cared.

CHAPTER SIX

"Your place or mine?" I asked Beck as we stood outside the hospital, huddled against the chill. The trial participants had been given their meds and sent on their way. My small bottle weighed heavy in the pocket of my jacket.

Hope in a bottle, or placebo? It was hell not knowing. Cruel, actually.

Jet lag finally had felled Logan. Benton Myles and Dr. Hunt were huddled with the Feds, leaving Beck and me at loose ends.

"My toothbrush is at your place," Beck said with a wary smile.

We'd had a fight about it. I wasn't comfortable with the commitment that implied. He'd said it was just a toothbrush. Even though I knew he was wrong, I was learning to choose my fights.

With my arms crossed across my chest, I stared into the darkness—night had fallen while we'd been dealing with the uglier side of life, the side I called home. "My knee doesn't seem so important now, does it?" I tamped down the anger with only slight success. It burned inside me until I felt sweat dripping down my sides despite the chill in the air.

"Your knee is the most important." The threat and our suspicions gave his words a hollow ring. "I would've stopped you regardless."

"But you would've given chase. I mean, had you actually trusted me, trusted my instincts."

"Yes."

At least he admitted the truth—a truth that gaped between us. "So, we lost our only lead, and someone's life hangs in the balance." I didn't look at him—I didn't trust myself to. "This one's on you, Detective."

He flinched away. "The chief made me your keeper. He made it clear my job rests on being able to keep you from...reacting inappropriately."

Inappropriately? Who gets to decide that? The seekers of truth or the lawyers who clean up the messes? "Not good for either of us." I hazarded a side-glance. He looked tired and troubled. "And not good if I'm actually going to be a cop."

"Looks bad, I know."

"Is bad."

"I know." He ran a hand over his eyes. "It could be you, Kate."

"Why would anyone target me?" I shrugged away the thought surprised that it really didn't matter one way or the other. "Death is nothing but a timing issue—something I live with every day."

His jaw took a hard set and a muscle worked in his cheek. This fight had been building for a long time—since I first set foot in Beck's precinct as anything other than a suspect.

I didn't want it, but I'd never stepped away from a fight.

"What about the other people in your life, Kate? The ones who care. You think your death would be nothing more than that? A timing issue?" His voice lowered to a deep growl.

"I didn't ask you to care."

He reeled back as if I'd slapped him.

I stepped into the void. "It's not my job to live my life in a way that makes you comfortable. I don't ask that from you; don't demand it from me. And that's not what this is about anyway. You think you're mad at me when you're really mad at yourself." My voice rose, the anger seeped like molten lava through the fissures in my control. "You fucked this up." I poked him in the chest. "You. Not me." Another poke.

He grabbed my fist and squeezed. He wanted to hurt me...to share the pain. I could feel it vibrating through him. He wasn't that guy, at least, not yet.

But I knew the urge. Although giving in to it never got you the result you were looking for. What should help only made it worse —one of life's cruel twists of fate. Grabbing his thumb, I loosened his grip and twisted my hand free.

"*You stopped me.*" A bouncing Betty stuffed with emotional shrapnel; the accusation hung at the apex of its flight between us. Then it exploded, shards of white-hot rage perforating control. "I'll never be any more than a damaged misfit with control issues to you," I shouted the words at him. My vision grayed and blurred. "I'll never be a cop. A detective. A *colleague.*" I wanted to kill him. *Now.* I panted with the effort to resist.

He stepped back, trying to move out of reach.

I moved forward, keeping the closeness between us. "I'm nothing but a charity case to you."

My fist balled. I raised my hand. Shivering with rage, I held my breath. Closed my eyes. Fought the urge. Then I let my hand fall.

Beck grabbed my arms, pinning them to my sides. "You need to calm down."

A trapped animal, I quieted. "Worst thing you can say to someone out of control."

As Beck relaxed, loosened his grip, I whirled and kicked him in the shin. "Let me go!"

He grunted, but he didn't let go.

Pain shot up my leg taking my breath. My knee!

My good leg buckled.

Beck eased me to the ground. When he released me, I rolled onto my back. With one hand on my knee, I eased it to my chest. Even through the thick denim of my jeans I could feel the heat. "Fuck."

Beck crumpled down next to me. He reached for my leg. "Is it—"

"Don't touch it." Pain and fear gruffed-up the words, which came out harsher than I intended. I didn't apologize. "Don't touch me."

"Want me to get a doctor?"

"No. Help me up."

"I'll need to touch you. Can you handle that?"

I ignored his hurt.

He held my arm while I leaned on him, testing the knee.

It held.

"This one's on you," I said. I couldn't let it go—the pain of his betrayal cut deep, so deep I was numb.

"You've made that clear." Not an apology. Not a denial.

I shrugged out of his grasp. "I need to get my bike."

I limped back inside the hospital and up the stairs to the tram. He let me go.

By the time I'd reached the platform, I was drenched in sweat, my knee pulsing with pain but holding my weight, or at least, some of it.

A young doctor, looking as bad as I felt, had taken my usual spot in the back as far away from everyone as possible, but close to the exit door. He gave me a tired nod of disinterest. The doors shut, the car bounced on the spindles, then steadied as the wire took its weight.

When I looked down, Beck was gone.

USUALLY DESPERATE FOR the safety of home, I'd race through town, my body bent over the bike absorbing its power. Tonight, I felt disconnected, out of sorts. Confident my handlebar-mounted GPS could recalculate as many times as I needed to allow time to calm myself, I took unfamiliar roads as I worked my way home.

Home.

Portland hadn't always been my home, but it felt more like it now than anyplace else. The rest of my family, Hank's widow and kids, lived in the Bronx, a world away. I had friends here: Stella, Logan, the Watchman...Beck.

Friends were a new thing. As an undercover cop for the NYPD, I'd learned not to cultivate friendships, not to get attached, until it had become an ingrained, perfected art.

And now, if I was to find my way back to me, I desperately needed attachments.

Death might be a timing issue, but life was more of one and filled with irony.

Beck. I'd hurt him. That should've been okay. He'd hurt me— he deserved it.

But it wasn't okay. His hurt and my guilt nestled close to my heart.

Time evaporated as I wandered. So did my unease. My focus returned, and I took stock of my surroundings, trying to determine where my wanderings had delivered me. Not home, but the next closest thing.

My studio.

The owner of the studio had given me a key. I don't know whether he understood that art played a big role in the battle to find me again or whether Stella strong-armed him, not that it mattered. I had run of the place, day or night.

Night was when I needed it...when the ghosts whispered, and fear filtered through all my empty places. Nights like tonight.

Three keys jangled on my keyring: my motorcycle key, my house key, and the studio key. I read the lettering on the tags to make sure. Anger still trickled through me and my hand shook as I aimed the key at the lock. Tonight I needed three tries and several deep breaths before the door opened, squeaking on its hinges. I left the lights off, navigating by feel, dodging shapes and shadows created by the filtered light from the streetlamp outside. The place smelled of paints and thinners, the dampness of clay, the heat of the kiln, of people's hearts and hopes. Art was about expressing one's essence—an unforgiving, exposing master.

In my love of it, I hoped it exposed the me I used to be.

Reaching the far back corner, I flicked on the light. I used to paint, or so I'd been told. Happy scenes, colorful and bright. Now, large looming shapes in black metal stared down at me with unseeing eyes—dark and brooding, their faces hidden. My art had taken a sinister turn—proof to the old adage that art imitates life.

Irritation buzzed through me as I tossed my keys and my phone on the worktable—a scarred slab of wood that took my stabs of irritation without a word. Angry words. Angry life.

Angry.

I was like an addict, the blood levels of my particular poison ebbing and flowing but never completely clearing. Stella and I were working on that. She'd told me my long-term indulging in anger had rewired my brain, and we had to switch the wires back. Most days her faith overcame my disbelief. Today wasn't one of them.

I shrugged out of my jacket, letting it drip over a stool as I turned to my work. Pieces to be cut. Welds to be made. One last figure then the circle would be complete.

Druids chanting an ancient prayer, or something darker? I didn't have an answer.

Even though anxious to get started, anxious to lose myself in something I completely controlled, I paused, as I always did. While the memories still flitted like birds at dusk, hurrying to find a roost before darkness engulfed them, I needed to capture them. I paced my workspace and I recited the day as I remembered it, memorializing the words in some tiny bit of digital space in my phone. If only storage space in my brain were that easy to access... Even though I depended on my phone, I hated it. I hated the journal Stella had given me, now almost filled with jumbled memories that my brain rather than my pen should've processed and cataloged. And I hated the letters that marched over my skin— they set me apart but kept me part of the whole.

But most of all I hated who I'd become. Keeping myself meant I'd had to let other things go: life, people...living.

But my life wasn't worth fighting for if I couldn't be relevant.

And to be relevant, I needed to be present, whole, not scattered words, snippets of time.

With one butt cheek on the stool, I closed my eyes and listened to what I'd recorded. The words tumbled, but they flowed. The day would be there for me tomorrow.

Exhausted, depressed, feeling a loss larger than myself, I clicked off the button on the recorder when the words stopped.

Beck.

I should call him, but I didn't know what to say. He was wrong, but I'd never felt him to be dishonest. Trust would have to be his truth. He'd have to decide. Damaged goods, could I be trusted?

Even I didn't know.

Already I felt myself closing off, shutting down the connection.

Safer by myself.

I grabbed the TIG welder, donned my safety gear, and fired up the light.

A bright light that could melt metal.

I wanted to be that light.

Sweat dripped off me by the time the light went out, the gas spent. The anger, too. As my focus settled back into the real world, my heart still clung to hope even if my brain had abandoned it.

I needed Beck. Needed the tether.

What would I do if he left? *Survive.* But would that be enough?

I pulled up my face shield, tugged off the heavy gloves, then wiped at the drops of sweat on the end of my nose with the back of my hand. One bead I missed trickled to the corner of my mouth. Funny how sweat tasted like tears.

Light tinged the frosted windows with pink. The night had flown. Heart and soul weren't the only things lost to art.

The hooded figure was almost complete. A productive night.

Too tired to refill the tank, I propped myself back on the stool and rubbed my knee. Fluid had rounded it, hiding the bones that normally jutted like broken, twisted beams from a half-demolished building.

The heat had lessened but was still there. The memories flooded back with the pain.

My iPhone screen was blank. The blue screen saver mocked me. An empty canvas. No photo of smiling loved ones. No missed calls. No messages waiting. As if my life was waiting to be written or to be rediscovered.

My finger hovered over the screen. I should call Beck. A bit untethered, adrift, I wanted to hear his voice. I didn't need him; at least that's what I told myself. I wanted him. Want was different from need. But both were part of being whole.

I balled my fist and let my hand drop. Call him and say what? To call searching for an affirmation of something he didn't know would leave us worse than we were.

When he'd had no time for thought, only action, the truth had shown itself. A truth neither of us could live with. And I didn't know what to do with that.

To avoid questions with no answers, I focused on ones that might have some. Before the group had disbanded at the hospital, I snapped a few photos of the note. The one... What was his name again? I could barely remember his face, much less a random sequence of letters. I pulled up my sleeve and angled my head to read. Benton Myles, with a "y". The familiarity I knew I should feel had faded until it was only a shadow that slightly colored what I'd lost.

Short-term memories were the worst. Logan had said something about my disease impacting the transfer into long-term, but I couldn't remember exactly what. Irony was, I was starting to remember that.

I read the note over three times, trying to excite a few neurons. Not sure I succeeded.

She didn't have to die. Another will. You can stop it. But you must hurry. Time is running, the clock ticking.

A memory echoed. Another note. Another time. A dead man. That one had been personal. *Hank.*

I shook that away and refocused on the words on the tiny screen. Was this one personal? I didn't see why it would be. I wasn't a key player. If I died, people might be sad, I didn't know, but the research wouldn't grind to a halt. That's what they wanted, I thought. Someone had said that's what they wanted.

How can we stop it? Who would be next?

Questions with no answers. And the only way to get answers was to ask more questions. But later. Too early still, the light outside barely pink.

What time would it be in London? I asked my phone and it told me—middle of the workday. I scanned my notes. Detective Inspector Potts. I finally found his name and contact info; the phone did the rest. The connection echoed the hollowness of distance.

After the third ring, a man answered, his words clipped, his tone tired. "Potts here."

"Detective Inspector Potts, this is Detective Kate Sawyer with the Portland Police Department. I'm following up on your investigation into the death of one of our residents, Dr. Rita Davenport." I read the words immortalized in my phone. They helped me sound confident, official.

"Yes, Detective. How can I be of assistance?" Wariness infused each word.

"That's what I wanted to ask you. What can I do on this end to help your investigation?"

"Well then," he said, the wariness much less evident. "Not used to getting that out of you Yanks. We're at a bit of a dead-end here."

"Have you located Dr. Davenport's computer?"

"No. It was not with her luggage being held at her hotel by the bell staff. A search of the surrounding area yielded nothing."

"Odd that she wouldn't have it with her. It held all her research."

"I agree. We're contacting as many of the people she interacted with at the colloquium as possible. As you might imagine, it's taking some time. They've scattered to the far corners."

I could hear his fatigue. "Are you still thinking suicide?"

"All indications point that way."

"Precisely why it would be the most unlikely." I didn't give him an opening to disagree. "Her colleagues seem to think that would be highly unlikely."

"All but one," the detective inspector said, letting his implication hang like a ripe apple on a low branch.

Hungry for information, I bit. "All but one?"

"Yes." Papers shuffled in the background as the detective inspector paused. "It just came to my attention that we had a missing person call the night Dr. Davenport died. One of our younger officers took the call. At first, he dismissed it. He didn't make a formal report as the gentleman who called had only seen the doctor an hour before, but he was concerned enough to call. When the officer came back on duty an hour ago and heard about the suicide, he connected the call with the deceased."

"Why was the caller concerned?"

"He said Dr. Davenport seemed ill, paranoid, and not at all herself."

"And he waited an hour to call?"

"He said they'd had an argument. Once he'd cooled down, he saw the situation more clearly."

After he'd shoved her in front of a train. "Who was this mysterious caller? Did he give you his name?"

"Yes. The officer remembered. Dr. Evans Hunt."

That name seared through the synapses. What had Hunt said? I squeezed my eyes shut as my hand tightened around my phone.

Remember!

The past was foggy. The hallway. Hunt had been odd to Logan, accusatory. *Yes!* Hunt had said he hadn't talked to Rita; he hadn't seen her.

"Is your officer sure the caller was Dr. Evans Hunt?"

"That's who he said he was."

"You've preserved the tapes?" I assumed the London constabulary had the same backups in place as we did.

"Of course."

"Could you drop me a copy?"

"It'll take a bit to retrieve it, but yes."

I hit my name on the contacts list on my iPhone and read off my email, then had him read it back to me. "Yes, that's it. Thank you. I'll work that angle here and get back to you."

We rang off.

The caller had to know he would be taped. If it had been someone pretending to be Dr. Hunt, that would be easy enough to ferret out. That made me believe the caller really was who he said he was.

So why had he lied?

CHAPTER SEVEN

AFTER BUYING A SODA AND SOME SUSHI AT THE AIRPORT, THEA shouldered her backpack and found a pillar to lean against while she ate. Something bothered her. Maybe it was the oddly threatening conversation with her father, but she didn't think that was it. Oh, he was an ass, and he loved to play the bullshit game, but he was still her father. Thea knew he'd stoop to low levels to chase a buck, but she didn't think he'd let her get hurt. Maybe she was wrong. Carter had always thought that Flynn would stop at nothing to get what he wanted. Hell, Carter had almost been a casualty—something about being tied up, naked, covered in honey, and left for the ants. Thea had stumbled upon him at a very opportune time. He blamed her father but could never prove it—not to her satisfaction anyway. Not that she hadn't believed him, but she wasn't going to pick Carter over her father. Not then, at least. But now? Now, she'd be happy to shoot them both. Although at this moment, it wasn't her father who raised the hackles on the back of her neck. Nor Carter either, for that matter.

No, she felt sure she was being followed.

As she offloaded her backpack, she took in her surroundings in a leisurely glance. Two men and one woman looked as if they were studiously avoiding looking in her direction. Carter used to tell her, watch for someone doing something forced or out of place. When she'd been with Carter, they'd been followed a lot. Came with the territory, he'd said.

She'd promised herself never again. And look where that had gotten her—a one-way ticket to Sumatra. Carter Livingston kept cropping up like an incurable rash. At least her shots were up to date.

Before she'd left the house, she'd had a hurried call with her in-country contact. He'd been surprised to hear from her but agreed to meet her with her gear and her gun when she arrived. Now she had to get there.

First, the tail. Identify, then engage. Once in country, Thea would be home, and that gave her a huge advantage. Besides, the longer they followed, the more she could learn. Another thing Carter had taught her. Funny how quickly she donned old clothing.

First, identify.

As if intent on her food, Thea opened the plastic tub of sushi and poked at the pieces with her chopsticks. As she did so, she scanned the room keeping her head bowed, hiding her interest. One man who had attracted her initial interest had wandered off. The other man was still there, sipping on his beer and focusing on a basketball game. She watched him for a solid two minutes. He didn't so much as glance her way. Only the woman remained a likely candidate. Sitting at a table in the middle of the concourse, she had no food, only a bottle of water that remained untouched. She held her phone in front of her face, pretending to be captured by whatever was on the screen. In reality, her eyes looked over the device, scanning, watching. When her gaze passed over Thea with only a slight pause, she felt a chill.

Funny, they sent a woman.

Thea weighed her odds. Used to dealing with men who often underestimated women, this one presented a new set of challenges. A woman working for the bad guys was a whole different level of low. She should know better.

With two plane rides, a boat ride, and the rest of the way by kayak and foot, Thea knew where the woman would make her move—and it wouldn't be on a crowded plane.

So she settled back to get some rest for the fight ahead.

———

DETECTIVE INSPECTOR POTTS' bombshell about Evans Hunt was significant enough to be immortalized on the inside of my left elbow. Unsure what to do with it, I wished Beck would call, wished he were here. Still too early to call—who, I didn't know—I decided to keep moving forward with what I did know. I scanned my phone for the photo of the medicine bottle with Beck's scrawled notes as to contact information, location, and all of that.

Grabbing a shop towel, I wrapped my forearm, then swiped the surface of the worktable. Shards of metal flashed as they caught the light. One pierced the side of my hand. I dug at it, pulling it free before it had a chance to work its way deeper. They did that, bits of metal, splinters of wood, the words I printed on my skin. A dot of blood welled. I wiped it on my jeans, leaving a red slash that looked like a brushstroke.

Where to start? I didn't have a computer, just my phone, that was risk enough, and it would have to do. The connection was slow, but so was I.

I started with the manufacturer. I thought about calling them. They were in Nevada. Early here; same there. Looked like I'd do it the hard way and that suited me.

Corporate records. Start with the website—a Nevada company.

Staring at my phone, I wandered to the back corner of my workspace. With my back against the wall and careful to hold my hurt leg straight, I sank down to sit on the floor, my legs in front of me. I pulled my backpack from under the nearby table and extracted the journal Stella had given me. Using the pen clipped to it, I made notes as I scrolled through pages with my thumb. The owners of Nitro DNA apparently didn't want any press. Several corporate shells protected them, and Nevada law protected the shells.

Several dead ends later, I was scrolling through grant applications in medical fields I didn't understand when I found a connection. Turns out ownership can't be hidden from the government, at least not where funding for cutting-edge science is concerned.

I scrolled down the list of the owners of Nitro DNA. I scribbled notes as fast as I could. All names I recognized. *Benton Myles. Flynn Janeway. Evans Hunt. Dr. Ward.* I double-checked his name to make sure. Yep, he was the guy who'd given Logan such a hard time at the hospital. And one other name, *Jasper Clarkson.* I didn't know him.

I needed to talk to Beck—he'd know where this piece fit in the puzzle.

My phone rang before I had time to make the call. I smiled at the caller ID. "Beck, I was just calling you."

A pause. "It's not Beck, Kate. It's Carla."

Carla? So hard to switch gears. Carla?

"Beck's partner." Her voice was tired, flat.

Beck's partner? The fading letters on my right forearm confirmed it. I forced a smile into my voice. "Hey, Carla. When I saw it was the precinct number, I thought it was Beck."

"Uh, yeah, anyway, Beck asked me to call and get you to come in. We'd like to get a sketch of the guy you chased yesterday."

Why hadn't he called himself? I knew but the memories weren't clear. "Yesterday?"

"Some guy grabbing cans or something?"

The whisper of a memory, its breath cool on my cheek. "Not sure I could describe him to you."

"It's okay. We've got this guy here with a new machine. It's non-invasive, measures brain activity. Voodoo to me, but he says his accuracy with rendering faces from memories folks don't even know they have is astounding. You game?"

Technology didn't surprise me anymore. Not after having stem cells injected into my brain. "If you think it'll help. What time?"

"Guy's here now."

"I'll leave in five." Silence hung between us for a moment while I worked up my courage. "Can I talk to Beck?"

"He's not here." Carla's voice held a softer tone. "Did you guys have a fight or something?"

"Why?"

"When he came in, he looked like forty miles of bad road. When he left, he looked worse."

"We've got a few rough spots to get through, same as anybody." Not quite the truth. Our rough spots weren't the same as anybody's. Nothing about us was normal. "Where'd he go?" I felt this moment overwriting the past few in my brain—I knew when the memories wanted to run. Desperate to hold onto them, I transferred her to speaker. I put my phone down and pulled up the browser. Tugging up my left sleeve, I wrote down what I had found. I couldn't forget.

"He got a call. Something about his daughter. You know the one?"

"Yeah." A downward spiral of drugs and bad decisions, she'd been lost.

"Anyway, knowing Beck as I do, it was bad. He didn't say anything. He talked to the chief and he left."

And he hadn't called me.

I felt it in my heart: he was gone.

CHAPTER EIGHT

Beck wasn't answering. I'd tried several times before leaving the studio. Should've called him earlier. I felt like a pig, but I couldn't remember why, which pissed me off. And I felt a little lost, which pissed me off even more.

I told myself I didn't need him. And I knew I lied.

While the bike throbbed underneath me, I plugged my earbuds into my phone and started the tape I'd recorded yesterday. Carla expected me to remember; I could at least try. As a precaution against wind noise, I donned my helmet. Securing the chinstrap took me a minute—I was out of practice. In my case, I considered brain buckets superfluous. A little bit of reckless that tied me to the me I used to be. Then, with my voice in my ear, I followed the GPS's red line toward the Central Precinct on Second.

The sun hung low just above the horizon, but it brightened by the minute. The city barely beginning to stir, the traffic was light, which made picking up the tail child's play.

A white BMW, not the typical nondescript stakeout car. A small SUV. A woman driving. Blond. Young. Meant to throw me off. She maintained the distance, not closing not hiding. This was a message, not a threat, but I kept her in my rearview in case I was wrong. Listening to yesterday, I took a circuitous route through town. The BMW stayed with me.

With no parking, the precinct wasn't exactly user-friendly. Flouting a few city ordinances, I bumped up the curb and parked my bike next to the door. One of the perks of being perceived as "different."

The young woman in the BMW slid past. She didn't look at me, but she was aware. I could see it in the rigidity of her posture and her straight-ahead focus, both forced. Jerking the top of my Sharpie with my teeth, I made a note of the license plate number on the palm of my left hand—it didn't have to stick, just be readable for a little bit.

The officer on duty waved me through, buzzing the doors open without a flinch as the metal detector squealed. I found Carla behind her desk, the desk across from hers empty. I'd never been here without Beck. Without his gruff displeasure the place held a sterile accusation

Carla glanced up as I stood nervously at her desk, feeling lost and oddly afraid. Fear wasn't something I normally allowed myself. Today I couldn't stop it.

"Hey." A small black woman with short braids all over her head, each one ending with a different colored bead, a quick smile and a hardness that lurked under the approachable exterior, she lifted her chin toward the chair next to her desk. "Take a seat," she said, but she knew I wouldn't. After a long stare, her gaze missing nothing, she shook her head, the downturn of her mouth an admonition. "Man, you two better get it square between you or you're gonna be worthless. You get any sleep?"

"I don't think so." I was a bit fuzzy on that.

"Gotta stop doing that. Your buddy, Logan, has been telling me that sleep is more important than we realized. They say your brain gets rid of all the trash and organizes all the new stuff while you've taken it offline and are catching some Zs."

"Maybe that's what I'm doing wrong."

She didn't smile—apparently my delivery needed some work. "You never know."

Irony once again—a random song on an endless loop. "Can you run a plate for me?"

"Sure." Carla arched one eyebrow, but she didn't miss a beat when I read the number from my palm. "Got it." She focused on her computer screen. "You can sit down while I input this."

"Why does everyone seem surprised when I act like a cop?"

She glanced up, a quick cut-the-bullshit look. "Growing pains. We're all getting used to each other. Now sit."

Keyed up, I eyed the chair. "I'll stand if it doesn't make you nervous."

"Do what you want." She leaned forward, her nose inches from the screen. "If you were like the last guy in that chair, strung out, and with a knife someone missed, *that* would make me nervous."

"I'm only half crazy. No weapons. You should be good." I didn't know Carla all that well. We'd met a couple of times, but no more, at least not that I remembered. She'd been cool but distant. Today, I felt a bit more warmth. While she worked, I looked at her desk —you could tell a lot about someone by what they chose to display in their workspace. One photo—a boy, young, maybe three or four. Nothing else. No one else.

We were both alone—no life partner. So was Beck.

Misfits.

I wasn't sure how a kid changed that, but I knew it did. My niece and nephew, Hank's kids, gave me a heartstring to hold onto.

Beck had his two daughters. Carla, a son.

I'd had Beck, or I used to. At the thought, I felt loss, but couldn't remember why. Only the pain remained. I turned my back to his empty desk. Without him I couldn't even be a cop. That's what the chief had said. The damn rule was emblazoned down my right calf. Beck made me look at it often.

If I weren't a cop...I let the thought disappear. Without my job, without my duties, I didn't have anything worth living for.

"Wouldn't you know?" Carla leaned back, her chair groaning in protest. "Stolen. Southwest. Report came in a few hours ago."

I wasn't surprised. "She wasn't trying to stay out of sight. I figured she didn't have anything to hide. Worth a shot, though."

"The officer who investigated did say several neighbors reported a red sports car, fancy and all showy, lingering in the neighborhood. At first, they didn't pay any attention."

"It being an expensive car and all." My turn for the sardonic grin. "I'm assuming no plates."

"No. A man driving. They described him as big, gray hair. Not sure how they'd know about the big part. He never got out of the car."

Being small myself, I didn't see a problem with that. Size always made an impression on me, but I chose not to voice that fact. "Who reported the car stolen?"

She squinted at the screen once more, her finger ticking off the lines as she read. "Missy Clarkson." Carla gave a low whistle.

"Should I know her?" Clarkson. The whisper of a memory.

"The daughter of Jasper Clarkson. Sixteen with a newly minted driver's license."

"I don't think it's a crime to give a kid a nice car." I popped the top off my Sharpie. Clenching it between my teeth I looked for a bit of skin. Inside my right elbow I printed the names: Missy Clarkson and Jasper Clarkson.

"All depends on how you want that kid to turn out."

I capped the Sharpie, stuffing it back in my pocket, then blew on the new ink until it had dried. "Maybe so. So why the whistle?"

With both hands, she pushed back, sliding her chair away from her desk, then around to face me. "Seriously? Jasper Clarkson? Don't you read the paper?"

"No. The news scares me." Clarkson. Clarkson. Where did I know him from? The chill of a connection. I opened my phone and scanned my messages. "Shit!"

"What?" Carla's features sharpened.

I read from my notes.

"So, all these dudes are investors in the company that's making individualized medicines under the FDA radar?" Carla didn't seem surprised.

I hadn't spilled Dr. Hunt's secret—didn't see the need. "Yeah. It's an interesting coincidence, which I don't believe in, by the way. But I can't see any motive for murdering Rita Davenport."

"Well, you're right about that. But it sure is interesting his daughter's car was used by someone to follow you."

"There's something going on. I just wish I knew what it is. So, who is this rich guy?" I checked my notes. "This Clarkson?"

"Jasper Clarkson is some big real estate developer dude. He's got projects all over the country, if not the world. He's always giving money to some cause and making sure he gets his picture in the paper doing it."

"Somebody told me that if you do a nice thing and everybody knows about it, then you don't get credit for it."

Carla quieted. "Who told you that?"

I didn't reach for the memory; I let it come. "The Watchman, I think. But I knew it from long ago like it was written on my soul or something." The Watchman—Joe—he'd saved me...and he'd saved himself. Almost died doing it.

Carla swiped at her eyes that were now bright. "My gran used to say the same thing—maybe yours did too."

I shrugged.

Carla straightened herself up and smiled away whatever had made her sad. "Your Watchman, how's he doing?"

Something sad touched me. "He's okay, but not like he was before. Weaker, like he wants to go to another place."

"Sometimes memories can eat at you until there's nothing left."

Memories, both good and bad—they came together, I suspected. It had occurred to me that I could be struggling to remember something I'd wanted to forget. Logan had told me to have courage. I'd told him to fuck off. "So why am I here?"

"The sketch artist? The guy stealing the soda cans?"

Curiously, I remembered most of our conversation about it. "I can only give the sketch artist the minimum. Stuff like that doesn't stick."

"According to him, it sticks whether you can access it or not."

"Are you sure? This would be short-term memory. It's not designed to last long."

"I'm only telling you what he told me."

"Well, let's find out."

TWENTY-FOUR HOURS, two planes, a boat, a kayak, and a hike to get home—in the dark, not that it mattered—Carter Livingston should have been dead to the world but sleep only teased. Stray straw covering the loose weave of his cot made him long for the feather mattress at his hotel off of Lowndes Square. The rusted bearings of the fan turning in lazy circles overhead, barely stirring the heavy, humid air grated on his already raw nerves.

He'd made a quick hit on London, taking in Rita Davenport's paper defense and gathering a few colleagues for a short catch-up session. They formed a loose consortium, working together to stay on the leading edge, the only place with any relevance.

And now, he was home and as twitchy as a flea in a skillet.

Something was off, but he couldn't place it.

A rustle outside focused his attention just as Hippo whined. His hand found the soft fur of the dog still curled next to his cot, her head raised, her body quivering. "What is it, girl?"

The dog answered with another whine, but she didn't alert.

Carter silenced the dog as he listened, swiveling his head like a radar homing on a ping. The jungle had quieted.

Something slipped through the silence. No, *someone.*

Bamboo shivered. He cocked his head. A hand slipped across the bark of a Moli'aina, then bent back a branch, only the thought of a sound, an expectation, really. A slight citrus scent carried on the barely-there breeze. Footfalls, whispers on the bed of leaves.

Friends didn't come quietly.

Carter eased from under the Army blanket covering his feet and rolled off the cot, then brushed back the netting. With a hand signal, he ordered the dog to stay. A whimper in protest, but she didn't move.

"Good girl." A whisper, nothing more.

Crouching, he stayed below the level of the windows as he crab-walked to the doorway. A rough curtain of plastic strips was all that protected him from the night.

Feeling up the wall, his hand closed over the handle of his machete hanging in its scabbard by the door. After easing the long blade loose, he tested the edge. Even though careful, he drew blood, the acrid tang so strong he could taste it. He set the trip-wire then slipped into the darkness. His back against the plywood walls of his shack he stilled and listened.

He pieced the sounds into a mental picture as the shaman had taught him.

Human.

How had they found him? On the trip home he'd taken every precaution. He hadn't been followed; he was certain.

The human moved, then paused, then moved again, working his way around the small clearing. Carter tested the air. No scent. The human kept down-breeze.

Carter eased down the length of his cabin, then rolled around the corner, using the building, such as it was, to protect his dash to the tree line. He moved to his left until his foot hit the flat rock he'd embedded in the ground. Angling off of that, he ran to the tree line—the cool shadows welcoming him, hiding him. It took him no more than ten seconds to find the tree, the one with the notch gouged in its side. His back to the tree, the notch between his shoulder blades, Carter pictured the landscape between himself and the human—a mental map of trees and shrubs he knew by heart.

With quiet skill from having lived and hunted in the jungle, he moved quickly, counting steps. Every tenth step, he paused. Lowering to his haunches, he'd feel carefully through the darkness until his fingers found the wires. Rising, he'd step carefully over, then move forward another ten steps. At each pause, he'd listen for signs that the human had been alerted to his presence. But the figure moved on, somehow avoiding the wires.

His machete heavy in his right hand. The air hung still, the humidity smothering. Things moved in the dark, scurrying through the dense blanket of plants and mosses that softened the jungle floor. Carter used the rustle to hide his movements as he circled back putting the human in front of him.

The birds and animals resting in the treetops made no noise as if they sensed the predator-and-prey dance unfolding below.

Carter ignored the bugs that swarmed, disturbed by his passing. Swinging his machete in slow arcs, the sharp blade made short, silent work of any foliage in his way.

The person paused, perhaps looking, listening. Carter closed the distance, relying on sound and touch, navigating through a familiar world. He could hear them now, smell their fear, their weary stench from a long trip—a hint of soap from their clothing.

No more than fifteen feet separated them, he guessed.

The figure stopped.

Carter used a tree to hide his presence. He heard them, fumbling through the dense leaf matting moldering on the jungle floor. A moment of realization. Blinding panic.

He threw himself to his stomach, his arms crossed over his head. A fraction of a second later, a flash of heat, then the roar of the explosive charge high above. He'd set the charge to blow the top of the tree, sending it crashing onto trespassers below.

The top should fall to his right. He dove left.

Branches fell across his calves as the treetop landed, the impact rolling through the earth beneath him.

After working his feet from under the branches, he then pulled his knees to his chest and rolled onto his back, his legs bent ready to piston his body upright. Braced on one hand, he leaned forward as he gripped his machete. He listened into the darkness. But the blast still echoed in his ears—a ringing that obscured other sounds.

He sensed a presence behind him just as he felt the press of cold steel against his neck.

"Hello, Carter."

Air escaped in a sigh—relief he couldn't hide.

Thea.

The voice held memories, good, very good, hot and desperate, then very bad—but it didn't hold a threat, at least not an immediate one. Okay, maybe a hint of hate—he didn't fault that—but no homicide, at least not yet. She wanted something, and that gave him an advantage.

"You're like a bad penny, man." Carter tried for indifference. He failed. Thea wouldn't have bought it anyway. No matter the feelings between them, they were always intense.

"Worst nightmare."

He'd been right. Thea Janeway's voice held a hint of hate, tempered with something softer. Carter relaxed but remained wary. "You could've let me know you were coming. I would've set a place at the table with the good china."

"You don't have a table."

His head swiveled her direction, keying in on the sound of her voice, gauging location and distance. "Now see, there's the difference between us, Thea. I'm metaphorical and you're—"

"—a grown-up. You're just a man-child and his dog chasing the world for the best high."

As if on cue, Hippo bounded out of the darkness. With an excited yelp, she launched herself at Thea. Thea dropped the knife, then caught the big dog mid-chest. She held on as the force threatened to tumble her over backward. "No! Hippo, down!"

Carter reached for her as he grabbed the dog. "Down!"

The dog immediately responded. Thea lost her balance, but Carter was able to ease her to the ground. "What is it?"

On her knees, she shrugged out of her backpack. Sitting back on her heels, Thea brushed the hair back from her forehead. "It's happened, Carter, just like you said it would."

A cold shot of adrenaline hit his heart. He'd hoped they'd have more time to prepare. "Fuck. Stupid bastards. They wouldn't listen."

"They've killed once. I'm carrying a sample from the victim. I hope it will give us a hint as to who requested the design or who created it. We've got to figure out who the killer is." She paused. "If possible."

His voice turned serious. "I've got people who can help."

"Somewhere in here is the key. But we've got another problem."

"Let me guess, they've threatened to do it again."

"The clock is ticking."

"Already infected?" Carter Livingston was many things, but he was never slow on the uptake.

"Most likely." Thea tugged on Carter's hand and he pulled her to her feet. "It's been a long trip. I can't keep the sample cold for that much longer."

"Then we'd better hurry."

Both of them jumped as an explosion ripped through the jungle.

"They're at your cabin. We've got to go." Thea grabbed Carter, pushing him farther into the jungle.

Carter whirled toward the sound. "They fucking blew up my house!" He turned back to Thea, but he was about thirty degrees off. "They fucking blew up my house. And you brought them here."

"I'll build you another. Come on Carter, we have to go. Now!"

"And you'll replace the fifty grand I have in computers and satellite hookups."

"For God's sake, Carter!"

"The equipment." He didn't even flinch as men crashed through foliage.

They sounded close—too close. "Okay." Thea tugged on his hand. "Let's go."

"Guns?" Carter remained rooted.

"Know any bad guys who don't carry guns?"

"Quite a few."

A shot whizzed through the foliage.

That got Carter's attention. He ducked, then turned and ran.

Thea tried to lead, but Carter muscled her behind him. "I know this jungle."

Thea resisted, but only slightly. "But you're blind."

Carter whispered to the dog. "Boat."

Behind them, their followers crashed through the brush. Periodically a small blast then yelps of pain pierced the silence. Carter had planted those trip wires everywhere—part of his eyes in the dark, he'd told Thea...before.

"Quite a perimeter defense you have," Thea gasped as she ran.

"One can never be too careful. We're stepping on powerful toes, Thea." Carter dodged and wove and didn't sound out of breath at all. "Do you know exactly who is after us?" Carter yanked her hand, then let go. He trailed his hands by his sides feeling his way through the trees.

"Haven't a clue. But the cops in Portland are on it."

"Which covers me with warm fuzzies."

Thea kept right on Carter's heels, the thrashing behind them growing louder. "Following a blind man through the forest. This whole thing was fucked up from the get-go."

"Eyes are not the only way to see."

He left the last part out, but Thea heard it anyway. "Your heart knows the way." Carter had made it clear he still carried hope of the two of them working together in the jungle. Thea had shared the dream. But she'd wanted him, all of him. Then she'd lost him to the shaman who'd promised him the moon. "They picked me up in Portland, but somehow they knew I was coming to find you." Thea managed to bark each word while she ducked and dodged the branches that slapped at her. Vines snaking through the brush grabbed at her ankles. Those tripped her twice.

Carter caught her each time, almost without breaking stride. "So, you played along."

Thea worked to keep up but felt she was shucking when she

should be jiving, slowing them both down. "Easiest way to find out what they wanted."

Carter managed a choked laugh. "Knowing you, I should've expected full-frontal. How's it working out so far?"

"Pretty much as expected." Her breath was ragged now, burning her throat. "You go ahead. I can't..."

They broke out of the jungle, the smell of the sea heavy, the light of the moon a ghostly shadow on the water. "We're here."

The dog leaped into the boat, followed by Thea. With a few turns, Carter unmoored the boat, then jumped aboard. The engine fired. "Hang on," he shouted above the noise as he opened the throttle. The propeller took a big bite as he lowered it into the water. The boat surged forward as the first shots pinged off the metal and hissed into the water at close range.

"Get down!" Thea shouted. Both hands clutching the gunwale, she folded herself over the dog. "Down," she ordered and the dog dropped to her belly. Facing forward, Thea braced against the wind as the boat fled across the water.

Carter grunted behind her.

"You okay?" she shouted, letting the wind carry her words back to him.

"Yeah. Your bill just jumped to 100K."

Ten seconds, maybe less—it seemed like an eternity—then they were out of range of the shooters on the beach. Carter turned back to hug the shore—a small boat didn't mix well with the open ocean.

"Any destination in mind?" As Thea turned to look at him, the wind whipped her hair, the tendrils popping her face with a sting.

Carter's eyes, a milky white in the moonlight, stared forward as if fixed on their destination. "Are we past the rocky outcropping to the left? I've never left it wide open like that. Don't know how to count the distance at full throttle."

Thea guesstimated their closure rate then waited five or six seconds. "Now."

Carter swung the boat hard to his left. "Parallel?"

"Ten degrees more."

He adjusted the course. "You came from town?"

"Yes." Thea put a hand on the dog, keeping her down.

"Let's work our way back that way. With that many armed men, I'd bet they have their own boat, and we're going to need a more seaworthy mode of transport."

"Where are we going?"

"Singapore. Access to big computing and that huge DNA database the Chinese have been building."

"I'm sure I don't have to tell you the database is in Shanghai." Thea's heart sank, but her pulse quickened. "You're not going in through the front door, are you?"

"Somehow I left my invitation at home. Not to worry, someone left the backdoor open for us."

"Just like that?"

"Just like that. I know a guy."

Thea idly stroked the big dog. "We're coming up on the point. Swing out twenty degrees and throttle back. With only your machete between us we're going to need surprise on our side. Too bad you opted for a Lab—right now we could use a rabid German Shepherd."

"Don't be dissing my dog. Hippo has her uses."

The boat slowed, making an arcing adjustment to starboard. "The bench to your right opens. See if there is anything in there you might like."

As she eased out two watertight gunnysacks, Hippo slipped by her to take up her position leaning against Carter's left leg. His hand dropped to stroke the dog's head. Thea watched them for a moment. A perfect team. She'd been a part of that once. Or maybe she'd been fooling herself.

"Look, there." Carter's voice brought her back.

Peering into the darkness, she could make out the sleek outline of a low-slung yacht, no lights, only a faint glow from the electronics on the bridge. They'd anchored two hundred yards or so from shore. "How did you?" She dropped her voice to a whisper.

"The waves. I heard it."

"There's movement on the deck. A man. No, two. Guns. No, make that automatic weapons."

"I guess we'll just have to be a bit more careful then." Carter eased the small craft closer.

CHAPTER NINE

The guy had set up his equipment in one of the interrogation rooms. There was that irony again. Young, bouncing with enthusiasm, his blue eyes bright, his manner undeterred, he wasn't what I expected. He extended a hand. "I'm Doctor Bill."

"Dr. Bill?" The guy looked all of sixteen, maybe.

"And you're Detective Sawyer."

"Right." His handshake was firm, his skin warm and dry. Mine was the opposite. I took the chair he indicated. "Is this going to hurt?" Leaning forward, I tucked my hands under my thighs to keep them still.

"Not at all. We're going to tap onto a couple of the electrodes they're using for your stem cell therapy." He touched the back of my head at the hollow of my neck. "These right here. They are embedded in the visual cortex. We want to read activity in the inferotemporal region."

Apparently, I had regions I'd never heard of and couldn't pronounce. "You've done this before."

He leaned away from me so he could catch my look. "In Macaque monkeys. As you might imagine, not a lot of folks have electrodes planted in their brains."

"So happy to help." For a moment, he read my look, then gave me a grin. Experience allowed me to interpret—the unbridled joy of working with an unusual lab rat. "And the monkeys?"

"Good as new. Not to worry."

My brain, not his. "Monkeys remember faces?"

"We're not as far removed as you might think. And it turns out that we have very specific face neurons that respond to different facial features—a high brow, a wide mouth, the space between someone's eyes—things like that. Odd, I know. But that's how we can access faces so quickly and remember. And we've been able to model it mathematically. It's stunning how accurate the model and the neuronal correlations are."

"It's that easy to read my thoughts?"

"Only when it comes to remembering faces. The other stuff will remain sacred, I assure you. We have yet to crack that code."

"Stuff? Is that a technical term?" I wasn't sure keeping it all secret was a good thing—many days I'd love for someone to tell me what I was thinking. Logan had told me that my disease precluded accessing memories, but not the formation of them. And it didn't destroy memories, at least not until the brain tissue died.

He kept telling me that hadn't happened. I wasn't so sure.

As the young doctor hooked me up, I did what I always did—I pretended I was somewhere else. But with my memories what they were, I didn't have anywhere else to go, and I found myself thinking about Beck. Where was he? What horrible thing had taken him away? Why wouldn't he answer my calls?

"Okay." Dr. Bill placed his hand on my arm. "Are you good?"

I laughed.

He looked like he understood. "I promise this will be the easiest thing you do today." He sat across from me, our knees almost touching. "This is how it works. All you have to do is try to think about yesterday." Someone had briefed him. He led me through the day.

His story swirling around me, I let my mind drift, catching the details as I could. They were fresh—I'd been listening to them on the ride over. Even still, some faded while others stood in stark relief. Was that normal? Did other people process like that? Or was that part of my disease? With no normal to tie any of this to, I wallowed like an unmoored boat.

He wound down, then shifted behind his machine. A printer whirred to life.

"I'm sorry. My memory isn't the best."

He grabbed a paper from the printer and held it up. "What do you think?"

Stunned, I struggled for words. Visual cues helped the memory—pictures easier to hold onto than words. I'd seen the guy. His ghost stared back at me. "That's him."

Dr. Bill didn't seem surprised. He gave me a copy of the photo and assured me he'd upload one to Carla. No time like the present to start searching the databases, he'd said. He'd packed up and the room was mine. Straddling a stool, I listened again to my memories from yesterday. Then I looked at my notes: three leads, no partner. Carla would follow the picture of the can guy. I needed more info from Logan to figure out what to do with the corporate information I'd uncovered. That left Jasper Clarkson.

Swallowing my pride, I tried Beck again. Still no answer. I listened to his message all the way through. When I got to the beep, I disconnected. His voice affected me in ways I didn't want to admit. I was bad for both of us. But knowing that didn't make me want him any less.

I rooted in the small pocket of my backpack until my hand closed over metal—my badge. A detective, it said.

Time I started acting like one.

WITH ONE HAND, Thea held onto the small boat as it rocked in the swells, the water lapping on the sides. With the other, she stroked the dog, more to calm herself than control Hippo. How much did she trust Carter? Maybe enough to trust him with her life but not with her heart. He was good in a fight.

"Still see only two?"

Carter had leaned forward to whisper in her ear. She heard him easily over the soft idle of the outboard. "Three. One on the stern. One on the bow. One roving. Looks like no one is on the bridge."

He cut the engine, letting momentum carry the boat the last thirty feet. Thea stood with her feet braced as wide as she could get them in the narrow boat. As they approached the idle craft, she leaned forward, placing her hands against the metal. Pushing, she kept the boats from touching. Then, hand over hand, she eased the smaller boat alongside the other as Carter paddled silently. She'd worked the bow toward the stern of the larger boat, keeping it tight, invisible from above unless someone leaned far over the railing.

"Me first," she said. "I'll take the guy in the stern. Then the dog comes over. Then you." She quickly tied the boat to a ladder railing, then gave it a hard tug, checking her knot.

Carter didn't say anything. He didn't need to—they'd done this before—different island; different boat; different bad guys.

Thea pulled a sheathed ten-inch blade with a heavy metal handle from the gunnysack. With one foot on a ladder rung and one hand holding the rail, she reconsidered. A knife against three men with automatic weapons tilted the odds a bit too far against her. A Glock would improve them. She found one nestled in the side pocket of Carter's bag of tricks. The gun felt balanced, weighted just right for her hand. Knowing Carter, she also knew a round would already be chambered. She stuffed the gun in the zippered pocket on her right pant leg. Pockets and pissed off were two essentials to remaining alive while in Carter Livingston's company.

The salt spray coating the metal made the going slow, which was fine with Thea. As she mounted the ladder, Carter kept the boat steady, one arm on either side of her, his body pressed against hers. *Never one to miss an opportunity*, Thea thought, which made her smile. Carter was almost childlike in his lack of guile. But that was the only thing about him that was childlike. That thought made her smile wider.

She listened, trying to catch footfalls above the sound of the water lapping against the sides. Carter had his talents, but keeping watch wasn't one of them, for obvious reasons. She was on her own. Footfalls sounded above, moving from her left. The dog whimpered from below. She pressed herself against the boat and held her breath. Her heart pounded in her ears. She risked a glance down. Carter held a rifle steady, trained in her direction—presumably at a spot above her where Carter thought one of the bad guys might appear. His aim looked a trifle low, but Thea didn't risk trying to alert him. Regardless of his aim, if he took a shot she'd be in a boatload of trouble.

If the man above so much as glanced over the railing...

Seconds ground by. Finally, the footfalls moved past and to her right, toward the stern. Thea paused long enough to shoot Carter a wicked look. Even though he wouldn't see it, he'd feel it.

One rung. A pause. Another rung. Thea eased her way to the top. A whiff of smoke. She closed her eyes and absorbed the world around her. Wind from her right. He'd passed from left to right. He'd be on the stern taking a smoke. She had no idea where the other two were. The one on the bow hadn't left his post while she had watched, so unless called away, he would probably remain there. The third one, the roving shooter, he was a wildcard.

Reaching the top rung, she pressed against the side of the boat while she unsheathed her knife. With the blade clutched between her thumb and forefinger, the point down, the handle in front, she eased upward just enough to get one eye above the deck line. A pair of boots off to her right, the toes pointing slightly away. If his peripheral vision was any good, and if he glanced down, he could see her.

Clouds scudded above providing protection from a full moon. Walking up the rungs, Thea accordioned her body so that her feet were as high as she could get them, her butt hanging low, her muscles tensed. Hanging by one hand, clutching the knife, she peered upward through the strands of wet hair glued to her forehead. A deep breath. No second thoughts. Thea pushed upward, standing on the second-highest rung.

The man paused, his hand halfway to his lips, smoke curling from the tip of the cigarette clutched between two fingers. His eyes widened. His mouth opened.

Thea flicked the knife. As it arced end over end, the blade caught the reflection of a red position light on the stern, strobing as it flew. The butt end caught the man mid-forehead with a meaty thunk. His eyes rolled back. His knees buckled, and he crumpled to the deck.

Scrambling over the railing, she hurried. The knife wasn't as heavy as her throwing blade back home. She figured surprise probably felled the guy more than the force, so she didn't have much time. Her knees hit hard as she dropped down beside him, already snaking her nylon belt from the loops. With a few quick turns, she secured his hands behind him. As he began to stir, she stuffed a handkerchief in his mouth.

"You there." The voice came from behind her. Male. Cold. The roving shooter, no doubt. "Back away. Hold your hands where I can see them."

On the balls of her feet, her knees bent, Thea slowly rotated as she held her hands out to the side.

"Up. Keep them up." The shooter motioned with his gun— something black, semi-automatic, if not fully. Young, with military training and one of those butt-ugly Marine haircuts, he wore a half-bemused expression.

Thea raised her hands and gave him her widest grin.

His eyes narrowed. "What are you doing here?"

"When somebody comes after me, trying to kill me, I like to know why. The who part is equally fascinating." She swiped at the hair tickling her eyes to get him used to movement. The zipper on her pants-leg pocket was only half closed, but still, she'd need a few seconds to grab the Glock.

The man behind her groaned. Two to one would make things

interesting, but Thea didn't have time for interesting now. Who knew how soon the landing party would return, empty-handed and angry, and even she and Carter couldn't handle those odds.

She made a move for her gun.

"Don't!"

She froze.

"What the?"

Hippo scrambled over the railing. With a growl that made Thea's hair stand up, the dog launched through the air. She hit the shooter chest-high, taking him down before he could get his gun raised or a shot off.

Thea grabbed her Glock, then covered the distance between herself and the shooter in one large stride. She coiled, then uncoiled, catching the shooter in the temple with the butt-end of her pistol. His body went limp.

Knowing Carter wouldn't be far behind, Thea reached over the railing and found his hand. She pulled him up and over. "I've got one on the ground, gagged with hands tied. Take care of the second one. He's out cold but not for long. The dog will show you. I'm going after the third one."

Before he could object, Thea collected her knife and drifted toward the bow. Her heart pounded in the silence. No movement. No hushed call to his patrol members.

Neither good signs.

Thea had been taught to stop and stay still when she sensed danger. This guy must've read from the same manual. A light mist started as the wind picked up. Enough water to make the deck slippery as snot. Thea swiped the sleeve of her jacket across her eyes. The damp fabric helped a little...enough.

She slowed her breathing, one ear cocked to catch the sound. A foot at a time, her back pressed to the cabin area of the boat. The cold of the metal leaked into already cold flesh through the thin fabric of her jacket. Beads of sweat dripped into her eyes. She blinked them away, welcoming the sting. The walkway narrowed toward the bow. At the end of the cabin area, with the expanse of the bow deck in front of her, Thea stopped. The knife felt heavy in her hand. Instead of pocketing the Glock, she kept it at the ready. Something told her this one would be different—the other two were too easy. Just like happy, easy never hung around for long.

The boat rolled slightly in the swell. In the distance a light burned, gossamered by the light mist until Thea couldn't figure whether she imagined it or if it was real. Somewhere out there, life was normal. People going about their business never wondering whether this would be their moment, the end of their bean row as Thea's grandmother used to say. The thought made her smile. Somehow, she thought her grandmother would be both appalled and proud of her. Not that her grandmother's opinion would tip the scales of Justice over much.

Thea inched her head around the corner. No one. The deck was clear. Where had he gone? Oblivious, had he gone in search of his friends, maybe to join them in a smoke on the fantail? Carter hadn't called out, so either he was dead or waiting.

That meant the odds were good the third shooter had hidden, waiting.

But where?

Thea eased farther out. She narrowed her eyes against the mist, focusing. Switching the Glock from her left hand to her right, she held it at the ready. The knife fit through a belt loop, the hilt secured it—not ideal, but she wasn't going to give up a weapon.

Her eyes kept a constant scan, pausing for a few seconds every ten degrees, looking for movement. A few more inches out. A flash in front of her. *There!*

Searing pain burned across her right shoulder. Thea dove for the deck. She rolled then scrambled, using a barrel for cover. *No waiting! He'll expect you to hide.* Ignoring the pain, the flush of warmth spreading, she dove and rolled again, keeping her eyes on the shooter's position. He hadn't moved. In the darkness, she hoped he hadn't seen her. Her position now was at least 100 degrees to his right flank. Gritting her teeth against the pain and keeping low, she worked her way closer. Several large open boxes helped hide her. Gun boxes. She needed to hurry.

A bird call sounded. Carter. Yes, she needed to hurry. The landing party—he must've heard them. She paused to listen. Nothing. Using the box as cover, she peeked around the back side. Squinting, she could just make out the outline of a man's head and maybe the curve of a shoulder; that was it. Without thinking, she lifted the pistol and pulled the trigger.

A pop. The man fell forward.

Thea sat back on her heels but kept the gun high. She felt her arm which had started to shake. The bullet had passed through the meaty part of her shoulder, taking a slice out of the delt she'd been working so hard to perfect.

Hippo bounded into view with Carter on her heels. They both gave the shooter the once over. "Dead," Carter announced.

"I don't shoot to miss."

"Why'd you kill him and not the others?"

"He shot first—there are rules about that sort of thing. Maybe not out here, though. But it's damn hard to get a dead guy to give you any info. And right now, we are in desperate need of info."

He zeroed in on her voice. Stopping in front of her, he extended a hand. Thea let him pull her to her feet.

He pulled her toward the stairs leading up to the bridge. "No, right now we have a desperate need for speed. I hope they left the keys in this thing."

ONE OF THE great things about having a bad memory is I could claim forgetfulness, and everyone would buy it. That might come in handy as what I had planned broke just about every condition of my employment. Beck had made me Sharpie-tattoo every rule on my right calf. Besides me, only he knew that. He wasn't here. And he wasn't answering his phone.

A low whistle escaped as I eased the bike to the curb in front of what the GPS had said was Jasper Clarkson's humble abode. Larger than most Holiday Inns, built of rock and wood, with a long porch and a go-away attitude, the house reeked of old money and revenge. But it didn't have the air of inherited money. No, the spit-and-polish patina was a bit too bourgeois for that. The garish statues in the center of the curved drive—nymphs frolicking in a fountain, also hinted at a less-than-blue-blood upbringing. No gate to keep the riffraff out, which surprised me. Every other house in the neighborhood hid behind hedged fences and large gates. Guess that's why the car was an easy target. With the houses so far apart, who would hear? And now it made sense that the neighbors wouldn't give a second thought to a fancy car lurking.

Jasper? Who would name their kid Jasper? That was a huge chip to carry through the brutality of childhood. Jasper Clarkson had found a way to get back at the world. If money were a measure, he'd certainly won the game and rubbed everyone's nose in it.

I wondered what kind of man needed to flaunt his wealth but then almost invited curiosity seekers to wander up the drive and enjoy the grounds.

The front door looked like it had been carried on the backs of slaves all the way from some cathedral on the moors. At a loss after searching for a bell, I finally lifted the lion's head to the right of the door. A muffled bell sounded deep inside the house.

The door creaked open and I took a step back. Now I knew why a gate was unnecessary—the butler or doorman or whatever he was would scare kids on Halloween and adults on every other day. Or maybe it was the semi-automatic slung across his chest. While I didn't possess much personal knowledge regarding real estate moguls, I wasn't aware of any who flaunted armed house staff, which begged more than a few questions about Mr. Jasper Clarkson and his business practices.

The man in the doorway gave me an expectant glare as I rooted in my pocket. When I produced my badge, his glare turned icy.

"I'm here about the car reported stolen this morning." The truth, sort of. But the implication was rock solid. The chief himself had told me never to go anywhere on official police business on my own. As far as I was concerned, this was unofficial, but I didn't feel the need to share that. "I'd like to see Mr. Clarkson."

"It was his daughter's car."

"But he owns it." I found a card in my back pocket. Dog-eared with a number I didn't recognize scribbled on the back and a stain that looked like coffee on the corner, it was all I had. I presented it. "Detective Kate Sawyer."

His left eye twitched as he stared at my card, then he stepped aside. "You'll wait in the library." He ushered me across the large foyer. The thick rug in greens and blues muffled sound and protected the burnished wood beneath it. The furniture looked old and expensive, meant to impress. Clearly, I was the wrong audience. Front and center on the far wall, hugged by the curve of a banistered staircase, hung an oil painting—a portrait, a full-body, full-frontal female nude.

"Impressive."

The doorman noticed my interest. A wisp of a smile. "Mrs. Clarkson."

That left me slack-jawed. Every dignitary who walked through the door would see...not to mention her children and their friends. The man who would put his wife in her altogether on display was growing more interesting by the second.

The doorman waited by an open doorway for me to join him. "Wait in here. I'll see if Mr. Clarkson is available."

Alone, I used the time to make a quick circuit. The room was an art director's dream, staged to perfection. With its curated knickknacks and antiques positioned to be seen, the room was totally sterile as if no one lived here but rather acted out a scripted existence. I'd wandered onto the set. To play what part?

As I worked through what I knew and the bits I couldn't quite remember, I warmed my hands in front of the fire banked in the oversized stone fireplace at the far end of the room. Even in summer, I bet this room would hold a chill. One of the seams of the hunter green with gold-embossed pattern wallpaper had started to pucker in the dampness. Keeping up a façade required vigilance.

Uncomfortable with my back to the doorway, I kept my body angled so I could see anyone who entered. The minutes ticked by —the pendulum clock behind the large desk announced each one. After twenty had passed, I decided the guy was intentionally keeping me waiting—a game I was terrible at playing. The anger, always a fire in my core, licked flames higher and higher, melting my patience and my resolve. Hard enough to fight the assholes of the world without battling myself. Why wasn't Beck here? Where had he gone? Why wouldn't he at least answer the phone? Worries bit at me, shredding my focus.

"Detective Sawyer."

I jumped at the booming voice.

A man, tall, white-haired, ruddy complected, with a warm smile and cold eyes, strode my direction. When he stopped in front of me, he didn't extend a hand. He also didn't waste a glance at my badge, so I pocketed it. Instead, he kept his eyes on me, searching my face for something. "I've heard about you."

A cold chill. Flying low and out of sight was my comfort zone. "How so?"

"You've been in the news. Quite a success story."

Success story? In the news? Had I? "Not quite on par with yours." A glance around the room, taking in its opulence, made my point. "Real estate must be a good gig."

"Not real estate per se. Planned communities."

"Excuse me?"

"Here in the States, my team and I design whole communities from the ground up. Each has all the varieties of housing from multi-family to individual estates. We plan everything—the schools, the recreational facilities, the shopping. Many of our projects are built around lakes."

"You design those, too?"

"Of course." He'd missed the mock in my question.

"Carefully constructed, man-made water features." His smile was meant to disarm.

Wrong audience, but he didn't need to know that. "You only do business here in the U.S.?"

"Of course not." He seemed slightly offended. "My company is one of the largest in the world. We have properties and partners in every important country." He preened in anticipation of my admiration.

Like I said, not the right audience. "About that car? The one that was stolen?"

He waved a hand, dismissing me, then poured himself a liberal dose of something amber and presumably alcoholic from the bar. He held up a crystal decanter of some sort. "Wanna snort?"

I did. Desperately. "Boss frowns on that."

He raised a glass in half-toast as if to say rule followers were to be pitied at best. I concurred, but life dealt us each a hand that had to be played. Not that rules hindered me—hard to follow what I ignored or couldn't remember. "So, the car?"

"Not important." He paused with his glass halfway to his lips and skewered me with an impenetrable look. "I told the chief that. My kid's car. Not a biggie. I can get her another."

"I understand." I pulled out my notepad Stella had given me and poised my Sharpie over a pristine page. "Anything you could give us would be most appreciated. We have information that leads us to believe the perpetrator might have information about another crime."

An eyebrow ticked up. "Really? That's rather mundane, isn't it? Someone stealing a car to perpetrate a crime?"

"Still a crime. Gotta be solved."

"And you got stuck doing cleanup."

With a casual shrug, I did my best to look irritated—not hard, considering.

He poured himself another dose of liquid courage or whatever. "As I said, it was my kid's car. She has a habit of leaving it out, keys in the ignition like Portland was a fucking fairyland or something."

And she lived in the castle with the Devil King. "And did she do that last night?"

He threw back the drink. "Yeah." He didn't look at me.

"Did you notice anybody odd lurking around, any strange cars?"

"I worked late."

"And your daughter? She was home with her mother?" A snort of derision.

"Okay. Home with the staff?"

"The staff goes home at night. My wife doesn't like witnesses."

An interesting choice of words. "And your wife? Where was she?"

"How the hell..." He stopped himself. He turned a painted-on smile my direction. "You'll have to ask her to get the exact timeline."

He had no idea. "Perhaps, then, I should speak with your daughter?"

"Over my dead body." He said it with a smile, so it took a moment for the words to register. "She's a minor. You need my permission."

"And she really wants that car back, I bet."

For a moment I could see his indecision—a soft spot for his daughter. Duly noted.

"I can buy her another one."

"No doubt. So, nothing you can add?"

"What crime is the car implicated in?"

"Ongoing investigation. I'm sure you understand."

He had to accept that, but that didn't mean he liked it. His rigid posture, the painted-on smile told me he didn't. "Brace will see you to the door."

I followed his glance—the doorman. Brace was a name that begged more than one question. I didn't ask. At the doorway, I turned. "One last question."

Clarkson paused, his glass halfway to his mouth.

"You're an investor in..." The words fled, the memories evaporating. I checked my phone. "Nitro DNA."

His eyes widened slightly. "Not a crime."

"Maybe not."

<hr>

UNSURE where I wanted to go or what I should do, I paused outside the front door, which shut behind me with a whoosh like a bank vault. The day still held a chill. I pulled on my gloves which I'd retrieved from my jacket pocket. Killing time. Trying not to worry. A headache bloomed, and I felt oddly cold.

Had it been smart to play that card with Clarkson?

My thoughts refused any efforts to corral them. Like old times without the warm fuzzies.

Being on my own felt liberating yet disconcerting. Being a cop, acting like one, felt like home. My bike sill angled at the curb, and I started down the hill toward it. Halfway down the hill, I turned, walking backward for a bit, drinking in the house. As I turned away, I thought I caught a movement in the first-floor window on the left. When I looked back, all was still. I looked for a bit to see if I imagined it. Nothing. I must've been seeing things. Not unheard of.

I continued down the drive to my bike. With more research to do, I figured the central library would be as good a destination as any, especially with Beck...away.

I'd just donned my helmet and was securing the chinstrap when a figure stepped out of the bushes to my right. Young, blonde, stick-thin, wringing her hands, she wore a thin T-shirt that had seen years of wear, the decals unreadable, jeans with so many holes only a thread held her on the right side of decency, and a shy smile with a haunted look. "You want to know about the car?"

"Are you Missy?"

She nodded, eyes on alert, scanning. "He told me to leave the car out, keys in it."

"Your father?"

"Who else?" She didn't try to hide her derision. "Have you found my car? I really need it."

Something about her plucked a heartstring. She needed food, and maybe a big hug, not that I was in the hugging business, but still… "Where do you need to go?"

She glanced back at the house. "Away."

Yeah, me too. Both of us running from an overwhelming reality. "Going alone? World's not a safe place for a beautiful young woman."

"Safety in numbers?" She flashed a fierce look. "We'll be fine."

Not going alone. Okay. "Any idea why your father wanted you to leave the car out?"

"So somebody could steal it?" Even though she gave me the attitude that question deserved, she did manage to stifle an eye-roll.

"Detective Sawyer!" that booming voice again. This time it made my heart stop. I'd done something wrong; I just didn't know what. Jasper Clarkson strode down the driveway, his phone held aloft. "The chief wants to speak with you."

The girl shrank back as her father approached. He ignored her. Instead, he focused on me as he handed me the phone. "You'll want to take this call."

I felt pretty sure he was wrong about that, but I took the phone. "Sawyer."

"Detective." The chief's voice was lethal. "You will come to the station and turn in your badge immediately."

"What for?" Righteous indignation welled in my chest. "I'm just doing my job." Had I done something wrong? Apparently, the chief thought so, but I couldn't remember. I pressed the heel of my left hand to my temple. The pressure helped the headache but didn't stop the hammering of my heart.

"A condition of your badge was that you never go alone. You know that."

Did I? I hiked my pants to show my right calf where I'd written the important stuff. A quick scan. It was there in mocking block letters. Why the fuck couldn't I remember? "Sir, you can't." I turned my back so I didn't have to see Clarkson's gloat and lowered my voice. "I'm nothing without my job. It's all I have." I gripped the phone so tight I felt sure it would explode in my hand. The shivering started from someplace deep, visceral, necessary—the place where my soul lived.

"You've overplayed your hand, Sawyer. We can't have you grilling children against their parents' wishes."

"I wasn't..."

"Mr. Clarkson is a very influential part of this community. You've stepped on the wrong toes. Come see me." The line went dead.

Without looking at him, I handed the phone back to Mr. Clarkson.

He wanted me out of the way. I wondered why.

CHAPTER TEN

THE SLEEK SHIP CUT THROUGH THE ROLLING SWELLS LIKE A STEEL blade through skin, following the nuance but staying the course. Thea set the throttles and the autopilot, then boosted herself into the captain's chair. Raking a hand through her tangles, she allowed herself a heavy sigh. Actually, it was more self-satisfied than heavy. The smell of rain rode in on the wind off the sea. Weak light from the full moon obscured by a thickening layer of broken clouds above kept her nerves on edge. Ramming something at thirty knots was not the way she hoped to be jettisoned out of this world, not that anyone really got to choose. She had the radar sweeping, but in these swells it would be far from perfect. Hanging with Carter was definitely not conducive to her longevity.

Thea had helped Carter drag the two men still alive into the back stateroom. The dead guy, they'd offered to the sharks—out of sight, out of mind. Thea hadn't minded killing him. Given the chance, he would've gladly sent her soul winging to the Underworld, so over-board he went. Cruising into Singapore Harbor with a dead body...or three...to explain would be problematic. She hoped Carter would take care of the other two—they couldn't be left alive to sing to the police. She knew she could dispatch them with no remorse, but she didn't want to face that dark side of her soul. Fantasy of a different version of herself, the mild-mannered lab rat, was far more comfortable. As her mother had grown weaker, she'd often told Thea she was far more like her father. The truth had hit home, but not set well.

Even above the wind, Thea could hear an occasional scream. Carter would get the info they needed. Thea preferred not thinking about exactly how—not that she was squeamish. Right now, she was warring with what she knew to be true and what she wished was true—she needed to fix that. But not now—this was kill or be killed.

Tamping down all signs of weakness, Thea used the pain in her shoulder where the bullet had gouged flesh to focus her. Pain was good. She could use pain.

Blocking out Carter and what he was doing, she worked to keep the ship on course, turning slightly into the waves so she crossed them at a ninety-degree angle as much as possible. The seas were building, slapping the boat, breaking over the bow as if angry at what they'd done.

But it took evil to fight evil. Surely, the Fates understood.

Logic was comforting, but Thea knew she'd pay a price eventually.

"Fun, wasn't it?" With his hands on either side of the doorway, Carter leaned in, jolting her from her self-defeating argument—she was who she was, and life would have to deal. Hippo snaked through his legs, then greeted Thea with a lick on her hand. The smell of wet dog filled the small space as she stroked the dog's head.

How could the logically wrong place feel so emotionally right? The same question applied to Carter Livingston as well. "I've laid in the course for Singapore. Your job is to get us a flight to Shanghai."

"I know what you're thinking," he said.

"Did you hear me?"

"You're thinking this is really great fun. This is where you should be. I'm your person, as they say. But that really bothers you."

"I didn't get a Ph.D. from a rather illustrious institution only to squander it to run through the jungle with you. It would be a waste to die from a curare-tipped arrow while you're high on some newly discovered obscure hallucinogen that you think will earn you a fortune as an alternative to bored first-world denizens."

"Oh, hell, Thea. This is where you're supposed to be. Look at you, you're practically having an orgasm over being shot at. And for the record, curare is so twentieth century."

Thea couldn't decide whether he was trying to irritate her or was simply being himself. The more she thought about it, she realized that it was pretty much the same thing. "You don't know what you're talking about. You can't see me."

"There are other ways to see."

"You said that before."

"You didn't listen, so it bears repeating. Anyway, this is the life you crave; you know it, you just won't admit it. And you got that fancy diploma, so when you go back to the Land That Critical Thought Forgot, they'll listen to you."

That was more truth than Thea was comfortable with. "The Land That Critical Thought Forgot. Cute." Thea agreed, but she wouldn't let Carter "see" it.

"Yeah, you know, where if they didn't discover it, then it can't possibly be valid."

"Close, but you got that wrong. If they didn't *patent* it, it can't possibly be valid."

"You made my point. That is precisely the problem with modern medicine—it's all about money."

Thea couldn't argue. In fact, she could put an exclamation point on his premise. And that was a big problem. "What did you get out of our two guests?"

"Mercenaries."

"That much was obvious." A large swell caught them a bit too much on the starboard side, jerking Thea's attention back as she fought the wheel, her feet braced, her grip tight.

Carter braced himself in the doorway. Hippo slid up against the stand of Thea's captain's chair, then kept on her stomach until the rolling settled out.

"Anything else?" Thea asked once she'd regained control.

"Payment and instructions all done very slick with no face-to-face."

Okay, he was being deliberately obtuse. "Mercenaries usually don't go off killing people unless they know who they're working for. That way, at least they have some leverage." Thea squinted into the darkness through the beads of water on the windscreen that quickly raced away driven by the wind only to be replaced by more. She amused herself with thoughts of ways to inflict a bit of pain on Carter Livingston. If there was a more irritating man...

He slapped his thigh, jolting the dog to her feet. "I told you that you were meant for this."

Thea rolled her eyes, which was lost on Carter but made her feel better.

"Before he died, one did mention a lawyer in Vancouver."

"Canada?"

"No, sounded like he thought the dude was stateside."

Vancouver, Washington, a stone's throw from Portland. Thea swallowed hard. "We killed two people?"

"Three." Carter rushed on before she could kill him, too. "Singapore is heavily patrolled. We're in a stolen vessel, which, while it hasn't been reported as stolen yet—"

"It's stolen. Mercenaries don't use their own boats."

"Okay, as I said, a stolen vessel, which will be hard to explain. Two pretty bunged-up men with a few missing fingers and teeth and a serious case of finger-pointing would be impossible to pass off. So, they followed the first guy over the railing."

"I didn't need the details." Seeing lights ahead through the rain, Thea pulled back the throttle, maintaining enough speed to keep the boat from foundering, which was more than she was comfortable with. "We're closing on the harbor pretty fast." No matter how hard she tried, Thea couldn't keep the edge in her voice as it wavered.

"Relax." Feeling along the instrument panel, Carter moved to stand beside her. "I live here. I've got friends who will look the other way. Especially when I give them the boat—there's bound to be a finder's fee for returning it."

Thea grabbed Carter's hand and put it on the wheel. "Hold this. I'm going to check out the paperwork if there is any."

Based on their closure rate, Thea figured she had five minutes.

A quick search through all the obvious places yielded nothing. "We'll have to run the registration."

"I got a guy who can do that," Carter said, totally casual as if he did this every day.

Thea didn't want to think of his everyday life. It was probably way more fun than hers.

"You have no idea how much leverage being blind can be," Carter continued as if anticipating a red-carpet greeting which Thea doubted. "When you're not able-bodied, nobody sees you. If they do, they help you or overlook what you might have done because people who aren't perfect make everyone else uncomfortable."

"The quicker you're out of their sight." Thea smiled at her unintended irony. Curiously Carter did, too.

"Exactly."

The water calmed as they entered the harbor and Thea throttled back. One minute later, a harbor police boat pulled alongside.

"Here we go," she said. Once again, she'd put her life in the hands of Carter Livingston.

As I walked through the precinct, everyone I met avoided my eyes. Well, everyone but one. A young cop, so green he held his chest out and his shoulders back and looked like he might salute, nodded, and said, "Detective Sawyer," before his gaze skittered away. I didn't think that was a good sign. But maybe it was him and not me. As I said, social cues still confounded me.

Carla rounded the corner with a mug of steaming coffee. "Good luck," she said as she passed. That spark of warm connection I'd felt before had gone stone cold. Hoping for...something...I watched her until she took her seat at her desk, her back to me.

The chief was waiting for me, manning the door to his office with the glare of a jailer checking in his last prisoner.

I took the offensive. "Chief, you can't—"

"I can do any damn thing I want." He slammed the door so hard it rattled the glass panes of his front wall. He jerked closed the blinds, then turned to face me. With a wide stance and arms crossed, he blocked the door. "I run the force, or have you forgotten that?"

Trapped. I scanned the small space, looking for some way out. Through him was the only route. Not ideal, but I didn't put it past myself. Shifting from foot to foot to hide my discomfort, I held my ground. "I haven't forgotten. If I had, you'd make sure to remind me."

His features rearranged into a scowl.

I fought the urge to swipe his legs from under him and run. For some reason, I thought to add, "Sir."

He rolled his eyes. "Beck's not here. I told you not to go anywhere without Beck."

"I haven't spoken with you about that, sir."

"This isn't a democracy." He sighed but took it down a notch. "I told Beck not to let you go anywhere without him."

"Was that personal time, too, sir?"

"Of course not." He moved past me and took a seat behind his desk.

The look he gave me wasn't new. Everyone knew I wasn't right; I struggled with memory, anger, control, and God knew what, and they didn't know how to deal with that. Well, I didn't, either. But they didn't have to live with me—I did. Not sure where that got me other than a pity party of one, which I never allowed myself. "Beck isn't here, sir. I have to be able to do my job."

"Maybe you forgot the rules, Detective."

I could see in his face that he used my title to soften the blow. It didn't. It just pissed me off. And, I didn't forget the rules—they were etched on my calf. But I was a cop. Without that part of me, I didn't know if I had anything left. It was all I'd been and everything I was. "I'm a cop, sir. Employed by this force. A detective, you just said so yourself. I've got to do my job—even if my partner disappears."

He cocked his head. Kindness softened his growl. "You're getting better."

"Hard to say, sir. Each day seems like the last. Progression isn't obvious when you live it." I stopped shifting. My nervousness balled cold in my stomach. "About Beck going AWOL, sir?"

"He didn't tell you?"

I started to explain but then decided against it. The details had disappeared, leaving me with only the sense that whatever had happened had been bad. I assumed his daughter. I think Carla had confirmed, but I wasn't sure. He hadn't called, and he wasn't answering; that much I did remember. "What?"

"Not my story to tell." He leveled his gaze. "But you need to hear it. Not from me, but from Beck."

His words held a warning—no, caution, maybe. And a hint of fear. "I've known him for a long time. He's more than an employee. He's a good friend." The chief wiped a hand across his eyes.

I could see his age and it surprised me. Full of energy and riding on pissed-off, he always seemed younger. *This job could eat your soul.* Beck's voice whispered a distant memory.

"I was his sergeant at the Academy." He shook his head, and the worry intensified. "He had his own set of rules even then."

"Where has he gone?"

"I don't know." The chief returned as the friend retreated. "We can't save everybody. Now, about you. I need your badge."

Panic squeezed my chest until I couldn't breathe. "Please," I whispered. "Don't do that."

"Kate, I have to." He rose from his chair. Placing both hands on his desk, he leaned toward me. "You have some control issues, and I can't run the risk."

Control issues.

The anger, tamped to an ember, flared. Heat licked at my control. My vision telescoped.

Before I had time to react, the chief rounded his desk and grabbed my arm. "Give me your badge."

"Don't." I flinched away, but he held tight. His size and strength held me prisoner. I whirled, then brought my elbow down on his arm, breaking his hold.

He yowled in surprise. His hand dropped as he rubbed his elbow. "Shit!"

I backed toward the door, horrified at what I had done. Where had that come from? "I don't like to be touched." Not an apology, an explanation. I wasn't sorry, so I didn't say so.

"You just proved my point." The chief quit rubbing his arm and held out his hand. "Your badge, Kate."

"An officer is allowed to protect himself." Quoting a displaced memory verbatim, I made it sound like one of the Ten Commandments.

"Not from her superiors."

"Even then. Especially then...sir." I fought for breath, for control. "Would you treat Beck the same?"

"Of course not! You're not him."

"To you, I am. Or I should be. Beck and I are both detectives."

"I owed him. Did him a favor." Realizing he was sliding into a hole he couldn't scramble out of, the chief clamped his mouth shut. A tic worked in his cheek. Control seemed to be in short supply in his small office. I could've told him arguing with crazy makes you feel like you're riding the same train.

He snapped the fingers of his open hand. "Your badge." That's the chief—never one to back down from a losing argument.

"Don't you want to know why Jasper Clarkson wants me out of the way so badly?"

The chief raised his eyebrows. "No."

"Doesn't it strike you as a bit of an overreaction?"

"Rich people have their ways. And they don't like to be molested by detectives." He snapped his fingers. "Your badge."

Before I could blink, he snatched it from my hand.

But he wasn't taking my life. Not before I got me back.

First, I needed Beck home. Without him, I couldn't be me.

I shifted through the door then ran.

THE BIKE PULSED beneath me as I opened the throttle. The day had brightened as my mood headed in the other direction. *How could he?*

Each time I glanced at my forearm, the words *He didn't tell you* mocked me. That's what the chief had said, his words burned into my gray matter like a brand on a young steer. However, unlike the other important memories, these were not memorialized in my meticulous print. Instead, the words dripped down my arm in an angry admonition. I'd scrawled them hurriedly, in agitation, anger and fear. They'd caught each emotion.

Everybody thought I was worthy of taking a bullet, of dying. I rubbed my aching knee. The problem was, nobody thought I was worthy of truly living, of dealing with the unholy mess of every day. To the chief, I was a charity case, a political poster child, to be trotted out in front of the ignorant. *Look, we hire the disabled.* They should pay me by the photo op; that way, we'd all come clean.

I hit the Harrison Bridge then popped onto the 84, heading east as fast as the BMW would carry me. *He had to know what taking my badge would do to me. I'd disappear.*

A uniform radaring my lane waved as I flew past. I wouldn't help him make this month's quota—he wouldn't gun me. Most cops knew me, knew my bike, and left well enough alone. *Beck would know what to do.*

Taking the ramp at eighty, I flew onto the 5, heading north. Past the airport, across the river, I slowed when I hit Washington.

Beck was gone.

That thought tamed the others that had been ping-ponging around inside my empty skull. Shivers raced through me. *I might not get him back.*

What would I do then? He'd become a part of me—a major part of a life I disdained but desperately needed.

The details had faded, but the fear remained. *What had I done?* I couldn't remember.

With no destination in mind, nothing to do, nowhere to turn, I pulled a U-turn and set the GPS for home.

This time I took the Burnside Bridge off the 84. The Portland sign greeted me, the white stag caught in a perpetual leap. I knew the urge. Sometimes leaping off this bridge or some other place high enough that my body would reach terminal velocity before it hit the ground seemed like the only way to end the pain. But pain was good. It kept life in front of me. And that, too was a good thing. So, for now, I'd leave the leaping to the stag.

My condo building was a few blocks down on the right. A cylinder of glass and steel, it stood out from the lower brick ware-houses surrounding it. Most of the citizens hated the conflicting styles, but for me, it made finding home a lot easier. I parked next to the elevator in the garage—this spot I didn't need to note on the key tag. I took the stairs up one floor, stopping at the desk for my mail. "Anybody looking for me?"

A long-running joke as I never got any mail. Even though my witness protection anonymity had blown up with my last case, I'd pretty much killed anybody interested in finding me.

"Actually,..." The clerk turned and pulled an envelope from the file behind him. "You do have a message. Didn't come through the post, though. Came by messenger."

I didn't like the sound of that. After a few moments and with no real options I could think of, I took the envelope. "Thanks." I held it aloft. White. My name in block letters. Black ink. Not sealed. No return address. I forced a smile. "Probably a come-on from one of the local restaurants. Or maybe a death threat."

If he had a preference, the clerk didn't let on. But then again, I needed remedial social cues training, so I could've missed it.

"Oh, by the way, your friend is upstairs," the kid called as I retreated toward the elevator.

"My friend?" Hope flared. *Beck.*

"Yeah, the guy with the saxophone."

"Oh." The Watchman, not Beck. Hope dashed. That was the worst thing about hope; it rarely lived up to its promise.

The Watchman waited for me in front of the far wall made of floor-to-ceiling glass. My favorite spot, I understood its draw. Standing there, I felt like I could see heaven. On a clear day, Mt. Rainer would be visible in the far distance, the stunted form of Mt. St. Helens in the foreground. Today was not that clear, so the Watchman was left with a view of the Willamette River and the city rolling away.

After throwing all three deadbolts and moving the potted plants in front of the door so I wouldn't keep checking it as my memory faded, I shucked my shoes, then joined him at the window as we drank in the view. "What do you see?" I asked, the envelope burning a hole in my back pocket.

"Trouble." A homeless schizophrenic, the Watchman was all I had left except for the hospital crowd, of course. But they wanted something from me—I was never sure exactly what, but that was the feeling that stayed with me long after I'd left there. The Watchman wanted only the comfort of friendship—that I could do. Most days, anyway—as long as he didn't want a hug. That seemed good enough for him.

Wearing his trademark duster and worn but serviceable steel-toed boots, he let his arms hang by his sides and didn't look at me. His gray hair looked newly cut in uneven layers. His chin, cleanly shaved, sported a thin dark line of crusted blood. He looked like he carried the weight of the world—but he always looked that way. A bit of newly acquired weight fleshed out his cheeks a bit, and they'd lost some pallor—both good signs. "You've gained some weight."

"Your buddy Stella makes sure I stay on my meds and eat three squares."

"She's good that way."

He gave me some side-eye. "Couldn't tell it from you."

"I'm incorrigible; She told me so herself."

That tickled his smile. "When folks are trying to help, it's not a bad thing to let them."

"Depends on their motivation." So far, counting everyone as an enemy until they'd proven otherwise had kept me alive. Making exceptions to that rule had proven to be more difficult than I'd imagined. "The students at the cosmetology school hit you a bit hard."

"Price is right."

Free as I recalled, but my recall wasn't the best. "And you get what you pay for." My cognitive therapist loved having me memorize platitudes and clichés. Better than fairy tales, I guessed.

"I like being around the kids. So young. Life hasn't kicked them in the gut yet. Not sure how that really makes me feel, but today I found the sun and ignored the inevitability."

I touched his hand, the one so close to my own that I imagined the warmth. The corner of his mouth ticked up. "Tough day?"

I started to give him the normal bullshit, but then he squeezed my hand as he flicked a glance my way. His eyes were old, faded blue, yet filled with a wisdom that came from riding through Hell and living. "Kate."

So I told him. Consulting my notes, my phone, random scribbles on my body, and, yes, my memories, I pieced together my day the best I could.

After a few moments' thought, he said, "Well, you are an overachiever; that's for sure."

I didn't laugh. To be honest, I didn't know exactly what he

meant, but after all of that, laughing wasn't even a remote possibility. Reliving it in the retelling only made it even more real.

"What's in the letter?"

"Out of all of that, that's the thing you think is important?" A razor's edge of pain pierced through my knee. All the other injuries from the past—a past forgotten but unwilling to leave me be—ached. My stash was where I left it—in a tin on the coffee table. I parked myself on the edge of the couch and concentrated on rolling two joints. The smoke from a natural leaf did what no manufactured drug had ever done—it took the pain so only I remained, in peace, torment free. It could even smooth my thoughts until life felt real, manageable. Which, of course, it wasn't, but the fantasy was nice.

"You have the best stuff." The Watchman pulled on the joint, breathing in the smoke, holding it, then letting it out slowly. He'd taken a knife in the gut. I'd been there. We both carried the pain.

"Medical grade. They tell me the THC slows production of the amyloids in my head. Somehow, it reduces inflammation and protects nerve cells from dying."

"My mother always told me to choose my friends wisely." The Watchman seemed amused as he took another drag. "A bad day."

Not a question; I got that. I pulled, inhaling the smoke, holding it in my lungs until I felt calm sift through the crazy. I repeated the process until the horrible had fled, and the pain only tapped a reminder.

"You ready for the letter now?"

"Why are you so hung up on that damn letter?" I tilted my head back, then blew a perfect ring of smoke.

"Someone went to a lot of trouble to make sure you got it."

"Yeah, well, my mother went to a lot of trouble to make sure I learned my manners, but I'm not too hung up on it."

I pulled out the offending envelope, threatening in its blandness—no identifying marks except my name in block print. Not sealed, so no DNA from licking the glue to close it.

The whole thing had one thing written all over it: bad news.

CHAPTER ELEVEN

T{HEA} PULLED THE THROTTLES TO IDLE AND WATCHED WITH HER heart in her throat as the harbor police boarded. Two of them. Both male. Each stood wide and adjusted his crotch, then pushed his belt down. "Why do men do that?"

"What?" Carter asked.

"Grab their balls."

"Nervous."

"Really off-putting." Thea watched the officers. The lead dog motioned for the other to fan out to the rear.

"Reflexive—a primal protection."

Funny, men instinctively protected their balls; women went for their kids. Making the male and the female necessary for procreation was life's cruelest joke. Asking opposites to join together in a common goal was asking too much. Men and women—diametric in their approaches. Thea shook her head. "You did cleanup, right? Blood might be a bit hard to explain."

"Don't worry. I got this." Carter sounded confident.

Thea didn't want to know what that meant, so she didn't ask for details.

"What does the front guy look like?" Carter asked. "Eyes too close together? Split lip but repaired, sorta like a cleft palate, maybe?"

Thea squinted into the darkness. "Yeah. Not to profile or anything, but he looks like he'd sell his mother for a good dinner in Hong Kong."

"With a happy ending."

Thea shuddered. "Well, I don't have a mother to sell. And no way I could give that guy a happy ending without puking. So..."

"We'll give him a boat." Carter moved toward the door. "Where is he?"

"Coming up the stairs."

Not for the first time, Thea saw her life parade before her eyes. Carter Livingston had that effect. But no matter the horrible demise she had pictured, rotting in a Chinese jail had not been on her short list. Of course, with her mother literally dead and her father dead for all practical purposes, no one would be there to mourn.

Ending up like Rita with a colleague as her next-of-kin wasn't a great option either.

Too many choices, no time.

The cops' footfalls on the metal stairs sounded a rhythm her heart mimed.

As if Carter could sense her thoughts, he reached over, finding her hand. He gave it a squeeze. "Have I ever let you down?" His grin told her they both knew the answer to that.

In so many ways and so many times, Carter Livingston.

The first cop, the one with the lopsided lip, gave her a sneer. "I see you've brought a peace offering, Carter."

Carter snorted. "The girl? Hell, you can have her. More trouble than she's worth."

On the opposite end of the deer-in-the-headlights spectrum, Thea struggled to keep her expression bland, the homicide hidden. Of course, she figured the cop would wrongly interpret her expression as a challenge, but it was the best she could do.

"You got papers?" The cop turned to Carter. From his tone it was clear he knew the answer.

"I don't need papers. We weren't even planning on coming here. At least not until we stumbled across this fine yacht floating around the South China Sea all by itself."

"Abandoned?" A flicker of interest lit the cop's dark eyes, but he didn't seem surprised. "Pirates?"

The South China Sea had become a hotbed of piracy amid the international dispute, with China forcefully exerting control. Pirates? Mercenaries? Not too far off, Thea reasoned.

"She's stolen," Carter continued. "We checked. Hell of a finder's fee offered."

That they hadn't checked.

The first cop licked his lips as the second one shouldered into the small space, too late to catch the conversation. "Stay outside," the first cop ordered, and the second man disappeared.

Thea and the first cop watched the second one go down the stairs and out to stand on the bow decking, well out of earshot. Regardless, the first cop slid the door shut, trapping the three of them in the bridge. Quickly, the heat rose, the acrid smell of the three of them and the dog filling the small space. A mosquito buzzed near Thea's right ear. As the least irritating creature in the room, she let it live.

"I could arrest you." The cop sounded unconvinced as if his decision was already made.

Thea's patience expired. "For what?"

Carter kept his hand at his side but motioned Thea to silence. Not her world, she knew that. But seriously? They hadn't had time to search the boat. If she knew Carter—and she did—they wouldn't find anything without a forensics team. There was nothing quite as irritating as ineffectual men preening in pretended power, which they did all the time, quite frankly.

"I beseech you." Carter put a hand over his heart and gave a slight bow. "That you will accept the boat as a humble gesture of our gratitude for overlooking any transgression we may have unwittingly made."

Thea wanted to laugh out loud then shoot them both, but the blood warming in her backpack stopped her. Lives were on the line —this wasn't the time to indulge her fantasies.

"Dock at the police pier." The cop slid the door open halfway.

"We'd prefer to take the inflatable."

Carter kept his voice calm, almost nonchalant. His ability to function in front of a firing squad had always impressed Thea— impressed her and attracted her.

"As you wish." The cop had already lost interest in the two of them as he eyed the instruments. *Probably visions of sugarplums dancing in his head*, thought Thea as she grabbed her backpack and followed Carter through the door. The dog trotted after them as if the cop no longer held their lives in the balance.

Thea wouldn't breathe until they'd hit land and disappeared.

THE LETTER.

Time stopped as I stared at it, feeling as if the Watchman had asked me to read the verdict in my own trial. The Watchman gave a hint of a smile when I thrust the envelope at him. "You read it."

A light shake of the head. "Your message. Probably personal."

No doubt.

After rooting in the kitchen, I came up with a pair of scissors that I washed. I took the last toke, then carefully saved the roach in an ashtray on the counter. With the scissors, I meticulously nipped off one end of the envelope. Not sure why I was being so careful—the thing was a smorgasbord of trace at this point, including mine. Maybe it was just habit. Or delaying the inevitable.

Finally, I squeezed the envelope slightly and slid out the paper inside. Holding it by the corner, I shook it open. It unfolded in front of me, displaying a familiar scrawl.

Beck. My heart took the hit.

He was short and to the point. *I'm sorry. Need time to think. Don't try to find me. Regardless, I will always love you. Try to accept that.*

Not a threat—a *fait accompli.*

Letting the paper flutter to the coffee table, I sank onto the sofa.

"What?" The Watchman sat down next to me. He gestured toward the letter. "May I?"

Frozen, paralyzed with a loss I never acknowledged, I didn't respond. I couldn't.

He's not coming back.

Emotional arrows rained down; a barrage fired from atop a castle wall that found soft flesh.

Without Beck, I couldn't be me.

"He doesn't mince words, does he?" The Watchman tossed the offending message on the table. "Any idea what this is about?"

I drew my feet up and to the side, tucking them under me. My knee howled in protest, so I let that foot dangle off the couch. Wrapping my arms around me, I focused on grabbing gnats of memories that buzzed around my head. A hurt whisper was all I could manage. "He didn't trust me."

"Trust takes time." The Watchman laid an arm across my shoulders, his touch soft, undemanding. When I didn't resist, he let my body absorb the weight of his arm; then he pulled me into him.

I put my head on his chest—an instinct for comfort I'd long ago forgotten. Curiously, it worked. Human touch, human connection, all part of being human. Obvious things a damaged brain could lose. "I'm pretty hard to trust."

"Maybe for Beck."

"But if he doesn't trust me...if he won't be my partner, I'm out. Chief said so. He took my badge."

The Watchman didn't ask why. Instead, he curled into me, resting his head on mine.

"I'm losing the battle on all fronts. They'll stop the trials unless I catch the killer."

"There's no 'I' in 'we,'" the Watchman whispered.

"What?"

"Something my brother, the ultimate team player, used to say." His voice turned sad.

Something bad had happened to his brother. Something the Watchman felt responsible for. The details eluded me, but I remembered the pain.

"What I mean, Kate, is this battle you're fighting, it's not just your battle. You have a team of people who care, who are willing to step up for you. Your odds of success vastly improve if you let them in. If you let us help."

"But what if I hurt you, Beck, Logan, Stella, everyone?"

"So you don't trust yourself."

I pulled away from him, the truth a wedge between us.

He held tight. "How can anyone trust you if you're not the first passenger on the train?"

A knock on the door cut off my sharp reply. Offense was the best defense when running from the truth. "Who could that be? The desk didn't call to get permission to allow anyone up here." I uncoiled from the couch, then pulled my Glock from under the last sofa cushion.

"You got that thing set on stun?" the Watchman asked, a bit of wildness widening his eyes. "I thought you said no guns."

"It's okay." I patted his knee, my focus already shifting to the door.

My stockinged feet slid on the hardwood without a sound. Beside the door, I flattened my back against the wall, my gun held in both hands at the ready in front of me. The knock came again. Louder now, more insistent.

I motioned the Watchman to move to the kitchen, where he'd be out of the line of any fire, then waited while he took refuge behind the counter. "Who is it?" I called.

"Kate. It's Carla. From the Precinct. Beck's partner."

"What do you want?"

"Let me in."

A fellow cop. Could I trust her? There was that word again. With a glance at the Watchman, and still keeping the business end of my pistol pointed at the door, I leaned across and tugged the plants aside. Then one by one, the locks yielded. After a couple of deep breaths, I opened the door.

Carla's eyes flicked to the gun.

"I know I said no guns, but at home, I make an exception."

"You got a right to protect what's yours." Careful to push the barrel aside, Carla stepped inside, then past me. "Wow, awesome digs." A movement in the kitchen caught her attention. Her hand covered the gun she wore on her hip, then dropped when she saw who waited there. "Hey, Joe. You good?"

"Holding my own." The Watchman stepped from behind the counter to shake her hand, his face solemn. "What brings a member of the local constabulary to this humble abode?"

Joe could lay it on thick, but Carla seemed to like it. "I need Kate."

As the last deadbolt clicked into place, I turned to face her. "Need me?" Rooted to the spot, I put the gun back in its hiding place. "Whatever for? The facial recognition guy find something alarming floating around my synapses?" My heart hammered against the cage of my chest.

"We got a dead body in the river." Her chin tilted up in defiance.

"What's that got to do with me?"

Her voice softened. "Kate, I think you might know him."

"So, where is it we're going?" Thea held on to the slippery rope strung along the side of the inflatable with one hand and the throttle of the outboard with the other. She didn't have an extra hand to wipe the rain out of her eyes or push back the hair that glued to her face. "You could've gotten us a better ride." She had to shout over the noise of the motor.

Carter, with one hand comforting the dog that lay on her belly on the bottom of the boat and the other resting comfortably on one knee, peered into the gloom as if he could actually see something. "We are invisible." His words rode the wind back to her.

"So is everything." Thea squinted into the night. The harbor would've been well lit, with position lights to guide them. But Carter had insisted on leaving the protection of the lights, instead preferring the cover of darkness. "Take a heading of one eight zero. Look for a light. It'll be alternating orange and green. Pull in there."

"We're going into open ocean in this?" She thought of the squall line, the rain. The ocean would be angry and building.

"It's not far. One of the islands. Posted Private, nobody goes there." There were dozens and dozens of tiny atolls south of Singapore. A good place to hide.

The lights of the city provided a half-light that allowed Thea to navigate, if not confidently, at least somewhat certain she wouldn't rip the thin rubber on a protruding stick or metal spike. Instead of wasting energy griping at Carter, she focused on the lights on the shore, using them to keep her distance from the shore while looking for their signal.

Thea moved, widening her feet to provide more stability. Her foot found metal.

Two of the AK-47s from the yacht.

"When did you stash the automatics in here?" she shouted at Carter.

"Before I joined you on the bridge. Preparation is the key to success."

Along with a shitload of luck, thought Thea.

"The cop back there, he plays both sides," Carter said as if making small talk at a posh cocktail party. "He would've taken our vessel, then had the shore patrol arrest us for illegally entering the country. He's not my regular guy, but we play the cards in front of us."

"Is your life always like this?" Thea shouted as she throttled back, keeping the engine to a low hum.

"Only when you show up." Carter turned. She could see somehow that fact made him happy.

What a fucked-up pair we are. Thea repeated that over and over to herself, but she knew it wasn't true. For a moment, she stared at the figure in front of her. How could she both hate and love someone so much? A fine line. A dark splotch on the back of Carter's jacket drew her attention. "You've been shot." She sounded a bit more concerned than made her comfortable.

"Yeah. Not the worst I've taken. Do you see the light?" Carter asked a fraction of a second after Thea spied it.

"Coming up. Two o'clock. We're fifty feet from shore." She pushed the handle away from her, using the propeller on the end of it to steer them toward shore. "We need to get you some help."

"Idle it in. Here." He waited, giving her time to look, then tossed a pistol to her. "Locked and loaded."

"So this isn't your guy either?" Thea checked that a round was chambered then tucked the gun into the waistband of her pants as she maneuvered the small craft. Fighting the swells took attention and strength she was losing fast. Her shoulder hurt like a mother; she needed to get Carter to a hospital and the blood to a cooler. The quickest way to do all that was to shut up and do what Carter said. There'd be an appropriate time to make her feelings known.

A cold ball of worry for Carter nestled in her stomach as she fed on the adrenaline surge. They needed to hurry.

Thea felt the crunch of sand brush against the bottom of the boat. She raised the propeller higher, then as they rode a slight swell toward shore, she killed the engine. After rotating the motor, she dropped the boom with the now dead propeller inside the craft. She palmed the gun, holding it beside her leg, her finger caressing the trigger guard.

A single figure stood at the end of a dock waving a lantern. Orange. Green. Orange. A dark wall of trees stood behind the dock. If Carter had wanted a secluded place, he'd gotten it. "I got him. What should I do?"

A lone bird called.

Carter's shoulders slumped as he pressed a hand to the dark spot and stretched against it. "Go ahead and tie it up. It's my guy."

"The bird call?" Thea angled the craft toward the dock.

"No, anybody can mimic that. He gets his knockoff Gucci cologne made special by some herbalist in the Old City. Stinks like bat shit, but he says it has special powers of seduction. I can smell him."

Thea shuddered at the thought. "Is this your normal meeting place?"

"Never the same place twice."

Thea didn't like it—Carter was going in double-blind.

The man on the dock kneeled then leaned over the edge. He gave her a toothless grin, which Thea interpreted to mean the man had heard every word.

"It really doesn't smell that bad," she said as she tossed him a guide rope.

The man bobbed his head at Thea's feeble gloss-over. "Stink like bad-ass shit. But work like magic."

Carter tensed but kept his manner easy. Only Thea picked up on it.

Something was wrong.

She curled her finger around the trigger. "Carter, you and the dog first. I'll tie up." Thea looked up at the guy on the dock. "Help him out, will you?"

He skittered to the front of the boat and extended his hand.

"Eleven o'clock, a foot high," Thea barked as she threw a rope around a bollard that was almost rusted through. Between the bollard and the splintered, weathered wood, it was a toss-up as to which one would fail first. Pretending to secure the boat, she kept an eye on the two men. A low growl. The dog wasn't happy either.

The man on the dock grabbed Carter's hand. He raised his

other arm. A flash of metal glinted in the light. "Attack!" Thea ordered the dog.

The dog leaped. Teeth sank into the man's raised arm. Carter pulled and the man and dog tumbled into the water.

Thea grabbed one of the automatics and trained it on the tree line.

There would be others.

As soon as she thought it, tiny darts of light flashed from the tree line. The jungle erupted in a cacophony of indignation—birds and critters rousted from sleep and catapulted into panic.

Thea crouched below the dock, only the top of her head above the boards so she could see. A flurry of flashes from the left. Bullets tore through the trees, whizzed overhead then hissed into the water—another salvo from about twenty feet left of the first.

With her eyes never leaving the spots where the shooters hid, confident in the darkness, Thea grabbed both of the automatics. Raising only high enough to level the gun, she braced her elbows on the dock and let loose, first on the original shooters, then on the second. Then she ducked down behind the dock.

Retaliation came quickly. Bullets gouged the wood as the shooters sighted on her muzzle flash. This time though, Thea thought the firing was not quite so fierce. She popped up, repeating her firing strategy—first to the left, then to the right, then back down—but this time more quickly.

As she ducked down, several bullets flew over her head.

"You okay?" Carter asked, his voice muffled as he hunkered down as low as he could, his left arm draped over the side of the boat.

"Yep. You got the dog?"

"Yep."

"The guy who went in?"

"Dead. Friendly fire."

Thea popped back up, letting loose another salvo, this one quicker still. The gun clicked on an empty clip. She ducked back down, reaching for the second automatic. "Stay still. No movement, no noise."

A couple of quick bursts rained wood splinters on them.

Thea worked on her breathing, slow and steady. She watched Carter who cocked an ear, listening. Slowly, the jungle settled.

A couple more bursts. More wood splinters. A few hissed into the water. Thankfully none had yet found the tender rubber of the inflatable. A few more eternal minutes passed.

Thea's heart rate evened out, the adrenaline now only a trickle.

The rubber under her hand vibrated—two quick taps. Carter.

They were coming.

CHAPTER TWELVE

"You want me for an ID?" I asked Carla. Despite my best efforts, disappointment added a hard edge to every word. When Carla had first walked through the door and told us about the body in the river, I hoped she wanted help, cop-type help. I could tell from the Watchman's long face he'd hoped the same. I motioned Carla toward a chair opposite the couch. "Sit."

She took the turquoise one closest to the window, my favorite. "You guys been smoking in here?"

"Medicinal, for pain and brain, as the good doctor says." I took my former position on the couch, facing her across the coffee table. The Watchman paced, which didn't help. Well, at least not me anyway. As his drugs wore off, movement held the crazy back, or so he'd told me.

"You good though?" Carla eyed me like a perp.

"One joint for pain. Brain is fully functional, using the term loosely, of course." And the MJ did something to keep it that way —a drop in the treatment bucket, but it helped. Couldn't remember how, though. My brain obviously didn't think it horrifying enough to remember, and I hadn't deemed it necessary to take up epithelial real estate, which on my frame was limited, so I was left with the knowing, but not knowing.

She seemed to deflate a bit as she leaned back. "So do you actually believe all the shit you spout?"

That got a guffaw out of the Watchman as he momentarily paused mid-pace. "I like her." He hooked a thumb at Carla but directed the comment to me.

"Good taste." I liked her, too. Good for me, but probably bad for her. Most of the people I liked ended up hurt or dead.

The Watchman resumed pacing, this time with his hands clasped behind his back and a slight smile replacing his frown.

I gave Carla's comment some thought. The shock of losing my badge, of losing Beck, had worn down to a dull, throbbing emptiness. With the panic gelling into realization, I now could think... maybe even without my normal desperate need to protect myself. "Most of the time, I believe my own bullshit. I have to."

"Why?"

"Keeps everyone safe." I toyed with the idea of rolling another joint—anything to avoid her stare and the hit of reality. The first joint had taken the edge off, but the pain was still there, all of it—a nagging reminder of my own stupidity. "Besides, it's easier that way, easier for everybody."

"Not you."

It was like she'd cracked open my head and peered into my fear. "Maybe I'm afraid not to believe my crazy act. I'm just playing down to others' expectations."

She pursed her lips and nodded as if confirming a supposition. "Then you'd have to admit you're getting a lot better and maybe even scarier; then you'd have to live up to it."

No use arguing with the truth. "Being a victim is easier."

She eyed me long and hard. "No, I don't think so."

This head game was making me itch. "Do you really have a body or was that an excuse to get into my home and crawl into my head a bit?"

"Both."

That got my attention and brought the Watchman to a standstill.

Carla, obviously enjoying the attention, extended her legs so she could reach into the pocket of her khakis. "I got something for you." She pulled out her hand, then opened her fist.

A bit of gold.

I looked at her unsure what to think, afraid of what to hope.

"It's your badge." She extended it toward me. "Take it."

The metal was warm from being in her pocket. "Where'd you get it?"

"Some detective you are." Pressing both hands on her knees, she pushed herself up, then looked around. "You got any firewater around here? I don't normally go to the mat with the Boss Man. Left me a bit shook."

I pointed to the bar. The Watchman bolted into the kitchen, presumably to get ice. "Sorry, my manners—"

"Are unnecessary among friends." Carla whistled at the bottles lined in a row. "Righteous."

"Pick your favorite poison." I stared at the badge in my hand—a pot-metal key to me. "You fought the chief...for me?"

"What he did was wrong." Carla chose the Macallan 25. The Watchman brought her a small bowl of ice. She deposited a single cube in a tumbler holding one finger of the amber liquid, then returned to her chair.

Afraid to speak, I let her savor the Scotch—after twenty-five years, it deserved a bit of reverence.

The first sip, she held in her mouth for a moment letting the fumes invade her olfactory senses—so much of taste had to do with smell. The second, she let slide down her throat. "Wow."

"An appropriate word from both of us."

She leaned forward, her elbows on her knees, the glass dangling from one hand as she gripped the lip with three fingers. "Being a female cop is still being an outsider in the good-old-boys club. While the guys are well-intentioned, they're pretty stupid when it comes to women, what we can do, and how we handle stuff. So they make assumptions that aren't right. And worse, the higher they go, the more self-defensive they get. Chief's first goal is to protect his ass. Second is the work."

"Is that how he thinks?"

Carla shrugged. "That's how he acts."

Actions were more telling than words. I made a mental note, not that it would stick. "What does that have to do with me?"

"I've been watching you." She rotated her hand, swirling the liquid in her glass. The ice made a comforting sound, like a wind chime in a soft breeze. "You're getting a lot better. Making good decisions. Beck told me what happened at the hospital. I told him I thought you showed great restraint. If he'd done that to me, he'd a-been looking for a doctor with a steady hand."

I couldn't remember exactly what had happened, only that the hurt had burrowed in like a splinter. *Not my fault.* "So you're my new keeper?" That should've elated me, but, for some reason, it rankled.

"Hell no." She leaned back, went for another sip, then stopped. She put the glass on the coffee table. "Enough to calm the nerves. But we got a body to process and I bet a murder to solve."

"Where do I fit?"

"You don't need a keeper." Carla spat the words as if they offended her. "Going out to Clarkson's house was good police work."

"Chief was mad as hell."

"Clarkson's a big shot and the chief was missing a chunk out of his ass."

"And a backbone," the Watchman said.

"The more pressure applied, the weaker it gets." Carla shot him a collegial smile. The Watchman had some sort of police background, but the details eluded me.

Clearly, Carla remembered what I'd forgotten.

Her theories held water. I wanted to believe them. I needed to believe them. What was I afraid of?

"I need your help," Carla said, turning up the serious in her tone. "Beck has gone off all Lone Ranger, which opens up an opportunity for us to team up. We can show them how it's done."

My emotions must've trotted across my face.

She gave me a look filled with a history I didn't know but could feel. "Now's the hour, Kate. You fight, or you're lost."

THEA RESTED the automatic on the boards of the dock and sighted down the barrel. With less than half a clip, she'd have to make her shots count. In the front of the boat, Carter held the dog, both of them tensed but relaxing into the inevitable. Thea read that in their postures, their easy breathing.

Three of a kind.

"They're coming," Carter hissed.

It took five full seconds for Thea to hear what Carter had picked up—a gentle swishing of the grasses, light, measured foot-falls, the snap of a twig barely audible.

"Clear of the tree line," Carter whispered.

"All of them?"

A quick lift of his shoulders in the moonlight to say, "Hell if I know." So helpful. The dog whined. Carter silenced her with a hand signal.

Thea's heart caught the rhythm of the slight swells as they lifted the boat, rolled under it, then let it slide back, pausing before the next swell lifted it. Her vision tunneled—she'd avoided looking at any lights that would diminish her night vision, but she'd still be shooting at movement. If she killed an innocent in Singapore... Probably wouldn't be any worse than killing a not-so-innocent...and a whole lot better than offing someone in China.

Carter turned her direction. If he gave her a hand signal, she'd shoot him first.

She raised slightly, processed the movement, and squeezed the trigger, panning the stream of lead across an arc starting at her far left. Her kill zone extended past the last sighting of a shooter on her right.

Screams. Bodies fell. It was hard to tell the human from the agitated cries as bullets shredded the jungle growth. Birds took flight. Creatures howled. Men died. Thea tried to block out the sounds, but she knew, in the darkest nights, when sleep wouldn't come, she would hear, and she would remember.

She let off the trigger and the hail of lead stopped. Once again, the jungle quieted. With an ear cocked for sound, Thea waited, the gun trained higher to take out anyone who'd made it through. A few moments whispered past with the stillness of a year. "Anything?" she hissed.

Carter shook his head. With a sharp movement, he ordered the dog ashore. The dog leaped. Carter boosted her with a shove to the rear and the dog disappeared into the night. Thea heard his grunt, the effort the movement cost him. The dark stain had grown larger.

They needed to hurry.

The dog yipped. Coast was clear.

Thea pressed Carter down as he shifted to stand next to her. "Give me a minute." She slung the gun over her shoulder, letting it hang on its strap, then she grabbed one of the support beams under the dock. Her feet dangled in the water as she monkey-barred from beam to beam, progress hidden by the structure above. Only when she'd reached the far side at the closest point to land did she leverage herself up for a look.

A man with his back to her, epaulets on his shoulder, peered into the night, his gun trained on the point where he expected her to surface.

The boss.

That made what she was going to do so much easier. The inert form of the dog at his feet made it even easier still. She slipped her knife from its scabbard. Her foot found a purchase, wedged in the vee of a brace. Her fingers fit through a gap in the boards—a strong enough grip to hold her weight. Holding the knife by the blade, she pulled herself up, steadied, then whipped her hand through. The blade arced, turning over once. It caught the light before burying itself in the man's upper back. His shoulder blades snapped together as he stiffened, then his body tumbled over the edge.

He hit before she could sound a warning to Carter below. He grunted. "Fuck." He didn't whisper. "Is that the last of them?"

Thea didn't answer as she dropped. Her feet sank, but not so much she couldn't move through the knee-deep water. Using the reeds at the edge of the bank to hide her, she moved away from the dock, watching, waiting, gun at the ready.

Nothing.

The dog whimpered—she'd only been stunned.

Thea took a deep breath in relief—Carter might forgive her for the loss of his house. But his dog? He'd see she roasted on a spit in the fires of Hell.

An engine fired up in the distance—somewhere through the jungle. A boat?

Damn! "Did you hear that?" Thea asked as Carter got a leg over the edge of the dock, then rolled the rest of his body onto it.

"Yeah. A boat on the other side of the island."

"Get the guy." Thea lifted her chin where the bossman had done a swan dive.

"He's dead. Where's the dog?"

"I know he's dead. He was also the ringleader. I've got to figure out who is sending these guys after us and how they know what they know, or we can kiss our asses goodbye."

"You think he's going to carry a business card or something?"

"Shut up, Carter and do as I say. Do I mess in your business?"

"Yes." His tone said, "fuck you," but he did as she asked. The body floated nearby. Carter grabbed a foot. He worked the body around until he could grasp the man under the armpits and pull him on the dock. He got his torso where Thea could check him out but left the man's feet dangling. "Hurry. Half the Chinese Army will be looking for us."

"Chinese? We're a bit far from their territory."

"Trust me." Following the whimper and the scratching of the dog's claws on the wood as she tried to get to him, Carter crabbed over to Hippo.

She'd done nothing but trust Carter, and well, that hadn't turned out so well. Last time she'd cheated death. This time she had a feeling death would be pissed and out to even the score. "How's the dog?" Thea asked as she patted down the dead man, searching pockets. In his breast pocket, she found a pill bottle.

"Stunned. Goose egg on her head." His voice held a lethal edge.

She shook a few pills into her hand.

Red and blue with illegible tiny letters printed on the capsule.

Fuck! The hara-kiri of betrayal laid her wide.

She stood and tugged her phone out of her pocket.

"Whoa, whoa, whoa!" Carter was on her the moment he heard her press the first button. He grabbed the phone. "Are you crazy?"

"What the fuck?" Thea whirled on him.

"My question exactly." Carter faced her, his nose six inches from hers.

Thea stopped seeing red and logic returned. "Okay. Got it. I know better. These guys have known our every step. If I fire up my phone, they'll know we're alive and be able to track us."

"They'll know soon enough." Carter gently touched her face. "It's the tracking issue I'm more concerned with. If it makes you feel any better, I know how hard this stuff is on you."

"You mean the being hunted?"

"No, the killing."

"They wanted to kill us. My goal was to extend the same courtesy but trot out my manners first. Did you get my knife? It wasn't in the dead guy."

"Here." He handed the blade back to her. "A bit dirty but none the worse for wear."

Thea slid the steel against the fabric of her pants leg, wiping off the man's blood. "The guy got the worse end." She secured the blade once again in the scabbard. Keeping low with the gun at the ready, even though the clip had to be damn near empty, she traversed the ground between the dock and the tree line. Dozens of bodies, dark mounds, none of them moving. Thea tripped over one more as she made her way back. She reached down and rolled the man over. Wrong. A boy. A kid in a uniform. A Chinese Army uniform. "We got a problem. Bad guys are using wolf's clothing." *And kids to do their dirty work. Who are these guys?*

Carter moved to stand beside her. He cradled the dog. "Well, let's make it look like we all play for the same team."

AFTER TWO UNIFORMS waved her through, Carla eased her cruiser down a ramp, stopping just short of the river. I'd been fidgeting in the passenger seat—enclosed places stole my breath.

"You going to jump out of this thing?"

I pulled my hand from the door latch like a guilty child. "Maybe."

"I'm guessing not using a seatbelt is part of the same quick escape thing?" Until now, she hadn't said a word about the incessant call of the car, alerting her to the fact I was in mortal danger without being strapped to it earning herself a get-out-of-jail-free card.

"Sorry," I said it but didn't mean it—a social skill I'd picked up recently. Didn't understand it, but it seemed to defuse awkward situations, and this seemed awkward—for her more than me.

She killed the engine, silencing the irritating recrimination, and we both leaned forward in blissful silence, taking in the scene in front of us.

Two temporary vapor lights on articulating poles hung over the scene like vultures. The body, covered by a tarp, rested half in and half out of the water. The medical examiner's team assembled just off to the left, waiting while a photographer recorded every inch. Other techs canvased the edges of the crime scene looking for footprints, tire tracks, anything that might give us a clue.

"You got an ID?" I asked, thinking she didn't but not sure.

"Not yet. The guy who found him, just a kid really, high on something, told us the vic wore scrubs, purple like the hospital."

My heart lurched. My friends worked at the hospital. "Let's go see if I've seen him around." I opened the door.

Carla gave me a look I couldn't read—almost like she wanted to say something, then thought better of it.

CHAPTER THIRTEEN

"WHERE ARE WE GOING?" THEA CLUNG TO THE STEERING wheel. As the Jeep jounced through potholes, muddy water splashed, coating the windscreen. She drove as fast as she dared through unfamiliar jungle with only the light of the moon. "You're sure this is the way?" Stupid thing to ask a blind man, she thought, but given the lack of light and his heightened senses compensating for the one he lost, he could probably see better than she.

Not a comforting thought.

The small army she'd obliterated had left an interesting array of vehicles, none of them with the keys left in them. A private island, who would need so many trucks? The Jeep had been the third one she'd tried to hotwire. City living had eroded her skills. Flynn would be less than proud. "What is this place?"

"Pirate base. A place to call home while trolling the South China Sea for spoils."

She started to ask if they were safe there but thought better of it. Safe was a relative term and she and Carter had long squabbled over the definition.

They'd lost five minutes max while she had worked her magic, so she wasn't going to beat herself up over it. "Are you going to tell me exactly where we're going and who we're to meet?" The wool uniform was a size too small and stank of fear. The bullet had stopped the owner's heart. Not much blood.

Carter held the strap attached to the roll cage at his ear—he wore his uniform with ease. The dog rode it out on the floorboards. Carter's head lolled forward.

"Carter!" Thea shook him.

He lifted his head, but his eyes were at half-mast. "Just ahead. I smell curry."

Thea thought he was hallucinating. She fought to keep the Jeep from sliding off the mud track and worked her way through her options. A stolen yacht. Three dead guys. The bad guys were only a half-step behind and gaining. And Thea's body count was enough for any decent policeman to take her out in the jungle, torture her a bit, have some fun, then kill her slowly. Carter was totally out of it, and only he knew, in theory, their destination and, hopefully, a way out of this country and back to one that at least believed in innocent until proven guilty. They were lost in a jungle, low on ammo, without even a Girl Scout first aid kit to staunch the bleeding from the bullet Carter had taken in the back. The cloth and binding she'd used wouldn't hold for long.

The engine coughed.

Thea mashed the gas a few times.

It coughed again, sputtered, then died.

And they were out of gas.

Out of habit, she turned the ignition off. "We're pretty much fucked."

Carter let loose of the handhold and pointed with a trembling hand. "There."

Thea squinted. Then she stood. Bending over the steering wheel, she wiped the front of the windscreen before plopping back down. A deep breath. Concentration. And she saw it.

A light!

Faint and flickering as the wind shifted the fronds of the trees, but it was there.

"You still smell curry?"

"Green. My favorite. Shell never forgets." The dog whimpered as she nuzzled Carter.

"You think the men after us got here first?"

"And left the curry?" Carter laughed, but it came out all choked. "They're not looking for David or even me. They're looking for you."

"Yeah, but the question is why?"

"I have a feeling it has to do with what you're carrying."

Thea pulled her backpack from the rear set and checked the temp. Cool but rising. "It's just some blood."

"Obviously, someone feels threatened by that. Let's find out why."

"And David can help us?" Thea leaped out of the Jeep. The mud was like snot. She went to one knee in front of the Jeep before she found her footing. "Come on, Carter. Gotta fill you full of green curry. If that doesn't cure what ails you, I don't know what will."

"Shell is a shaman. She'll know what to do. And David knows more about the nuances of the DNA helix than anyone I know."

"A shaman hacker and a shady biogenetics guy weaponizing DNA. But of course." Thea took most of Carter's weight as she levered him through the opening that passed for a door in a jungle Jeep. "Can you walk?"

"With your help."

Careful to hide her injured shoulder from him, she took his weight, his arm around her neck, and secured him with her good arm around his waist. Still, the pain stung. Gritting her teeth, she pushed it aside, used it to focus. With her shoulder braced in his armpit, his breath hot on her cheek, they started for the light. Hippo trotted in front of them. Periodically, she would circle back to check on their progress, which was slow. Thea had found better footing just to the side of the road, but carrying Carter took all her strength. They slipped once, both falling to their knees. Thea didn't think she'd get him back on his feet, but somehow, she managed.

The dog circled back, this time touching Thea with her nose as if to say "Hurry."

"I know, girl. I know."

Carter's chin rested on his chest and the rest of him on Thea—his strength had all but vanished. The light was still a hundred yards away, maybe more.

Thea's knees buckled. She crumpled to the ground. Carter landed across her lap. Eye to eye with the dog, she had an idea. Why she hadn't thought of it before? "Help, Hippo. Get help. Go get Shell." If Carter had been here before, if he knew Shell, it was a sure bet Hippo did too.

The dog turned and bounded into the jungle.

THE NIGHT TURNED COLD. Maybe it was colder by the water. Maybe death chilled the air. Either way, I wished I'd brought a jacket.

As if reading my thoughts, Carla opened the trunk, pulled out a Portland PD fleece, and tossed it to me. "Just washed it."

"Hunter orange. We're safe from those stalking the wily stag but targets for anyone else gunning for an above-the-fold-story in tomorrow's paper." I zipped it up to my chin, then transferring my badge to the zippered pocket. I needed it close, where I could touch it.

The medical examiner's team and the other techs didn't even pause as we approached. The photog squatted next to something in the mud, her flash strobing with each snap. I stood within listening distance as Carla approached the knot of people.

"Who's running the scene?"

"I am. Officer Petrillo." A young officer, still so green he glowed, pushed himself off his cruiser. *The young kid who'd saluted me outside the chief's office*, I thought. I wasn't sure, but a memory flashed, searing, leaving a glowing outline like a bright light on a dark night. Before it faded, I compared it to reality. Yep, same kid.

"Petrillo." Carla seemed surprised. "Anyone else?"

"No, ma'am."

Carla glanced back at me. "My partner," she turned back to the young cop, "and I have it now."

"The chief told me..." He trailed off.

Carla's shoulders rose around her ears as she lowered her chin.

The kid wilted. "Yes, ma'am. It's all yours."

Carla addressed the M.E.'s team. "I'm trying to get an I.D. on our vic. Can one of you walk Detective Sawyer here through the scene so we don't mess up anything that might be helpful?"

A young gal culled herself from the herd. I followed her footsteps, careful not to destroy any possible evidence or add too much of my own. Her Wellingtons were the perfect choice as she waded into the shallow waters, then bent over the yellow-tarped form.

I stayed on the bank, my heart pounding as the young woman peeled back the covering. The light shining from above and at a slight angle flattened his features and cast shadows where none should be. Time in the water had puffed him up. Death had stolen his color, leaving his skin a pale blue. His hair floated, moving with the water—tendrils like snakes around Medusa's head. I angled for a better look.

I knew him.

I glanced up. Carla watched me intently.

"Our Coke can guy from the hospital." Somehow his face swam out of my memory. I took another look. Yep, it was him all right.

Carla nodded. "He sure looked liked the photo that guy took from your memory, but I needed you to be sure."

"It's him." I half-remembered the memory download. "How long has he been in the water?"

"Not sure until the M.E. gets a closer look, but prelim, and off the record, he thinks twelve hours, give or take, of course."

She must've seen me shiver as she handed me an unused tarp to wrap around my shoulders. "You're living in the wrong place if cold is not your thing. Here it can seep inside until it wraps itself around your bones."

"It normally doesn't bother me." Standing shoulder to shoulder, we both stared down at the body.

"We stepped on somebody's toes." Carla included herself in the *we*.

Technically, I had stepped on someone's toes. I'd culled the guy from the herd and chased him, alerting everyone to the fact that I'd noticed him. "And they're tidying up loose ends." I pulled the tarp tighter. Why was I so cold? This was an average spring evening, or so I'd been told.

"Any idea who might be cleaning up?" Carla asked. Her voice sounded casual, the question anything but.

I worked my left arm out from under the tarp so I could see it, then hiked up the sleeve of the fleece, and started reading. "Okay, we got Myles Benton, Clarkson, some researcher that went all passive-aggressive with Logan in the hall at the hospital—"

"And some lawyer dude in Vancouver." One of the techs materialized in front of me. Between gloved fingers, he held out a water-logged business card. The print was still easy to read, but something written in ink on the back had faded to illegibility. I knew better than to touch it, so I angled a look. "Walter Westmore. Anybody know who he is?"

Carla pursed her lips and shrugged.

"I've heard it." I reached back, trying to remember. I pulled my phone from my pocket and pulled up my notes. Nobody moved while I scanned. Nothing. I closed my eyes, taking myself back. My studio. I was searching online. Corporate records. I'd wanted to tell Beck something. What was it? *Nitro DNA. Grant money.* "Give me a minute." I returned to the car and pulled my notebook out of my backpack.

Wandering back to Carla, I read my notes. Once I got closer, I started reading out loud. "The company located in Nevada that made the drug used to kill Rita Davenport..." I looked up to make sure Carla followed me. She didn't. I backtracked and brought her up to speed as much as I could. Thankfully, I'd made copious notes from the meeting at the hospital, fewer from my solo research, which pissed me off. She asked a few questions, but not many.

"So, what about the company? Nitro DNA?"

"It's based in Nevada where you can bury ownership beneath a whole bunch of layers of bullshit."

"Nevada. Long way from here." Carla jammed her hands in her pockets.

Why the woman wasn't cold in her T-shirt, I couldn't fathom. I was dying. Shivers racked through me, and my hands shook. Somehow, I kept the waver out of my voice. "Not that far. You can hide ownership, but you still need a registered agent."

"And?" She looked like she knew the punch line but let me have the minor victory.

I pointed to the card. "Walter Westmore Esquire."

THEA CRADLED CARTER. He was out now, his breathing shallow, but his pulse steady if a bit thready. A shaman. One of his hallucinogenic friends. Terrific. "Carter." No response. She stroked his face. Still nothing. "You have to make it. Fight, Carter." She eased him to his side so she could check the makeshift bandage he'd wrapped around himself while she drove, covering the one she'd applied earlier, which was soaked with blood. The blood still seeped, but it was better. Still, time slipped away. She had no idea exactly where they were. And no way to get back to the boat to take him to Singapore, although she doubted he'd receive much care in jail. She tugged her backpack closer. The cooling canister was almost out of coolant—the blood wouldn't last long in the heat.

Her focus wandered as her strength ebbed. Her shoulder numb, the muscle refusing to cooperate, she was down to one arm. She couldn't carry him, and she couldn't leave him. So she guessed they'd just die where they'd landed.

Her give-up complete, a sound grabbed her attention.

A bark! The dog!

The bark was muffled, distant. The dog barked again. This time closer. Thea had only a moment to brace herself when the dog hurtled out of the darkness, bowling her over and laying her back in the mud.

"First thing we do is break you of that habit," she said as Hippo licked her face. The dog landed mostly on Carter, where he lay across her lap. That didn't seem to bother either of them.

"Hard not to smile, though." The voice was male—not what she expected. And with a New Zealand lilt. "Such unbridled love."

Thea couldn't hold both Carter and the gun. She'd made a choice. Now, with the unexpected man in front of her, she wished she'd made a different one. He was huge, a massive body topped with a tangle of wild red hair that blended into a beard he'd probably been working on since puberty.

"Where's Shell?" Thea asked, throwing a dart into the darkness.

"When the dog showed up, we figured Carter almost carked it, so she's pulling out her cures." His voice matched his appearance, menacing but not aggressive. The man reached down, hooking Carter under each arm, then lifted him as easily as he would a two-year-old. "Didn't expect to see you, at least not walking and talking. He said he'd kill you the next time he saw you."

"There's a lot of wishful homicide going around."

While he didn't smile, his features, the ones she could see, softened. Perhaps it was just a lightening of his eyes, but hard to tell in the darkness.

"Not the first time he's shown up at Death's door?" Thea stood and brushed at the mud, only making it worse. "This stuff is like slime." She looked up in time to see the man disappear into the jungle. She grabbed the backpack, then followed him. At first, the darkness confused her, but she followed the sound and found him just as he broke into a small clearing. "You must be David."

He didn't acknowledge her and, really, she knew better. Only a piker or a Fed asked these shady hacker dudes anything personal.

They lived light and fast, skulking through the Dark Web, safe among their peers—safe being a relative term.

A hut that could've been built by the same drunk with a hammer who built Carter's squatted in the middle of a small clearing. Probably used the same plans, too, although that was giving all of them too much credit, thought Thea. This one even listed to one side and had plastic strips guarding all its inhabitants from marauders. Not that she was surprised—there was no reason to build a strong door if someone could punch their way through the walls.

David, or whoever he was, angled sideways through the door to the hut, slipping his broad shoulders through, then easing Carter inside. He didn't look back.

Thea wasn't one to be left out in the dark.

One step inside, and her mouth dropped. The place was walled with servers all blinking and processing; their hum sounding like a swarm of locusts. Air-conditioning units circled the walls above. Dripping moisture, they barely kept up. "How?"

"Solar. Undersea cables. Tapped into a supercomputer in a safe location. Shell has a lab in the back. Give her the blood." David laid Carter down on a cot.

A woman materialized next to David. As small as he was big, they made an odd pair but somehow fit. Maybe the way they folded toward each other. Or maybe the soft touch as she laid a hand on his arm. "How is he?"

"Better than last time." David stepped to the side, giving her access.

Dark hair pulled tightly back from a round, unlined face. Angelic, was all Thea could think of. The lady, who Thea assumed was Shell, moved with the guileless grace of a fawn. She touched Carter in various spots, then held her hands over him while she closed her eyes. "He'll be fine." She said something to David in a dialect Thea didn't understand, then she turned to Thea. "David will make some tonics, I believe you call them. Carter has lost some blood; he is very tired. Let him rest. Tomorrow he will be better."

"He needs blood, a hospital."

The woman smiled. "He has blood. I will help him make more. This is my hospital."

Thea didn't have any more fight left. Carter trusted these people; he'd put his faith in faith healers. Now, he put his life in their hands. There wasn't much else Thea could do. "Thank you. I don't mean to be insulting." One knee started wobbling. She shifted her weight to the other, which wasn't much stronger.

"And you." The woman grabbed Thea's arm. Her grip was strong, her flesh warm, her touch comforting. "You need food and sleep—after I tend to that shoulder. You are safe here for the moment."

"They'll be back." Thea didn't have the energy or really the knowledge to explain or to identify their attackers.

"Doubtful. They are cowards. They will wait until you leave."

"Cowards?"

"We are protected here. We tend to the men who use this island. In return...." Shell led Thea to a small table she hadn't noticed, captured as she was by the amazing array of computing power.

"They keep your presence unknown."

"Sit."

Thea wanted to know how well they were protected. But the knowledge wouldn't change anything—other than maybe make her ulcer flare up. "People followed me. They know we are here."

Shell gave David a look and he disappeared into the back room.

"You sit. Let me work." Thea did as asked, unmoving, unflinching, as Shell went to work on the shoulder. Searing pain followed by...something cool and soothing that took the heat away. "That's amazing." Thea glanced at her shoulder. The angry red was gone, replaced by the flush of pink. "How did you do that?"

Shell smiled. "All that we need, nature can provide."

Thea couldn't disagree. Her stomach grumbled when Shell pushed a large bowl in front of her and began ladling from a pot.

"Green curry. Carter's favorite. But you eat what you need, I can make more for him tomorrow. His body does not have the energy for food now." Once she'd filled the bowl, she disappeared around the corner, then reappearing with a bowl of white rice. "The white is good for you. We laugh that Westerners think the brown is the good part."

"The U.S. will go down in history as the birthplace of bad nutritional information. High carb, low fat got us a population of diabetics. God knows what other bullshit they're ladling on a trusting populace." Thea thought about her own little corner of the vast medical conspiracy. So many charlatans happy to outright lie to perpetuate hope in a false premise to protect their own pot of gold.

"You have some blood for me to analyze?" Shell crossed her hands in front of her and waited.

"You have a lab too?" Thea said through a mouth full of the best curry she'd ever had.

"Enough of one."

Thea would have loved to get a peek at it, but first food, then sleep.

Shell handed her backpack to her, then stepped back.

Thea pulled out the cool canister. "The blood came from a woman we think was attacked with weaponized DNA."

Shell's mouth thinned to an angry line. "Humans must always turn good to bad."

"Cain and Abel," Thea said, surprising herself. She hadn't thought of that little bit of arcana in a long time. "And only *some* humans. We're trying to trace the virus carrying the DNA design. Somehow, we have to use it to catch our killer. If we don't..."

"He kills again." Shell reached a finger under the chain around her neck that disappeared into her décolletage. She lifted it, exposing a perfect tiny Nautilus shell, which she wrapped in her hand. "A comfort that bad never lasts."

No but it can leave good hanging on the edge of extinction. Thea resisted pointing out the obvious irony in the shell. "Evil is like energy—you can't diminish it; it merely takes a new form." Thea paused shoveling the curry into her mouth, her spoon poised in front of her face. She glanced up at Shell. "The killer has already targeted and infected his next victim."

"So, we are not only racing against him, but against time."

Thea thought it could be any one of them. Their DNA, along with that of each participant in the trial, was in the database. No one had found a breach, at least not that she knew. Regardless, from the outside or the inside, someone had access to the delicate information.

But who? A traitor in their midst? Thea, with as jaundiced a view of life as she had, couldn't imagine one of the team turning on the others with such ruthlessness.

And who would they be racing to save, if that was even possible?

CHAPTER FOURTEEN

CARLA AND I HAD TAKEN REFUGE IN THE CAR, KEEPING OUT OF the way as the M.E.'s techs worked the scene. I cranked the heat up to high, rubbing my hands in front of the vents as the air warmed.

Carla had her laptop open on her lap. "You cold?" She seemed comfortable in shirt sleeves.

"Too hot for you?" Now, the shiver had reached my voice, and it quavered.

"No, it's fine." She focused on the screen. "Let's do a little digging into Mr. Walter Westmore, Esquire."

"Lawyers," I muttered, unsure why. I couldn't remember any experience with lawyers, good or bad. It just seemed everyone had a negative knee-jerk reaction to them. Perhaps with good reason—most politicians were lawyers...or thieves, to the extent those were mutually exclusive.

From Carla's low whistle then a grumbling growl, I realized I might have been a tad optimistic when it came to Mr. Westmore.

"This dude is on a first-name basis with the Grievance Boards in three states."

I wasn't exactly sure what that meant, but Carla's tone told me it wasn't a good thing. "Let me guess, Oregon, Washington, and Nevada."

"You got it. He's licensed in all three except his license is suspended in Nevada." She leaned closer to the screen, the light painting her face in blue. "And Oregon."

"Hence his office across the river in Washington. What'd he do?"

"Mostly mismanagement of client trust accounts. He does have an address in Carson City, so technically, he can be a registered agent in Nevada, and you don't need a law license to do that."

"Helpful. Give me the address." She read it off and I pulled it up on my phone. It sounded legit, with a suite number and all. It wasn't. "One of those mailing stores."

"Figures." She looked through the window at the techs working. "How about the Washington address?"

I worked my phone magic. "Google Earth shows it to be legit. His name's even on the sign out front."

"It's too late now to pay him a visit, but first thing tomorrow." She gave me a side- eye. "You game?"

"Thought you'd never ask." I leaned into the air vent and pulled the neck of my fleece open, inviting some of the warmth inside.

"Man, you need to eat or something? It's hot enough to grow orchids in here."

I fisted a hand and wiped an arc through the condensation fogging the side window next to me. "Probably." I couldn't remember when I'd last eaten. Maybe breakfast yesterday? My stomach was no help—I'd quit listening to it, so it had quit talking to me. "Looks like the photog found something. They're casting some prints."

Carla and I joined the photographer. We all bent over the tech pouring casting material into what looked to be tire tracks. I let Carla do the talking.

"What did you find?" she asked the girl holding the camera.

"Some tire prints, as you can see. Footprints also—some tennis shoe prints. Tire looks like a motorcycle. I'll know more tomorrow after we've run them through the system. Might be able to give you a make on the tennis shoes and the tires. Fairly distinctive."

As I watched her talk, I wondered how old she was. Just barely out of Pull-Ups, by my guess. But her manner exuded competence, which was all I cared about.

"But fairly broad with regard to the tires," I chimed in, curious how I knew that. Maybe sometimes I focused too hard on the remembering, paid too much attention to what I knew and what I didn't. Others didn't seem to focus quite as much.

"You'd still be surprised. Certain manufacturers favor certain types of tires. Porsche and Pirelli, that sort of thing."

"A bit of a stretch."

"But it's something." Carla stopped the argument with a hand on my arm. "Thank you," she said to the photographer. "When you process the photos will you email copies to both Detective Sawyer and me?"

"Sure."

The tech doing the casting nodded as well. "I'll let you know when we have a clear ID."

I raised my phone. "Do you mind?" I wanted a snap of the guy just in case. Not sure in case of what, but it seemed like a good idea.

"Go ahead." The photographer inched back so I had a clear shot.

I snapped a few then pocketed the phone. "Thanks." Nobody asked what I was going to do with the photos. Trust. I'd forgotten. Beck had always second-guessed me, so not being questioned was a new thing.

I beat Carla back to the car and turned the key to fire up the heat before she got in.

She slid in behind the wheel. "You sure you're not coming down with something?"

As she backed the car up the ramp, I waited for the cold to ease and scrolled through my emails hoping for something from Beck. Instead I found the tape of the missing person's call the detective inspector had promised. I cued it up, then played it so Carla could hear it, too.

When it had finished, she asked, "Who was that?"

"Dr. Evans Hunt, director of the program I'm in at the hospital and Rita Davenport's superior."

"He saw her the night she died?" Carla fixed me with a stare.

"Yeah, and he lied about it."

"You think..." Carla put the car in gear and eased toward the road.

"I don't know what to think, but right now, I'd say everyone involved in the trial is a suspect."

"I hate it when I can't count on the good guys," Carla muttered as she wheeled into traffic.

Me too, but it wouldn't help to tell her what she already knew. "You've known Beck a long time, right?"

"Went to the Academy together, so yeah, we've been through some shit." When she flipped around to look forward through the windshield, she didn't meet my eyes. "Why?"

"You know why. What's he gotten himself into?"

"Sometimes the past, it doesn't stay past, you know?" Clearly, she was uncomfortable, her face pinched with concentration as she walked through a verbal minefield.

A sarcastic reply sprung to mind, but I stifled it. My past was rarely present. "It can bite you, for sure." Mine had bitten me and I never even saw it coming—not until someone had parked a stiff in my bathtub. I waited. Pressing Carla seemed like a bad thing.

She wandered through town, taking an indirect way to my place—at least that's where I assumed we were going. Still several blocks away, she pulled to the curb. Out of habit, she reached for the key, then, with a glance my direction, left the engine running, the heat on high.

She swiveled so she half-faced me. I could see my worry echoed in her eyes.

"If he asks, man, this didn't come from me. You got it?"

THEA AWOKE WITH A START. A sound. What was it?

After polishing off two bowls of curry and rice, she'd fallen asleep where she'd sat with her head resting on her arm on the table. Her back shrieked at the insult, but she didn't move. Curiously, the pain in her shoulder had disappeared. She stretched and windmilled her arm. Nothing.

Something had awakened her. What was it?

She listened. A shifting. The dog whimpered.

Carter.

Thea knelt beside the cot, pressing a hand to his forehead. "You're burning up," she whispered as if he could hear.

He moaned.

"I'm going to get Shell." Thea rocked back on her heels and stood. "Hippo, guard."

The dog's stare left Thea certain it would've been accompanied with an eye-roll if dogs could do that.

The cottage was small, filled with equipment. Shell had said she had a lab. With all the servers, the heat was oppressive and much too damaging for a lab, especially one capable of analyzing delicate bodily fluids. In the tropics, where would the coolest place be?

Thea peeked around the corner where she had seen Shell disappear last night. A galley kitchen opened into a small sleeping area bounded by waist-high solid walls with netting above. Two cots, both empty, were the only hints of human habitation. A hooked rug covered the middle of the small room.

The last time they'd been in this situation, what had Carter told her to do? Thea closed her eyes. *Listen, Thea. Don't trust only your eyes.* How was she so easily able to summon him? The answer made her uncomfortable. The last human on the planet she wanted to be connected to was Carter Livingston. He wasn't good for her blood pressure or her longevity. But everything else...

She closed her mind and opened her ears. At first, the sounds of the jungle at rest muffled everything else. Trees moved, branches rubbing in the breeze. Birds called softly. Bugs, too. Small animals moved in the treetops. Thea forced herself to listen past the jungle noise. Slowly, other noises let themselves be heard. The hum of the servers in the other room. The crackle of electricity as it arced through lines most likely exceeding their max capacity. And something else. A soft shuffle. Something moved through dirt or sand.

Thea squatted next to the rug, patting the edges. Once she knew what she was looking for, the handhold wasn't hard to find. She raised the trap door. Made of green wood, it took both hands and what little strength she'd recovered to lift it. On her knees, holding the door a couple of feet open, she found herself face-to-face with the business end of a side-by-side double barrel. "From the bore it looks like a twelve-gauge Beretta. Pretty fancy for the jungle."

David eyed her, holding the site for a moment longer than necessary as if to intimidate, then lowered the gun. "Figured you were fine where you were. And Carter might need you."

Her gun leaned in the corner. Her knife stuck in the ground next to it. They'd left her with nothing. She cocked an eyebrow at him. His heavy-handed manner grated, but she needed his help, so she could put up with him a bit longer. "An unarmed first line of defense. Always a good thing."

"We don't know you. Only through Carter." He stepped back but didn't offer her a steadying hand, leaving her on her own to navigate the hand-hewn stairs.

Thea could only imagine what Carter had told them, not that it mattered. This wasn't a popularity contest; it was a matter of survival. David didn't stop her when she went for her gun, checked the state of her ammo, then slung it on its strap over her shoulder. The knife she tucked where she could reach it.

Shell, perched on a stool and bent over her equipment, hadn't acknowledged Thea's intrusion. "I've got the virus and have isolated the DNA strand. Interesting design." Her voice sounded fresh, excited—a dog on the scent of a killer.

"You did all that here?" Thea asked as she cataloged the equipment scattered on tables around the underground bunker. Her gaze rested on several boxes of ammo tucked under one of the tables. They were expecting trouble.

"It's a short strand design. The killer is keeping it simple, targeting a specific, easily activated genetic defect." Shell looked at Thea for confirmation. "You're the geneticist."

"Yes, the lady who they killed, Dr. Rita Davenport, carried a Parkinson's genetic profile along with the specific anomaly for paranoia. Not all with the genetic profile for Parkinson's have it. But it can have fatal consequences."

Shell took off her glasses and rubbed the bridge of her nose. "Fatal isn't the important thing here. Most paranoids don't suffer some horrible fatality. How did she die, this Dr. Davenport?"

"Jumped in front of a subway train."

Shell flinched. "The key for your killer is the immediacy of the consequence to the trigger. If he triggers cancer or Alzheimer's, the gestation would be too long."

"And the causal link too remote." Thea grabbed a stool and straddled it. "He wants us to know he's doing it."

"Might make him easier to catch." David had taken a perch on the second of the steps leading to the room above.

"My equipment isn't sophisticated, nor am I," Shell said, rubbing a hand over her eyes. "This sort of thing is a bit out of my normal realm. I'm really just learning. Curiosity more than anything."

"So you can't tell us more?"

"I can tell Carter what to look for, but he's the one you need. Someone put the request for this design on the web, looking for biohackers who could build it. Carter has the network and the entrée to ferret out the person who designed it."

"And through them, the person who ordered it." Thea felt the first glimmer of hope that they actually had a trail to follow.

Shell doused it. "Doubtful. The IP address will be spoofed for sure."

Thea popped off the stool. "Then why are we here?" She wanted to move, to pace, but there was nowhere to go in the tiny dirt box.

"You get the designer, and he can tell you how the order came and where he sent the design to be made. Follow the clues, Thea."

Shell sounded...unperturbed. Like she didn't know someone would die if Thea failed. Someone Thea *knew*. The bastard had already killed Rita—Thea's friend and mentor. Stiff, sad, all-buttoned-up Rita, who pined after a man who only talked to her when she had something to give.

Maybe he'd taken all she had. He'd pushed them all to the breaking point—Rita had taken the brunt of it.

Thea vibrated where she stood. Could Evans Hunt be behind all of this? He could do it, for sure. But why? She shook the thought away. This trial was his baby; all he cared about. He wouldn't sabotage it...would he? Money could make men do crazier things. Thea had seen it multiple times. Her father sprang to mind, making her anger flare.

David's voice broke through. "To get the clues, it's Carter you need right now." He levered himself off the step. "Shell can give him the scent. Let's go see if he's up to doing some bird-dogging."

He tromped up the stairs, his body disappearing from the head down, which struck Thea as odd. She motioned Shell to precede her, then brought up the rear. At the top, she flicked off the light, then stepped into the room. Turning, she lowered the wooden cover. The rug had been nailed to it, making the whole hiding thing relatively quick and easy.

Shell and David had thought it through.

"Well, I'll be goddamned!" David's anger boomed through the small structure.

Thea shrugged her gun into position and rushed around the corner.

Shell and David gave her wide eyes.

"What?" Thea tried to see around them, but they formed a human wall. "Carter?"

"Carter is gone."

———

THE HEAT and our breath had fogged the windows but didn't touch the cold that had me shivering out of my skin. I gritted my teeth to keep them from chattering. Carla stared at me, making me self-conscious—scrutiny wasn't my thing. God knew I got a lot of it. Guess I should be used to it, but I wondered if that was even possible.

"You sure you're okay?" Carla asked, delaying.

"Okay is a relative term. I'll live. Just tired. Probably hungry. And my knee hurts like a mother." Not to mention the broken heart thing, which I didn't...mention. That whole bit of pain was jumbled up with all the other, graying out the memory of what caused it. Someone had told me that was our body's way of allowing us to move forward: it forgot the pain of childbirth so you'd do it again. Maybe it forgot the hurt of a broken heart, so you'd risk another. "So, about Beck?"

She killed the engine, which killed the heat, then crossed her arms and pressed back against the driver's door as if trying to put as much distance between her and the apparent bombshell she was sitting on that would explode between us.

I'd numbed myself—that's the only way I knew how to deal at this point. Reality hadn't exactly been my friend. And the future would sabotage each day if I let it...so I didn't.

"We'd been out of the Academy maybe ten years."

"So not that long ago?" Math was still a higher mental exercise that eluded me. Besides, I thought Beck was around forty, but we'd never discussed it. Hadn't seemed to matter since I was rarely sure how old I was.

"Yeah, nine years, give or take. Beck was busy with his family— his girls were teenagers. His wife was one of *those*. Resented every hour he spent 'solving other people's problems' as she said. He was handling it, but he wasn't happy, and he was stretched to the max."

"Hardwired to pissed off?" He'd let me see enough hints to feel the heat from the fire he'd walked through.

"Hair-trigger, man." Carla shook her head. "I tried—hell, we all did—to get him to back off, take some time, get his family under control or get out. But it was like work was the only place he felt..."

"Himself."

Her eyes flicked to mine. "Yeah." She shifted back to looking out the window. She'd wiped a small round hole in the condensation.

I didn't think she saw anything but looking kept her from focusing on what she was doing, what she felt was the betrayal of a good friend...a brother. I knew the cost and gave her struggle the appropriate reverence by keeping my trap shut.

"Anyway, his daughter started picking up the tension between her parents. Man, she was good. She knew exactly where to stick the knife in her dad and just how far to turn it. When he wasn't home, which was often—as you know, a detective's hours suck— she started acting out, disobeying curfews, all the stupid teenager stuff. Truth was she needed her dad bad, but he didn't have one ounce extra to give."

"And she was too young to appreciate it."

"Yeah." Carla sighed the word, her breath misting just a bit in the air that had gone cold. "So when she got picked up for soliciting, he took it personal."

"Soliciting? Carla, it *was* personal. Not much worse a kid could do to a parent who's a cop except ending up dead."

She seemed to shrink into herself. "Man, I got a kid."

The silence between us held the rest of her worry.

"He's doing okay?"

"Honor roll. My mom. I couldn't do all this without her. My job keeps a roof over our heads and food on the table; my mother keeps us all sane."

"Beck didn't have that. His kids didn't either. Yours will be fine. You will be fine."

Her smile broke the tension. "I know. It's just, when something happens to someone close to you, you feel like maybe you want to do everything not to invite it into your own house. But you want to help your friend."

"What did Beck do?" The surety hung heavy on my heart. I knew. I just didn't want to know. My hand sought the door handle —the need to escape almost overwhelming.

"He went looking for the guy who was pimping her. We all knew him. He was...well, trust me when I say you so do not want that sort of evil around your teenage daughter. Slimy, a smooth talker. Handsome. The young girls had no defense when he turned his attention their way."

"Teenagers, the perfect targets. Convinced they know everything, and yet they know just enough to find trouble, but not enough to get out of it."

"Beck blamed himself. He said the reason teenagers are like that is to make sure they get their parents' attention when they need it most—when the trouble they find isn't a black eye on the playground."

Never having experienced that particular form of toxic guilt, I didn't have anything to offer.

"Beck and I had busted him before. Got him stone-cold for killing one of his girls. Only fourteen. His lawyer was a greasy one. Cooked up some stuff, said we'd crossed the line, had violated the guy's rights. I don't even remember which amendment he said we'd violated. With those guys, it's always something." She spat the words. "We done it all by the book. Chief was our superior. He didn't go to the mat for us. Said it was too hot."

"Shit." A ball of dread wound tight in my stomach.

"Beck found the pimp, Johnny Do Right—our name for him, not his. He was one of those suck-ups who would shine you on all the while selling crack to your kid behind your back. He could rub every nerve raw, know what I mean?"

I nodded.

"He always said if the girls did right by him, then he'd do right by them. God, I hated that guy. We all did. And he was coated in more Teflon than Bill Clinton. All the shit just ran right off him, and he'd smile and thumb his nose at us." She shifted away from the memory. "Can I ask you a question?"

"Okay." I really wanted to know what Beck had done, but I had to let Carla get there in her own way and her own time.

"What's it like to kill somebody?"

A hard question to answer, especially since the doing it and the thinking about it were two different things. "In the heat of the moment, when you're absolutely sure you're doing the right thing —it's you or them—it's easy. It's not taking a human life; it's saving your ass or someone else's, maybe even someone you love. It feels so right."

"And after?"

"In taking that person's life, you don't realize that you've made them a part of yours. You never get rid of them. No matter what they did. No matter who they were. They were like you...human. And you took that. There's a very personal price for that."

"Is it worth it?"

"Hell, yeah. It's why we're cops. To protect and serve." I reached across and squeezed her arm. "When you're sure, pull the trigger. But by God be sure." I let her arm go. "He killed him, didn't he? Beck killed your Johnny Do Right."

"Yeah. It was bad."

"Who knows about it?"

"Just the chief, Beck, and me."

"And I bet, at that point, Chief stuck his neck out."

"Better than that. He made it disappear."

Oh man, worse than that. Now, Beck owed him. Big time. Nothing worse than having that sort of marker hanging over your head.

For some reason, Beck's bit of vigilantism didn't bother me. I'd done the same, sort of. Besides, I colored outside the lines, too. Someday it would bite me in the ass and life as I knew it would come crashing down, but hopefully, I'd go out doing the wrong thing for the right reasons.

Beck would get that. Maybe that's what we saw in each other.

"Did his daughter know what her father had done?"

Carla pursed her lips. "She suspected. Even confronted me about it. Stupid kid. Never really appreciated what her dad did for her."

"Goes with being a teenager." I stared out the window for a moment trying to understand the emotional toll this must've taken on everybody. "Did Beck know his daughter suspected?"

Carla let out the breath I hadn't realized she'd been holding. "No. I sure wasn't going to tell him. Can't imagine how that would eat away at a father like Beck."

"How *did* she know?"

"Said she was there, hiding, her father never saw her."

"Where's the daughter now?"

"Nobody really knows. Somewhere here in town. Pops up every now and again when she wants money. She's in her twenties now. Old enough to take responsibility for her own bad decisions."

"It still haunts her father." I'd seem him fight that demon as it ate him from the inside. I'd seen it in some of his paintings. I'd seen it in the haunt in his eyes when he didn't think I was looking.

"You never stop being a parent, no matter what they've done."

"But if she's here..."

"He's a cop; he could've found her? Is that what you think?" Carla finally met my gaze. "You don't have any kids, do you?"

I shook my head.

She gave me a nod as if that explained everything. "He could've found her, maybe. And then what? If she didn't want to be found..."

"I get it. An addict's gotta want the help." My turn to stare out the window. *Beck.* He needed help but wouldn't ask for it. Seems his daughter learned at the feet of the master. "The pimp, whatever his name was, is dead. Beck's secret is buried. What launched him off?" *And why won't he answer my calls? Was he over me or afraid to drag me into whatever it was?*

"Seems his secret wasn't buried quite deep enough."

"They never are." I felt the lick of anger building. "Someone threatened him?"

"Yeah."

From the hard look in her eyes, I knew it was worse. "They've got proof?"

"So they say."

"There's more, isn't there?" I didn't wait for Carla's nod. I knew. "They have his daughter."

CHAPTER FIFTEEN

"Where's the dog?" Thea asked.

"The dog?" David whirled around the small space like a missile looking for a target.

Shell looked like she understood. "If he were taken, they would've killed the dog."

"And the dog's not here." Thea stopped in the middle of the room and quieted her emotions to let thought through.

"He was hurt," David insisted, anger tightening his voice. "Maybe delirious. Perhaps he wandered off? Someone lured him away. Maybe even the damn dog." He still seemed to favor finding a head to bash.

Thea shook her head and smiled at a private joke. "He went to take a leak."

"What?" David's face scrunched into a frown.

Shell looked amused.

"Listen." Thea could hear Carter. A whistle to the dog. A twig breaking where he stepped. He felt safe here; he wasn't trying to be quiet. But his pain was real, his breathing labored against it. Thea heard it all and had processed it just as Carter parted the plastic strips guarding the doorway and stepped into the room, the dog on his heels.

One step inside, he stopped. "Thea? And Shell?" The dog wiggled around his legs to greet Thea with a lick on her hand. "And David, too. You're all here."

"How do you know?" David asked. "We haven't made a sound."

"Shell always smells like coconut. Your anger crackles like electrical current. And Thea needs a shower."

"You're not exactly daisy-fresh yourself." Thea took a sniff of her clothes. Carter was right. A shower then sleep, but neither were in her immediate future. "You feel better?"

"My bladder was about to burst. That bullet in my back hurts like crazy, but I'll live."

Shell took his arm and guided him to a chair in front of the computer. "Here, sit. I couldn't take the bullet out. It's right up against your spine. You're one lucky man, but it's too close to important structures for me to remove."

Carter felt the chair, then the shelf in front of him, his hands coming to rest on a keyboard. Then he traced the outline of the screen—a mid-sized laptop...powerful portability. "I'm assuming you have work for me to do?"

Shell moved another chair next to Carter's. "You sit," she said to Thea. "Walk him through it. Watch for mistakes."

"Mistakes!" Carter feigned offense.

Thea eased in beside him. "He sees better than we do. His eyes don't fool him." She leaned into him, her shoulder touching his. He was warm. Perhaps a bit too warm. "You sure you're okay?"

"No, but I will be once we get the information we need."

She listened while Shell told Carter what she'd found. "It's a small section of DNA." She recited the gene pair sequence from memory. They used a coronavirus to carry the strand and infect the victim."

"And the sequence is a specific trigger for the—" Thea asked.

"Paranoia in Parkinson's," David answered. "I recognize it. I've been working with Eddie Chan in Singapore crunching the data from the Chinese DNA database looking for anomalies and what we might be able to tie a genetic footprint to. Like needles in a huge haystack, but fascinating."

"He's not in China?" Thea asked. "Odd that the Chinese would let someone outside the country access that kind of info."

"They don't know where Eddie is."

"Okay," Thea said, knowing better than to ask more. "Tell me something, anything, that will help me find who did this to Rita."

Carter stiffened, his hands poised on the keyboard. He stared straight ahead. "They killed Rita?" His voice was soft, hurt, with a hard hint of revenge.

Thea squeezed his forearm. "I'm sorry. I thought you knew." He looked stricken. Of course, Rita had been at Carter's meeting in London—that's where they suspected she'd been infected, not that Thea would breathe a word of that to him. For all she thought she knew about her colleagues, the insights that had eluded her were coming at her hard and fast.

"We were at Cal Tech together more than a few years ago." His tone hinted at more.

Thea let it lie. "Then help me find her killer, for Rita, and before he kills again."

Carter took a deep breath then winced against it. He settled into business mode—Thea knew the look. "Okay, the design request would've been put up on Virorg.com."

"What?" Thea asked, her nose wrinkling.

"It's a webroom where someone can challenge virologists to come up with a specific design. It'll come with a set of design parameters, but they'll be loose. We need to wander around and see if we can find a design request that fits Shell's parameters. Hopefully, we'll be able to track the designer and get more info."

"Wouldn't they hide that sort of thing?"

"No reason. The other members won't know what the design will do to the recipient. None of this is outwardly toxic or bad—it won't be obvious."

"Like the flu, it can be mild in some, or non-existent, but in others it can kill."

"A rather broad-brush analogy," Carter said as his fingers flew over the keyboard. "But apt if indelicate. The request will be written in SBOL, an open-source language similar to XML, and popular with the synthetic biology crowd. It'll seem like a standard vaccine request. Once the design is accepted, it'll go into the database for anyone to see."

"Even info on the person requesting the design?"

"Yeah, but that'll be a spoofed IP address and not worth our time to try to chase. But if we get the designer, we've got someone real to try to extract info from." Carter seemed confident.

Thea fed on his confidence. "I can't believe they put all this in a database for all the world to see."

"There are two theories at work in the DNA world. Many feel we ought to go to great lengths to protect our DNA and keep the work out of our molecular business. The other thinks we ought to create a huge database of all the DNA we can find and map. That way, our knowledge base increases exponentially."

"And if an evil-doer uses DNA to attack someone..."

"We'll have a better idea as to how to craft the antidote. Where we sit is a short boat ride away from the largest thriving bio-marketplace. My guy is in the middle of it with connections all over the place. I'm asking Eddie to find the designer."

"This is scarier than I even imagined." Thea leaned back in her chair and watched the Chinese characters march across the screen as Carter typed. Her Mandarin was rusty, so she caught the gist but lost the nuances.

"I'm on the front line trying to head off a war nobody knows is coming." Carter was in deep. He stopped typing long enough to cover one of Thea's hands with his. "You want in; I can feel it."

Thea tugged her hand back, but she didn't deny it. Saving humanity seemed like a worthy effort for an MIT Ph.D.

While they'd been working, or, more rightly, while Thea had been watching Carter work, David had taken the dog to the kitchen for some food, and Shell had worked her special kind of magic with green curry and coconut milk. She set a bowl at

Carter's elbow. "You missed this last night." She touched him lightly, his forehead, his chest, and smiled slightly. "You are better, yes. But you must eat."

Carter finished a few more lines of characters. "Shell, can you read this back?" He took the bowl. "I'm famished. Thank you."

"What do we do now?" Thea asked—nervous energy, the need to do *something* prodded her.

"We wait."

THE WATCHMAN SNORED SOFTLY on my couch as I let myself in through the unlocked door. The lock had been a bone of contention between us. He didn't see the point in locking out whatever life had sent for you. After finding a stiff in my bathtub and almost becoming one myself, I had a slightly different take on personal safety. Five locks on my door and he couldn't throw one. I gave each its due, double, then triple checking them. Then the notes and the potted plants in front of the door. Yeah, I was a bit anal. I also went through this routine so often sometimes I couldn't figure out whether my memory was yesterday's or today's or some other day's. The visuals confirmed I'd secured the apartment as much as possible without having a metal door and a drop bar. Even I thought that might be overkill.

Jesus, I was cold.

I tossed my backpack on the chair then went and layered up—a long-sleeve shirt, a sweatshirt, then a puffy vest for good measure. Coffee sounded good, so I set about making some.

The Watchman stirred then sat up, rubbing his face.

With measured care I set two mugs next to the pot. "I'm sorry. I didn't mean to awaken you."

"That's the frou-frou coffee you like, right?" Sleep gruffed-up his voice. "The one with vanilla in it? Smells delicious."

Maybe it was the aroma that called him from slumber. With my nose over the pot, I pulled in air. I could barely smell it. Didn't matter. I needed to talk with him. I poured him a mug—cream and sweetener until it looked like coffee ice cream and probably tasted like it too.

"Here." I handed him his, then pulled a chair so I could face him, our knees almost touching but for the coffee table.

"You look like you're about to explode." Wrapping his hands around the mug, he raised it to his lips and took a sip. His smile told me I got the formula right.

Sometimes I remembered, sometimes not, but I was never sure I got it right when I did. Having confidence in an inconsistency was a skill I had yet to learn.

"I need your help." I, too, cradled my mug and downed the hot liquid as quickly as I could without serious bodily harm. I pulled a quilted throw across my lap, tucking it in around my thighs.

"I gathered as much." He leaned forward, his interest clearly piqued.

"It's Beck." Reading from my arm, my notebook, which I'd retrieved from my backpack, and the notes I'd tapped into the phone, I gave him the short and sweet.

"So, this daughter of his..." He leaned back.

I fetched the pot from the kitchen and refilled his mug, then my own. "Samantha." A magazine on the table looked like a good enough coaster for the still-hot pot. It'd cool quick enough. After making sure the pot would stay there, I double-checked her name from a spot on my arm underneath where I'd first written Beck's name and number. "Yep. Goes by Sami."

"Yeah, you got a description?"

I switched to my notebook—my arm wasn't large enough to hold that volume of information. The highlights, yes, but that was it. I tilted the book to catch the light. Writing in the car hadn't made for an easy read. "Five feet eight, one-sixty. Wavy brown hair, sometimes with a poor peroxide job. Pretty tatted up. Most distinguishing is a phoenix on her chest."

"Not easy to see considering she's probably bundled up in this weather. It has a bite to it."

"The head of the bird is a focal point." I glanced up. "I'll leave it at that."

An eyebrow raised, then as quickly dropped back into place. Living on the streets broadened one's view. "Any idea what crowd she ran with?"

"She had a pimp." I checked my notes. "Went by Johnny Do Right."

He snorted as if to say, "Of course she did."

"You knew him?"

"Knew of him. A badass with a big grin. Thought he had a lock on life 'till someone stuck him. Actually, they cut his femoral artery. Hell of a way to die. You know it's happening and can't stop it. When the artery is severed," he made a cutting motion across his groin at the top of his right leg, "both ends retract into the leg. You can't reach them to cut off the flow before you bleed out."

"Nice."

Beck had done that.

A shiver chattered my teeth and I took a gulp of coffee.

The Watchman frowned. "Never knew you to be squeamish. You coming down with something?"

As if in answer, I sneezed, catching it in the crook of my elbow.

"You need some food, then some sleep...and maybe a nice long bath," he needled with a hint of a smile.

Since the dead guy showed up in my tub, I hadn't been able to work myself up to relaxing in the thing.

"Two out of three, I can do. So, you knew of the pimp?"

"Ran girls in the Southeast until someone took a grudge and made it personal."

I eyed him over the lip of my mug and worked to keep my voice steady. "Any word on who took him out?"

"Not that I recall. The street was curiously quiet about it. Guess everybody knew he had it coming. Hell, I bet the line of those who wanted to erase him would wrap around a city block... twice. So, everybody clammed up and no one pointed a finger."

I started breathing again. "You think you could ask around, hit up some of your friends on the street to see if they've seen Sami?"

He set his half-empty mug on the table. "Why do you want to find her so bad? Beck told you to stay away. I believe his exact words were 'don't try to find me.'"

"I have an authority issue." That got a grin. "Besides, we don't turn our backs on our friends." That was a lesson I'd proven in spades with the Watchman and he'd returned the favor.

"I'll ask around, but you gotta promise me you'll eat, shower, and sleep. A springtime cold is no fun."

I swiveled to look at the front door. Had I locked it? Plants in place. Door locked.

"You're safe here, Kate."

Rita thought she was safe, too.

I shook my head. So not like me to be worried about bad guys —I could handle them. If someone tried to push me in front of the subway train, worst-case scenario, we'd meet our Maker together.

The demons that kept me awake nights were already inside, eating away at my memories and my resolve. Those guys scared the piss out of me. Couldn't see them coming, and if I couldn't see them, how could I fight them?

A flash of memory snapped across my synapses. Two kids. Christmas music. Laughter.

Not my memory—Hank's.

With my fists clenched and my eyes squeezed shut, I focused on something I knew was mine. The Watchman. A gash down his middle. Blood... Of course, the memory would be horrible—those stayed. And tonight, with the Watchman close, my brain had latched onto a terrifying memory. But the Watchman had lived. We both had.

In my head, Hank retreated. I'd learned to control his memories, but not my own. Some sort of irony there that was lost on me, but at least I recognized it.

Tonight was a fuzzy night. I could feel the memories fraying at the edges. Reaching for some warmth, I abandoned my coffee and pulled the throw tighter around me.

The Watchman leaned over and pressed a hand against my forehead. "You're burning up."

A shiver racked through me. "And you're full of it."

"Let me make you some soup." He stared down at me with a look of resolve.

"Sure, knock yourself out." Pressing pillows around me, I fortified myself against...life, and men who were being pushy or irritating right now. My eyes drifted closed as I curled into the chair, resting my head on the top of the back cushion. Pots clanged and banged as the Watchman pulled what sounded like everything out of the cabinets.

I awakened sometime later to a soft clink, followed by four more. The lights were dark, the house quiet.

The Watchman had let himself out.

The soup, in a bowl in front of me, was cold.

"Why did Evans Hunt want you to find me?" Carter asked Thea while he waited for a reply from his contact.

"He said we'd need your computing prowess to get to the bottom of all this." Thea was a bit surprised at the question. "He said your skills were absolutely necessary if we were to sort through all the DNA, looking for anomalies that could be easily targeted and have immediate repercussions."

Carter rolled his head back, cradling it in the lace of his fingers. He put his feet up on the desk, crossing them at the ankle. His chair groaned in protest, which he ignored.

"Doesn't your back hurt? The bullet?" His recovery seemed impossible. Of course, her shoulder hadn't given her even a twinge since Shell ministered to it.

"Naw, Shell's got this stuff."

Thea made a mental note to get some of Shell's "stuff." It'd be a godsend to folks with hard-to-heal sores, among other things.

Carter stared unseeing at the ceiling. "This is a simple sleuthing problem. No huge data crunching involved. Just know the right people to ask. Even Dr. Hunt, in his exalted position, could figure out who to query."

"Maybe he thought you would know. The Dark Web and all of that. It's not like these designers hang out a shingle or anything."

"True, but he could've called." Carter fished in his pocket, then tossed his cellphone on the desk. "I was just with him in London. We exchanged current info. He seemed insistent that he know how to reach me."

"Funny," Thea said, joining the chase, "he told me I was the only one who could find you."

"Bullshit. He didn't phone. He didn't write." Carter's feet hit the floor, making Thea jump. "But he sent you on a long and perilous journey. I wonder why."

Thea didn't like the implication of the obvious answer. "My tail kept their distance; yet they knew exactly where I was going. You guys have taken a ton of precautions against being found, living off the grid, as it were, hiding your IP addresses, bouncing messages around the globe?" She glanced at Carter for confirmation. He nodded once. "How did they know?"

Carter didn't answer, letting Thea continue on her roll. "They brought explosives, an odd thing to bring on a manhunt."

"Unless your job is to destroy any evidence."

"Of what?" Exasperated, Thea jumped to her feet. "Dr. Hunt is my colleague." She didn't want to admit she also had her doubts... well, maybe an inkling of a doubt about Dr. Hunt as well.

Carter followed her as she paced around the tiny space as if he could actually see her. Thea knew it was the sound he followed, but it was still a bit unnerving.

She'd never known Carter to leap to conclusions he couldn't support. "You're saying my colleague, my mentor, tried to have us both killed. Why?"

"We obviously know something—something we shouldn't, something that threatens Dr. Evans Hunt and could blow the lid off this whole thing."

"But what?" Thea plopped back down in her chair. "Okay, let's assume you're right. We need to figure out what it is we know that is so incendiary. Let's start with London. You said you saw him there."

"Yeah, I held one of my impromptu think tanks in the back room at a hash shop. It's always fun to get some brilliant minds together, get them high, then step back and see what happens." Carter smiled at the memory.

Thea's eyes widened. "They all smoked pot?" She couldn't imagine Rita partaking—control was her thing.

"Yeah, pretty much. Rita put up a bit of a fight, but your Dr. Hunt got her to pull a couple of times on his joint. That was all she had."

"Who rolled the joints?" Thea's voice sharpened.

Carter turned toward her. "Why?"

Thea explained their theory as to how Rita was infected.

Carter took it like an unexpected gut punch. "Damn." He pursed his lips. "We all were messing about, joking, jawing, that sort of thing. David was on one side of Rita, Hunt on the other. Either of them could've rolled it—they both were giving her a bit of a hard time."

"David?"

"Yeah, David was there. First time he'd come in a while. As you may have noticed, his social skills are a bit...blunt."

"David. Like this David?" Thea glanced toward the door. She could still hear David playing with the dog outside.

"Yeah."

"What's his specialty exactly?"

"Gene editing. CRISPR especially."

"Okay." Thea drew the word out as her brain went into overdrive. "Editing is a rather fundamental part of this whole weaponized DNA thing. That's sort of coincidental, don't you think?"

"Shit!" The same thought hit them both at the same time.

"Where's the canister the blood was in?" Thea started tossing things on the floor, looking under abandoned clothing, her backpack.

"They're not looking for you," Carter said as he bolted toward the door. "Or for me. They're looking for David."

"Us they could find." Thea found the canister around the corner in the tiny kitchen.

David pushed aside the plastic strips and whistled. "Come, Hippo."

"David, get inside quick," Carter said, keeping his voice steady, but his tone brooked no argument.

The dog almost bowled Carter over. At the last minute, Carter sidestepped the big animal and segued right into an even bigger one—David as he charged through the doorway, tearing a couple of plastic strips off in his haste. "What's the matter? Shell? She's okay?" David caught Carter before he fell, lifting him and setting him back on his feet.

Carter pressed a hand to the big man's chest. "Yeah, she's fine. Just catching forty winks downstairs. For someone to get to her, they'd have to get through us first. Not happening."

Thea unscrewed the bottom of the canister. Using a screwdriver she found plunged into a board by the doorway, she pried the lining out of it, then tipped it over her open palm. A tiny device fell into her hand. Flynn had been in her house. She'd left him alone with her backpack. Dammit, she knew better!

"Fuck." She looked up at the two men watching her. "They've been tracking me all along."

CHAPTER SIXTEEN

Logan was late.

I paced across his office and tried to breathe slowly and not panic. First Rita had died, now Logan was...not here. Not that scientists were known for their punctuality, but Logan was usually waiting.

Carla had confirmed a nine o'clock trip to visit the shyster lawyer—I couldn't remember his name and was too worried to look. I glanced at my phone. I had an hour and a half to work through Logan's tests; then, I had to bolt. The precinct was just down the hill, but it would take some time with the tram and all.

Voices raised in anger drew my attention. Not close but getting closer.

"Goddamn it, Logan. You and your *trial* are threatening to derail all of the research and testing thus far!" The man had a high-pitched voice unknown to me.

I stepped out into the hall in time to see Logan, the tails of his lab coat flying as he turned on the much shorter and rounder, but equally angry man. Red flushed his face. His chest heaved. I recognized him but couldn't place the where or the who.

"No, *Dr. Ward,* what we will shut down is the system in place where researchers, testing facilities, doctors, and Big Pharma all profit from the billions flowing into their pockets while the patients get screwed. For all that money and time, you guys haven't produced one viable drug to treat the tangle diseases that are running rampant."

Dr. Ward. I hiked up my sleeves and searched for his name.

"The new Biogen drug—"

"Diminished amyloids but does nothing to improve cognition. Do you think the patients give a farthing about plaques if their ability to think and speak and wipe their asses doesn't improve?" Logan punctuated each word with a poke in the man's chest.

A crowd was gathering, ringing the two men.

"More testing—"

"Will do nothing but line your pockets. What about the *patients,* Dr. Ward?"

"You are implying I am profiting at the expense of the suffering."

"I'm not implying it. I'm pretty sure I stated it plainly."

A few snickers waved through the crowd.

As I elbowed my way to the front, the shorter man took a swing at Logan catching him on the jaw. He let out a yelp as Logan staggered, caught by surprise more than anything I wagered. I waited, letting Logan have his shot, a right hook to the man's soft belly. Air left him in a whoosh as he doubled over.

I stepped between the two men, keeping my eye on the shorter one as he coiled for a counterpunch. With one hand on Logan's chest and the other hand holding back the other man the same way, I tried reason. "Come on, guys. Enough." They struggled to overcome my locked elbows as I strong-armed them apart. "Anyone want to help here?" I beseeched the crowd.

A security guard stepped forward. When he saw me, he gave me a wide-eye. "You again. I should've known. Any guns this time?"

I didn't know him or at least didn't recognize him. "No guns today, at least not yet. But the day is young." I lifted my chin toward the short guy. "You take Shorty here. I got this one."

Once I was sure the guard had a tight grip on whatever-his-name-was, I locked a vise on Logan's arm and pulled him away. The crowd dispersed and I pushed and pulled Logan into his office, then slammed the door. "What the hell was that about?"

Logan rubbed his arm where I had held him. "That guy and others like him give medicine a bad name. They milk the system with research that shows no real efficacy. They test drugs that don't work. They *know* they won't work—they're treating the tangle diseases as having one etiology while they really have so many, many different causative factors. All because of the grant money coming down from NIH or the pharmaceutical companies. Nobody is willing to kill that fatted calf. All the while, patients die."

The door seemed like a good perch, so I leaned against it. "What's his beef with you?"

"First, our drug works. It will remove or counter the inflammatory effects of one particular pathogen that is strongly correlated with cognitive decline. That pathogen is something we are all exposed to. Hell, they've even found it in ancient man along with the amyloids that we postulate are the brain's immune response to the inflammation caused by the pathogen."

"But that's not the whole answer, is it?" If it were that easy, I'd be back to my old self.

"No, but it's a huge step. There are also genetic factors, in addition to other sources of inflammation. The real beef Dr. Ward has with us concerns our testing protocol. We've developed various tests that can prove or disprove a drug's efficacy simply and quickly."

"Cutting out a lot of time and money."

Logan took a seat on the couch. "And a lot of folks whose careers, whose livelihoods, rest on keeping the system as it is."

I sat next to him. "I see. You think the ass in the hallway would try to sabotage the trial?"

Logan glanced toward the door as if looking into the hallway. "I wouldn't have thought so, not until recently. And attacking me in the hallway was a sure sign of desperation." His gaze met mine. "I really couldn't say."

"What about killing Rita?"

"Desperation has driven folks to do a lot worse, though right now, I can't think of anything worse."

"Anybody else close to this trial who might feel equally threatened?"

"The list is longer than my arm. We have our proponents, but we also have poked a big stick in a huge beehive—a whole government and corporate structure."

"Corporate?"

"Sure, the big pharmaceutical companies could see billions they've spent have no return at all. Thea can give you the inside story."

"Speaking of, have you heard from Thea?"

Logan brushed at an invisible spot on his scrubs, avoiding my eyes. "Not since just after she got off the plane in Singapore. She was being tailed but had the situation in hand."

I felt my eyebrows shoot toward my hairline. "And that doesn't bother you?"

"The internet is mostly nonexistent where she was going. Forget cell service."

"When can we expect to hear from her?"

"When she has something to tell us, I guess." Logan socked at a tattered pillow on the couch. "Hunt should be shot for sending her. I don't know what he was thinking."

"Don't we need..." I lifted my sleeve and tilted my head to read, "...Carter Livingston to help with the investigation?"

"I don't know. Carter is a loose cannon."

None of this made sense. I wasn't sure if it was me or if all of this really didn't make any sense. We had people running in all different directions. "You think someone might want us all going in opposite directions on different continents?"

Logan tossed the pillow to the far end of the couch. "I hadn't thought of that. Any theories?"

"No. Tell me about Thea and her corporate angle."

"Her father, Flynn Janeway, heads a huge pharmaceutical company based across the hill in Beaverton."

As a cop, I could see a problem with that. "She and her father are close, then?"

"Loathe each other. Opposite ends of this particular war and probably everything else."

That made me feel better, but not completely. "What's the name of his company?"

"Bio-something. Hang on." He rifled through the scraps of paper covering his desk then handed one to me. "A start-up looking to find something to hit out of the park."

"Nothing so far?"

"No. Janeway cashed out big time when his last company went public. Word has it he bet the ranch on this new venture. Even went so far as to dose his wife with an unapproved and experimental drug."

I pulled off the cap with my teeth, then aimed my Sharpie at a small square of exposed flesh on my left upper arm, then paused. "Seriously?"

"According to Thea. Morals are an impediment in the pharmaceutical business."

I blocked the name in tiny letters, snapped the cap back, on and shoved the marker into my back pocket. "You know you're going to die in here, and it will take a backhoe to dig you out." I stared at the tall piles of magazines leaning like Pisa.

"I've carefully stacked them so that the center of gravity stays within the base. These will never fall."

"Never is an invitation for life to teach you otherwise." I parked a butt cheek on the chair.

"Look at you." He smiled like a proud father.

Probably more fun now to talk to with more of me available. I shivered and pulled the zipper of my puffy jacket higher. "You are a borderline hoarder, just saying."

He looked around. "You have a point." He leaned forward.

"Speaking of which, we need to go through your normal battery of cognition tests."

I punched up the time on my phone. "You've got thirty minutes. I've got to get to work; Carla will be waiting for me."

Logan raised an eyebrow but didn't ask. "Let's get started then."

We worked through the basics pretty quickly: day, date, who was president, where I lived, could I draw the face of a clock, and then put the hands for various times.

Logan leaned back. "You've made amazing progress. And the memories, how are they?"

I knew he was asking about Hank's that pushed their way in from time to time. "When I'm nervous or tired, they are worse. The rest of the time I can bury them."

He seemed relieved, not that I'd forgiven him for giving me the last dose of my brother's stem cells—the ones harvested after he died. Those memories were a life sentence. Hopefully, the cure would be worth the price.

"We have the smell thing left, that's it." Logan produced a tray of small vials. He pulled one out and waved it under my nose. "What's this?"

I breathed in through my nose then shook my head. "I got nothing."

"Really?"

I sneezed. "Might be coming down with something, though."

"Could explain it." He tried another. "How about this?"

"Nope, still nothing."

He capped the tube, slipping it into its designated slot then leaned back. "We'll need some bloodwork."

Alarm jolted my heart. "Why?"

He shrugged, but I could tell he was worried.

"Nothing to worry about. Just routine. I'll walk you down to the lab."

Just routine? Right.

My heart hammered as hope fled.

God, I was so cold.

"WE GOTTA GO! WE GOTTA GO!" Carter shouted. His hand sought the dog's collar.

Thea grabbed her backpack.

"David, grab your laptop," Carter's voice was calmer now. "You know something you shouldn't. We need to know what that is."

Thea whirled. David was gone.

"Where the fuck *is* he?" Carter shouted.

"Gone to get Shell, I would imagine."

Gunfire sounded in the distance—automatic fire returned by single shot.

"David and Shell's 'protection' is outmanned and out gunned. We've got to hurry." Thea's heart rate slowed, her vision sharpened, her mind cleared to deal with the problem at hand. Her father had always told her that, when the shit hit the fan, there were two kinds of personalities—those who panicked and were doomed and those who didn't and thus weren't. She was the latter —a fact that had saved Carter Livingston's skin and her own, more times than she remembered.

"Fuck!" Carter paused in the doorway, listening. "Get him and Shell."

Thea had already headed to the top of the stairs. Then she heard it—an odd thump like a large firework being launched into the sky. "Incoming." In a few strides she had Carter by the shirt and the dog by the collar. She threw them both down the stairs then

dove after them. Someone grabbed her shirt, yanking her to the side and cushioning her fall. She curled up, shielding her head with her arms and held her breath.

A mortar. So close, the whistle of it screamed in the night.

Thea's heart pounded. She pressed against the earthen wall. A direct hit would be a firestorm. The whistle so loud. Hands pressed to her ears.

An explosion rumbled through the earth and rent the air. Then nothing. No heat. No flames. Silence.

"It went long." Thea bounced to her feet. "Hurry. They've got to recalibrate." She shoved Carter up the stairs. Then the dog. "Don't think that's the only one they have," she said to David as he helped Shell up then followed.

Thea gave a quick look around the space. A notebook caught her attention. Tucking it in the waistband of her pants under her shirt, she followed. Smoke filled the kitchen and computer room. The mortar had hit close. David folded the laptop Carter had been using. Carter grabbed the dog. Shell filled another pack with clips.

"We got ten seconds, fifteen max. Best guess." Thea opened her pack. "Give me your laptop. Shell's pack is full."

David hesitated.

She grabbed some clips, stuffing them in various pockets. "Now!" She extended a hand and snapped her fingers. The thump of another mortar. "Incoming!" Thea shouted.

She yanked the computer from David. Moving for the door, she stuffed the computer in her backpack, then grabbed Carter's hand, guiding it to the strap on her backpack. "Hold onto me and keep up." At the door, she didn't even pause, leaping into the darkness.

Carter knew her well—he jumped as she did, then hit the ground with a grunt. The pain robbed him of half a step. "The dog?" he asked, his breathing labored, his voice sharpened.

Thea managed a glance back as she darted and weaved, pushing and pulling Carter, knowing each tug and push hit him with the sharp sting of a dagger point. "To your left, on your heel."

David had grabbed Shell, positioning her behind him. They were ten yards behind, no more.

The mortar hit the shack. Instinctively, Thea covered her head. The flash. An instant to orient herself and cover her head and brace for the concussion. It hit with the power of Thor's hammer, knocking them to the ground. Thea hit hard. The force robbed her of breath.

Move! Run!

Splinters of wood, metal and fire rained down like God had indeed seen and found fault.

The hair on the back of Thea's neck stood up. She could almost feel someone hiding in the trees ahead sighting on them, intent on picking them off one at a time...or someone behind. The timing between launch and impact and the path of the first mortar had told her not only the direction the assholes came from but also how far away they were, more or less. *Devil's in the details.*

Clouds hid the moon, dimming the light to almost nothing. She picked herself up and grabbed Carter by the jacket, hoisting him to his feet. She ignored his grunt of pain.

A red dot traced a tiny circle over his heart. Thea shoved him backward, then threw herself backward. The shot whistled between them. "I got you. Run!"

They zigzagged through the night.

Another flash to her right. "Down!"

Carter fell to the ground. Thea whirled, sighted, and fired a burst.

No sign of David or Shell. No friendly fire. "Run now!"

Carter bolted ahead with Thea on his heels. Thea half-cringed, steeling herself for the bullet that never came. "Twenty feet trees straight ahead. Angle ten degrees." The darkness hid so much. Thea hoped it wasn't another tree.

Finally, the coolness of the cover of trees sheltered them and they stopped.

Hands on their knees, they bent, gasping for air.

The dog barked twice—tiny yips.

Thea looked back at the smoldering remnants of the shack. A line of dark figures advanced, the glow of the fire behind them.

"What do you see?" Carter whispered. "Shell and David?"

"No sign. Ten targets. Too far."

"We wait."

"Fuck. I knew you'd say that." Thea checked her ammo and took a breath.

"How well do you know David?"

"Why? Carter squatted, his back against a tree. The dog sidled in next to him.

"He could be dead. He could've circled back to get behind them. Or he could've cut and run. Our lives could hinge on which path he chose. Any guess?"

"Flip of the coin."

CARLA WAITED in front of the Central Precinct in the same unmarked ride she had yesterday, the engine running. The doors were locked, so I tapped on the passenger window.

"Worried about the riffraff that might climb inside?" I asked through the glass.

"You'd be surprised. And not riffraff, but hipsters thinking I'm their Uber."

"In this ride?" I slipped inside and closed my door.

"No barrier to entry." She hit the lock switch. "You don't look any better today than yesterday," she said as she eased the car into traffic, and I turned the heat on high.

"Nice to see you, too." A headache bloomed behind my right eye, sharp like an ice pick jammed in my temple. Guess I'd die if someone did that; this only made me want to. I rubbed my arm where it ached from the blood draw. Logan said he'd get back to me. I tried not to think about it.

Carla killed the radio and kept quiet on the ride across the river, actually across both the Willamette and the Columbia, to Vancouver, Washington. We wandered through neighborhoods that apparently even Google maps didn't want to go into before pulling up in front of a disreputable strip center. Carla parked where we could see the lawyer's office, but not where he would notice he was being watched.

The whole center looked like it was hunkered down awaiting the wrecking ball. A neon sign over a beauty salon sizzled, one half of it shorted out. A liquor store, the windows blacked out and covered with bars, looked like it had been hit too many times. No doubt if anyone walked through the door with an attitude, they'd be met with the business end of a double-barrel. Police could respond, but not necessarily deter—a dilemma that frustrated me as one of the protect-and-defend crowd. The middle two retail spaces sported frosted windows and For Rent signs. A few cars dotted the lot.

A slim female, her face hidden behind the shield of her helmet, her blonde hair streaming from the bottom, fired up a BMW like mine, but hers was vintage, mid to late seventies, I'd say. She'd been parked in front of the salon. With her toes barely touching the ground, she maneuvered the bike, then eased past us, giving a nod.

Something about her stirred a memory, but it flitted just out of reach.

"Mr. Westmore isn't exactly living high on his law license, is he?" Carla leaned forward, taking in the surroundings.

I did the same. "See anything worrisome?"

"Not anything other than this whole place struggling under a shitload of despair."

"Tell me about it. We stay here too long, we're going to need some Xanax." That got the hint of a grin. I cracked my door. "You want the front or the back?"

"You look a little more down and out than I do." Carla glanced at me. "No offense."

"None taken. I'll ask him for help with my recent drug bust. Or maybe a felony assault charge?"

"Drugs. Felony assault might scare him." She showed me a photo on her phone.

He was a weasel, too small to be a badass. "Got it. I'll distract him while you come in the back. See if there are any files to pilfer. But first, we really should wait for backup." At her look, I smiled.

"But that's not our style. So, why don't we set up my phone to video the building, catching the ends, to see who might make a run for it?"

Carla pursed her lips. "I like it. Show me."

So I did. Wedging my phone between the window and the doorframe on my side of the car, I set it to continuous record, thankful for the big rubber case the Watchman had insisted on the last time he watched me decompensate after something happened to my phone. It made sure the phone wouldn't slip from its precarious position.

"How'd you know how to do that? Seems so simple, but I never thought of it."

"When no one trusts you and you return the favor, you improvise."

"Man, that's harsh."

"I gotta be me," I said as I spread my arms wide, but Carla had already slipped out of the car. Hands jammed in her jacket pockets, she hurried, head on a swivel, around the side of the building.

"Guess that's my cue," I whispered. Last time I'd let myself into an office, I'd killed a man and almost lost Stella. Not exactly a feel-good experience to build on. I double-checked the phone was recording, then let myself out of the car, easing the door shut.

A lone car, a dinged-up Mercedes at least twenty years old, painted flat black with black rims, occupied the spot directly in front of the door. The stenciling on the glass door, old and curled, spelled out Walter Westmore, Esquire. As I pushed through, a bell announced my arrival. No one manned the battered front desk, a refugee of many an office surplus store from the looks of it. A dark path in the commercial-grade carpet led to a hallway. I thought I heard a door click closed, but I may have been imagining Carla letting herself in the back.

"Hello?" The headache still thumped behind my eye. I did my best to ignore it. A car out front. Door open. Someone should be here.

The chill of silence answered me. A frisson of *watch out* gave me a dose of adrenaline.

Maybe he was in the head.

I cocked an ear. Nothing. A peek into the hallway. The coast was clear. And no one tried to take my head off. I took that as a good sign, considering I'd given up my gun. Chief's orders that still rankled. Although I might not trust myself, I wanted others to trust me enough to use my judgment. Probably a cake-and-eat-it-too kind of wish.

The first office was empty—no furniture, no human. Not even a tacky photo on the wall or a telephone. Carla and I arrived at the second office at the same time, she through a secondary entrance which stood open, and me through the front. She held her gun at the ready and almost lowered it on me.

I raised my hands. "It's me."

"I can see that." She holstered the gun. "We got a problem. A man with half his head blown off is sprawled out in the back room. Blood is still fresh. The place has been trashed. Files everywhere—a paper explosion."

"Somebody's tying up loose ends. But they must've been interrupted—this office hasn't been touched."

"Interrupted by whom?"

"Maybe us. We weren't exactly trying to hide. If the guy was smart, he posted a lookout to watch the front."

"The motorcycle," we said in unison.

"But was the girl the lookout or the shooter?" I wondered out loud as I scanned the office.

"You be good while I call this in." Carla brushed past me.

"Check the video on the phone. See if we chased someone out the back." I heard the chime of the bell as she went for her phone in the car.

I had five minutes, max.

I'd tucked a pair of light gloves in my pocket before I'd left. I pulled them on and hit the first drawer. A cellphone that I pocketed. A few pens and a pad of paper printed with Westmore's contact info. I flipped the pages. All blank. Nothing taped above or behind the drawer. The middle drawer was locked but easily popped open with the letter opener I found in the far drawer. The middle drawer held a handheld recording device and a single tape.

Jackpot.

I scooped them up and zipped them in my inside pocket.

The desk yielded nothing else. With letter opener in hand, I did a quick scan of the rest of the office. On my second pass, something caught my eye. Westmore's chair. A tufted, leather high-back—standard-issue lawyer ostentation. At the seam where the seat met the back, a bit of leather had pulled loose.

I dropped to my knees and swiveled the chair so I could see it better in the light from the overhead bulb. With the point of the letter opener, I picked at the bit of loose leather. It came loose easily. Once I had enough free that I could work my arm up between the stuffing and the backing, I reached in. Nothing. I pulled my arm out and started over, this time reaching between the stuffing and the tufted leather of the front of the chair. backing of the chair. Three-quarters of the way up, in to my arm pit, my fingers touched a slim bit of paper. Grasping it between two fingers, I maneuvered it out.

An envelope.

I sat back on my heels and shook out the contents.

A dossier. With photos. My heart hitched.

Beck.

Also in the envelope, Mr. Westmore had included what looked to be a list of real estate assets. I had no idea how this tied into anything, but, if he hid them, I wanted them.

The bell dinged, announcing Carla's return. I stuffed the papers under my shirt against my back, securing them in the waistband of my pants then pulled my jacket back down. Trusting Carla completely didn't seem like the right thing to do. Call it instinct. But the chief had taken my badge—why hadn't he been the one to give it back? Maybe he didn't want to grovel; I got that. So he sent Carla. But the chief had shut me down when it came to Clarkson.

The bigwig clearly held his leash. For sure, politics had something to do with it. But maybe not all to do with it, and it was that question and Beck in the crosshairs that had me feeling pretty wary of everybody.

Good guys couldn't always be trusted. Not the chief. Not Carla. Somebody spilled the beans to Westmore.

"The cavalry is on its way," Carla announced as she strode into the room. "Nobody ran. You up for a look around?"

I showed her my gloved hands. "Waiting for you."

As I joined her in a search of places I'd searched before, I didn't feel bad. As I suspected, there was nothing left to find in the office. We moved on to the file room in the back. The jagged edge of a memory stopped me in the doorway.

Like Stella's.

I pulled in air and then stepped carefully around the body, avoiding the pool of blood, focusing on the present, which was only slightly better than the past. "He hasn't been here long."

"What I said," Carla didn't seem irritated. "I'd say we leave the blood-soaked papers and files and stuff on the floor for the M. E. Don't want to disturb any trace."

I agreed. Didn't want to, though. "I'll hit the file cabinet. What do you say you look outside for any fresh footprints, tire tracks; you know the drill." I smiled to take the sting out of my bossiness. The right take-charge balance ever elusive.

Carla left me alone with my thoughts and the dead guy.

Something was bugging me. I'd found the low-hanging fruit. For sure our premise that the shooter had been interrupted was most likely the way it went down. And there had to have been a lookout...

The girl on the bike.

I pulled out my Sharpie and made a note on my right calf.

The shooter wouldn't have heard us until I'd come in the front door. So they bolted out the back. But Carla said no one showed on the video.

"What's out back?"

"Property is bounded by six-foot chain-link with a foot of concertina wire on the top. Looks like it belongs to the building behind. A bank."

"Make sense. Neighborhood's a bit down on its luck. No alley?"

"Nope. No way out except around the front."

We saw one. So where was the other?

CHAPTER SEVENTEEN

"WHY IS IT THE BODY COUNT INCREASES EXPONENTIALLY WHEN I'm around you?" Thea asked as she calmed her heartbeat and leveled the gun, training it on the shack but scanning the open field. They'd come from that direction. Regulating her breathing, she waited for that whites-of-their-eyes moment.

"We are living on the cutting edge of a war where billions are at stake." Carter's teeth flashed in the dark. "It's live or die, man."

He should know. Thea only heard about it from the safety of her lab. Carter lived it, apparently. And now it had found its way into her world, no matter how much she'd tried to protect herself.

If the bad guys, now getting close enough to warrant attention, were sent by the guys who wanted to shut the program down, then monetize the ideas such that very few of the afflicted could afford the cure, they deserved to die.

"What are they waiting for?" Thea asked as the line of guys seemed to wander around.

A low thunk answered her.

Another mortar!

"You had to ask," Carter said, sounding actually happy. An adrenaline junkie, this was right up his alley.

Thea stood and raked the line. Men fell; some ducked and ran.

"Run, Carter!" She dragged him after her as she worked her way deeper into the jungle.

She ducked as the mortar exploded a hundred yards to their right. "Good thing these guys are bad at math." She almost laughed.

Automatic fire behind them drew her attention.

David. She turned to make sure. He'd arisen like a phoenix from the fire. "He just bought himself a get-out-of-jail-free card."

Someone rose up behind him. Thea squinted then shouted an alarm. Too late.

David crumpled to the ground.

Shell bolted from the trees. She made a sound that etched itself on Thea's soul. The sound of a heart tearing apart.

Thea ran from the cover of the trees.

"Thea! No!" Almost the same pain in Carter's voice.

But Thea ran. She thumbed her weapon to single-shot mode. Anger drove her, pinpointed her vision, slowed the world. She'd make them pay. One shot. Blood bloomed. A man died. Another shot. Another man fell. Thea raced by Shell.

Shots erupted from the smoldering timbers of the shack. Thea ran into them, ducking and weaving only slightly. They gave her a firing line. A dark figure hid in burned and shattered timbers. Thea stopped and shouldered her gun.

The noise disappeared.

She squeezed the trigger as the figure half-rose from his crouch.

His head exploded.

Behind her, the firing had stopped. Not a figure moved as Thea walked over to Shell, who lay over David's body. Shell's pain, her horrible loss...words simply were not adequate. Thea reached and tugged at Shell's arm. "We've got to go."

When Shell looked up, she seemed grateful Thea hadn't offered any thin words of empathy or any platitudes. "His soul has already gone. The spirits watched over him. They will comfort him." Her voice was calm, but tears streamed down her face.

Thea helped her to her feet. "Stay low; we've got to move quickly." Thea pushed Shell ahead of her. "Head straight for the trees." Thea didn't crouch. Instead, she stood tall enough to scan for reinforcements lured by the sound of battle—she had no idea how many men had been sent after them. And she had no idea exactly what they were looking for. At first, she'd thought David, but they'd killed him.

"I need my backpack," Shell whispered after she'd gone ten yards or so.

Thea knew time would be wasted arguing. "Where is it?"

"The man who shot David," her voice wavered. "He took it."

"Stay right here. I'll be back."

Shell squatted and nodded. Thea retraced her steps. She'd nailed the guy—too late, and that would haunt her, but she'd gotten him. From David's body, she angled south toward the cabin. The killer hadn't made it far. A quick search yielded Shell's backpack.

Shell waited where Thea had left her. She clutched her backpack to her chest.

"Go quickly now. Stay low," Thea whispered, her order clear. She kept close, protecting Shell as best she could. They made it to the tree line. Nobody followed. Nobody shot at them. Nobody launched any more mortars. The jungle had fallen eerily quiet.

Carter waited where Thea had left him. "Thea?" he whispered, his voice holding an edge.

"I'm here. With Shell."

Her voice brought him to her. The bear hug surprised her, but not as much as the long deep kiss. When he pulled back, his voice was hoarse with emotion. "Don't you ever do that again."

"You will want her to," Shell said, her voice steady, composed.

"David?" Carter asked.

Thea laid a hand lightly on his arm. "I'm sorry."

"Damn. Shell..."

"We will have time to mourn later. Now, we must go."

"Carter," Thea took charge. "I need to get word back to my colleagues."

"You know who is behind this?"

"No. But I know who's in this up to his ass. Is he calling the shots? I don't know. But his heavy touch is a tad too familiar."

Carter rubbed a hand over his face. "Flynn. That goddamn son of a bitch!"

"Who is this Flynn?" Shell asked.

"My father." Thea shouldered her weapon and grabbed Carter's hand. "Let's get to civilization before he has a chance to hurt anyone else."

***

"YOU GOT THIS?" I asked Carla. We'd searched as much of the lawyer's office as we dared. The M.E. would sift through the rest. We'd have to wait, but time slipped past. The clock ticked on one of us. But who? Who would I lose next? And how much time did we have before the little bit of DNA exploded? I pressed a palm to my right temple as I shivered.

"You sure you're okay?" Concern softened Carla's normal brusqueness. Her words even rang with sincerity.

"No, I'm not okay. Got a bitch of a headache and, as you said, may be coming down with something. I don't know. Hell of a time. If I could just catch the fucking idiot playing with us, I'd be a whole lot better!" My voice rose to a near shout on the last part. I didn't apologize. Either she felt the same, or we wouldn't be partners for long. "I need some air. You got this?" I repeated.

"Sure. Sure. Nothing to do here but wait."

The backdoor banged against the wall as I pushed through. One step to avoid the bounce back, and I stopped. Just as Carla said, chain-link fence topped by concertina wire enveloped the strip center on three sides. Was it the bank that was paranoid or our dead shyster? Didn't really matter. What did matter was the missing accomplice.

My gut told me there had to be one. No proof, of course, but I intended to solve that. Walking slowly along the back of the building, I scanned for footprints. At the doors to the empty spaces, I paused, pulling and turning. Each of them locked, neither of them showing any pattern in the dust that might indicate someone had opened them recently.

That left the hair salon at the far end.

The backdoor opened easily. The backroom was empty, so I eased inside. A young woman, lopsided haircut—long on one side and shaved on the other, dashed into the room. When she saw me, she drew up short.

"I parked around back."

"Cool. Front desk is through there." She hooked a thumb over her shoulder. "I'm mixing some color."

"I need that color now! Seven Ash, Seven Brown. Stat," a voice tinged with self-importance bellowed from the front room.

The girl jumped. "Gotta run." She bolted to a small sink, tubes lining the shelves above it.

I left her to her business. My right eye squinted against the headache, but other than that, I tried to make myself look casual as I strode to the front of the space. The girl at the desk looked up with a bored expression. She popped her gum as she waited.

While I formulated a reply, I turned my back to the door and scanned the space. Three stations, two of them filled, lined the wall to the right. Two nail techs worked on the left side, both of them busy as well. Popular joint in the middle of a not-so-popular neighborhood. Something about the place didn't jibe.

Two male hairdressers, all the rest female. Only two of them didn't glance at me.

An eighties soundtrack played, the volume a bit too loud.

One of the hairdressers flicked on a hairdryer. I didn't even flinch. But it did draw my attention. At that moment, the client seated in one of the chairs to my right rose and pointed a gun at me. "What do you want here?"

A tall girl, tats on most of her exposed flesh, sunken cheeks, greasy hair, and dead eyes, she looked like she could handle the gun but little else. And she clearly hadn't availed herself of the establishment's services.

For the first time in a long time, not looking like a cop was a good thing. Some of my former life on the streets undercover for the NYPD resurfaced; I fell into old habits. "I'm looking for work. Was told I could score some good stuff here and maybe work the streets."

The girl gave me the once-over. "Aren't you a bit old?"

"Desperation feeds on everybody." I hiked the sleeves of my jacket exposing my forearms. The bruise I had from my earlier blood draw might give me a bit of street cred with this crowd. "I'm new in town. The bank turned down my loan application." I let loose a half-crazy sounding cackle. "I need a hit and I'm willing to work it off." Shivers racked my body. Still so cold. The headache had closed my right eye. The effect would help if I could hold it together. I let my gaze wander the room. "Can you help me?"

One of the hairdressers, a tall, thin white guy with a tiny Hitler mustache and a meanness about him, lifted his chin. "Yeah, I can always use another lady." The way he said "lady" made me want to wring his neck. "What's your poison?"

I let the shivers run free. "I could use a quick hit of smack. Calm me down, you know? Then we can talk turkey."

He opened a cabinet filled with paraphernalia and enough stuff to get him to sing like a soprano. As I hoped, the girl let her guard down.

Two steps and I'd wrung the gun from her grasp and turned the tables.

Stepping back, I put a safe distance between all of us as I kept my eye on the rest of the patrons. "Everybody stand down, hands where I can see them." I reached into my pocket and flashed my badge.

"Shit," my would-be dealer growled. "A fucking pig."

"Noun, you got right, but I'm a bit offended by the adjective." With the gun, I motioned for him to step away from the cabinet. I gave a low whistle. "You got enough stuff in there to move you to a federal address for long enough you'll be on Medicare by the time they let you out. Bet it won't be your first offense either." I fought off another round of shivers. The cold seeped into every cell. Must've picked up the flu or something.

"Yeah." The guy tried to sound bored, but his eyes darted around like a caged rabbit's. "You gonna take me in? I got a good attorney—he'll chew your ass so bad you'll wish you'd picked a different door to walk through."

I pursed my lips. "You talking about the guy next door?" It was a long shot, but it made sense. Mr. Westmore looked for symbiotic relationships in all the wrong places. I doubted he could've resisted this one. These guys must've been like an annuity for him. "He's got half his head missing, and brains and blood splattered all over his back office."

The dealer couldn't hide his shock. His eyes darted toward the lawyer's office as if he could see through the wall. Sirens sounded in the distance, getting closer by the second.

"I'd let you take a look for yourself, but time's short. Like I said, I want information."

The guy was smart enough to see the crack in the door I offered. "About what?"

"Two things. A girl, early to mid-twenties, big phoenix tattooed on her chest." His eyes gave him away—he knew her. "Street name and where I can find her."

The sirens were closer now. I urged him with the gun. "When they get here, the deal is off the table."

"Destiny. Hangs out over by the Pearl. Folks over there got money and needs, know what I mean?" He gave me a grin.

If I shot him now, who would miss him?

I resisted the urge. He wasn't worth the jail time—but I wasn't done with him, that much I knew. "Nice. You keep that up, and I'll walk out of here, leaving you to plead your case with..." Cop cars screeched into the parking lot, lights strobing. "...them."

Dealer dude held up his hands. "What's the second thing?"

Without taking my eyes off everyone, I pulled up the crime scene photos I'd taken of the dead guy. Squatting down, I pushed my phone across to him. "Any of you know this guy? He also was a client of the lawyer next door. I'm sure one of you has seen him around."

They passed around my phone, then pushed it back to me.

"That's Frankie…or was," the girl who'd pulled the gun on me said. "Homeless dude. Slept with the crew under the Morrison Bridge. He wasn't too bright—they all looked after him." She looked genuinely sad. "He wouldn't hurt anybody. What'd he do to get himself killed?"

"Crossed paths with the wrong guy, I guess. You know if he had a job or family or anything?"

"No family that I know of, but you can ask his friends. He took random jobs every now and then, but nothing steady. Folks liked him. He was childlike, wouldn't hurt a fly."

I sidestepped to the door, pushing it open with my foot. In the parking lot, cops already worked to set up a crime scene. Carla took center stage, barking orders. I tucked the gun in the waistband of my pants at the small of my back. "Nice doing business with you." For a few seconds, I focused on each face, hoping they stayed long enough for me to hunt them all down and put them behind bars or in a detox program, whichever was appropriate. Last but not least, the dealer guy tried to meet my gaze, but his eyes skittered to look over my shoulder. I spent the most amount of energy trying to imprint his mug into my synapses.

That one I planned on sending straight to Hell.

"Kate, you okay?" Carla called.

I turned my back on the hair salon and marched toward the light. "Yeah," I answered. When I got closer, I hooked my thumb back toward the salon. "Just asking questions. Girl had a gun in there." I handed the piece to Carla. "Might want to grab her and check it out."

Carla motioned to a couple of uniforms, sending two around back.

"Take one with you if you go in the front." I gave her a description of the girl with the gun. I left out the dealer and his stash. He'd be mine.

"I'd sure like to know who our dead guy was and what game this lawyer was playing that got his head blown off."

"Maybe we could start with the girl on the bike?"

Carla gave me a sideways look. "Where would you start?"

"With the motorcycle. How many mid-'70s R-90S BMWs do you think there are in this town?"

My phone vibrated in my pocket. I dove a hand for it as hope flared.

Beck!

I squinted at the number. Not Beck. Logan. I swiped to answer. "Kate here."

"Hey." Logan's tone sounded flat with defeat.

A cold ball settled in my stomach. "What is it?" I knew it wasn't good.

"Kate, can you come to my office? We need to talk. We've identified the target."

<hr>

CHAPTER EIGHTEEN

<hr>

THEA FELT AN UNACCUSTOMED WEAKNESS AS SHE SWUNG THE machete, hacking a new path through the jungle. Carter and Shell followed silently behind. Whoever was after them would be watching the roads.

"How many places on this island could a boat dock?" Thea whispered through heavy breathing. She and Carter had left a blanket of dead bodies at one. They'd also left their boat, such as it was. Whether the inflatable had come through the hail of gunfire intact was anybody's guess. Right now, it was the only boat they had.

"We are surrounded by beaches," Shell whispered back.

"What are you thinking?" Carter asked, his voice just above a whisper—he never was one to back down from a fight...even when outnumbered, overmatched, and looking at death square in the eye.

Whatever happened to "live to fight another day?" Thea wanted to ask him even though she knew it would do no good. Her shoulders screamed in protest as she lifted the blade then brought it down in a chop.

"It's not far," Shell said as if reading Thea's thoughts.

"That's good. I haven't much left."

"Your body, it is healing. It needs energy for that."

"Right now, we need all the energy we can muster to stay alive." Thea's arms shook against the weight of the blade. Sweat streamed into her eyes. Every bit of clothing stuck to her. She wanted a shower, then food, then to inflict punishment on somebody... anybody. The next chop, the one where Thea was certain she couldn't lift the blade one more time, broke through the dense undergrowth, offering a sliver of moon-drenched beach. Thea arrowed the machete into the ground then crossed both hands on the hilt. Leaning on it, she worked to regain breath and strength.

"What are you thinking?" Carter stepped in next to her, keeping in the cover of the trees. "This beach is too exposed."

"There is a jetty to our left about two kilometers," Shell said. "I have kept the blood you brought in your canister. I gave it a recharge with the coolant I had left. It will not last long. The bits I have found are not your complete picture. We need to get it to Eddie Chan."

Putting hands on her hips, Thea surveyed the empty beach. A long way from home and running out of options—what else was new? "You and David wouldn't have a boat or anything?"

"No, we counted on a friend on a neighboring island to ferry supplies in, and us in and out when needed."

Thea had no intention of reaching out to him. Who knew which side he favored?

"I know what you're thinking," Carter said. "I agree, but he'd be a good backup if things get worse."

"Worse?" Thea wasn't sure exactly how much worse they could get. Her mind slowed; thoughts formed the hint of a plan. "Okay, you two work down the beach toward the jetty. Keep to the trees." Thea extracted the Glock from the pocket in her pants. "Shell, can you use this?" In answer, Thea felt the burn of the woman's disdain. "Got it. But shoot first, okay?"

"You're going back for the boat, aren't you?" Carter squeezed her arm.

"I'll pick you up on the lee side of the jetty." She extracted her arm, this time gently. "If I don't come within the hour, find a way to get Shell and my backpack to Eddie Chan." She handed him the pack. Thea didn't have to tell Carter that this was so much more important than one life—countless lives hung in the balance.

For once, he didn't argue—and he didn't kiss her again. Thea didn't know if she had the will to leave him a second time after one of those kisses.

KATE. *We need to talk.*

With Logan's words haunting me I stepped into the gondola for the ride up Pill Hill. The doors whooshed closed behind me, and the small glass enclosure jerked then swayed as the wire took its weight for the ascent to the top. I couldn't stop myself from shaking.

So very cold.

Lifting my eyes, I focused on the platform at the top and ignored the few people taking the ride with me. Everybody stared into their phones. I concentrated on my escape. Being locked in this thing always set my nerves on edge. Today was worse than usual.

The sun peeked through the clouds casting a dappled light. It didn't help. Darkness—I sensed it closing in. I couldn't see it yet, but I could feel it—and I could taste the cold, bitter, metallic tang of fear.

The killer had shown his hand.

Had he targeted someone I loved? Beck? Stella? Logan? Oddly I found little worry about myself. Every moment of every day I lived under a death sentence. The timing, while it would be less than ideal, didn't bother me.

Death would come when he was meant to.

Just let me catch this killer first.

But what if the ticking clock beat in someone who carried a piece of my heart?

The vulnerability took my breath. I would stop them. I would be in time. I would kill if I had to.

The gondola bumped its arrival. I squeezed sideways through the doors before they fully opened. My usual routine, nobody took notice. Fueled by nervous energy, I strode up the ramp as fast as my knee would let me. At the first juncture, I veered left to the medical building.

As if on autopilot, I found Logan's office, a huge feat, considering. But actually, I had to consult my notes less and less to find him. I was getting better; I could feel it. The life I wanted shimmered just out of reach but was coming into focus.

Flanked by pillars of leaning paper—reports, magazines, published studies, doctoral theses—Logan slouched in his chair. He'd aged a decade in a few days. When had I last seen him? This morning? Yesterday? The day before? I wasn't sure and didn't want to look. It wasn't important.

"You know," I said as I strode through the open door, "you're going to die in here. One of these piles will fall and bury you. I keep telling you that, but you keep ignoring me. Nobody will know you're gone until you start to stink." He watched me with bloodshot eyes. He didn't smile, so I forged ahead. "You know how you told me to read? That it would help me to rebuild the plasticity of the brain? I believe those were your words." I tried not to look at him—as if avoiding him and filling the air with words would forestall the inevitable. "Well, I read this story. It was about really old men on some remote island in Polynesia. Anyway, once they reached a certain age, I don't know exactly what that was, but it was more like when they felt they'd reached the end of their usefulness, they'd gather under this big old tree." Logan's eyes followed me, but they had no light. I parked a cheek on the arm of one of the chairs, out of danger from falling journals and such. "Every now and again, an old branch high up in the tree would fall and kill one of the old men. Deadfall they called it. Totally random. Creepy, don't you think?" I wound down waiting for a response.

Logan blinked at me as if processing, then motioned to the chair. "Sit," he said. "Please," he added as an afterthought. "You think life is random like that?" He seemed to be struggling with something.

Filled with dread and propelled by the prod of the worst-case scenario, I paced, refusing his offer to sit. "Seems like it to me. You're the hotshot genetics guy, but seriously, three billion base pairs. Sounds pretty random, how they pair up, how they express, what sort of deficiencies they have."

"Lots of room for...miscalculations," Logan agreed. "But hardly random."

"Well, maybe under your microscope life is all neat and tidy and explainable. But out there?" I gestured toward the window that was so dirty it looked opaque. "It's one big random mess. Do I get run over by a truck today? Does somebody I love get shot and die because they were in the wrong place at the wrong time, or they stepped on the wrong toes? Will I have a job tomorrow? Will I be fully present or...not?" I shrugged. "Random."

Logan snorted in a self-deprecating, the-joke's-on-me sort of way. He raked his hands through his hair. He had great hair—the kind most women ached to muss. "I studied my whole life to acquire knowledge." He looked up. His eyes held a world of hurt. "Knowledge is power, right? And with power we create order." That last bit he said with the vehemence of an invective to the gods or something.

"You guys play God, that's the problem—it's like unleashing the genie from the bottle. And you think you can control it." I crossed my arms and tried to breathe. My heart in my throat, I slid into the seat. "So, what's so bad you had to look me in the eye?"

THEA LEFT Carter and Shell in a small rocky hollow on the leeward side of the jetty. She'd taken her bearings and then charged off through the jungle, this time taking animal paths and narrow two-track roads when she found them. Without Shell and David to protect, Thea didn't worry too much about cover. She'd give them the first shot. After that, all bets were off. This way she could move more quickly.

Time was not on their side.

By her calculation, the boat and the small pier where she and Carter had left it was not directly across the island. Angling to her right maybe thirty degrees would take her there. If she cut off the northern tip of land, she should arrive about where she needed to be. A calculated guess in a weakened state. Thea put her odds of being spot-on at minimal—she just hoped she'd be close.

At least she had the moon.

And her automatic. As her long stride ate up ground, she checked the clip then flipped it to semi-automatic. Not much ammo left—she'd have to be judicious.

Once she hit the road she'd taken to get to Shell and David's, she hung a right. Sticking to the tree line, she pushed her pace into an easy lope. Keeping the road in sight, she counted down the minutes—she'd given herself an hour.

The jungle creatures sheltered her, silencing their cries and moving soundlessly as they flitted, unalarmed.

By the time Thea hit the beach, she had twenty minutes left. If the inflatable had taken a bullet...she shook the thought away. More careful now, Thea worked her way down the beach. The bodies she'd left had spent a full day in the sun—she could smell them.

She was close.

With the pier bathed in moonlight, Thea crouched in thick underbrush, stilling herself, taking in a calming breath, letting it out slowly. Only the fronds of several palms brushed together in the light breeze. No movement. No sign of human life. Of course, the hiding places were many...

The inflatable rose and fell with the small swells. Their luck held.

Just a little while longer, Thea implored the powers that watched over them.

The sandy expanse between herself and the boat grew seemingly wider as she stared at it. She shook her head at herself then shook off caution as she slung her gun across her back on its strap. Crouching low, she made a run for it. Zigging and zagging, she tripped over a body. Her feet never stopped churning as she crabbed through the sand. She dove into the boat.

Nobody shot at her. Nothing moved.

She rolled onto her back, sucking in air.

A voice, deadly calm, cold, sounded from the darkness. "I knew you'd come back for the boat."

CHAPTER NINETEEN

"Kate, I'm so sorry." Logan looked at me with all the pain I held.

"Is it Beck?" My voice was so tight, the words barely sneaked out. My heart froze. How would I go on?

"What?" Logan looked taken aback. "No. No. Of course not." He reached across his desk and took my hand. "Damn you're cold." His eyes caught mine. "It's already started."

"It's me," I whispered as reality hit. I must've smiled.

"Odd way to handle it," Logan said.

I shrugged. "Every day I live waiting for this sort of thing to hit. It's almost a relief when it finally comes."

He opened his mouth to say something, then clamped it shut and shook his head. "With you, I never get what I expect."

"Where would be the fun in that?" I didn't feel bad or scared or anything really. "All I want is the chance to catch the psycho who's doing this."

"Oh no. I need you right here. We've got the virus and the DNA snippet from the blood draw yesterday, but we haven't a clue what it's targeting."

My eyebrows crunched together. I'd half stopped listening

when he'd said no. "No" so didn't work for me. "How is that important?"

"If we don't know what it triggered, we don't know how to turn it off—and we don't know what it's going to do to you."

A shiver chased through me. "For one thing it's making me damn cold." I rubbed my arms trying to generate some heat or blood flow—any sign of life would do at this point. Keeping Logan thinking I would do what he wanted would get me out of here. "Who would know besides the guy started this whole game?"

"The Chinese, if they would help us. They've been collecting DNA for years. Their database is phenomenal. They've been doing a deep dive into epigenetics and synthetic biology for far longer than we have."

"Since you have the DNA, can't you craft an antidote?"

Logan looked a bit surprised by my question. "Your logical thought progression is...progressing."

"We will snatch defeat from the jaws of victory."

"Seriously, Kate."

"Yes, I'm seeing more of the puzzle of life, but not for long unless you guys figure out something or a psychopath has a change of heart."

"We play inside the box—this would take far longer than we have."

"So, we need Thea and her friend." Logan nodded. "Have you spoken with her?"

"I've tried to reach her," Benton Myles said as he breezed into the conversation. "Kate, I'm so sorry."

I turned to stare into his startlingly green eyes, dark with concern...or calculation. Frankly, I hadn't liked the guy when I met him—something about him wasn't right. Maybe that's why his name had finally stuck. He reeked of false sincerity. I liked him even less now. "And did you speak with her?"

He shook his head. "She didn't answer. Kate, I can help you. I have resources, but you need to cooperate."

"Cooperate?" Such a nice-sounding word, but it rarely meant

what I thought it did. Through the course of my illness, cooperate had become synonymous with surrender. Not one of my better things. When they passed out the fight-or-flight all I got was the fight.

"Nothing alarming. My people will take care of you. We've got geneticists, doctors, technicians all over the world who can fashion an antidote."

Logan rose out of his chair. "I don't want Kate leaving the hospital."

"She'll have to come with me." Myles's tone turned cold. "I can help her, Dr. Faricy. I can play outside the box. Isn't that what you said you needed?"

How long had he been listening outside the office door before he'd made his presence known? The guy was pinging all kinds of bad on my radar. What was his play here? Only one way to find out.

"Kate?" Logan didn't like the choice we'd been put to or the position he'd been put in. "Are you okay with that?"

Calm, Kate. Calm. Hank's voice. Odd he should come now. *You got this.*

His voice worked. Panic fled; the world came into focus.

At this point, facing down the guy who could make or break the trial, Logan couldn't be expected to have any balls. I got it. "I don't see that I have much choice, Logan. You said it yourself—we need what Benton is offering." I softened his guilt with a hand on his arm. "I've got this."

Whether he could read my subtext or not, he seemed a bit more at ease when he let me go.

With a hand on my elbow and a proprietary air, Myles steered me into the hallway, joining the flow of lab coats. "I'm very sorry." His breath hot on my cheek, he sounded not the least bit sorry.

"You said that already." With my free hand, I pried his fingers from around my arm. "Tell me about your wife."

He winced as if I'd hit him. "She died." Clipped tones hiding a world of hurt.

"ALS."

He stared straight ahead as we navigated the sea of people. "Brutal disease. We had just moved into our dream home in one of those fancy communities—golf course, club, a lake, even a riding stable which my wife was giddy about. We'd been there a couple of years, and she started having problems with balance, muscle control...so unlike her. I took her to specialists all over the world, begging for help. Nothing they could do, they all said. We'd have eighteen months. Eighteen months of watching her lose all that she was, all that she could do. Then she was gone. Nothing I could do. Never will I ever let that happen again."

I had no doubt he meant it. "And the trial?"

He flicked a glance my way. His eyes held anger...and hate. The tilt of his jaw telegraphed his arrogance...and his fight. A man in his situation could be my best friend or my worst enemy. "Your man said she was too sick, hadn't enough time left."

"Was he right?"

Myles stopped, pulling me to a halt with him. The flow of people parted to continue around us. "Now we'll never know, will we?" Then he turned on his heel and charged off, leaving me to catch up.

"You hate him, don't you?" I asked when I'd once again installed myself at his shoulder—the pace a little fast for my bum knee, which was screaming for my attention. Before he could answer, a man coming the other way lowered his shoulder and lunged into me.

Myles grabbed me, keeping me from falling. "Hey, watch where you're going!"

The man turned. In white-coated fury, his face beet red, his contempt on full display, he glared at us for a moment, then whirled and disappeared into the sea of his colleagues.

"Asshole!" Myles threw the word after the man. "You okay?"

"Fine." The man's face filtered through my memory. I knew him.

Myles nodded then charged off again. Once again, I caught up. "You and Dr. Hunt, that's eating at you, isn't it?"

"Why do you ask?" He acted unconcerned.

"Revenge is a strong motive."

That stopped him again. "For what?" He narrowed his eyes and moved into my space.

I didn't back down. "Murder." I shrugged. "Well, two murders and an attempted one. Could turn into a third depending on how it all turns out."

"You think I killed Rita?" He didn't ask about the second murder.

"Means, motive, opportunity—you check all three boxes."

He backed off, looking interested but not guilty, and not, for that matter, overly concerned. "Is that what you think?"

"Just considering the possibility."

He raked his hand through his short hair. Underneath all the bravado, the guy didn't look great.

I knew suffering when I saw it. "Did you kill her?"

"Felt like it. Not her per se, but somebody...somebody who had anything to do with this trial." When he looked at me, his mask slipped just a little to reveal the raw emotion underneath. "I couldn't do it."

"Not into killing?"

He gave me a smile that chilled my blood. "I'm like anybody— with the right motivation, I could kill."

Honesty! So unexpected from Benton Myles. "But you didn't?"

"My wife asked me not to."

"Her dying wish." The man himself was a mystery but I was starting to understand his rules.

"She didn't want anyone else to go through what we did. For some odd reason she thought I could accomplish that." His shoulders slumped in defeat. Letting her down would be impossible. He'd die before that happened.

"What do you want with me?"

"To help you."

"To help keep me alive?"

"No. If Rita is any indication this killer acts fast—we don't have the time to start from scratch. The only way to save you and the trial is to find him and learn what he already knows."

"You want to help me catch him?" Was the guy for real? Or was he luring me away from my pack to...eliminate me or my participation in the hunt? "How long have you and Flynn Janeway known each other?"

He didn't miss a beat. "Several years. I invest in many medical start-ups. A few years back, some Silicon Valley types got all atwitter over the longevity breakthroughs—or at least the tantalizing possibilities. I threw some money in the pot. Janeway was a part of it. Frankly, life is too painful. I can't fathom wanting to experience a hundred years or more of it."

If anybody understood, I did. "Man, I'm down with that way of thinking."

His shoulders lost some of the tension. His guardedness dropped enough for him to take a deep breath. "Yeah, life is cruel."

While we were in the middle of a bonding moment, albeit over our own mortality, which was kind of a downer, I decided to strike. "What's your beef with Dr. Ward?" The guy who'd lowered his shoulder—for some odd reason, his name popped into my head when summoned.

A corner of his mouth ticked up. "Don't ever let anyone tell you that you aren't a good cop. I'd say you're damned good."

The compliment slid right off as easily as he'd trotted it out. "Back there in the hallway. He wasn't sending me a message."

"No, we're in the longevity thing together. When he heard I'd invested in your trial, he went all passive-aggressive, not that I could give a damn."

"I'm not sure I'm remembering correctly, but I think he has a bunch of his income reliant on various trials of Alzheimer's treatments. Our trial, if it works, will cut way into that."

For the first time, he flashed a smile, and I could see the charisma he'd hidden. "Let's make that happen."

Could I trust him? Should I? Did I have a choice? "What role do you see yourself playing?" I wasn't sure he'd tell me.

"What do you need?"

"I need a very complete dossier on Jasper Clarkson. I don't have to tell you who he is. I believe he is also a co-investor. Why you guys want to be modern-day Methuselahs is beyond me." I caught him looking at me, his thoughts hidden, his expression calculating. "That's the right guy, isn't it—Methuselah?"

"Your memory serves you well."

I couldn't help but laugh, but he did have a point—it was getting better. Would it stick? Or would it tease me, then drop me back into a dark hole? Either outcome would be far easier to live with than the not knowing. "So, Clarkson. I want to know his bank balances, his liabilities, his girlfriends, what the problem is between him and his wife. Is his kid a troublemaker, a good kid, or both? You know the drill."

"His blood type and the size of his pecker?" Myles lifted one eyebrow.

"At the very least."

"Why do you want to know?" The question sounded casual, but the tension in his body indicated it was anything but.

"You said you wanted to help."

We stepped through the front doors into the deepening darkness. He pulled me to the side out of the flow of folks on a shift change. Most everyone ignored us. "I can't help if I don't know what you're thinking."

"Get me what I want; then I'll be able to tell you what I'm thinking. Now I've got questions. Some answers would be nice." I jammed my hands in my pockets and headed down the path that would take me down the hill toward town.

"The gondola is quicker."

I ignored him. No way would I let him trap me in that glass cage.

"Need a lift?"

Apparently, he was going to let me go—something I'd not been sure of before. That, of course, didn't mean he'd let me get away. "No, thanks." I felt him watching me until I'd rounded a corner and the night had swallowed me.

Once I was sure he couldn't see me, I veered off the path into the trees—I'd go over ground. And for sure, I wouldn't head home —he knew where I lived and could have goons waiting.

Besides, I needed the Watchman, and I knew where he lived.

<hr>

AT THE VOICE, Thea went still. Her hand, down by her thigh, found the hilt of her knife and closed around it. "You. Why am I not surprised?"

Her father leaned forward, his face catching the moonlight. The angle of the light accentuated the bags under his eyes, the softness at his jawline. His hair had been mashed under a hat, his forehead still showing the mark where the band had bitten a bit too tightly. "What? Not happy to see me?"

Goaded by his grin, Thea scrambled her feet underneath her, then launched herself forward, bringing her knife up to his throat.

Flynn had anticipated her move. He swiped away her hand holding the knife, then twisted it behind her.

The pain teared her eyes. Thea cocked her other elbow, then torqued her body. With all her strength, all her weight behind her elbow, she aimed for his nose.

He never saw it coming. Hard bone met cartilage. Flynn fell back in the boat, his hands instinctively cupping his nose.

Freed, Thea skittered back out of reach and flipped her gun from her shoulder, aiming it at his heart.

As blood dripped, Flynn eyed her. "You've learned a few tricks since we last sparred."

"An arrogant male, sure in his physical superiority, is no match for a woman."

He capitulated with a shrug. Letting go of his nose, he dabbed at the blood with the back of a hand as it slowed. "I know you won't believe me, but I'm here to help you."

Thea almost laughed...almost. She knew her father well enough when he was playing her. Now didn't seem like his normal game. "Why?"

Flynn looked around. "You're doing okay on your own, but time is running out. I've got the yacht waiting just around the corner."

"Give it to me but give it to me straight. One hint of your normal bullshit and I'll pull the trigger. No remorse. Not even a hint."

He seemed to accept that. He'd taken her mother's life—well, she'd been dying, and nobody could have stopped that, Thea gave him that much. But Flynn had hastened her end, and worse, hadn't given Thea a chance to say goodbye or to be there. Both deserving of a bullet to the heart by her way of thinking.

"Somebody's targeting your trial. They've hit another person critical to the outcome."

Thea's focus sharpened. "Who?"

"I don't know. But the key is in David's computer. That's why the whole setup to get you to find him."

"I could find Carter, and Carter could find David." She gave her father a long stare and tried to keep the same demeanor, the half-nonchalance and whole skepticism—she had David's computer—well, Carter and Shell had his computer as they had her backpack. "It had to be somebody close to me or to the trial, a colleague perhaps?"

"Or somebody who'd been with both of them in London. Who knows what was said?"

Thea accepted that. "Doesn't narrow the field very much." She lifted her chin. "You fit the profile, and you were in London. You wanted to find Carter; you told me so yourself."

"True on all of it. I came to your house to try to get you to tell me where Carter was. I wanted to keep you out of it."

"And when I wouldn't play nice, you planted the bug in the canister of blood."

"I'm here, and I can help."

Or mess up the whole deal. If the key was in David's computer, she needed to get back to Shell and Carter to tell them. But she'd be delivering everything she had right into her father's hands. But what choice did she have? She'd never make it back in time to help Carter and Shell now. "You know who's after David and his computer?"

"No, it could be anybody, but I do know it's somebody close to you. It has to be."

"That doesn't let you off the hook."

"No, it doesn't." He didn't further any plea.

Not pushing and prodding went against her father's normal MO. Maybe he really did care. Thea wanted to believe him, but too much rested on the decision she made. "They killed David."

Flynn deflated a hint. "Damn! I'm sorry, Thea. Carter and Shell? Are they okay?"

Her father was in tighter than she'd thought. Thea didn't know what to make of it. Maybe Carter and Shell might be able to shed some light, or at least some confidence. "Is his computer gone?"

"I don't know," she lied. Shell had made her go back for it. "We were taking mortar fire. Shell packed her backpack. David carried only weaponry."

"Mortar fire?"

"Whoever they are, they are well-funded." Thea motioned with her gun. "Fire up the motor, we need to go."

Thea, facing rearward, kept her gun trained on her father who manned the small tiller. The change in the waves alerted her to the presence of the boat before she sensed its bulk behind her. "How many men?"

"Ten, fully armed. Rounding up mercenaries on short notice isn't as easy as it sounds."

Thea tried to resist falling into a familial ease. Murder and mayhem—the ties that bind. She was only marginally successful. "You do know how many lives are at stake here?"

"Intimately."

Thea had lost a mother, but Flynn had lost a woman he'd loved. Wallowing in her own pain, Thea hadn't considered the depth of that and the weight her father shouldered for his part in her mother's death. A lifetime of battling the shrewd businessman, Thea had lost sight of the man he used to be...and perhaps still was.

Time would tell.

"One more chance?" he asked over the sound of the engine and the slap of the waves as he powered back.

The man knew her far too well.

CHAPTER TWENTY

The Watchman still called an abandoned warehouse between the Pearl and the river home. Recently, fire had mostly gutted it—we both had almost died—but with nowhere to go, many of the homeless stayed taking shelter in what was left.

The Watchman liked the top floor where he could see the stars, or so he'd once told me. He also had told me that if anyone came up the stairs, which somehow had been spared by the fire, he'd jump out one of the windows—the short way down and the easy way out. On any given day, I could peer into that abyss, but the Watchman, with his guilt and schizophrenia, lived every moment with his toes curling over the edge, poised to jump. Stella had said he was one missed pill away. The thought terrified me. Vulnerability—I hated it, didn't want it, but my heart brought it to me anyway.

Once again, I found him staring out the window. The fire had shattered the glass, letting the cold of night drift in on the dampness.

"What do you see?" I asked again—different view, I expected a different answer.

He didn't seem surprised to see me. "Trouble."

Same answer. He stared out at the Pearl District with its refurbished warehouses, shiny condo buildings, and bright lights beckoning all to the chic stores and upscale restaurants—a world away yet seeming so close I could reach out and touch them. But we were invisible to them.

"What's bugging you?"

"The world is out of balance."

"Worse every day."

He turned and grabbed me, his eyes wild, his power and vehemence hitting my fight response big-time. "We have to do something."

I clenched my hands at my sides and fought to still myself—I was used to the Watchman and his...moods. "You take your pill today?"

Some of the rational fought away the crazy in his eyes. "I don't know." He looked stricken. He fished in his pocket for his pill packet, a plastic box with tiny compartments labeled for each day of the week. Stella had set him up with it. My job was to see that we stocked it up for the week on Sundays and then that he never fell too far behind. "Today's Wednesday, right?" he asked as he counted the pills.

"No, Thursday."

"You sure?"

Used to not being sure of anything, I pulled out my phone and double-checked. I held up the screen so he could see. "Yep, Thursday."

"I lost Wednesday." His voice carried the feeling of true loss.

One day missed was one day's joy foregone, and we only had so many. "You got a haircut."

He brightened. "I did! I remember." He stared at his pill dispenser again, his brows furrowed. "Damn, one behind, though."

"One is okay. Remember what Stella said?"

He nodded as he shook out the pill into his palm, then popped it in his mouth and swallowed it dry. "I'm okay, right?"

I gave him a hug. He let me hold him longer than normal. "You are way more than okay. We got this." I tugged on his arm. "Come on. Can you light the fire—I can't seem to shake this coldness." Now that I knew what caused it, it didn't bother me as much—but its presence kept prodding with a reminder of the shortness of time.

By my calculations, the killer had given Rita three days, maybe four.

At best, I was already two days in.

In no time, he had his Hibachi fired up and warming the air around it. I held my hands as close as I dared.

"You're looking a bit ragged," he said as the light of the fire chased away the shadows I'd used to hide me.

"No sleep. Something happened to Beck—I can't remember what. And I've got a murderer intent on killing again to shut down Logan's trial."

"It's your trial, too."

I didn't mention that time worked against me on that one. "I'm only one of hundreds of millions."

"That many?" If he hadn't been sitting, warming himself as well, he would've bowed.

"The world's a big place. Any word on Beck's daughter I asked you about?"

His brows furrowed. "I've lost a day. I'm so sorry."

"No worries." I filled him in on her description again and what I knew about her.

"Oh, I remember. I asked around. Seems there's been a cop asking around as well. Driven everybody underground."

"Shit." Beck knew better. But right now, he was no longer a cop. Now, he was a father on the warpath to protect his daughter. "What about where she's turning tricks? Somewhere in the Pearl?"

"I got my friends out on the street. When they see her, they'll let me know."

"Okay." I didn't tell him if the word didn't come quickly, it would be worthless. "While we wait, I need you to help me with the Morrison Bridge Gang. Seems to me I have a very thin memory of my last interaction with them not going so great until you showed up."

"They thought you killed one of their group."

"Did I?" Life kept presenting me with versions of myself that made me uncomfortable at best and alarmed me at worst.

"No." He put a hand on my arm. "But if you had, you would've been justified. I know you, Kate."

"Glad somebody does."

"You doing this for Beck?"

A silly question, but I thought I knew what he meant—catching the killer was more important. "Sure, but I can't shake the feeling the two are related somehow. A bunch of rich guys are pulling strings around here. One of them has the chief dancing, which makes me think Beck is somehow wrapped up in it. I can't tell you why without betraying a confidence, so you'll have to trust me. Can you do that?"

"You're the only person on this planet I would trust with my life."

I was pretty sure I'd saved his life once, or maybe twice, but we didn't talk about it. "All the rich guys are tied to a pharmaceutical company that is in this whole synthetic biology thing up to its last dollar. They're all in."

"Which makes them dangerous."

"Maybe if we find the girl, we can find Beck, and he can shed some light. If someone could just give me a pinhole of illumination, I could run with it."

"Nice words." He looked impressed. "The trial is working."

"I don't know if I'm getting the drug or the placebo."

"It's working, Kate." He sounded like he needed that almost as much as I did. "Where does she hang out?"

"One of the warehouses around here, but she spends her nights hooking in the Pearl."

"Okay. Some of those pimps are shoot-first kinds of guys. You up for that?"

"No guns, remember?"

He took that in stride with a grin. "Surprise. We'll use that. So what do you need with the Morrison Bridge Gang?"

"We pulled one of their own out of the river."

He whistled. "They're going to think you are the harbinger of death. Hope they don't decide to put you out of their misery."

"An offering to stop the carnage? If that would work, I'd gladly let them do it."

THEA STOOD at the railing of Flynn's boat, her back to the spray, her eyes fixed on her father as he manned the bridge. They'd picked up Shell, Carter, and the dog. For a moment, she had thought she'd have to tranquilize Carter to get him on a boat with her father, but he acquiesced.

Her phone vibrated in her pocket. Damn, the iPhones really were waterproof.

A number flashed. Not one of her contacts, but a Portland area code. "Janeway."

A sigh and a short pause. "I'm so glad you answered."

"Kate?"

"Benton Myles told me he'd called you, but you hadn't picked up."

Thea held her phone out and searched the call log. "I've not received any calls nor any messages."

"There's a lot of lying going on around here."

"To be fair, I've been pretty far out of reach. But what do you mean 'a lot of lying?'" Thea picked up on Kate's tone—things had gone from serious to worse.

"Dr. Hunt. He lied about seeing Rita after the conference and right before she...died."

Thea didn't want to believe it. Words wouldn't come as she

stared at her father manning the helm. The boat cleaved through the night. The lights of Singapore beckoned—they hadn't far to go.

"How'd you find out?"

"Missing persons call to the police in London. I heard the tape myself—it was him. He said he'd seen her after the conference, she was acting weird and ran, then he didn't see her again and couldn't contact her. He got worried and called it in."

"That's two reports of her paranoia. I'm outside of Singapore with..." she glanced at her father, "...Carter. We met up with some of his colleagues. One of them, David Thorne, said he was familiar with the genetic variant in some Parkinson's carriers that, when triggered, causes paranoia."

In the firelight, Kate checked her recent notes running down one arm and on part of her left calf. There it was, just inside her left ankle. "You speculated as much."

"We know how the killer got to Rita, but we don't know who's next or what their weakness might be. It's like finding one particular fish in the vastness of the ocean."

Kate really didn't need to be reminded. "Maybe when we find out who, we can back into the what and disable the trigger before..."

"That's the theory, but we are running into all kinds of...interference. They killed David, shot Carter, and now we're barely keeping ahead of them as we try to find a geneticist David was working with here in Singapore...who, by the way, is tapping into the Chinese database without the proper authority."

"Sounds like a good friend to have. Carter's okay?"

"Apparently." Thea watched as Carter slid open the door to the bridge and relaxed into one of the captain's chairs near her father. Neither sported ruffled feathers. In fact, they seemed a bit chummy. "He's got his shaman with him."

"Do I need to know?" Kate asked, sounding at a loss.

"No," Thea laughed. "We're chasing this guy down here to see if he can map the design of the DNA structure used to cause Rita's paranoia, then look for similar designs, or, if he's really good, he can find the designer. Apparently, each of them has their own way of doing things."

"A signature of sorts." Kate sounded like she followed along.

Thea didn't know how much Kate understood or remembered but right now, talking to her seemed nothing out of the ordinary. "Exactly."

"Then the designer could...?"

"Put us onto the manufacturer—the one who received the request and farmed it out."

"They would know who ordered it."

"Maybe, but I'm counting on them telling us where they sent it and if that person has ordered any other designs."

"Two birds, one stone."

"Yep." Thea needed to get into David's computer. If their theory was correct, there was something in there the bad guys wanted. "Any theories on why Evans would lie?" she asked, knowing Kate had as many answers as she did...and probably could come up with as many theories as well.

"Only two really: guilt of his involvement or fear of being implicated."

"Rita had a thing for Evans." Thea felt like a traitor. Rita had confessed her attraction in confidence after a few too many glasses of wine—a very rare occurrence and one that was never repeated.

"Reciprocated?" Kate's voice had sharpened.

"No. Evans cares only for his medicine. People are simply a means to that end. Honestly, I don't think he even realizes what he does and how it can hurt people."

"All very human, but I still would like to know why he lied." Kate took a deep breath then coughed as she inhaled some of the smoke from the Watchman's Hibachi. "Sorry. You say you're one step ahead of the bad guys?"

Thea watched her father and Carter chat like old friends. *Or maybe in their grasp,* she thought, but couldn't say it—not now, not yet. "They sent some Asian mercenaries after us."

"How'd they know where you were? Did they follow you?"

"Please, I'm better than that. No, they planted a bug in the container of Rita's blood."

"Who had access to that before you left?"

Thea could almost picture Kate hiking up her pant leg and jotting notes in her perfect block lettering on a bit of exposed flesh. "Benton Myles, Evans...and my father."

"Really? Your father? I've only heard a bit about him. What's his angle?"

"Whatever you've heard, he's worse. His angle is making obscene profits off human suffering." Carter looked like he was deep in conversation with Flynn—they'd be at it a bit before they pulled into the harbor. Still gripping the phone, Thea slipped into the darkness, heading toward the cabin. Maybe Shell could help her get into David's computer.

"You do know your father and Myles are investors in some company that is formulating a longevity drug?"

"The Fountain of Youth."

Kate sort of snorted, which Thea interpreted as a laugh. "Not terribly creative."

"And perhaps a tad arrogant." Thea joined the bit of light-heartedness.

It didn't last in Kate's voice very long. "There are a whole bunch of rich guys—"

"And a researcher named Dr. Ward." Kate double-checked the name. She'd gotten it right.

"He's a wart." Thea didn't try to hide her disdain.

"He still could be a clever wart."

"Have you tied that or any of them to the formulation of the DNA?" Thea asked, knowing she and Carter were the keys to that. But if Kate had found something...

"No. But Benton Myles has been making a nuisance of himself around here."

"What does he want?"

"To help me find the killer."

"That's rare. How are you coming with that?"

"At this point, just poking sticks in beehives."

"We both need to hurry—the killer is going to target somebody else soon, if he hasn't already."

Kate held her secret close. If Thea knew, she might hurry, and hurry led to carelessness. "Right. Keep safe and let me know what you find."

CHAPTER TWENTY-ONE

As I put my phone back in my pocket, I caught the Watchman staring at me. "It's you, isn't it?"

"What?"

"The next one. I could hear your friend talking." The Watchman's hands shook as he picked at a button on his duster, his growing agitation starting to show. "He put a fucking time bomb inside you."

I grabbed his hand, pulling it away before he tore off a button he might need, and held it in mine.

"Damn, you're cold," he said, his worry tightening his voice and driving his bit of crazy to the surface.

I squeezed his hand then extracted mine. "Yeah, no sleep. No food."

"A bit of DNA triggering crazy shit." He put his hands over his heart. "Katie, I can't lose you."

"Me either," I said with a tight smile. "We don't have much time. Will you help me?" For the first time, I saw the pain that losing me would cause to someone else. I didn't know what to do with that.

"You need to be in the hospital." The Watchman poked at the

fire with a charred board. The light from the flames danced across his face, hiding the hurt and the pain.

"That's what Logan said."

"But you ran away."

He knew me better than I knew myself. "I actually left with someone who indicated to Logan that he would help me. Turns out, he implied help with my medical issue to get Logan to agree, but what he really wants is to help me find the killer. I'd love to know why."

"I already don't like him." The Watchman's hands had stopped searching for mischief, signaling his return to some semblance of control. His meds worked quickly—I'd seen it before.

"For some reason he thinks I'm his best shot, but I need to find Beck. I need his help."

"You can find the killer without Beck. You and I both know that. This is about saving Beck, saving him before that time bomb goes off in your body."

"Sometimes, other people are more important, you know." I leaned as close to the fire as I dared and tried to push aside the worry. Something clawed at me from the inside, something deep and evil—I sensed it more than felt it. It had begun.

The Watchman didn't argue.

"Here." I tugged at the lawyer's papers I'd lodged at the small of my back. The tape was mine, as was the dossier on Beck. "You've got more experience than me, and probably more synapses talking, so help me go through this." I filled him in on the slimy and now-deceased Walter Westmore. I glossed over the how and who of Beck's participation in all of this. Some secrets needed to be kept close—the juicier a secret, the farther it traveled. I spread the papers around the fire. On hands and knees, we both worked our way around the paper circle—me first, the Watchman trailing. He took more time than I did, so once finished, I sat on my haunches and let my mind free-associate. When the Watchman sat beside me and pocketed his readers, I asked, "Theories?"

"The guy is seriously into real estate."

Most of the papers dealt with planned communities scattered around the country, each owned by a different LLC—all of them listing Mr. Westmore as its registered agent. "Hardly indicting." I deflated. "A smoking gun would've been preferable. Real estate doesn't factor into this at all, at least not that I can see. We're talking about a discovery that will change the way tangle diseases are treated." At least I'd gotten my hands on the blackmail stuff the greaser had on Beck—that made it all worth it. Of course, I'd left Carla out in the cold, but I justified it—Beck's business, his to share. If Carla had a hand to play in all of this, she had yet to show it—so keeping Beck's private info private seemed justified...at least that's what I told myself. With my hands on my knees, I sat back. "You up for a quick trip to visit with the Morrison Bridge Gang?"

THEA EASED along the railing toward the stern, her hand firmly gripping the hilt of her knife. One of her father's men slipped by her, both hands cradling his automatic weapon, ready for...whatever. Something about this whole setup seemed too pat, too... prepared. Maybe it was her healthy wariness about her father, maybe it was fear and bone-numbing fatigue, but, either way, she didn't like any of it. And Carter being so cozy with the man who'd left him to be eaten by ants...what was that about? Carter and his games. But who would be left out to die this time?

Thea knocked softly on Shell's cabin door. "Shell? You still awake?"

The lock clicked and the door opened a few inches. Shell took a look around, then, seeing Thea by herself, she opened it wider, lowering the small pistol she'd held at the ready. "Carter gave it to me," she said, anticipating Thea's question.

Thea locked the door behind her, knowing, as flimsy as it was, it would be little protection should one or two of the goons decide they wanted inside. "What did he tell you to do?"

"Shoot anyone but you." She perched on the edge of a massive bed covered in gold-threaded silk. The room had every amenity: antique furniture Thea couldn't identify gave warmth to the high tech. A television showed alternating images of fine art, mostly Van Gogh. The bathroom boasted all the modern conveniences, sleek, opulent, and perfectly designed for the small space. Thea eyed the bar in the corner. "Any food?"

Topping off the tank just might help them get through what came next. Knowing her father and Carter, what came next would require all the cunning and strength she had.

"Plates and plates. The fridge is there." Shell pointed to a mahogany cabinet.

Thea bent to the task, pulling out all the offerings and arranging them on the bed. "You have to eat. We both do."

Shell seemed to hear the words Thea didn't want to say. *This is going to get worse before it gets better.* However, Thea couldn't imagine the pain of losing one's partner. The worst for Shell might have already happened. Both women fell to eating. Mostly Thai, mostly spicy, the food amped Thea's energy. "Do you have my backpack?" Thea said through a mouthful of something so spicy it brought tears.

Shell reached under the bed and handed it to her. "Your father wanted it. He thought it was David's."

"You told my father no? I love you already."

"A formidable man with no soul," Shell said with amazing accuracy. "But he is hurting. Don't doubt the power of hurt to bring out the good."

Thea listened but didn't believe, not completely. "Actions speak louder."

"Give him a chance."

"I will—if it doesn't kill us." Thea opened the top of her backpack and pulled out the computer she'd stuffed in when they fled the cabin. In her haste, she hadn't gotten a good look at it. "Is this David's computer?" she asked Shell, thinking she recognized it, but knowing she couldn't possibly. The tiny butterfly sticker next to the trackpad stopped her.

Rita's computer! She held it out for Shell to see. "This isn't David's, is it?"

"No. Your friend gave it to him in London. She wanted us both to review some research she had done. Then you arrived and told us she'd been killed, then the trouble started. I knew what they had to be after. David grabbed the guns. I grabbed this." The tiny woman looked so calm, so wise.

"It wasn't David's computer they were after?"

"No. Rita told him to be careful, there might be trouble."

Thea gave her a big hug. "Thank you! This will tell us what they were after, I know it." With the laptop on her thighs, she pushed away the food, then booted up the computer. The first screen asked for a password. Thea stared at its blinking accusation.

Now she knew why she was here.

But who arranged it? Who was after her, and what exactly did Rita have in her computer that folks were willing to kill for? They'd just put all their research, all their data out there for public comment. "Well, let's see what Rita was hiding," Thea said half to herself. "Take that little popper and guard the door. Shoot first; ask questions later. This was a setup pure and simple, designed to get us to right here, right now. They killed David so he wouldn't interfere. Let's kill them before they get another of us." Shell nodded, her expression determined. Thea put her gun where she could get to it in an instant, then angled herself to face the open blinds of the outside balcony. They wouldn't come through the front door.

Rita had made her memorize the complicated password. Thea typed it in. She guessed she'd have a minute or two—they had to be watching her. Why had she taken the time to eat? Stupid!

With practiced precision, she worked through Rita's files—she knew what she was looking for. Rita would've left a trail. Thea followed the trail, simple cues only she would know until she arrived at the end—a file titled JC DATA. A Word file, it opened quickly. Rita had left a summary for her. As she heard boots on the outside walkway, Thea scanned quickly. As glass shattered, she slammed the computer shut and grabbed her gun.

The first guy through with a gun drawn wore black and held no resemblance to anyone she knew. She stroked the trigger and he fell at her feet. The next guy through, shoved from behind, his hands in the air, was her father. "Don't shoot." His split lip oozed blood. Red welts on his face would turn black and blue in time. He'd put up a fight.

Thea thought about shooting then decided to wait. Carter had been with him. She kept her gun aimed at his chest. "Where's Carter?"

"They have him on the bridge. A hostage in case I proved unworthy." He seemed to think that was mildly humorous.

Thea didn't share his lack of regard for their predicament. "Did the crew mutiny?"

"Just can't get good help these days." Flynn wore his bravado with a practiced air.

"And no time for a thorough background check." They'd set him up good and simple.

A man with military bearing, short-cropped haircut, also wearing black but sporting an insincere air of contrition, said, "Ms. Janeway, I'm terribly sorry for the bother, but I must request you give me your gun, then that computer."

Thea laid her gun down on the deck then extended the computer to him. "All you had to do was ask."

"Thea!" her father barked. "If they killed for what's on that computer, don't you want to know what it is?"

"No. I want to go home. This is your kind of game, Flynn. I want no part of it."

The head mercenary pulled out his gun, aimed, and fired. Flynn yowled and dropped to the deck, clutching his leg. The bullet had pierced the fleshy part of his thigh. Not much blood—he'd live.

The man turned his gun on Thea. "I need the password."

"That's not my computer."

This time he pointed at Shell.

"Okay," Thea said, raising her hands in surrender. "Okay." The man handed the computer back to her. Thea gave Shell a look, then she took a deep breath and opened the lid to the laptop.

Smoke bloomed—the sizzle of an electrical fire.

Thea let it drop from her hands. She bent to retrieve it but grabbed her gun instead. Crouching, she squeezed the trigger, aiming just higher than Flynn's head. Bodies fell. She inched forward toward the balcony door. Laying on her stomach, she took a breath, then held it. Inching out, she fired a blast one direction, then the other. Screams, then silence.

She turned back to the stateroom. The head mercenary moved, then groaned. Thea eased over to him. "Who hired you?"

"I don't know."

She pointed her gun at his head. "Sure?"

He nodded. She pulled the trigger. The pin clicked on an empty chamber. The man laughed. She pulled out her knife and buried it in his chest.

"Come on," she hissed to Shell and her father. "Let's get Carter and get out of here."

Shell checked the chamber in her gun. Flynn, grimacing in pain, on his belly, used his elbows to pull himself over to the computer. "Whose was this?"

"Rita's. Leave it."

"But the hard drive."

"The program was developed by the Army. Trust me, there isn't anything left of that computer worth saving."

"How?"

"If you don't close it down using set protocols, it will self-destruct when next opened. Safeguards sensitive information."

"Would've been nice to know."

Thea shrugged. "Let's go. I haven't killed all of them...yet."

Gunfire erupted toward the bow of the ship. "Carter!" Thea pulled her knife from the man's chest then grabbed the gun of one of his henchmen who had fallen behind him. "Shell, take my backpack and get him to the inflatable on the stern. Carter and I will meet you there. Flynn, I hope you can walk."

Keeping to the shadows, Thea stepped over the bodies as she moved across the balcony then dropped to the walkway below. Nobody met her. Nobody moved. The sounds of the scuffle stopped. Silence, scary in the absence of sound, enveloped her. All she could hear was the lapping of the water as the ship moved through it, and her heart pounding.

Carter.

Was she ready to lose him?

She inched down the walkway, the light from the bridge casting a glow across her path ahead. Still no movement. No sign of life.

To her left, behind a storage chest lashed to the railing, Thea sensed movement. Two strides, she dove into the shadow, gun first. "Drop it, asshole!"

The business end of a weapon punched into her side—not hard but enough to get her attention. "You first."

Thea's knees almost buckled as she lowered her gun. "Carter, it's me."

"I know. You're upwind. Haven't you learned anything?"

Weak with relief, she almost laughed. "A few things, but I could use a refresher."

"Where are the others?"

"You trust Flynn?"

"About as far as I can throw him, but we need him."

"He and Shell are heading toward the inflatable. Once again, we make an escape from the Singapore Harbor Police." Thea looked forward. They'd almost made the mouth of the harbor. She stepped onto the bridge and pulled the throttles to idle, then killed the engines. "Somebody will find this beauty, but we need to be gone."

CHAPTER TWENTY-TWO

Each time I ventured out at night I was amazed at its cloak. The Watchman and I hurried across Burnside, past the line that never seemed to shorten at Voodoo Donuts, heading east, keeping the Willamette on our left and the lights of the center of town on our right. The few folks we met going the other direction didn't throw even a glance our way.

We'd become invisible.

Of course, past a certain time of night as it blended into the nascent day, everyone became invisible or wished they did. Self-protection—as if sinners were nocturnal creatures. Some did their dirty work using darkness as a cover. Others, so smug in their arrogance, so confident in their deceptive normality, worked their dirty deeds illuminated by the light of day. Most of us never saw them coming.

That's who I was looking for. He wouldn't hide in darkness. No, he would use our naiveté as a shield from suspicion—a foe with a friend's smile.

But which "friend" was he?

We kept to the smaller streets and alleyways, working our way closer to the river. The Morrison Bridge gang was a tight-knit group. Some down on their luck, some struggling with their health, all sticking together, supporting each other with the ferocity of family. They didn't like me. Hence the Watchman to ease the tension. Everybody liked the Watchman. He looked after everybody and played a mean sax—a pretty disarming combination.

The group stirred, perhaps sensing our approach. The outlines of bodies materialized from the shadows—some had been sleeping, others standing watch.

"Hey, Joe." A woman, her voice wary, stepped into the dim glow from the streetlights overhead. Long, dirty hair, clothes decorated with street grime, her face clean, her eyes clear, she spread her feet and braced herself, protecting her clan. She lifted her chin toward me. "You again. What brings you here? Last time it was death. Hope you're on a better mission this time."

I glanced at the Watchman...Joe to everyone but me. He'd need to take the lead, but was he up to it? He gave me a wink and my worry subsided.

"Kate here has a problem," he started.

The woman shrugged and cut him off. "What does that have to do with me?"

Joe got his back up—no words, just a look, and it shut her down. She shrank within herself. Silently, her gang had gathered around us. I didn't like it, but I tried to stifle my twitchiness. A shiver racked through me, chattering my teeth.

"You okay?" The woman eyed me with a hint of care and a larger hint of worry.

"No, but don't worry, you won't catch what I got."

"Kate, here—" the Watchman started, but I cut him off with a shake of my head. He understood and clammed up—my burden to carry.

I pulled out my phone and found the photos of Frankie. Death once again. "I'm really sorry." I held out the phone to her.

She didn't take it, preferring instead to clasp her hands behind her back and bend over the device to look. I understood—you touch it, you own it. After letting me scroll through, she stepped back. "You like working for death or what?"

"I'm a cop. Death sits at my shoulder." I figured that was enough. "I found who murdered your friend..." I glanced at the Watchman for help.

"Benny," he filled in. "Kate has a memory thing she's dealing with—it's brutal," he said to the rest of them.

I brushed off their shuffles and grunts of sympathy. "I found Benny's killer, and I intend to find this gentleman's as well."

"Frankie. That's Frankie." The lady's voice broke. "Nice man, a boy really. He was simple—that's how my gran used to say. He was sorta like a Labrador retriever she once had—he wouldn't hurt anybody, but if you fed him, you owned him."

That somebody would use someone like Frankie to do all kinds of wrong was...well, wrong. So wrong. "He obviously followed the wrong person home and ended up dead." I pocketed my phone. "I need your help figuring out who he might have been doing an odd job at the hospital for. That's where I crossed paths with him. Next thing I knew..." I let it hang. Someone had murdered him—we all knew it. I would fix it. "When did you guys last see Frankie?"

The lady glanced around at her gang. "It's okay. Tell the lady what you know."

"Frankie, he came around about a week ago," a male voice from the shadows offered.

"Yeah, he bought us all lattes like we were fancy." This time a female voice. "He did that when he came into a bit of cash. Lattes, pizzas. One time he bought tickets to the beer festival in Pioneer Square." She giggled at that.

I could only imagine the bridge dwellers mingling with the craft beer crowd. The images, the friction points, made me smile... and they made me miss knowing Frankie. "Any idea how he came into the latte cash?"

"Yeah, some gal on a fancy bike came trolling. She asked a bunch of us if we wanted to do some janitorial work at the hospital, but she picked Frankie."

"Blonde?" I asked.

"Yeah, how'd you know?"

"Been seeing her around. Tell me about the bike."

"Old, lots of chrome. I think it was a BMW, but it looked nothing like the new ones, nothing like yours."

"You know my bike?"

"I seen you around. It's great being like me—nobody sees us."

I wanted to tell her I knew who she was, I'd seen her watching, but why burst her bubble? I was way more like them than I was like anyone in the world in which I walked. If I said that, then they'd all know.

A vintage BMW. I pulled up a photo of that model BMW and held it up for him to see. "Like this?"

"Exactly."

Time to find Blondie.

THEA DIDN'T WANT to think about how many laws they'd broken in getting this far. Nor how many bodies littered the island they'd left behind. "You know how to find Eddie Chan?" Thea asked Carter, who strode ahead, holding Hippo by a service-dog handle.

"That's not how it works here."

Thea didn't like the sound of that, but she had no other alternatives. With a finger on the trigger, she held the small automatic but kept it out of sight, hidden behind her backpack.

She tried to remember the twists and turns but Carter led them into an old part of the city that was a maze of Eastern medicinal merchants selling everything from shark fin to God knew what from tiny stalls lining the street. Overhead, lanterns swung from wires that looped from one side to the other then back again. The young ladies dressed in chic black dresses and expensive shoes and the young men following them, pretending their disinterest, gave way to men in threadbare pants cinched at the waist with a section of rope topped by white shirts, yellowed from use, and ladies in baggy rough-cloth tops with wide-legged pants underneath. They held wide baskets and dickered loudly, pointing to the thing they needed to cure a family member or themselves—the ancient art of healing through nature. Patents and profits had cut that tether in the West. Thea wondered how many people had died from the synthetic drug when a natural compound would have cured?

These big glass and metal cities in the Far East contrasted with their foundations, their roots in the ancient. Yet, the people knew enough to honor their past and revere what it taught them, while still moving through the modern with an eye on the future. There was something to be said for that. When you lost your roots, you floated free at the whim of any wind.

Shell knew most of the purveyors, nodding and bowing as she passed. At least maybe she could get them all out of the maze if they had to run for it.

The smells and the sounds enveloped Thea—she loved the exotic, the being in a place so far from her comfort zone. Carter nailed it—this was what she loved; this is what she missed. Damn it.

Two turns later, the road narrowed to a path. They fell into single file, Carter in the lead, Thea protecting the rear. This had all the earmarks of a setup. "Carter!" she hissed.

He held up a hand. "This is it." Hippo tugged him through an open doorway to his right.

They funneled into the tiny shop one at a time. Thea could barely squeeze in. Shell chattered with the proprietor, pointing to various bowls holding ground substances. Flynn helped Thea watch the entrances—he took the back; Thea stayed by the front door.

She'd taken a second peek out the door when Shell presented her with a small plastic tub of a foul-smelling unguent. "For your shoulder. And for Carter—his wound, no good." She glanced at Flynn but left out any mention of his wounds.

"Jesus!" Thea reared back, pressing herself against the bamboo wall that bent under the pressure. The proprietor let loose a string of Malay—Thea didn't need the words to get the gist. She moved Shell to the side then stepped away from the wall, pulling it back to its previous semi-upright position. "Sorry." She bowed to the gentleman, which seemed to appease him. "That stuff stinks," she whispered to Shell.

"You need for infection."

"Antibiotics?" Thea questioned with a raised eyebrow.

Shell looked around, then shrugged. "This better."

"It certainly could clear a room." Thea lowered her gun as a man slipped through the front doorway.

He smiled at the gathering. "I see you all have met my grandfather," he said in a perfectly clipped British accent. Tall and thin, with wispy black hair, pallid skin, and a broad smile, he'd come unarmed.

Thea relaxed a bit but still held the gun where she could bring it to bear easily. "Eddie?"

"At your service," he said with a slight bow, overplaying the whole thing. His grandfather erupted once again. Eddie listened with deference. Bowing, his hands together, he backed out of the door. "Come, follow me. My place is not far." Once in the street, he looked us over. He pointed to Flynn. "Who are you?"

Thea made the introduction. "He joined us recently," she said, hoping Eddie picked up on her meaning.

"Fine, then he must stay here with Carter to turn away any unwelcome guests." Eddie wasn't asking—this was a condition of his help. Neither man argued.

Thea didn't like the group being split up, but she didn't want Flynn in the mix either.

He caught her arm as she moved by him to leave with Eddie and Shell. "He's not who you think he is."

Thea tightened her grip on the gun but otherwise didn't acknowledge her father's warning. Eddie led Thea and Shell deeper into the maze of shops, some of them topped by apartments, their facades painted bright blue and pink and radiant yellows. At the end, he pulled a ring of keys from his pocket and opened a metal gate. A courtyard, fragrant with flowers and herbs, opened before them. Birds flitted, and the curl of incense rose from a tiny shrine tucked in a corner. A house, two stories, modern windows, fresh paint, but not ostentatious curled around the garden.

"Your place?" Thea asked as she gave each window a stare, looking for movement, the hint of someone hiding behind a curtain, but she saw nothing.

Eddie didn't say anything as he led them across the slate patio to a far set of French doors. The coolness of the dimly lit interior welcomed them.

"I'm sorry for the subterfuge," a voice emanated from the darkness. Female. "It's one of the many precautions." A young woman, trim, dressed in a current style but adorned with a businesslike manner, stepped into the light. She nodded at the man who had brought us. "Thank you."

He nodded, bowed, then left the room.

The woman extended her hand. "I'm Eddie Chan."

CHAPTER TWENTY-THREE

Staying well clear of my condo, I'd taken refuge in the Detective Room at the Central Precinct. My password still worked, so I felt okay being there. They had enough bandwidth for my purposes. Although my computer had been born before me, it was up to the task. I only had to bang it on the side twice. A few lights sputtered overhead, but I didn't need them. The sun had yet to rise—after a couple of guys passed through around two, I'd been left on my own.

Even with nobody there, the stench of fear and despair permeated everything. Neither the cops nor the perps liked the process —demeaning, terrifying...a trail of broken lives. Focusing on catching the bad guys helped. Thinking about how they got there would suck you dry.

Carla found me, my nose a few inches from the screen. "You're going to ruin your eyes."

I glanced at her. "Seriously?" She looked fresh as a daisy but with a strong dose of badass. Her jeans had holes at the knees, and her muscle shirt peeking from under her jacket that had frayed at the neckline. The streak of a coffee stain bent over one breast. Her hair had been braided recently—the tight, twisted strands ended in gold beads this time. I liked them better than the multicolor.

"Eyes are important. Just cuz you got one body part on the fritz doesn't mean you..."

I stared at her.

"Never mind. How long you been here?" she asked as she poured herself a cup of coffee. "How many days since you went home, took a bath, and changed clothes?"

"That stuff is lethal," I said without looking up, avoiding her question.

"I'm used to it." She took a sip. "Damn!" She spit it back into her cup, then wiped her mouth with the back of her hand.

"Like I said."

She deposited the cup in the trash then started working on a new pot.

Still focusing on the screen in front of me, I filled her in on Benton Myles and our odd little confab at the hospital.

"You think he's looking for you?"

"Don't know. Didn't want to find out. He let me go, but I got the impression he wasn't going to let me melt into the darkness. A man like that has plans. I don't play well with others, as you know. Figure I'm safer here than most places."

That got a smile as she filled the pot and set it to brew. "Pretty optimistic, given that whole weird bit with Clarkson and the chief."

I leaned back in my chair and crossed my arms. Most likely I also sported a self-satisfied grin. "Speaking of." I leaned over and pulled a chair close...Beck's chair. I pushed the thought of him aside, but I swore as I did, I caught a whiff of his cologne. "Take a seat."

Carla brought us both cups of fresh coffee. "Clarkson? You been digging dirt on him? The chief will have your ass." Carla leaned in next to me. "What is all this?"

"You know that motorcycle, the vintage BMW we saw the blonde riding at the murder scene?"

"You traced it to Jasper Clarkson?" She slapped a big-eyed look on me.

"Not directly, but hear me out."

"Oh." She deflated a bit. "Who then?"

"Wait for it." I sorta liked jerking her chain. Having the upper hand wasn't a normal position for me. "That motorcycle has been cropping up in other interesting places."

"Do tell." Carla used a booted toe to pull out the lowest desk drawer then rested both feet on it as she settled in to listen.

Nervous, unused to being listened to, I fetched the pot and topped us both off, then returned it to sizzle on the hot plate. Moving felt good, helped me think. "The Watchman took me down to the Morrison Street Bridge tonight. I had a bead on our stiff, but I needed to work that one alone. Those folks are pretty skittish when the cops come sniffing around."

"You're a cop."

"But you look like one."

"Point taken." Carla gave me a look. Beck used to give me that same look when I went off all Lone Ranger—his words not mine. The memories seemed to be coming easier—not that the bone-numbing cold was any better. The coffee didn't touch it. I'd sorta gotten the shivering thing under control—to most, I must look like a junkie crashing. Not exactly the confidence-building look I was going for, so I stifled myself as best I could. "He went by Frankie. The gang agreed he was a bit mentally challenged, but everyone liked him. Because of that, he often got odd jobs."

"Like collecting soda cans at the hospital?"

"Exactly. One of the people who knew Frankie the best told me a blonde on a shiny BMW motorcycle came by offering that little bit of employment—cash, of course."

"Of course." Carla's feet hit the floor as she sat up. "Our same blonde?"

"Well, same bike. I showed them a picture I found on the internet."

"Well, damn." She bumped my shoulder with hers. "Good work, detective."

"There's more." Once again, I went through the refill drill.

"You still cold?" Carla asked, her eyes narrowing in suspicion.

"No," I lied. "Real short on sleep. It's catching up to me."

She seemed to accept that. If everyone knew I was on borrowed time, they'd think I was martyring myself. Didn't they understand finding Beck was more important than me? Way more important? For me, as well as them.

"You find any bikes like that in Portland or at least somewhere around here?"

My smile gave me away. "You know how the rich like their toys."

Her eyebrows shot skyward. "You traced that bike to Jasper Clarkson?"

"No..." I let her disappointment show, then I delivered my punch line. "To his wife."

Carla fell back, sloshing her coffee on her sweatshirt. She brushed at the stain with one hand. "You're shitting me? The *wife?*"

"Surprised me, too. When I spoke with him, I got the distinct impression the two of them were on the outs."

Carla leaned back, breathing in the aroma from her coffee cup. "You think she's working to further the family interests, or she's got her own agenda?"

"Good question." I shot her some side-eye. "I'm thinking we need to pay the Missus a visit. I just can't see what their connection is to the trial. What's their beef with us?"

Carla shook her head, her eyes wide. "The chief will take your badge for sure this time."

"If we solve the murders—we've got three—he'd have a hell of a time explaining that, don't you think?" Losing my badge—yesterday, the idea ruined me. It was yesterday, wasn't it? Or the day before? The weird snippet of rogue DNA threatening to explode somewhere in my body that would make me do who-knew-what telescoped time and reordered priorities.

"I don't know. He was pretty torqued." I could tell Carla didn't want to get caught in the same net with me—especially if I went against the chief's orders.

"Makes you wonder why, doesn't it?" She had a touch of red drying on one of her braids. Ketchup? And then I remembered—she had a son. Nobody else, just a son. She couldn't afford to lose her job.

"Yeah, I think about that, but I don't like where it takes me." Carla crushed her empty coffee cup, then hurled it at the can. It bounced off the rim.

"I can't remember, but didn't you say something about Clarkson's money?" I couldn't see how money would factor in. The chief was appointed.

"Nothing pertinent, just the idea that money exerts power."

I debated my next move. The nothing-to-lose thing freed me up a bit. But Carla didn't have the same luxury. "You know when we were at the lawyer's office, and you went out to check the video?"

"I'm not going to like this, am I?"

"That depends on whether you can see the big picture." I tugged out the dossier and other papers I took, including the tape. "I found these hidden in the stuffing of his desk chair."

"You took evidence from a murder scene?" Carla didn't get angry. Instead, she grabbed my arm. "This better be good, Kate."

I lowered my voice even though no one had joined us. "It's evidence against Beck. You know, when he..." I trailed off. Saying it made it even more real, and I was having a hard enough time figuring out how to process what he'd done and conform that to the man I knew him to be.

"What?" Carla whispered as well. "All of it?"

I nodded. "I couldn't leave that for the guys to find." Carla didn't respond. I took that as a good sign but forged ahead before she changed her mind. "Look, it's all on me. You weren't even there."

"I'm not worried about that. You can't live life worrying about what the asshole might do to you. I've been down this road before. Landing on my feet is my superpower." She shot me a smile.

I looked for a tremor in her grin, but all I saw was conviction. "Your son?"

"If I give up the fight, what kind of example will I be setting for him? He's going to need all the warrior skills I can give him. Life is stacked against us, you, too. This world was built by white men for white men. The rest of us have a tougher slog."

I couldn't remember all the details of my battles, but somewhere deep inside, I knew she spoke the truth.

She looked me in the eye long and hard. "You thinking what I'm thinking?"

"Well, I'm not too good at stringing things together yet, but it's coming. Here's how I see it. You and the chief were the only two who knew about Beck and...what he did, right?"

"His daughter suspected."

"But you didn't give him up?"

"Of course not."

"So, you didn't tell her and you haven't told anybody else either, have you?" A head shake. "And the chief covered it up?"

"Somebody found out," Carla said, jumping to my conclusion.

"And the only guy I see who makes the chief jump out of his skin..."

"Clarkson. But we've got only the thinnest of ties with the murders."

"When it comes to Rita's, I agree. But we'll connect it. But with Frankie's and the lawyer's? We've got eyewitness accounts. Hell, we saw that damn motorcycle ourselves."

"It's within our authority to call in Mrs. Clarkson for questioning."

"The chief will have kittens." I tested her.

Carla rolled her eyes. "I knew you were going to suggest we draw outside the lines."

I angled my computer screen so she could see. "Mrs. Clarkson is quite the Instagram influencer. Turns out today she's doing some sort of promo thing, Designers for the Downtrodden."

Carla's eyes widened one more time. If she kept doing that, they might stay that way—at least some female relative in the dim, dark past had told me...I thought. Or maybe Hank remembered that. Our family was the same, so I didn't feel that odd disconnection when his memories wove among mine.

Carla smiled. "They really calling it that?"

"Naw. Creative license. It's going down at Pioneer Place about four o'clock this afternoon. You in?"

"You go down, I'm going with you."

<hr>

"I'M VERY sorry for the subterfuge," Eddie pressed down her dress, then gave her long hair a flip with one hand. "One can never be too careful."

"The Chinese?" Thea asked.

"Among others. They have the largest DNA database in the world, and they don't want to share. It's amazing...the data they have. From here, I can tap into it—had a few close calls, but while it's a security item for them, it's not one of the top targets of hackers and other countries." She gave a thin smile. "Including your own."

"I'd say from where you're sitting, you shouldn't cast aspersions."

"Well, even in your country, culpability rests on motivation."

Thea raised a hand—the other she kept on her gun. The whole thing had her nerves jangling. They were trapped at the end of a road that was nothing more than a long alley. "We speak the same language. The more we have at our disposal, the more we learn."

"And the more we know."

Shell put a hand on Thea's arm. "Don't worry. The threat won't come from Eddie."

"Come," Eddie barked, then disappeared through a set of

slatted double doors set in the back wall. She grabbed a lab coat... in bright pink...off a hook along the hallway. Other hooks held more coats, all white. "Help yourselves, please. And kick off your shoes." Eddie left her pumps and continued down the hall barefoot. Thea hurried, struggling with the laces on her boots. By the time she shucked the boots, and the socks—her feet had been laced into the watertight boots since Portland—they stunk worse than a teenage boy's—the others had disappeared from sight. Thea shrugged her gun from across her back into her waiting hands then followed them. Fear tickled the back of her neck. She pulled in several deep, slow breaths, calming herself, slowing her heartbeat, focusing through the fog of fatigue.

She heard the pop, followed by the sound of a body falling.

I knew it! Fuck! The words silent shouts as she fought against an almost overwhelming desire to run. *Don't let it be Shell!*

With her back pressed against the wall, Thea held the gun with both hands against her chest as she closed her eyes and listened. Furniture being overturned, hushed threats filtering down the hall. Thea eased around to grab a quick glance then pressed back out of sight. The hall was empty.

She slipped around the corner, her gun at the ready. One barefoot step at a time, she advanced on the room. The door stood a few inches open. Thea weighed the risks and shook her head. Life never gave her enough time. She slipped through the doorway.

A small man, his back to her, had Shell on her knees with a handgun pressed to her head. Two other goons stood off to the side, their guns half-lowered, the perceived threat past.

Eddie Chan lay crumpled on the floor, her eyes glazed, a red stain blooming across her abdomen as blood seeped through her fingers pressed against her stomach.

Thea took in all of this in an instant.

With a short burst, she took out the guy threatening Shell. As she moved the gun to sight on the goons, she stroked the trigger. The pin clicked on an empty clip.

The men recovered quickly from their initial surprise. One

even gave her a lazy grin. Thea's knife arced from her hand—a perfect underhand flip that buried the blade in the man's chest. He died with that lazy grin. The other man, distracted by his partner's demise, reacted a fraction of a second too late as Thea launched herself at him, swinging her gun for his temple. He ducked. The gun glanced off his cheek, staggering him.

Thea hit him with her shoulder, driving him back. She landed on him as he fell back, then rolled off him, pulled her feet under her, and popped to her feet. He rolled to his left. As he pushed himself up on his hands and knees, Thea used everything she had, swinging her leg to catch him, a foot to his sternum.

Thea bit down on a shout of pain. Her foot! But she ignored it, stepping into another kick, this time a bit lower. Thea grabbed her gun by the barrel and swung the butt at his head.

He fell, inert.

Thea grabbed his gun—an automatic like her own—then rushed to Shell, who huddled over Eddie. Dropping to her knees, Thea whispered, "How is she?"

Shell shook her head.

Eddie reached up and grabbed Thea. She lifted her head, straining with the effort.

"Don't." Thea pressed her back down. "We'll get you some help."

Eddie shrugged her off. "Reykjavík. Djang Warren. He's the blueprinter." She swallowed, her eyes starting to lose focus as if looking beyond Thea into the next life.

"Eddie, hang on!"

Shell put a hand on Thea's arm and shook her head. "It is too much."

"Djang," Eddie whispered. "I designed that. David mapped it and was following his map. He knew the design was mine. I designed another. Djang will blueprint and deal with the manufacturer who will send it to the person who requested it. He is the only one with the contact. He is in danger. Save him." Eddie's head lolled back. Thea thought she was gone when she mustered one last bit of energy. She grabbed Thea's shirt in her fist. "I didn't know. Please believe me. I thought..." Her head fell back, and she was gone.

"What did she think?" Thea asked Shell as she pulled her to her feet.

"That she was doing good. That is all she wanted."

CHAPTER TWENTY-FOUR

Mrs. Jasper Clarkson drew a crowd most A-listers dreamed of. Trucks from each of the local channels occupied prime locations near the action. As cops, we could've pushed that envelope, but Carla and I preferred the low-key route. Better to get the skinny if nobody cared who we were or why we were there.

While Carla worked her way to the front of the crowd circling the low platform that had been erected on Fifth just outside the dramatic glass entrance to the mall, I went to check out the VIP parking area. Cooling my heels earlier, I'd done some internet surfing at the library. Mrs. Clarkson and that BMW appeared everywhere together. Apparently, the bike was part of her persona.

Was she really that dumb or arrogant to let herself be seen at a murder scene straddling that ubiquitous bike?

Was I really remembering words like that? Something had changed. It was as if my brain was spinning, thoughts whirling, words coming. I'd made peace with the cold. If that was the price to pay to remember, I'd be willing to pay it. I might have to relocate to somewhere near the equator, but a small price.

Beck.

Okay, a very large price. Would I stay connected without my tether? I didn't want to try.

The day had warmed, thankfully, as I inched my way through the crowd. Glancing at faces, I looked for any I recognized.

Would I see him coming?

The crowd around me looked young, monied...bored. Designers for Change the banners read. Two worlds, no overlap. How did that work? Was this a play to get the well-off to buy silly creations and feel good doing it because a pittance of each sale would go to the less fortunate?

Why not go down to the soup kitchens, the shelters, and help them yourself?

I guess this way, the only contact would be through a credit card, so the wealthy remained unsullied. People were so...alarming.

A man in a rent-a-cop uniform stood, feet parted, arms crossed, his wide shoulders protecting the entrance to the parking area. "You got a pass?" he asked me. He tugged at his too-small shirt where it gapped between buttons across his chest. "You don't got a pass, you can't go in."

I palmed my badge, pulled it from my pocket, and opened my hand so only he could see it. "Will this do?"

With a frown, he stepped aside. "If you're here to make trouble..."

"Those would be the Feds. I'm local. Just looking to keep the mischief down."

He seemed relieved...maybe. A cop was a cop and this town had seen its share of heavy-handedness lately. Unrelated to me and my department, but all cops got caught in that net—bad business.

This being a smallish event, the lot held no more than fifty cars, most of them flashy iron that was hardly practical in Portland most of the year. The staff must've been left to fend for themselves. Toward the front of the lot, a section had been cordoned off. It held one bike...the BMW. A blonde, stick-thin, with a painted-on face and empty eyes, preened all over the thing, striking provocative poses for the cameras.

I waited at the back of the crowd until it thinned. The first chords of a show underway drew them toward the center of attention. I caught Mrs. Clarkson with a hand on her arm as she moved toward a makeup girl waiting to freshen her appearance. "Mrs. Clarkson?"

Up close, she looked like a Kabuki player—the pancake so thick it hid every vestige of the person who might live underneath. Her lashes, thick and black and curled to an impossible length, shaded her eyes. A bright red matte stained her lips, which had been injected to pouty perfection. "Bella, please." She flashed a practiced smile with no warmth until she got a good look at me. "Oh." Her smile morphed into a frown of impatience. "I've got to go. I'm up soon."

"You're the headliner. It'll be a bit. Gotta let the lessers whip the crowd into an appropriate frenzy."

She glanced toward the stage. "What can I do for you?" she said with a tone that told me her patience was evaporating as we spoke.

I still had an ace in my pocket, but I didn't want to flash the badge. Spooking a potential suspect before she could be squeezed for info didn't strike me as my best option. "I love your bike. I've had a bunch of BMWs. Right now, I have an F-800GS."

She batted her eyes and stared at me blankly. "You want to talk about the motorcycle?"

"It's like your thing, right? The R90S was one of the most important bikes of the '70s. The horsepower was unsurpassed."

"Yes, the most of any bike at the time," she said with a wave of dismissal.

She was wrong, of course. The most horsepower of the '70s belonged to the X-1, but it wasn't near the bike the BMW was. And then, at the end of the decade, the precursor to my bike was introduced. "Yeah, but the X-1..."

"Also a great BMW."

Wrong again. "How'd you pick the R90? You strike me as more of a crotch-rocket kind of gal."

For a moment she forgot where she was, what role she was playing. Or maybe I didn't strike her as much of a threat to go public with the holes in her carefully crafted persona. Maybe she didn't care anymore. "My daughter. She knows way more about all of this than I do. She thought it would give me an edge, something unique."

"She was right."

"According to her, that's a real unique bike."

"Really?" I feigned my disbelief. "You sure? I swear I saw it at a small strip center across the river in Vancouver."

She flipped her hair—so lacquered it hardly moved. "I'm sure you're mistaken. This is the only bike of its type in Portland, and I wouldn't be caught dead in *Vancouver*."

THEA WHIRLED at the sound of running behind her. On one knee, she trained her gun at the doorway. A dog burst through.

Hippo!

The thought registered as she tightened her finger on the trigger. She reared back. Her shot went high—high enough to miss Carter, who followed on Hippos heels. "Damn, girl, you shooting at dogs now?"

"Anything that moves. I haven't seen any friendlies since I left my house in Portland, so I'm in shoot-first-ask-questions-later mode."

Flynn peeked around the doorway. "We got to move." He took stock then settled a concerned look on his daughter. "What happened?"

"Goons were on our tail. Any idea how that happened?" She didn't hide her accusation.

"A setup. Who was the gal?"

"Eddie Chan."

Carter's hand found Hippo's head, stroking it, reaching for comfort. "Eddie's dead?"

"Later, Carter." Shell's voice held a no-nonsense edge. "We've got to go. They wanted Rita's computer. They didn't get it. Now, they're working up the food chain just like us."

"Eliminating anyone who can maybe point a finger," Carter said needlessly. We all got it.

Thea gathered Shell to her feet then put Carter's hand on the back of her belt. "Hold on. Don't slow me down." As Thea stepped by her father, she asked, "Takes a lot of money to launch this sort of offensive, hire all these mercenaries. Any idea about that?" Then added, "You take up the rear. If anyone follows, shoot them."

He didn't answer her question, not that she expected him to.

"How'd you get to Singapore?" Thea hissed over her shoulder.

Flynn fielded the question. "The company's G-650."

"It's waiting for you?" Thea led everyone down the hall, back the way they had come. At the end, just at the entrance to the drawing room where they'd met Eddie, Thea stepped over the body of the young man they'd met in the apothecary. A few short moments ago, he'd been full of life, a man with a purpose.

"Grab your shoes," Thea said to Shell as she stuffed her feet back in her boots, not bothering with the laces. She felt for Carter's grip on her belt, releasing it. "Stay here. I'll be back."

Thea made a quick reconnoiter of the room and the courtyard beyond. The gate to the street hung open on one hinge. Several young men and women lay where they had fallen. It was hard to tell which side any of them had sworn allegiance to—there was an unnerving lesson there, thought Thea. On any given day, depending on one's perspective, she herself could be seen as either good or bad.

As a scientist, Thea always looked for absolutes in a sea of incongruities but rarely found them. After coming this far, so sure of her battle, Thea wavered at the cost. So many lives. Each fighting for their own truth and losing. Thea would not lose. Not if she could help it. Kate's life hung in the balance. She had to protect the trial, Kate's chances. She wasn't sure why it all mattered so much, but she guessed that everyone came to the point at which they were forced to draw a line, to choose a side, and to invest, totally and completely.

Thea Janeway had reached that point.

The breakthroughs she and Carter fought for. The ones David and Rita had died for. They could save humanity...or destroy it. If there ever was a time to pledge allegiance, to choose a side, this was it.

Medical advances should not be abandoned because some sought them to do harm.

Those who wanted to subvert the system...they should be eradicated.

Lofty goals for the long term. What did they say? Wars weren't won in a day?

But battles were. If she let it, fatigue threatened to overcome her. One more battle. One more life to save. She focused on Kate, on her strength. Saving Kate. That was today's goal.

Up to now, the bad guys seemed to filter out of the darkness like cockroaches out of the walls of abandoned buildings. How many could there be? Thea prayed to whatever power that listened that they'd thinned the ranks and that she'd killed their leader. Getting from here to the airport, then into unrestricted airspace without somebody scrambling their fighters would be a major miracle.

The windows above the courtyard bothered Thea—anyone could be hiding behind the lace curtains. But there was no time to search all the floors, all the rooms. She hurried back to the others. "Come on. We've got to make it to the airport. Flynn, that plane better be ready to go, fueled to the max."

"I left it that way. Pilots are mine—not hired mercenaries. They are waiting. Sorta thought it'd be down to you and me on the run."

"If we're lucky." Thea shot him a look then hurried the others through the drawing room. On the far side, she took the lead. "I'm going to cross; then I'll cover you." She zig-zagged her way as fast as she could, then threw herself behind a large urn holding some sort of flowering shrub. With enough cover, she trained her gun on the windows above, watching for movement. "One at a time," she said as loud as she dared.

Carter came first, led by the dog. Just like him to want to be the one who took the bullet. No movement at the windows. He slid in beside Thea, then pulled the dog in close to him. Something about that made Thea smile. Before she motioned Shell across, she whispered to Carter. "You know a Djang Warren in Iceland?"

"Yep."

"Eddie said he's in trouble. He can help us, but we better get there first." With a quick hand wave, Thea motioned to Shell, who followed her zigzag lead. With gun at the ready, Thea kept her scan of the windows, moving from one to the next, then back again. Still no movement. She wasn't sure if this was good or bad.

"He's not in Iceland." Carter sounded far too calm.

"He's not?" If Thea could've spared a second of attention, she would've elbowed him.

"No, I'm supposed to meet him in Portland tomorrow. He sent me a text. Just got it."

"He's on his way?" Thea shuddered at the idea of some lab rat running through airports trying to avoid the guys after him. No skills, no chance.

"Don't worry. After the sophistication of the guys tracking us, I sent a detail to escort him and arranged private transportation."

Thea could only imagine what private transportation meant to Carter, but she didn't have the bandwidth to worry about the details or lack thereof. "He's safe?"

Carter smiled. "You could say that."

And that would have to do. Thea knew Carter knew the importance of their continued working up the food chain. "This Djang guy could give us who we want, at least that's the premise everyone seems to be operating under. What exactly is his role in the pipeline of weaponized DNA?"

"He's the sequencer, the blue printer. He can take Eddie's design and sequence it into the DNA properly."

"He delivers the end product." Thea let that sink in as she motioned for Flynn to come over. Could her father have had anything to do with the devastation up to this point?

Again, she kept an eye to the windows above.

If he had...well, if anyone were going to kill Flynn Janeway, it would be her.

CHAPTER TWENTY-FIVE

I worked my way through the small crowd to stand beside Carla at the front. "Ringside seats."

She licked an ice cream cone then thrust another one at me. "Eat this. You are wasting away before my eyes."

"How'd you know I'd get back before it melted?" Already drips of vanilla cream dribbled down the cone.

"Figured if you didn't, then I'd eat it." She eyed me until I started eating it, then asked, "What'd you find out?"

"Bike is here. Talked to Mrs. Clarkson." I raised a hand, forestalling the question I saw forming in that fear in her eyes. "Didn't tell her I was a cop, just acted like a motorhead. She didn't know jack about the bike. Said her daughter put her onto it—said it would be good for her image. I told her I'd seen a bike just like it in Vancouver. Either she's totally sociopathic, or she wasn't the one on the bike—she didn't bat an eye when I mentioned it."

"You think we ought to bring her in?" Carla worked around the swirl of her cone with gusto. "Man, I love soft-serve. We don't get enough of it, by my way of thinking." She shot me a bit of self-conscious side-eye.

"My fave as well. That and a shake so thick you have to eat it with a spoon."

Carla groaned. "We need to get to Ruby's soon." She watched me as I worked through the holes in my memory.

Ruby's. Stella. Tough night. Great shakes. "The diner, right?" I sounded triumphant, like a kid in the later rounds of a spelling bee, making us both laugh.

"You got it."

I shivered as the ice cream cold met my inner cold. Time was short. "I'm in, but soon, okay?" I scanned the crowd in that casual cop sort of way, looking for things amiss. I didn't find anything amiss, but I found something, rather someone, looking out of place.

The Watchman.

Typically nocturnal and shy, he generally avoided crowds. He caught me looking at him and motioned me over. "You okay here?" I asked Carla.

"Sure." She followed my gaze. "You go on. Meet me at the station later? Let's figure out our next move, okay? I'm thinking the daughter and the mother together. Get a good catfight going."

"You know we can't talk to the daughter, not without parental approval anyway. She's a minor. More hoops to jump through. I doubt good old mom will serve up her kid." I caught a couple of drips of sweet vanilla cream with my tongue as they ran over my fingers.

"I know. Glad you do as well." Carla waved me away.

I couldn't tell whether her style of telling me what to do or making sure I knew where the boundaries were pissed me off or made me feel good. Not as much in my face as Beck's approach... something about that thought jangled a bell. He'd been an ass. We'd fought. I'd let myself be drawn down to his level. He'd left.

He'd done bad things...before.

I had to stop him. No way I'd let him go down the same path. The chief, Carla...me...we wouldn't be able to save him a second time.

The chief? Was he saving his own ass? Offering up Beck?

This time, he'd go down.

I couldn't let that happen.

The crowd tightened as Mrs. Clarkson took the stage to a collective roar, so it took me a bit of time to wiggle my way through to the Watchman. I tossed the reminder of my cone in a can—the cold made my shivers worse.

"I've been looking for you." He looked calm, the wild in his eyes a distant memory.

"And you thought to look for me here?" My voice rose in question. I rubbed my arms and danced in front of him. Some odd chanting competed for my attention. It sounded far away...or deep inside. "You hear that?" I asked the Watchman.

"What?"

I pressed the heels of my hands to my ears. The voices still whispered. "Nothing," I said as I let my hands drop.

"It's getting worse, isn't it?" He looked concerned. Clear-eyed and concerned. He held his sax in one hand, his ankle-length duster partially hiding it.

"Have you been playing?" Usually more comfortable squatting on a corner under cover of night, a daytime gig would be a big step forward for him.

He nodded. "Yeah, just over at Pioneer Square." Pride straightened his spine.

"Good for you!"

"Quite lucrative, too."

"People at night are having too much fun to stop and listen. During the day, not so much. So, why were you looking for me?"

"I got a bead on your girl."

I grabbed his arm and squeezed. "Beck's daughter? Where?"

"Her father has been busting up folks all over the Pearl trying to find her. She don't want to be found, not by him anyway. You get my drift?"

"I can't promise what you're asking." I took a deep breath and worked for the words. "Beck is a father. His daughter holds a place in his heart nobody else can touch. If I know where she is, and if he asks, I'll not lie...I couldn't do that to him."

He gave me a look a father might reserve for a daughter when she'd exceeded his expectations—or I might've imagined it. Not too many folks ever gave me attaboys. "We need to move. You've put your life on the line to save Beck from I don't know what, but that's your choice, and I respect that. You need to respect that we haven't much time."

The voices, still soft, mocked me. They'd get louder. Something had driven Rita Davenport to jump in front of a speeding train on what was arguably the biggest day of her professional career.

My adrenaline surged. I could fight them. *Brave, Kate. Courage wins the day.*

Hank.

A memory. We'd been kids, but the context was lost...only the words remained. His thoughts inside me, could he help me in real time? Or was this something from the past to help now? Either way, what did it matter? I clung to him, to his words, to the strength in them. I knew how to fight the voices.

I can fight this. I can!

I stared at the Watchman, blinking until my eyes focused, and the real-world sounds drowned out the craziness. "Where do we start?"

He turned on his heel, his duster swirling behind him. "Follow me."

In a few minutes, we'd left the crush of interest behind, and the street crowd thinned enough that we could walk side by side. "How'd you find me?"

"I saw the bikes. Thought maybe they might attract you. A long shot, but it worked."

"Did you go by the condo first?" I'd first met the Watchman as he staked out a corner near my building where he could watch me. Sounds creepy, I know, but he'd taken a shine to the NY cop part of me. Turns out our friendship had been mutually beneficial—he'd known the before me. Those memories had been lost to me, but we came back together when it mattered.

And now, it seemed it mattered more than ever.

"Yeah, a couple of goons hanging around. Figured they might be looking for you and had spooked you off." He nudged me with an elbow.

"Don't have time to teach them a lesson." about The dude with a broken heart and a need to tilt at windmills. But how far would he go?

Would he kill to torpedo Dr. Evans Hunt's program?

Kill because his wife was denied...and died?

Couldn't he see her case was a lost cause?

Was love really blind?

I'd forgiven Beck for outright murder, justified it away by saying the pimp deserved it, Beck was a father protecting his daughter. Explanations, justifications...so easy when emotion ruled. But in the light of cold logic they fell apart.

Logic. Emotion. Surely the place we all could happily live existed somewhere between the two.

"Where is she?"

"Witch's Castle." He looked around. "Where's your bike?"

Where had I left it? I pulled the key from my pocket and read my last entry on the tag. "Pill Hill gondola parking lot."

He stopped, gave me a look, then reversed course. "Can you handle me on the back of that thing?" He didn't look happy at the prospect.

"If you promise not to panic," I said half-jokingly.

"I'll try," he answered with no mirth whatsoever.

This would be fun.

We'd found the bike, then established a delicate balance as I motored slowly through town, testing the Watchman's comfort levels, his ease of following the bike's flow. As we hit the edge of town, the air cooled in the canopy of trees, and the Watchman relaxed against me, his arms loose around my waist. "You know the Witch's Castle?"

I knew where it was—at the far end of Forest Park—but I didn't know the history, not exactly. Pain, murder, tragedy...I didn't want to know. My life had enough of those elements, and they weren't the ones I wanted to hang onto.

Once we hit the less-traveled roads of the park, I eased open the throttle and let the bike run a bit. The Watchman didn't tighten his grip. Instead, he seemed to lean into the turns, enjoying the power of the bike, the velocity over the ground. His chin rested on my shoulder as I made my way to the far end of the park.

"Park here." His voice startled me.

I pulled over and hid the bike in the trees.

"We'll hoof it from here," the Watchman said as he took the lead.

The Witch's Castle was a small stone structure that long ago had lost its roof and the glass from its windows, but not its aura of mystery. "Not much of a shelter," I said as we looked at it from the cover of the surrounding forest.

"Depends on who you're running from." A trail of smoke streamed from the chimney—milky white against the clouds, no one would notice it. Not unless they were looking for it. "Looks like somebody's home." The Watchman seemed pleased his intel had panned out.

Frankly, I was too.

The voice whispered. *Run, Kate. It's a trap. You'll never be you.*

I pressed the heels of my hands to my temples and tried not to laugh. A trap? Never be me? That was my life. I'd lost me a long, long time ago. "Follow me," I urged the Watchman behind me as I stepped into the open.

He grabbed me and pulled me back, his mouth close to my ear. "Wait. Look."

I followed where he pointed. A man in camo, dirty, his shoulders bowed from an invisible weight. I sucked in a breath.

Beck!

Seeing him, knowing he was alive—that was enough to flood a cascade of emotion through me. The need to hold him, to touch his face, to feel his body overwhelmed me. Curling my fingers into tight fists, I fought myself, my needs. If only I could run to him, hold him, explain something I'd lost, tell him how much I needed him, how I'd gladly sacrifice everything to see his daughter safe, his heart whole.

As if he sensed my internal war, the Watchman held me tighter. Emotions unleashed the waves of cold that tormented me as they rolled through my body.

"Damn," the Watchman whispered. "Hang on, Kate. Fight it."

You got this, Katie.

Hank's face, unlined with smooth cheeks, his eyes taunting. As a sister, I'd always been *lesser.* But he never left me behind. Never let me give up.

Fight, baby girl!

Waves of cold canceled each other out as they bounced around inside my body. For a moment, I felt strong, alive. *I could do this.*

Beck kept to the trees. When his gaze passed over our hiding place, I instinctively eased back, even though I knew he couldn't see us. The hard determination of the Watchman, the electricity of his silent force, filled me as if it could jump between us where our bodies touched.

Beck hung back. Using the trees, he worked his way around the perimeter until he'd gotten as close to the Witch's Castle as he could without showing himself. When he made his move, I made mine. "Stay here," I whispered to the Watchman, knowing he'd do so as long as he thought prudent. After that, all bets were off.

Bent at the waist, Beck crab-walked to the back wall of the Castle, then pressed his back against it.

I didn't see a gun. He shifted, and the waning light flashed off the steel of a blade. What was it they said about history? I racked my brain as I ran to the front opening of the small brick structure. *Some castle.* Barely large enough for a bed and a corner in which to cook. But maybe witches had fewer expectations than mere mortals.

After counting to three, I risked a quick look inside. I caught Beck as he slipped through a back window. His attention focused inside, he didn't notice me. I knew the look on his face, and it cut me to the core. Murder, revenge—they'd seized control, overriding the decent.

Beck dropped to the floor, crouching, his blade hidden against one forearm. One flick of his wrist and it would drop into his hand ready for its lethal work. Afraid to take my eyes off him, I let myself follow his gaze for a quick look.

A young woman curled, her knees to her chest, on the floor. The beaked head of a bird in bold colors peeked from the low neckline of her muscle shirt. The tip of a wing bent across her shoulder.

"Stay right there!" A young man who had been tending the fire banked in the open fireplace stood, brandishing his poker—a rusty length of metal that looked lethal enough but would do little to deter a father hell-bent on saving his daughter. The kid's eyes widened in recognition, but he stood his ground. "You need to leave. She's mine."

With a roar, Beck launched himself at the young man. "You fucker!" His voice was hoarse with emotion, with fury and hate, relief and worry.

The flash of his blade, his hand held low, propelled me from the doorway. "Beck! No!"

I grabbed his hand. His daughter groaned and shifted. The young man froze, his poker held high. Beck's eyes widened when he saw me. "How...?"

Though he tried to twist out of my grasp, I held tight. "No killing. Not this way. Not again." I saw in his eyes he understood... I knew.

"They did this to her." His arm shook with his effort to keep up the fight. Tears welled. His arm stiffened. The anger returned. "*He* did this to her."

The kid, all skin and bones and fearful bravado, waggled his poker at us.

I pulled Beck away. "Maybe. Regardless, whoever is responsible, we'll get them." With a finger, I touched his chin and turned his head so he looked at me. "We'll get them the right way. I need you." I glanced down at his daughter. "She needs you. Carla needs you."

"The chief?"

Odd he should mention him. "We'll talk about him later."

The kid, still brandishing his poker, lowered his voice. "Look, you guys need to leave. Take your little lovefest somewhere else. She made me promise that if you showed up, I'd run you off. She said it was important—life and death."

"Yeah, her life, your death," Beck growled.

Men! With a shake of my head and a sigh, I backhanded the kid, my fist to his temple.

He never saw it coming. He dropped like a skeleton, bones tangling with one another.

"That kid needs a meal," I said as I let go of Beck and rubbed my hand.

Beck took my small one in his large mitt—his skin so warm, so soothing, his touch so...necessary. "You're cold." He gave me a look that seemed to see past my lies and into my soul.

"Ask her why," the Watchman said from the doorway.

I shot him a look. Beck frowned then looked pained.

His daughter moved and groaned, drawing his attention. He knelt by his daughter. "Honey. It's Dad." He reached to caress her face but paused, then pulled back before he touched her.

She shivered. Her head lolled back as she wrapped her arms around herself. "No, Dad. Go!"

I put a hand on Beck's shoulder. "She's crashing bad."

The Watchman eased in next to my shoulder. "I can help her." He looked to Beck for his assent. Beck looked to me. "You trust him?"

"With my life." This time, the shiver racing through me buckled my knees. The Watchman, with a steadying arm, held me upright until I regained control.

"What's the matter?" Beck reached across. The touch of his skin was electrifying.

I gave him the best smile I could. "Been a day."

The Watchman snorted but didn't divulge my secrets. Instead, he dropped to one knee next to Beck's daughter. "You know what she's on?"

Beck looked pained.

"Don't matter." The Watchman reached into his pocket and brought out a small vial of clear liquid. "I find kids all over. I can stabilize them and get them to the hospital. This stuff will bring her back slowly. She won't get the rush, but she won't crash." The Watchman waited for Beck's nod then placed a bit of the liquid under her tongue.

The pulse in her wrist was thready. I kept my fingers there, closing my eyes, counting, willing the beat to strengthen. After I don't know how long—a minute maybe two, but it seemed like hours—her skin warmed, her pulse steadied. "She's coming around." I opened my eyes to capture Beck's gaze. His intensity told me he felt the same sorry I did.

For a moment, my world righted and I could breathe.

The girl stirred. This time her eyes didn't dance so wildly. Instead they rested on each of us in turn until they got to her father. The wildness returned. "You have to go!"

"Who's that bag of shit over there?" Beck lifted his chin to indicate the boy, who still lay where he fell. "Your pimp?" He couldn't hide the contempt, that anger.

I shuddered, this time even more violently. My legs unable to hold me, I crumpled to the floor. Just a few minutes later...too late. Beck would've...the kid would've bled out...like the other.

"That's Joshua. He's trying to help me." Her voice stronger now, she unfolded and raised herself on an elbow—a pretty girl under the ugly crust of a hard life.

"Help you?" Her father spat the words.

"Beck." I tried to reach him in his anger, to pull him back. "Listen to her. There's a reason we're all here. Everything is related."

That touched the cop in him—I knew the look that shifted his features. "How?"

"I don't have all the pieces yet." I leveled a gaze at him. "You have to trust me on this one." That was a minefield—that much I remembered. Trust, such a leap of faith, especially considering the current stakes. "Trust me, Beck. I know what I'm doing." I shivered uncontrollably.

I could see the pain those words caused him, though I couldn't remember why.

"We need to get you inside, preferably by a fire."

I held his gaze.

He pursed his lips then nodded. "Baby," he said to his daughter. "What is going on? Who are you running from?"

"You."

"Why?" The hurt leaked out of him.

"If they get me, then they'll get you."

"What do you mean they'll get me?" This time Beck didn't hesitate, he didn't pull away. Instead, he gently brushed back the hair from her forehead.

She hugged herself tighter as her crash deepened. Her eyes took on a hint of wild. "I can't be trusted."

Beck put a hand on the Watchman. "It's not working. Help her."

The Watchman looked calm, in control. He checked her pupils. "It's okay. We'll titrate the dose." He gave Beck a reassuring look. "I've done this a lot." The Watchman took one look at me, then cut off the idea he saw forming. "No, we can't take her to the hospital. Not until we sort out who is in trouble." He gave me an exaggerated look.

Not hard to figure he wanted me in the hospital, but he knew me well enough to know that helping me accomplish my goal was the quickest way to get what he wanted...assuming time waited for me. "We all need to all get to a place we can see them coming and compare notes." I lifted my chin toward Beck. "You have a car?" He nodded. "You and the Watchman get your daughter back to the Watchman's place. We have help there, and we can see them coming." I angled a questioning look at the Watchman. He nodded. "What should we do about the kid?' We all looked at the boy on the floor. He'd started to move but was far from being able to ask his legs to carry his weight. "I vote for leaving him here. If we take him with us, we drag him further into what has proven to be a deadly game." I could tell the two men were as excited as I was at leaving him in the cold. He had shelter, but no help. His cheeks still held a hint of pink. He'd have one hell of a headache, but he seemed healthy enough to get back to town on his own. This time I didn't wait for a consensus. "Let's go."

I helped the men carry the girl and settle her in Beck's car. As the Watchman had promised, she seemed better, maybe not completely fine, but not crashing either. From the looks of her, the road back would be long and painful. Worth it, but really only she could decide that. I'd be there to pick up the pieces of her father if she made the wrong decision or couldn't fight the battles in front of her. Why did anybody have kids? Such vulnerability and no control.

"Damn! Sami!" I said, startling the three of them. I finally remembered her name! Not sure how that had happened, but I'd roll with it.

Beck grinned through his pain. "You're getting better."

I shrugged and resisted blurting out the reality—I was the killer's next victim and we were bantering on borrowed time. My load to tote—more important things to set my mind to. "Hard to know. I live with me every day." I could sense it, though, the memories lurking closer, but I didn't dare invest in hope. I knew the devastation that waited for me there.

Would life be that cruel?

CHAPTER TWENTY-SIX

Flynn's plane, the lights on, the engines spooling, waited on a far pad out of view of the main terminal at the airport. Thea resisted jumping out of the car while Flynn got them through the perimeter gate, bolting for it and running up the extended stairs that beckoned with a hollow promise of safety.

Her father ran this show. Her father, who had killed her mother and sacrificed all decency in the pursuit of the almighty dollar. What angle was he playing this time?

They'd taken one car, Flynn up front with the driver and Shell, Thea, and Carter squeezed in back with the dog across their laps. This put Thea at a disadvantage, trapped as she was under the butt of a large Lab.

Flynn leaned across the driver to talk with the guard. At the end of Thea's comfort level, the guard eyed them then motioned them through.

"What'd he say?" Thea whispered to Carter. She'd caught a few words, but not the nuance. Seated behind the driver, Carter was close enough to hear it all.

"A bit of an argument about the sufficiency of payment. Something about a wanting to live longer than that. A drug or something?"

Thea didn't elaborate on her father's latest pipe-dream. "Living for hundreds of years seems not to be just an American dream. Bartering for four lives with the elusive promise of eternal life. I wonder when they'll smell a rat?" Thea hoped they were long gone by then, but lately, her luck hadn't been carrying her quite that far.

But this time, her luck held.

Somewhere way out over the Pacific, maybe just south of Hawaii, Thea started to relax. Not really let-down-her-guard relax, but maybe take-a-deep-breath-and-stop-holding-her-gun relax. Still fighting the bullet in his back and the resulting loss of blood and... everything...Carter had found a place to curl up for some sleep. Hippo stood guard. Thea knew that dog would tear anyone limb from limb if they got too close, including herself. Being a loner, Thea had no idea what someone would have to do to inspire that kind of loyalty, but she didn't have it, that much she knew. For a moment, she felt a loss at the realization.

Flynn stood at the seat next to hers, dislodging her melancholy. "May, I?" he asked as if she had a choice.

"Your plane." Thea shrugged, making sure her gun was within reach. Although firing a powerful weapon in a small pressurized vessel was rarely a good idea.

"Thea, I'm asking your permission because I want it."

She relented, motioning for him to take the seat.

Once he took a seat, stretching the leg that had been creased by the bullet, the silence stretched to awkward. Flynn motioned for the attendant to bring two flutes of Champagne. After a time, when the flutes were nearing empty, Thea felt a bit of warmth seep in. It's so easy to hate, to blame. Much harder to accept your own fault and to hear a story you don't want to hear.

"Thea." Flynn's voice hitched, betraying him and opening a tiny crevice in his daughter's heart. "Your mother."

Thea could see his pain and it surprised her.

"I know we were divorced," her father continued. "I made choices she couldn't live with. But to the day she died, we loved each other beyond measure. She was the last person I spoke with at the end of a day. With her voice in my head and my heart I could sleep."

"How's the sleep thing now?" Thea asked then hated herself for her harshness.

"Not good," Flynn answered without a hint of response to her recrimination. "It's a shame wisdom is wasted on the old. What I could've done if I knew then..." He let his hand drift over to find hers for a brief connection. "I sacrificed all I loved to my need to provide, to be somebody, to make a huge difference, and be recognized for it."

"And rewarded." Thea wasn't ready to buy the schmaltz.

"That, too. I made mistakes, let ego lead me." He shook his head. "Stupid." He pulled in a deep breath. "Thea, I don't know whether you can forgive me. I know you think I gave that drug to your mother to try to prove it worked. I only cared that maybe it would work just that once. I couldn't imagine a life without your mother in it. As you knew, as you told me, it didn't work, wouldn't work. You were right. I was wrong. But it was the only thing I had to try to save her." He stopped, unable to go further.

Thea so wanted to believe him, so needed to believe him. "I didn't get to say goodbye."

"I know. And I'm beyond sorry for that. I didn't know that it would turn so bad, so quickly."

Thea had to laugh. "That is the story of my fucking life."

"You're a Janeway, what can I say?" Flynn motioned for more bubbles.

"Mother used to tell me that."

"Did she mean it poorly?" Flynn made sure Thea had the fullest glass.

After slipping through painful memories that were as real as yesterday, Thea shook her head. "No. I think she meant it as a warning, but not in a bad way."

Flynn settled back with his flute. "You're all I have, Thea. I made a muck of it with your mother. I was never the man she wanted me to be. For the years I have left, I will endeavor to be the man you need me to be. You amaze me. You have made the choices I didn't have the courage to make. You lead with your heart. You want to save the world."

Thea frowned and held her flute to the light. "What manner of truth serum is this? Frankly, Father, I like killing the bad guys. And that really worries me."

———

"KATE," Beck put a hand on my arm and backed up a bit, "you look like you want to crawl right in the middle of that fire."

I couldn't get close enough to the flames. Looking for warmth, I chose the second-best spot, with my knees almost touching the hot metal of the hibachi and my back pressed up against Beck's chest. "Beck." I sighed his name. As he folded me into his arms, I let the darkness envelop me. His last words that filtered through were, "Kate, I'm so sorry."

I don't know how long I slept, but I awakened with a start, bolting upright from Beck's embrace.

"Kate, what is it?" Beck rubbed his eyes, his face haggard, the light in his eyes a constant flame, but burning down. A month of shut-eye might not fill his tanks. The chills still chased through me, but not as bad as before.

The Watchman stood guard over Beck's daughter. What was her name? I searched the recesses...Sami. The voices whispered the word, their lust evident. *You can't have her!* They already had me, that would have to be enough.

How long had Beck and I slumbered? "What's the time?"

The Watchman didn't look concerned. "Deepest part of the night now, so not long until morning. You okay?"

"Never better," I said with a forced smile. Actually, I didn't know how I was. I felt myself brightening in the lights, then slipping into the shadows—an odd effect I'd not experienced before. Moments of absolute clarity, then the fog returned. I couldn't banish the bad or hold onto the good, but somehow, I knew, in the shadows between, I was slipping away.

My phone dinged. A text. I grabbed for it.

"Been doing that for a while," the Watchman commented.

"Why didn't you wake me up?" I shot him a look.

Unfazed, he asked, "And how much good would you have been to whoever is looking for you?"

I narrowed my eyes. "So you have any idea how much I hate people making my decisions for me?" Squinting, I held the phone close to the light of the fire and stared at the text. "It's from Thea." I scanned the lines of text. "She's on her way back. A lot to tell. Nothing adds up." I looked up into Beck's dark eyes. "Maybe we have two halves to the whole?"

He shrugged, looking lost and ready to kill somebody.

As fast as I could, which wasn't particularly fast, I told her to meet us at the Watchman's, giving detailed instructions as to how to find us and what to say to the men downstairs the Watchman had tasked with keeping the world away. Done, I pocketed my phone. "They're close. An hour or two at most." I glanced at the girl under the blanket. "How's Sami?"

"Stabilized, but she's going to need more sophisticated help than I can give." The Watchman didn't seem overly concerned, not yet anyway.

"Can she talk?"

He pursed his lips. "If she wants to."

I moved over to kneel next to the girl. Beck framed her other side. For a moment, I left my hands on my knees as I stared at her. Resting, with the weight she carried momentarily forgotten, she looked young, so very young. And Beck. Such anguish as he stared at his daughter. I couldn't fathom the depths of pain that kind of connection could bring. Heights of joy, too, of course, but good was always balanced by the weight of evil, of pain, of loss, of betrayal...and, if you were lucky, only worry. Most of the time I wished it wasn't so, but in reality, the balance point, the pendulum swing, gave us all a framework in which to live.

We chose our spot on the continuum.

And most of us could do precious little to escape our choice.

I searched for the girl's hand under the blanket. When I found it, I was surprised by its warmth. The cold had become...part of me.

She will betray you.

The voices whispered. Oddly, I felt detached. Maybe it was having grown used to Hank's thoughts invading my headspace, unwanted and alarming. More voices did little to unnerve me. I wondered if this was what Rita Davenport had dealt with. Is this what so terrified her that she jumped in front of a train to quiet them?

For once, would my affliction somehow be protective?

Such irony. But also proof of my theory about the balance between good and evil—or rather the dual purposes of both.

I squeezed the girl's hand and she stirred. "Sami?"

She stilled.

"Can't we just leave her alone, let her rest?" her father said, but his tone told me he knew the answer.

"Sami!" I jostled her just a bit.

She opened her eyes—dark and warm like her father's. Her brows scrunched into a frown as she looked around. When she settled her gaze on her father, she moved away. "You have to go!"

Beck leaned closer. "I'm not going anywhere, honey. I don't know what's wrong, but if you tell me, I can fix it."

She shook her head wildly. "No!" Her agitation increased.

I motioned for Beck to back away. For a moment, I thought he'd ignore me, but finally, he did as I asked. Trust...a tiny bit, but a huge step.

"Sami." I touched her on the face to draw her attention. "Let me help."

Her eyes lost their wild when she looked at me. A slight lift ticked up one corner of her mouth. "I know you."

"You do?"

"Yeah, you're the badass who got all those diamonds and saved everyone." With renewed clarity, she focused on our small group gathered around her. "You saved him." She pointed to the Watchman. "And Dad, too. You even walked into the hospital with a gun and demanded help. You're amazing."

For a moment I reveled in the girl's misplaced adulation. "Sometimes life puts us all in positions to step up and make a difference. That was mine. Right now, I'm a woman who has a genetic form of early-onset Alzheimer's that will eventually rob me of me...if it has time. I've also been targeted by a killer who has gotten something into my body that will most likely kill me or make me so crazy I'll do the deed myself. I don't have much time. I have three things I wanted to accomplish before that happens: I needed to find you, and your father, and then the killer. Two out of three. I haven't much time for the third. Will you help me?" Beck reached across and grabbed me. I shrugged him off. "You and Sami are more important. And stopping the killer before he strikes again. If he discredits the program...the therapy that just might make a huge difference and save millions of lives will be lost. Trust me, Beck. Just this once."

"What does Sami have to do with any of this?" Pain etched the lines in his face deeper. Giving in, trusting me, would cost him so much.

"I don't know. Let's ask her." I turned back to the girl who had been watching us with intensity. "Can you help me?" I asked.

"I don't know anything to help you." The idea tortured her.

"Let's see. Can you tell me what you meant when you told your father that if they get you, they would get him?"

Her attention flicked to her father. "I know what you did."

Beck sat back on his heels and swallowed hard.

"It's okay. I get it, dad, I really do. You helped a lot of girls, not just me."

"Why didn't you come home?" Pain filled each of Beck's words.

Sami looked away. "I couldn't." She bit her lip and shook her head.

"Can you tell me why?" I asked, putting myself right in the middle of family I wasn't a part of.

Sami shot a silent question to her father.

He nodded. "She knows."

"You know what he did?" The truth terrified her, so she left it unspoken.

"Yeah. Sometimes good people, very good people, do bad things. Maybe the end justifies the means, maybe not. That's one of those moral tightropes I've never been able to walk. I've always done what the moment required and let the consequences accrue."

"Is that how everybody does it?" The girl struggled with the moral ambiguity.

"No."

Something about my story bolstered her resolve—maybe it was the bit of badass in it, maybe it was the bit about each of us having a choice in each and every situation. Regardless, she relaxed into her truth. "I did something bad—no, something awful—and I've been running from it since."

"You told someone what your father did."

Her eyes widened. "How'd you know?"

"You've been running all this time to protect him, haven't you?"

Tears sprang to her eyes as she nodded, afraid to look at her father. "I was so mad, so scared. I'd never seen him like that."

"I'm sure it made you question everything. How old were you? Sixteen?"

"Not yet." She gulped down a sob. Finally, she hazarded a peek at her father. "Dad, I'm so, so sorry."

Beck patted her hand. "It's okay, honey."

"I know you did it for me."

"I did it for me, too. And that part of it was wrong. Do you understand that?"

With the heel of her hand, she wiped at her eyes. "I think so."

"Oh, baby!" Beck folded her into his arms, rocking her back and forth.

I gave them a minute but no more. "I'm sorry, but..."

They pulled apart. "Yes, we need to keep going," Beck said. With his hands on her shoulders, he forced Sami to look at him. "You got this."

She gulped a few times, pulling herself together. When she looked at me, her eyes were clear. "You want to know who I told."

CHAPTER TWENTY-SEVEN

THEA NEVER WAS MUCH OF A SITTER, AND LONG PLANE RIDES trapped in the belly of a metal beast did nothing to alleviate her fidgeting. "Sit down," Carter said, leaving the hint of an order in his bark. "You're making it impossible for any of us to rest."

Thea thought about picking the fight she was aching for but decided her energy would be wasted on this battle. Without an apology, she slid into the seat next to Carter after she'd nudged the dog out of the way with a foot. "My butt hurts." Her shoulder had started to ache again—Shell had exhausted her supply of magic unguent. "How's your back?"

"Hurts."

Carter's response wasn't what she wanted to hear—he never complained.

"Can't leave the bullet in there."

"Probably not."

"It'll move when you move..."

Carter grabbed her hand. "It'll be okay, Thea."

He didn't make light of her concern or rub it in—a sign of new maturity that attracted Thea even more. Vulnerability—well outside Thea's comfort zone. How did one love without risking devastation? Thea recognized an impossibility when she saw one, but that never stopped her from looking for a way to achieve it.

"Sometimes you just have to give yourself up and trust," Carter said, reading her mind.

Was the fact he could see into her deepest, darkest depths a good thing or a bad thing? Thea wasn't sure, not that she could do much about it. Her heart overrode self-preservation.

Of course, that was no guarantee she wouldn't shoot him at some point.

She glanced back at her father who appeared to have nodded off. He looked uncomfortable folded into the seat—they'd given Shell the single stateroom in the rear. After watching for signs Flynn was faking his slumber and seeing none, Thea leaned into Carter. "I need your help."

"Fire away."

"You have your computer?" A permanent appendage, the tough Toshiba went everywhere Carter did. He gave her a look befitting the question. "Right. Well, we'll have to use the sat network on the plane—I need to access a file."

"Easy enough."

"But I need you to do all your magic so Flynn can't somehow capture the keystrokes, passwords, even the site I'm going to. Can you do that?"

"Please, woman, you insult me." Carter perked up at having something to do. "Your family, Thea..."

"If Flynn were your father?"

"I'd probably have killed him years ago, but yeah, I'd do the same thing. I totally get it, especially now."

"And you don't know the half of it." Thea rose as Carter shifted. His grimace belied his pain. Pushing her worry away, she asked, "Your computer?"

With a tilt of his head, Carter indicated the upper bin above them.

Careful to try not to draw her father's attention, Thea eased Carter's backpack out of the tight space and handed it to him. She retook her seat and looked over his shoulder as he booted up the machine.

"You're like a vulture." Carter chuckled. "The password?" he asked as he worked through various screens Thea didn't recognize.

Thea gave it to him—this wasn't her first ride on Flynn's corporate jet. The last one had been to spread her mother's ashes in Colorado. "You're sure he won't be able to track us?"

Carter gave her a stare. "This is super important, isn't it? Like more important than just keeping him out of your business?"

"Rita had a backup for her computer."

"And you're the only one who can get in."

"I'm the only one who knows it exists...and yes, if something happens to me, whatever it is in that computer that someone will follow me to the ends of the earth, killing anyone in his way, dies with me."

"And the killer gets away with it."

"But he doesn't get what he wants, so there is that."

"Little consolation." Once again, Carter hunched over the keyboard. "A minute more before I get a safe connection. I'm putting in a few extra steps to make sure anything we do is completely untraceable."

"You're sure?" To Thea, digging in Rita's private files seemed the worst sort of violation, even though Rita had specifically given her access...*in case.* Had she known? She must have.

Rita, why didn't you say something?

Only silence replied.

"There." Carter motioned for Thea to put down her table, then he slid the computer across. "It's ready. Just use it like you would a normal computer."

"What's protecting my keystrokes and all that?"

"I don't have time to explain, but in short, the program I'm running—a Carter Livingston design"— he pressed a hand to his chest in a show of no humility at all "—packetizes your inputs. The keystrokes are encrypted on this end. The packets are sent to spoofed IP addresses, bouncing around the world. Each forward transmission is protected using software much like but way more sophisticated than a VPN. Eventually, all of this ends at a server farm I control and whose location is known to one person, and that would be me. From there, my own software executes your inputs in the packet, then the packet is destroyed, and its internal temporary storage location overwritten."

"That's the simple explanation?" Thea started through the protocol Rita had made her memorize. It felt like she was keying in some doomsday code or something—the end of Rita's world for sure. But what had she gotten into that had gotten her killed?

CHAPTER TWENTY-EIGHT

With her father's help, Sami pushed herself to a seated position. The Watchman put a blanket around her shoulders as she held her hands toward the fire. She didn't seem bothered by the fact that blanket probably hadn't seen a dry cleaner in more years than she'd been on this planet.

"It was a while ago," she started, avoiding eye contact with her father.

"Honey," Beck patted her shoulder, clearly not at ease, "it's okay. What a bad time that was."

Sami shot him a look I could read on the other side of the room—bad would win the award as the understatement of the year. I'm not sure what kind of trauma seeing your father kill someone would inflict, but clearly, it drove her back underground, back to the reality-numbing drugs she could find. We had way more in common than she could fathom.

Of course, I didn't need the drugs—my reality disappeared of its own will.

Though lately things had been sticking, reality hard to dodge. I liked it, but I didn't. The cold though, that had come to stay. Damn, few things are more miserable than bone-numbing cold. I'd experienced many of them, so perspective was easy to keep.

I stayed still, absorbing the warmth of the fire, not wanting to inject myself in the give-and-take but so needing to know who the hell the kid told about her father and his transgressions. The Watchman, unconcerned about the drama unfolding, tossed another piece of wood on the fire. He'd managed to figure out how to vent it somewhat, but still, the smoke was thickening, constricting my throat and stinging my eyes.

"After..." Sami's voice broke and she swallowed hard a few times. "I didn't know what to do, where to go. You and Mother..." She trailed off as she gave her father a knowing look. "You both were so angry, so hurt, so caught up..."

"In our own pain, I know." Beck wanted to hold her, I could see it in him, but he kept the distance she'd established—a safe zone in which to confess. He resisted the "I'm sorry" that would be a hollow apology.

I made myself small and quiet.

"There was this girl, privileged and all, very professional. Said she was paying for blood."

"Blood?" I asked, unable to help myself.

"Yeah, she said it was for a company developing a drug to help old people live longer. They wanted 'young blood.' Unlike the blood centers, she didn't care about my drug use. I let her practically drain me dry. The money was good, so I thought, what the heck?" Sami shifted. She found my eyes. I smiled in hopefully an encouraging, nonjudgmental sort of way. Who was I to say somebody else's struggle was somehow less or bad or committing them to eternity in hell? "I never envisioned myself selling my blood to score hits."

"Certainly not the path I wanted for you," Beck said. "All I wanted for you was to be who you wanted to be."

Sami looked at him, her love evident. "When you're fifteen, you need a little guidance."

"Parenting and girls don't come with an instruction manual."

Sami shrugged, accepting that. "Anyway, this girl. She flashed wealth. Blonde, skinny, pinched face and a pout. At first, I didn't like her—just a kid wanting to piss off her parents and soil her hands among the downtrodden. I got it, but I didn't like it. Life is a mirror, right?" she said to her dad, clearly referencing an inside something.

Pain pulled his answering smile tight.

"You warmed up to her," I said, at the end of my patience rope.

"Yeah." Sami didn't look contrite. Life was what it was. "I was lonely, needed a friend. She seemed...safe."

"No agenda?"

Beck shot me a look. Not hard to read. I sat back, hugging my knees and trying to quit being an impatient cop.

"Yeah." Sami smiled a self-deprecating smile. "Funny how life sends wolves disguised as sheep to teach you something."

The kid was wise beyond her years—the street had a way of doing that.

"She betrayed you?" I asked, shifting away from Beck's glare.

"You could say that." Sami sighed, shifting the weight of the truth that weighed heavy. "She had this whole sob story about her father being an asshole, totally into making money and nothing else."

"Classic." I tried to commiserate. Really, societal pressures worked both ways. Men bought into the Great Provider role— some of them were built for it. "What was he into? Any idea?"

"Pretty much anything, but real estate mostly."

I tried to remain calm. "And her mother, where was she?"

"Around. At first, they had a good relationship, then social media discovered her mother and that was that."

"Instagram?"

Sami eyed me before answering. "You already know who I'm talking about."

"An idea. So, what happened?"

"You can tell the rest of the story." She looked at me with wise eyes. "I bought the whole play." She shook her head.

"Not your fault. Those folks know exactly when to strike; like predators they have an innate sense as to when their prey is most vulnerable."

She looked at me, only half believing. "Never happened to you, I bet."

"Almost cost me my life."

That refocused her and seemed to lighten her load. "Anyway, once I'd confided in her, she laughed at me. Told me how stupid I was."

"And then she disappeared." I finished her story. The kid obviously knew how important owning a cop or two could be. In her father's hands, that kind of information was a ticket to all kinds of bad acting. To implicate the chief followed easily from the initial story. Jasper Clarkson had the chief by the balls. Beck wasn't playing cricket. He'd be glad to sacrifice himself if he could save his daughter.

I knew the feeling.

Shivers racked my body.

"There's not much time," the Watchman whispered.

I ignored him, focusing on Sami. "You felt, if you kept running, they'd never get the goods on your dad."

"Perhaps foolish. I'd already given them enough ammunition."

Beck wrapped his daughter in a hug. "Honey, I would never want you to suffer the punishment for my sin."

"Oh, I'm far from blameless." Sami smiled as her eyes lost a bit of brightness.

"She needs you," I whispered to the Watchman.

Beck and I backed out of the way, giving him access to keep her stabilized until we could get her proper help. Still captured by the cold, I didn't move far from the fire. Beck added his warmth with an arm around my shoulders, pulling me close. "I'm sorry," he whispered, his lips moving against my hair. "I was wrong to doubt you. Your police skills come from somewhere deep inside. Even when your brain misfires, you somehow know what to do..."

"Who to shoot?" I added, hoping for some desperately needed levity.

"That, too." He dipped his head, pressing his cheek to mine. "You going to tell me what's up with the shakes?"

"I don't know. Part of it, I guess."

"We've got to get you to Logan."

"He's not the one with the answer."

He weighed that, then let it lie. "You hearing Hank much these days?" Another tack to see if I was scared.

"Oddly, no, not too much."

"But some?" He wouldn't let it go.

"Here and there."

"Okay. You'll tell me in time." He seemed sure of that.

If there is time. A voice inside. Not threatening. Not alarming. Not Hank.

No, this one was me. With so many voices in my head, hearing my own always caught me off guard. "I need to bring you up to speed." He listened without interrupting. Only once did he hold up a finger to pause my story while he retrieved his notebook from an inner pocket. With his pencil poised, he motioned for me to continue. And somehow, I did—the continuity flowed, the facts seemed to be all there. Unused to trusting my recall, I checked all the important details against the record in my phone and random notes tattooing my body.

Yep, I'd gotten it right. Of course, I'd get better now...just in time to...move on to the next adventure—if the killer had their way. A mere mortal, I wasn't sure what that would be like, but I wasn't afraid. And for the first time, I knew the loss I'd feel. Beck. The Watchman. Logan. Stella. Even Carla. They all had believed, helped...been friends. As such each had a piece of my heart, and leaving that behind, not being able to touch them and the part of me they held anymore would be excruciating.

Life: unbridled joy and living hell. There was that yin and yang again.

Balance. Until the world went on tilt.

Beck read back over his notes—his way to process. I used to find it irritating. Tonight, I found it comforting. When I jumped too soon, he was the steadying force that made me to review and think. A good team.

"The records you found in the lawyer's office?"

"A rather detailed dossier on you with a tape." I lowered my voice. "Sami." I practically mouthed the word, but it whispered out on a breath. "But the dossier had more details."

Anger pulled the skin on his face taut, accentuating the cliffs of his cheekbones. The man needed a good meal...several actually. Worry and stress and probably no sleep had worn him down to raw revenge—not a good look. "You're saying someone embellished it."

"There were details of the cover-up. I'm under the impression only two people besides yourself knew the whole story—the chief and Carla."

The Watchman flicked a glance my way—a hint of warning.

"Carla would never." Beck sounded sure.

"That leaves one."

"I'd like to see those papers."

Beck's eyebrows lifted when I pulled them from their hiding place against the small of my back. "Too important to leave lying around."

He smiled, then shifted away to read them in the light of the fire. I waited, warming myself, not really thinking about anything, and trying to keep Hank from highjacking my thoughts. Beck sidled back over more quickly than I anticipated. "You're right. Can I keep these?"

"Yours to do with what you will." I fished the tape from my pocket and handed it to him.

"Just like that?"

"Can't say I wouldn't have done the same thing. I'd like to think you'd have my back—you might not be happy about it, but you'd... help...however you deemed appropriate. This is my call."

He didn't toss them on the fire as I expected him to.

"Just don't kill him."

"You have my word." He held up the other papers. "These were hidden along with the papers about me?" I nodded. "You have any idea what the connection might be?"

"I've turned that around in my head a thousand times, but I can't for the life of me figure out what our program has to do with a bunch of real estate deals around the globe."

"I think I can answer that," Thea Janeway said, her head appearing as she climbed the ladder to the Watchman's lair.

"Thea!" I started to rise, but she waved me back down, then clambered the rest of the way up the ladder to join me by the fire.

"How'd you get in here?" the Watchman asked.

"Are you kidding? These are Carter's people."

Thea seemed amped on exhaustion and, from the looks of the stains on her clothes, battle. "Everyone's okay?"

Thea took a moment before she answered. "Where to start?"

"Give us what we need to know now. We can get to the details later."

Thea moved in beside me where I'd made room by the fire. "I left Carter downstairs with the dog. My father went home or somewhere." She shrugged. "Rita was doing some research on the side. She got interested in clusters of cases of mainly Alzheimer's but some of the other tangle diseases—a case or two of Parkinson's and several of ALS."

"Clusters?"

"Yeah, more cases than would normally be expected based on stats from the general population—way more." She brushed her hair back and eyed the rest of the folks hanging on her words. "I know you and the detective here, but who are they? She motioned to Sami and the Watchman.

"Colleagues and casualties, but on our side." My guess had her last shower in Portland before she left. And she has some exotic, Far Eastern odor about her. Medicinal maybe? "And Rita was chasing the cause?"

"Yeah, she mentioned it to Evans, and it triggered some research he'd done in the South Pacific decades ago when ethnobotany was his calling." Thea waved all that away. "Anyway, it turns out the increased cases correlate to algae blooms."

"What?"

"You know those fancy planned developments that developers build around a nice sized man-made lake? The rich folks live on the lake. The not-so-rich...don't." I nodded, encouraging her to move on as the dots weren't connecting. At first, I thought it might just be me having a hard time following, but the look on Beck's face told me I wasn't alone.

"Anyway, those lakes are pretty much self-contained with no fresh water coming in. So when the summer gets cooking they suffer something called an algae bloom, only it isn't actually algae. It's cyanobacteria."

"And Evans found a tie-in all those years ago," I said. I'd need more details later, but I got the gist.

"Yeah, living close to that stuff, swimming around in it, ingesting it...very bad for the brain."

"Do you think Evans is involved in this?"

Thea thought for a moment. "I wouldn't see how. Some of the facts sure pointed to him."

"He lied about seeing Rita the night she died." I still wasn't sure what to make of that, although it looked damning.

"Not a stellar moment. Either he was afraid of being included in the suspect list and perhaps losing a bit of professional luster, or he was protecting her."

"How so?"

"We all live by our wits. That's the seat of our professional reputation—how well our brains work."

"And if you go buggy..." I knew how that eroded folks' confidence.

"You're done," Thea confirmed, not realizing the same sort of assessment applied in my world. "I can't fathom any motivation Evans might have to torpedo his own program."

"But he didn't do that, did he?" Finally, I saw it all. "Nobody did."

Thea looked at me as the light dawned. "Of course! They were after Rita all along. It was personal."

"The notes, the threats, they were just to keep us moving forward. Most of all, they were to get you on the path of that computer. You could get into it. You could destroy Rita's research."

"Which I did." Thea didn't look all that displeased.

I sensed something more. "A backup?"

Thea looked around the room. "Until I'm sure who's playing for which team, I refuse to say."

"Understood." I stood and brushed myself off, delaying when I would leave the warm embrace of the fire for a moment longer. "Well, let's go get our killer."

CHAPTER TWENTY-NINE

JASPER CLARKSON'S MANSION LOOMED OUT OF THE DARKNESS, A sinister presence. The dramatic lighting only enhanced the ominous portent. I idled my bike the last one hundred yards, then parked it at the curb. Beck, with Thea and Carter...and the dog, which he had not wanted in his car...parked down the street.

Beck materialized out of the darkness. "I called Carla. No answer."

I held up my phone. "I know why." Clarkson, perhaps sensing the battle was lost, the troops dead or on the run, had snatched Carla and now used her as a calling card to entice Beck's and my presence...alone.

"Fuck." He stared at the house as if wishing it would melt right in front of us.

"What did you do with the others?"

"Gave them my car. They're headed to the hospital to help Logan." He pressed his lips together. "They didn't argue, which I found very odd—they looked ready to finish the fight. Hell, even the dog had her badass on." He was quiet for a moment. "It's you, isn't it?" he said quietly as if raising his voice would implore the Fates to make it so.

"Who?" Coy never worked with Beck, but I thought I'd give it a go. Right now, though I'd like to shoot Logan—well, after he manufactured my cure. For Thea and Carter to abandon the battle with victory in sight, the incentive must've been overwhelming. Frankly, Thea would be the lynchpin in the prosecutor's case, so having her out of the way gave me one less distraction.

"I thought so." Beck could see past my bullshit almost every time. "Well, we're here. Might as well finish the job. That's the quickest way to get you back to the hospital." He took a deep breath, then let it out slowly. "We should've waited for a warrant."

"The chief would've blocked us, and we'd be right here, just a few hours later. Time isn't on our side." Conversation would do nothing now, so I started up the sweeping drive to the front door.

After a moment, Beck kept pace. "You're going to get us in real trouble someday."

I smiled at his implication—we were a team, and he was all in. "Maybe. This job gets to you. So often, the bad guys get away to keep doing harm. Some technicality, some tiny mistake, trumped up into a violation of Constitutional rights. Over time, doing the wrong thing for the right reasons seems okay, justified even." I put a hand on his arm, drawing his attention. "We need to retire before then. A beach where we can do our thing."

"You got it." Beck tried for jaunty but failed. "How are you feeling?"

"Remarkably clear-headed. Seriously cold but...okay. Don't worry. Logan's got this. He'll reverse-engineer it in time. But," I motioned toward the house, "getting the man who ordered the hit would help tremendously."

Beck focused on the house. "Okay. Any ideas?"

"Play it by ear?"

This time, his grin hit and stayed. "I like that plan."

"Beware the butler." I pressed the bell. I could tell Beck thought I was kidding. The joke would be on him soon enough.

Once again, Lurch or whatever-his-name-was opened the door.

Brace.

His name was Brace.

I remembered.

He didn't seem surprised to see us. He stepped aside, motioning us inside. The look on Beck's face was a Kodak moment.

I didn't let myself wallow in it for more than a second or two. "The library?" I asked as Beck and I peered into the entryway bracketed by two grand staircases, one on either side, that met at the first-floor landing.

"Please." That was new.

We breezed around the butler. "You take the right? I'll take the left."

Beck and I ran up the staircases, leaving the butler behind. On the landing, we paused. "Probably better together," Beck said, careful to leave out any implication.

We'd left Lurch flatfooted, but he was gaining on us as he spoke in hushed tones into a tiny headset mic. Beck pulled out his gun, hesitated for a moment, then grabbed his backup shooter from his ankle holster and handed it to me. "This way." He motioned behind me to a long hallway. We threw open the doors as we half ran. The sound of running behind us grew closer—three men, maybe four—out numbered but not impossible odds.

The second-to-the-last doorway opened on a room that looked like a drawing room from days gone by—skirted tables, Tiffany lamps, a lounging chaise and overstuffed chairs all in Laura Ashley —a decades-old style in a centuries-old room.

Carla, her chin on her chest, sat in a chair positioned right where anyone who opened the door would see her. Rope wound around her chest, lashing her to the spot and looping down to tie her feet to the legs. Her hands hidden behind her, presumably they too were bound. She didn't move.

Beck moved to rush to her. I grabbed his arm. "Stop. Slowly."

The thick pile of the carpet bordered on a '70s shag and could hide all kinds of pressure plates or tripwires.

"He got us here. What kind of game is this?" Beck growled but heeded my warning.

My gun at the ready, I whirled at footfalls behind us. Jasper Clarkson slowed when he saw us. Another man trailing him ducked behind him, but not fast enough.

The chief!

Neither man had a gun.

"We were waiting for you in the library." Clarkson had lost his arrogance. He looked over my shoulder, ignoring my gun. "What the hell?" His gaze flicked back to mine. "Who the hell is that?"

"As if you don't know." Beck stepped forward where Clarkson could see him. He didn't seem surprised to see the chief.

"She's one of mine. Carla, Beck's partner." The chief remembered who he was if only for a moment.

Beck looked ready to rip his head off. "Tell me how to get to Carla."

Clarkson looked at the chief. "What does he mean?"

"Any concealed devices?" I interpreted.

"I have no idea. This is the women's wing of the house. I never venture in here and have no idea how this poor woman ended up here."

A motorcycle engine fired up behind the house. The light from a single lamp streaked across the room. I handed Beck his gun. "I do."

I took off at a run.

One of the great things about super-protected neighborhoods for the rich and famous included their lack of ingress and egress—one way in, one way out made the neighborhood safer, or so the theory went. I couldn't speak to its validity, but today, I threw a few thank-yous to the Powers That Be. One way out sure made following and catching up a whole lot easier. Several blocks down the hill, I finally spied the taillight of the bike three or four blocks in front. My bike won the horsepower contest, and from the looks of the rider and her awkward shifts in and out of the turns, I had the skill contest won as well.

Feeling a rush to catch up and beat the crap out of whoever hid her blonde hair under the helmet—the few tendrils steaming in the airflow gave her away—I worked to slow down, to think.

But mom or daughter?

I settled in behind the bike. A quick glance over her shoulder and the rider ahead goosed it, almost losing the bike around the next corner as she fishtailed. The rider should've picked a path into town with traffic to snarl my abilities to follow and alleys to dart down. Instead, she took a turn to the left, riding higher up the hills into the deep, thick forest blanketing the slopes. A local road I was unfamiliar with, it soon gave way to very narrow asphalt less than a car wide. In some cases, the asphalt had crumbled, leaving only dirt. The houses set back from the road into the trees wouldn't provide any cover. As it climbed, the road narrowed even more, the trees encroaching on room to maneuver as the curves tightened.

I'd catch her before the top where the path would drop down toward Beaverton on the other side. Relaxing into the flow, I focused on slowing then accelerating through the turns, laying the bike over so my inside knee almost touched the ground, watching for gravel that wouldn't hold. It'd been awhile since I'd pushed myself and the bike this way. Muscle memory is a great thing—I didn't have to rely on the sketchy neurons in my head. The joy of feeling one with the bike—I'd missed that shot of adrenaline, that feeling of mastery. For a moment, I lost myself.

One tight turn and I found myself climbing up the ass of the other motorcycle. I could see the rider's eyes flick to my reflection in the rearview mirror mounted by her left hand. She didn't seem alarmed. She didn't open the throttle further.

Perhaps she knew she'd smear herself across the road and break every bone coming up against one of the trees. So I settled in, waiting for a turn where she'd have to slow sufficiently that if I hit her back tire, she wouldn't die. The whine of the engines echoed softly, bouncing among the trees that streaked by in the thin beams of our headlights. The world reduced to tiny flashes, the happy growl of the engine, and the beat of my pulse which I could feel in my temples. My focus telescoped, the world slowed—there was nothing but me, the bike, the wind...and the red dot of the taillight I followed like a cat playing with a light pointer, coiled to pounce.

Approaching the top of the hill, the grade flattened, and the trees thinned, opening to a small grassy area, the edges hidden in the darkness. Without warning, the bike ahead of me swerved to the left, then sharply to the right.

She opened the throttle wide. The engine responded with a whine. Her rear tire spun in the gravel, giving me precious seconds to respond. I knew what she was going to do. A cliff lurked in the darkness, it had to. I could only imagine the drop.

I gunned my engine aiming for her broadside, then braced for impact.

Hunched over the handlebars, her chest almost resting on the bike, the rider stared straight ahead, focusing on oblivion.

She never even flinched when my front tire hit her bike just behind her leg, throwing the rear of the bike out from under her. Without traction, the wheel whined through the air. The impact threw me and my bike to the right—heading toward the darkness...the cliff. Without thinking, I stood on the brake and grabbed the handbrakes while shutting the throttle. I heaved my weight to the side and laid the bike over—pulling my leg up so it wouldn't get caught between the bike and the ground. The momentum and the weight would be enough to strip skin off at best, wrench a knee—and it was my bad knee—at worst.

The weight of the bike pulled me toward the edge.

I kicked at the bike, trying to free myself. My pant leg! It caught on something! I kicked and struggled but couldn't free myself.

My strike had knocked the other bike to the side. It stopped ten feet or so before the edge. My bike glanced off it but kept sliding.

I could see it now—earth, then air and darkness beyond. I shut my eyes and braced to slip over the edge.

Only a few feet more.

I clawed at the sand and gravel but couldn't find a hold.

I held my breath.

A thump. An abrupt stop that took my wind for a moment. I didn't know how or why we stopped, but the bike had to be teetering on the edge. With my knee against the seat, I levered myself back and away. At first, whatever was holding me held tight, then it gave, and I fell back. On my back, I propped myself up on one elbow.

For a moment my bike was there...then it was gone. It crashed and clanged against trees and rocks as gravity did its thing.

Breathing hard, I fell back.

Sensing movement to my left, I rolled to my right. A tree limb crashed where I had just been and splintered. I grabbed a short section of the wood as I rolled onto my feet. I turned and propelled myself at the woman. Gasping against the pain in my knee, I swung for her knees as I drove forward. Wood met bone. She crumpled with a yelp, landing on her hands and knees. Her helmet protected her from a foot to the chin, so I aimed lower. My foot caught the soft flesh of her stomach. As the air whooshed out of her, she fell on her side, then rolled onto her back.

I landed on her, my knee in her stomach. Careful to stay out of reach of her legs and feet, I wrenched an arm around and pressed hard against her locked elbow.

"Stop!" she gasped as she struggled for air.

I pushed harder.

She tried to roll to loosen the pain, but my knee and my weight kept her pinned. "I want to die," she wailed. "Why didn't you let me?"

"Too easy an out for what you've done." Cartilage ground as I put a tad more pressure on the joint. "Helmet off."

With shaking fingers, she plucked at the strap. Finally, she worked it free. Slowly, she pulled off her helmet. As it cleared her head, I knocked it from her hand. It rolled into the darkness. I grabbed her chin and yanked her head around where I could see her face.

"Instagram fame wasn't enough? Surely that would carry you through your divorce. Your husband is rather wealthy." She glared at me. "Oh, wait, I know jerks like that. An airtight prenup, right?" I tsked.

"No, I'd get my half."

That surprised me. I turned deadly serious. "Then, why? Seems to me the algae blooms could've been solved fairly easily. Why kill Rita?"

"She knew too much."

"Ah, I guess it could cut into the bottom line if word got out that living in your family's planned developments would shoot your risk of Alzheimer's through the roof." I pushed on her elbow just because. For Rita. And for...well, not me so much, but for the pain I left behind. I realized the heavy weight of that now.

I managed to secure her, but I kept a knee on her just in case as I worked my phone free.

Beck answered on the first ring. "Kate! Are you okay?"

"No, I'm dead and the long-distance charges are racking up really quickly." I know that was mean, but for some reason, I couldn't see anything but the humor in being stuck in the middle of a forest on some random path with a bent-up bike and a suicidal female. "Seriously, how's Carla?"

"Fine. She told me what happened."

"Confirming Mr. Clarkson's innocence?"

"Yeah, those two women sure hated his guts."

My heart skipped. "Two? I've only got one of them. You left Sami with the Watchman, right?"

He sucked in a breath. "Fuck, the girl will know." He barked orders to someone in the background. The next voice I heard was Carla's. "Kate? You good?"

"Well," I glanced down at Mrs. Clarkson, now bound with my shoelaces and looking daggers at me. "I could use your help. You'll have to triangulate off my phone—I have only the vaguest idea where I am."

<hr>

I HEARD THE SIRENS, but they stopped down the hill. Several minutes more and I heard the voices calling to me. "Kate? Kate?" Carla sounded in charge and none the worse for wear.

"Up here. Follow the trail to the top. Can't miss us." I massaged my knee, but the pain still bit with a hot sting. So not good. The shivers had abated somewhat. And juiced on pissed-off and adrenaline, I didn't feel so cold. Also, so not good.

But no voices. Not the odd paranoid one, not the comforting one belonging to my brother. Just quiet—quiet I wasn't used to. The recent me I'd gotten to know was slipping away, retreating back into the haze. I pulled out my phone and started making a quick recording, putting the past day or two down as quickly as I could.

I'd just spun the final gossamer thread as thin beams of light flashed through the trees—Carla had brought help, not that we needed it.

She broke through the trees canvasing the area with her light. "Where's your bike?"

I pointed to the gouges in the edge of the drop-off.

She raised an eyebrow. "And you let her live?" she asked, tilting her head toward Mrs. Clarkson.

"Her death wish is strong. Figured it'd be worse to send her to prison for the rest of her life." Several men had followed Carla into the clearing. Two gathered up Mrs. Clarkson. The remaining two worked to get the bent-up bike back together enough so the wheels tracked, and they could get it down the hill. "Beck with you?" I asked, knowing the answer.

"No."

"You think..." I wouldn't give voice to the words, his deed, not ever, but especially not with listening ears.

"You can't protect that man from himself. He's gotta make the right choice."

Not the answer I wanted, but I heard the truth in it. "Can the men take Mrs. Clarkson the rest of the way? I think I need you to get me to the hospital pronto."

I heard her tell her men what to do as she moved back toward the trees. Two steps, my world started to spin. I bent at the waist, putting my hands on my knees. Didn't help. I felt the bile rise in my throat. My knees weakened. I dropped to one knee, the good one.

Then my world went dark.

CHAPTER THIRTY

SLOWLY, I CAME TO. THE SMELLS REGISTERED FIRST. FAMILIAR smells, antiseptic, with the sweet stink of fear. Next, the sounds, hushed, rubber-soled shoes and their muffled squeak where sole met linoleum, the rustle of people standing close, the smell of the street, dirt.

The hospital.

My eyelids weighed a hundred-fold of normal, or so it seemed. Concerted effort finally moved them, letting in a sliver of light. Shadowy figures moved through the light.

"Am I dead?" My voice sounded hoarse, distant, almost like somebody else's.

A hand grabbed mine. "Katie, thank God! And no, you're not dead."

Beck! "You didn't kill anybody, did you?"

He hung his head, pressing his forehead to my hand. "Not this time."

"Not ever, not if you're going to be my partner." I felt myself smile. Slowly, the weight of my eyelids diminished, and I blinked several times against the light. After a bit, focus returned. The Watchman stood on the left side of my bed, opposite Beck. He had a scratch or two across one cheek and a split lip that had swollen until he looked positively fashionable. "What does the other guy look like?" I gave him my best lopsided grin.

"There are rules about hitting young women." He ducked his head, trying to hide the truth.

"Rules are invalid if the young woman had murder on her mind."

"Wish I'd known that up front. Took me a bit."

"Hope you got the best of her." He smiled his answer. "Good. And Sami?"

"They admitted her to get her stable and to figure out what the hell she's been pumping into herself."

I felt Beck flinch, and I squeezed his hand.

"Next stop rehab," the Watchman concluded.

"And the young Miss Clarkson?"

"In a cell next to her mother," Carla announced as she strode into the room. "You gave us all a scare. How're you doing?"

I wiggled, testing various body parts. "Bruises and scrapes I'd bet, but workable."

"And the cold?"

"Gone." I didn't know what to make of that, so I didn't try. A mist of clarity still protected me, but like mountain fog on a cool summer morning, it would soon dissipate. I could feel it. Whatever held me here, whatever had opened the doorways and cleared the synapses, faded as the force of my genetic affliction slithered its tendrils into places they didn't belong.

But for the moment, I was here...all of me, all the memories, all that had happened.

As if on cue, a tap at the door sounded. A man peeked his head in. Benton Myles.

"May I come in?"

Beck eased back, pressing in next to my head like a dog guarding a loved one.

Benton met my gaze, holding it. "How are you, Kate?"

"Rather formal for a guy playing games with my head."

He didn't deny it. In fact, he looked like he'd been suffering a bit. His clothes were wrinkled, the stubble on his face clearly several days old; his hair had resisted finger-combing. Despite it all, his ego and his power emanated from him in waves.

"What do you mean, Kate?" Beck asked, his question riding on anger.

"You gotta let go of that, Beck," I said, then turned to give Benton a long look. "I'm not dying, am I?"

"No."

"What are you saying?" Beck demanded, his anger blooming.

"Let it go. Everybody here was playing their own angle, even you. Benton's got some magic something he got into me. The memories, they came back. I recognized my old self, my competence, my ability to remember. It was all there, still is, but I can feel it fading."

"What?" Beck's struggle to process flashed across his face. "He injected you with something, a drug? And it cured you?"

"Temporarily, I'm afraid. And I didn't inject her. I used the same methodology used to kill Rita, but this time for good," Benton said. "It worked remarkably well, better than we even hoped."

"You and Rita. You were working together," I said. It wasn't a question.

"Strictly off the grid."

"What's the connection?" Beck asked.

Benton smiled at me. "You tell him, Kate; you remember. And from the looks of you, it seems you also know." He crossed his arms then leaned against the doorjamb.

"Should I arrest him?" Carla asked, clearly feeling protective of me.

"We can wait on that. I don't think he's done anything other than treat me without my permission, and for his own good. But I'll pass on pressing charges." Frankly, the idea that his drug worked, even for a bit, gave me a tantalizing bit of hope. This time, I embraced it without fear.

I let go of Beck's hand and pushed myself up in bed. Beck

plumped pillows behind me, then pulled the blanket up, tucking it around me. I let my attention rest on each person in the room for a moment as I took them all in. My friends, my family...well, other than Benton Myles, but someday he might prove to be my savior. "Okay, the short version: Benton, you asked Rita to do some research about unexplained clusters of higher-than-normal incidences of Alzheimer's disease and the like. You were desperate to figure out what had triggered ALS in a woman as healthy, young, and vibrant as your wife. Unexpectedly, Rita found a connection— that fancy house in the planned development in upstate New York. In London, during the colloquium, you two met. She'd shared her findings, but you wanted her data...you wanted the proof. I don't know, but I figure you must've told Jasper Clarkson, the developer of the planned community, about Rita's findings?"

"A few months back, we had an investor meeting—the longevity research. I was blind with rage. The guy can be a complete ass, but to my surprise, he was totally gobsmacked when I told him about Rita's correlation. He told me he'd look into it. Underneath it all, at his core, he's a brilliant businessman. As such, he surely didn't want to be known as a guy who knowingly gave a bunch of people a horrifying disease."

"He must've mentioned it to his wife or kid, or they overheard him talking on the phone," I said, speculating, of course, but somehow, they got wind of it. "In London you wanted Rita's data, but she wouldn't give it to you."

"No, she'd gone a bit buggy, as they told you. She thought I would kill somebody."

"Was she right?"

He closed his eyes for a moment, resting his chin on his chest. When he reopened them, they were clear, guilt-free, revenge-free. "I honestly don't know."

"And then, when Rita was killed, you knew someone was trying to bury her discovery."

"I didn't know it for sure. It could've been about the trial or any one of many toes she took glee in stepping on."

"That's where I came in."

He smiled—it was dazzling. "The perfect setup."

"You played your hand well."

"I had help."

"Rita's computer...her data."

"I knew she and David were good friends. They kept it on the down-low. He seemed like the only person she could've given the computer to. I'd looked everywhere, talked to everyone. I hung my hopes for recovering it on a sighting one of her colleagues had of her and David having a nice dinner."

"Away from the madding crowd, so to speak."

He pushed himself off the doorjamb and filled a glass with water at the sink. "A long shot that paid off...and got David killed." His hand shook as he took a long swallow. "I never suspected the tenacity, the willingness to kill."

"If it's any consolation, I've seen it a lot and the human capacity for cruelty and complete disregard for life never ceases to amaze and horrify me."

"Dr. Hunt helped you find David, sending Thea after him and the computer. You both knew she could get into it." I paused. This next part I didn't like so much. "And you knew the killer would want that computer."

"Yes, but I thought I had her protected."

"How so?"

"I sent her father after her."

That was a twist I hadn't seen coming. "What?"

"He's...resourceful. And it worked. He saved Thea and Carter and someone else."

"But not David."

"That will weigh on me for the rest of my life."

"You made one other miscalculation."

Benton snorted. "Only one? I'm in way over my head in this sort of game."

"You didn't need to give me the drug—you damn near derailed

me. I was doing fine on my own. That drug has a few kinks you're going to need to work on."

"You figured that all out on your own?" Carla asked. Beck knew better than to be that sort of condescending.

I let her off lightly—we all were pretty much maxed. "I'm a pretty good cop."

"I'll say."

Everybody laughed which put a smile on my heart.

"Carla, I need you to strong-arm those two women—find out how the hell they bought and paid for an army of mercenaries half a world away."

"It's easier than you think," Benton Myles said. "Powerful people hire them all the time...mostly for protection."

I didn't want to think about armies of highly trained people out there willing to do ugly things for the highest bidder...so I didn't. The case against the two women was coming together. In time it would get stronger as the pieces fell into place. "I'm ready to blow this joint. We still have some work to do."

Beck caught his cue. "Okay, everybody out."

We didn't wait for the doctor or discharge papers or any of that. Carla left to deal with the females of the Clarkson clan and hopefully worm some answers out of them. The Watchman and Benton waited outside my room while Beck helped me skinny into my clothes. "We both need hot showers and clean clothes."

He helped me finish the buttons on my shirt then tugged me close. Wrapping me in his arms he said, "Preferably together."

I warmed to that idea quickly. "First, we need to talk to Thea. A few pieces are missing, and we need help tying either Mrs. Clarkson or the daughter to the request for the design of the drug they eventually used to kill Rita."

"They've holed up with Logan in his lab."

ONLY SLIGHTLY DIZZY, like coming off some powerful joy juice, I held Beck's arm as we navigated the hallways toward the medical office and research complex. My clothes, torn and filthy with splotches of blood, did little to inspire confidence, but they covered all the essentials. People flowing the opposite direction gave us nothing more than a curious glance. One lady dressed in scrubs looked like she wanted to ask if we needed help but then thought better of it. Leaving as I had, I half-expected the hospital police to hunt us down and reinstall me in my bed...or at least try to drag me back there. But what I had those doctors couldn't fix.

With me leading the charge, we actually all made it to Logan's lab. Thankfully, as one of the head dogs, his lab could accommodate our little gang along with all the people crowded in there already. Logan, disheveled and bleary-eyed, held court in the middle. I recognized Thea and Dr. Hunt in the gang that surrounded the lab table. The young man with the milky eyes and the dog must be Carter. The other two, a short lady with dark hair, crepey skin, and eyes that had witnessed a thousand years and a tall, gray-headed man with angular features and a bit of Thea in him...if she'd been devoid of warmth. He could be her father. Somehow, I'd thought both he and Dr. Hunt still resided on the suspect list, albeit at the bottom.

Logan spied me across the room. "Kate! Dear God! You need to be in the hospital—I admitted you myself with orders to handcuff you to the bed if they had to." He slipped sideways between Thea and Dr. Hunt as everyone turned to look our direction. Arriving in front of me, he put his hands on his hips. "I should've known the nurses would be no match." He turned serious. "How are you?"

"Benton can explain. But before that, can you do the honors? I've not been introduced."

Thea rescued Logan. Stepping in with her manners, she made the introductions and I did the same for my group.

"Who is the man hiding behind the computer screen in the back there?" I pointed to a dark corner of the lab.

"A colleague of mine," Carter said. "He prefers not to be named, but he can be trusted."

Thea confirmed, "Carter's on the inside; any friend of his is above reproach."

A bit shortsighted, but Thea hadn't seen that side of life as I had, for which I was grateful.

As to the other men in the room I hadn't known, I'd been right. I paused on Flynn Janeway. "I thought you went home."

"I came to help. Not sure how I can, but I'm here. I couldn't be anywhere else."

I wasn't sure whether I could believe him or not. The woman, Shell, caught my attention. "You worked with David Thorne. I'm very sorry for your loss."

She dipped her head. "Rita told him someone might kill to get that computer. We were ready, but they were too many."

Benton pushed to the front beside me. "David knew of the danger?"

"Yes. You are not to blame. Rita told David you might come somehow, but you were not the one to be afraid of. She did not say who that was—I'm not sure she knew. David couldn't get into the computer, only Thea. We thought we would be okay."

"Until Thea showed up," I said.

"Yes."

I didn't look at the man standing next to me. He'd manipulated us all, injected me with an unproven drug without my consent; and yet we had nothing but good to show for it. Did that make it right? If not, how would the scales of justice tip? "Benton, you twisted the facts to make us believe the trial was in danger," I continued. "That way you could convince Dr. Hunt to pressure Thea to find Carter, who would lead you all to David and Rita's computer."

"Like I said, a long shot."

"That worked like a charm."

"And here we are."

Logan snapped back. "Benton, you have to help me! We are

almost there, reverse-engineering the DNA strand Kate was infected with, but we've hit a wall, we can't go any further."

"That's because it wasn't one of my designs," the man in the back of the room said.

"You blueprinted the drug, for lack of a better word, that killed Rita?" I pushed through the throng to stand beside him. Young, very young with a hint of Asian yet with blond hair and darker skin.

"Unknowingly, yes. Don't worry, Carter will rip me a new one. I went outside the boundaries of our agreement to use our skills to find those who are doing exactly what I did. I will pay for it." He dipped his head. "I am ashamed."

"How?"

"How did Carter find me? He has a database of designs. All designers have a way of doing things that is unique to them."

"Like a signature?"

"Of sorts. It's a bit of arrogance, to be honest. Wanting the world to know how clever we are. Eddie Chan actually designed it; I blueprinted it for manufacture. David actually scoured the database of designs. He's the one who tied it to Eddie."

"And Eddie led to you." I angled a look at him. "What are you doing now?"

"Tracing the buyer."

I liked that. "And?"

"Getting close. Give me a little longer."

I had no doubt his trail would lead to the Clarksons, for sure the women, perhaps the husband...and the dead lawyer in Vancouver.

We had our answers—the proof would come. I turned a steely eye on the kid behind the computer. "Now you know how all of this can be used and traced. So put it to work doing good. The idea that anyone could weaponize someone's DNA like they did Rita's is terrifying. The faster the world of epigenetics moves and grows..."

Logan finished my thought, "...the more opportunities there

will be to use what we learn about genetic triggers, for good and for ill."

Yin and yang. The balance of life.

"Logan, you and Dr. Hunt are going to want to pick Benton's brain. I'd leave Mr. Janeway on the outside of that conversation." He raised an eyebrow at me. "Competing interests, I'm sure you understand."

I hooked my arm through Beck's. "Come on. I believe you said something about going home and cleaning up?"

CHAPTER THIRTY-ONE

THE SHOWER HAD BEEN MEDICINAL, THE SEX EVEN MORE SO. Wrapped in Beck's arms I stared out at the city lights. My bedroom, my man—we'd come full circle.

"What are you going to do about the chief?" I asked. His friend, his boss, his mentor, had betrayed him. "I'm sure he gave you up to try to save himself."

"Yeah." That one word carried so much hurt. "I don't know what I'm going to do. He put himself on the line to help me cover everything up. It's kinda hard to hold it against him."

"I'm not that forgiving," I said, but in my heart, I knew I was. "You won't kill him."

"No. Maybe I harped on you so much about learning to control yourself because one time, I hadn't been able to, and I carried the weight of that. I don't ever want you to have to bear that kind of pain."

"I think we can help each other." I waited for him to stiffen against me, ready to argue, but he didn't.

"We can." He took a deep breath. "You were right," Beck said, his lips teasing my ear.

"About?" I stifled a giggle as frissons of pleasure chased any last hint of the cold away.

"I doubted you, second-guessed you, didn't treat you as an equal."

"Can you do that now?"

"If you help me, yes." He shifted, wrapping me tighter in his embrace. "You were wrong, too."

"I was? About what?"

"You kicked me."

"I did?" I searched back in time but couldn't find the memory. They were fading as I knew they would.

It's okay, Katie. You got this.

Hank was back. And I was scared. But what I faced I'd faced before. Now I had the sweetness of possibility to get me through the darkness. I snagged my Sharpie off the nightstand then unwound a bit from Beck's embrace. In my neat tiny print on the inside of my left arm—the spot I saved for the most important information—I wrote a reminder about Benton Myles and his treatment that had worked for a while. Beck watched me over my shoulder, his warm chest pressed to the cool skin of my back. He felt good...right.

Yes, Hank. We got this! I sent the thoughts to my brother wherever he lived inside me. I didn't think he could answer back, but life had been weird enough lately for me to acknowledge the possibility. If our memories could be stored and transferred, what about our sentient selves?

The thought both intrigued and terrified me.

Science, a sword with two edges.

"You scared?" Beck asked, his chin on my shoulder.

I rolled back into his arms. "Sure. I'm always scared. I could disappear and there isn't a damned thing I can do about it."

"I'll be here. Through all of it, whatever it is."

I rested my head on his chest and listened to his heartbeat.

And I knew he would.

THE END

Thank you for reading *Deadfall*!

As you may know, reviews are SUPER helpful. They not only help potential readers make a choice, but they also help me win coveted spots on various advertising platforms.

So, if you would please, do me the favor of leaving a review at the outlet of your choice.

Read a short excerpt below

CHAPTER ONE

I'm a killer. The thought tortured Jake Walker.

Matt was dead. Jake's fault. At least that's how he saw it.

Bile rose in his throat at the image of his boss thrown back in his chair, one neat hole in the center of his forehead. A once brilliant mind reduced to splattered bits of gore. Jake's hands shook as he closed his laptop and gathered his things.

They had asked him to let the bad guys in the software, to allow them to wander and hide in the millions of lines of code. A huge gamble. He'd tried to warn them. Yes, he'd told them he knew where to look, how to follow, but still...the stakes were so high they were out of sight.

They told him to keep his head down and report what he saw. He'd done that. The game had been fun...until someone blew Matt's brains all over his office.

They hadn't told him the cat-and-mouse game could be deadly.

They promised they had his back. They were supposed to be the good guys.

They had dangled the carrot. This was Jake's chance to be somebody, they'd said. Jake was the only one with the skills, knowledge, and access. Ego and idealism—they got him in trouble every time.

Had his back. Fuck that.

He'd called the number. They'd said sit tight; they'd get back to him.

Right.

Jake Walker might be a fool, but he drew the line at being a martyr.

The bad guys killed with precision and then vanished as if they'd never been. A shiver of fear knifed through him. What chance did one pansy-ass software geek have?

Matt was dead.

Forced into action, Jake didn't really hold out much hope, but he clung to the flotsam of desperation with the strength of a drowning man. Jake willed himself to slow, to act casual as if nothing was wrong. He had to get out of here, to run, to find help.

He squeezed his eyes tight against the image of Matt branded on his brain with the singe of horror and guilt.

Right now he felt spotlighted, the lights of his office holding back the darkness of the night outside his window. Through the interior glass walls, he scanned the sea of cubicles. An ominous quiet lurked in the shadows. In the half-light, Jake felt exposed and at a disadvantage. If someone wanted to hide, the geometric patches of darkness cast by the security lights would shelter them —the overheads had been doused when the last of his staff had left hours ago.

A noise startled him. Frozen, Jake held his breath and waited.

The sound didn't repeat.

Perhaps it was the air conditioning kicking on. The noises of the empty building sounded strange, creaking, groaning as if collapsing without the human energy to keep it inflated. Or perhaps it was his imagination. But he hadn't imagined Matt, dead, half his brain splattered on the bookcase, the window, the photos of his wife and kids.

Jake pulled in a deep breath, squeezing his eyes shut, then let the air out with measured precision, willing his nerves to calm. When he opened his eyes, the world had steadied a bit.

He could do this.

As he stuffed the papers into his briefcase, his hand brushed against cold metal. A gun—a Glock 19, so new the oil still gleamed on the unmarred bluing. Jake had never owned a gun before. And he'd never broken the law—not intentionally anyway. He'd felt like a felon scoring the piece off the kid in Hell's Kitchen.

How the hell had he gotten into this?

Jake didn't even know who the killers were. But he'd chased them through the code, and he knew where they were and what they were trying to do. He had to stop them, but he needed help.

And he needed to get as far away from here as he could.

He knew they were there, watching, waiting. So clever how they by-passed the trading programs with all the tight checks and rechecks and security redundancies. And so easy, too. Had he not been looking, watching, no one would've known the bad guys even manipulated the inventory numbers, or made phantom trades to manipulate the price of oil. His trip to Oklahoma had confirmed the inventory anomalies—the only time he'd gone off the reservation. Well, that and the phone call to his IT contact in Conroe. But those were it. After that, nothing had felt the same.

He tried not to look out the window, to squint into the night, scanning for those who wanted to know how much he knew, who he told. He didn't know all of it, but he knew enough to be afraid. Big players: Drayton Lewis the tech magnate, Senator Herrera from Texas with a lifetime of political IOUs, and others—he could sense them, but he hadn't turned over their particular rock yet.

Hurry, Jake. Hurry.

Jake booted up his desktop, his foot bouncing a staccato

rhythm. They were clever, all right, clever to the point of arrogance. And that's how he'd found them.

With a few quick keystrokes he started the scrubbing program on his hard drive and the backup that would overwrite both drives. Then he stuffed the new laptop into his shoulder bag, killed the lights, and headed out the door.

With no one at work to help, Jake knew he had to get word to someone. Without a whole lot of luck, and some serious help, he was a dead man. Shelby would know what to do.

But the information could get her killed.

He'd thought long and hard about how to show her where to look. He'd been careful, but had he been careful enough?

At this point, out of time and using up luck by the second, he had no choice.

They had to be stopped, and, of everyone he knew, Shelby was the only one who could handle the heat and crack the code. Together they could outmaneuver these guys. His sister had more lives than a cat and a bite more vicious than a pissed-off Doberman. And she could dig—if anyone could take what he'd found and put names to it, she could.

The elevator dinged its arrival, tripping his heart, which already pounded. As the doors opened, he paused. Looking back, he took a quick look around; he couldn't help himself. He'd liked it here— writing the security for the trading programs, being a cog in the wheel of global trade. With a sigh, he flicked off the lights and stepped into the elevator.

The clock was ticking.

After the doors closed and he was alone with his thoughts, Jake punched the button for the fifth floor. The guard wouldn't be at the monitors—he still had a lot of real estate to check—nonetheless, Jake would have to be quick.

They watched.

The elevator slowed to a stop. Fifth floor. As the doors eased open Jake fought the instinct to cringe, to hide—he half expected they'd crawled inside his head and knew what he was doing. They'd been in every other crevice. He ran a hand through his hair. *Calm down. If they knew... Stop! Think!*

After punching the hold button to keep the car there, he ran for the mailroom. The pre-addressed FedEx box waited where he'd hidden it. Each floor had a mailroom. He'd chosen this one at random, but primarily because he had no connection with anyone or any department that had offices there. After wrapping the laptop quickly in two layers of bubble wrap, he shoved it in the box, sealed it, and then put it in the early pickup box. It'd be on its way before the workday got fully underway. Filling his shoulder bag with a thinner box so it looked as it had when he'd left his office, he took a deep breath and bolted for the waiting elevator. Less than thirty seconds and he was back riding down to the lobby.

Jake had calmed himself by the time the doors opened, disgorging him into the large marble and glass atrium that never warmed, not even in the heat of the New York summers. The perfect heart for a corporate collective where "survival of the fittest" and "he who dies with the most toys wins" were rules branded on men's souls.

His footfalls echoed as he strode across the lobby, working hard to act as if today was the same as any other. But it wasn't. After today, there would be no going back. And Jake was fine with that. If not exposed, the secrets would eat at him until there was nothing left. So, either way, he was doomed.

Sorry to draw you into this, Shelby.

A year apart, he and his sister been close once, until Shelby had taken up the sword against big business and Jake had sold himself to her devil. As much as he hated to admit it, his sister had been right.

The security guard met him at the door with a smile, pushing it open. "All work and no play, Mr. Walker."

Jake gripped the man's shoulder—a quick connection that felt final. "Some days are like that, Ethan."

The man nodded as if he had a clue. For a moment Jake was envious of the guard. *Four advanced degrees and I'm jealous of the night watchman*. Jake chided himself, but he recognized his emotion—the last dying gasp of idealism. But somehow having taken a stand, having put in motion things that would stop them, Jake felt better. A surging sense of relief rushed through him—he would do that, he was that kind of guy, even when his life was on the line.

Jake stepped through the door, stopping once outside the penumbra of light cast through the glass. The night air, muggy and dense, smothered him like a plastic sheet. Sweat popped, beading on his skin still cool from the air-conditioned office. The discomfort proved he was still alive, which, all things considered, was a good thing and by no means assured—although his prospects were looking up.

He'd done it. He'd really done it. The vise around his chest loosened, and he took a deep breath, letting it out slowly.

Night had scoured the streets of people. A random can, skittered by a silent breeze, made him jump. Jake crossed the strap of his shoulder bag across his chest. The doorways stood empty, the storefronts shuttered, One World Center a beacon of light standing high above.

New York's fabled financial district—the beating heart of capitalism. Now a sleeping lion, it would awake to consume its fill again tomorrow.

A frisson of fear shivered through him, making the hair on the back of his neck rise.

So close. He'd made it this far. All he had to do was get to the airport—a ticket to Houston in his breast pocket. He'd paid cash, but computers remembered, and there was always a trail if someone knew where to look and how to follow it. He ought to know—he was a master at that game.

Head facing forward, eyes scanning as he maintained an outwardly casual interest in his surroundings, he turned and strode toward the Ritz. It wasn't far. He could catch a cab there.

He whirled at a noise behind him. Pausing, his heart accelerating, he stared into the darkness.

CHAPTER TWO

Sam Donovan was in her usual position—flat on her back.

Even though she'd pulled the small plane into her hangar that hunkered between the larger Coast Guard Air Station Houston Hangar and the even larger NASA one, the heat from the floor burned through her thin shirt—a vestige of the sun on its path, the light angling in through the open hangar door. Her east-facing hangar took the worst of the morning sun.

Only June and already the temperature and humidity in this reclaimed swamp south of Houston were off the charts. Cicadas sang from hiding places among the leaves on the few trees stubborn enough to live despite little water and intense reflected heat. A lone seagull called. Moisture beaded on the relative cool of the hangar floor. Sam had no doubt that if she tossed some water on the tarmac, she'd hear it sizzle and pop in the summer skillet.

Seattle would be misty and cool....

How had her father convinced her to give up the bush-plane charter company and move to this hellhole? Sam shook her head in disgust. Her mother had come, too. They'd done it for family, even though theirs was as fractured as any, and more than most here in the sanctimonious South, which itched like a hair shirt.

Clearly, some boundaries needed to be drawn, but, when it came to her father, Sam wasn't good at drawing a line in the sand. Patrick Donovan was known for crossing most lines anyway. All other areas of her life were ordered, precise—each tool in its spot, each plane centered on the markings on the hangar floor. Yet, her father defied all efforts at pigeonholing. Something Sam found irritating and oddly admirable. Perhaps she wanted the father he couldn't be.

But, thankfully, right now she wasn't searching for the glue for a fractured family. Her current problem was something she could actually solve. The spring assembly on the tailwheel of her 1946 J-3 Cub had popped on landing this morning. Thank God she'd been making the landing and not her student. The memory of the plane's immediate turn when she set the tail down on rollout shivered through her. Experience and quick reflexes kept them from leaving the runway, ground looping, or worse.

Then she would have had to fix more than a spring.

"Wrench." Sam stuck out her hand.

Nothing.

"Geraldo! Dammit." The heat had eroded her good humor. She blinked at the sting of sweat that trickled into her eye. Wedged under the tail, she couldn't reach to wipe it away. She shook her open palm. "Geraldo. Wrench, please." Where was the boy?

"What manner of wrench would ya' be needin'?"

Sam froze, the voice a taper lighting her already short fuse. Her father.

She wriggled from under the plane's elevator, which sat low to the ground, and gazed at the man looming over her. Full head of white hair, ruddy complexion, a bit of a paunch, his chin held a bit too high, as if willing someone to take the first punch—Patrick Donovan in the flesh. Today the scar across his chin—an old oilfield battle wound inflicted when the pressure got too high on a well and it blew the valve, launching a spear of metal three-hundred yards—was etched in bright red. He'd been lucky. His partner, not as much—the metal shot through both his knees. But that scar on her father's chin had served as a bellwether of his mood for as long as Sam was wise enough to take heed. Red was not a good sign—something had amped him up and raised his blood pressure, although she couldn't see any other outward sign. In fact, if she didn't know better, he looked snake-bit, although he was working to cover it up with a grin that barely lifted his lips into an anemic curve. His eyes, bright green and normally dancing with a joke, looked flat and dark.

Lately, he'd kept his distance, ever since their last row, but that one was on him. By Sam's way of thinking, stealing someone's plane, even if you brought it back, was just plain bad form.

"Paddy. Been awhile." *Think of the Devil.* Sam shook her head and stifled the urge to cross herself. Like the Devil, Patrick

Donovan often rode in on a random thought. She had only herself to blame.

"Aye." A frown darkened his face briefly like a cloud passing across the sun.

"Whatever you're selling, I'm not buying." Sam leaned over to root through the toolbox at her father's feet. After finding the wrench she was looking for, she glanced around the hangar, scanning for Geraldo. The King Air, an older model twin turboprop that was her workhorse, still nestled tail-in in the far back corner. Her Jet Ranger, one of the older models but still an amazing workhorse, took up the center of the hangar, its rotors aligned along its body. The J-3 she was working on, a pre–World War II tube and fabric trainer, she'd pulled just inside the doorway. The floor with its new coat of Epoxy gleamed like china ready for the plating of a holiday meal. A small office, with a subsistence-level apartment above, jutted from the north side of the hangar.

Her helper had vanished.

Wrench in hand, Sam dove back under the plane. "What did you do with Geraldo?"

"The kid launched out of here looking for all the world like he'd been shot from a cannon."

The wrench fit over the bolt but slipped when she put her elbow to it. "Goddamn it!"

"Mary Catherine!" Paddy actually sounded a bit shocked, which irritated the hell out of her.

"Now I know you didn't come here to make nice," Sam growled from under the plane. She hated her name. Hated to be spoken to like a child. And was on the verge of hating her father for it, which didn't sit well with her at all. Sam counted to ten and then decided she needed another trip through—ten wasn't enough. This time she held each digit in her brain until thoughts of patricide passed.

"You'll need to remember that one when you confess to Father Flanagan," Paddy continued, unaware how close he was to dying. "He's been asking after you."

"Been working overtime on your soul, I'm sure. But tell him

not to worry on my account. I gave up hypocrisy for Lent. So Geraldo jackrabbited. Thank you for that. But, really, it's little wonder considering the last time you were here." Sam knew there wasn't much good that could come from worrying that knot, but she couldn't resist.

"Aye. You were a bit cheesed."

"More than a bit. You stole my plane."

Patrick Donovan, Paddy to his friends, pressed a hand to his chest in mock indignation. "Stole! I was just borrowin' it a wee bit. I returned it."

Sam needed a different wrench. After rolling out from under the stabilator, she returned the wrench to its slot in the toolbox. With a clean mechanic's rag, she worked at the oil staining her hands to little effect, then pressed herself to her feet. "With bullet holes in the stabilator, no explanation, and the DEA hot on your heels. Took me a month to get my plane out of impound."

Paddy spread his arms wide. "See there, nothing lost."

"Except for the legal fees and the revenue I would've earned had I had the plane in service, not to mention parts and labor." He started to argue, but Sam waved his words away. "I'm taking it you are not here to apologize."

"Ah, you be thankin' your mother for that tongue."

"Don't you be speakin' of Ma. She's a saint." Sam clamped her lips closed—words, once spoken, couldn't be unheard. Those said in anger often provoked regret.

His cheeks flushed, his eyes all misty, her father stared at her, seeming at a loss for words, and then he said, "I am sorry. Sometimes life..." He sighed and then started over. "Sometimes I miscalculate."

Despite being hardwired to the self-preservation mode, Sam lowered her shield a hint. She'd never seen him without a ready gambit. "Is that what you call it?" She softened her tone. Asking someone to be what they weren't never worked out well, not that she'd forgiven him for stealing the plane. She knew he hadn't planned it; it had just happened. But, despite the almost near perfect futility, she had a mind to try to teach him a lesson. Things had to change—*he* had to change—for all of them. He needed a good scare, but, if her father was afraid of anything, Sam had yet to see it.

Jamming his hands in his pockets, Paddy turned to look through the hangar door into the heat of the day. It shimmered off the tarmac in waves, distorting the world like a funhouse mirror. "I've made mistakes—left the wrong woman, trusted the wrong people, tiptoed on the wrong side of the line more than once. When I make my way to the Pearly Gates, I'm sure Saint Peter will have a one-way ticket to Purgatory for me." He angled a glance at his daughter. "I'm not saying I won't deserve it. But I will say, when I made my choices, I thought they were the right ones. Perhaps I didn't think it through."

Sam snorted. She'd heard it all before. "Thinkin'. Not your strong suit." She clamped her lips together. He was doing it again, sucking her in, poking at the beehive of worry that she might have far more Patrick Donovan blood coursing through her veins than made her comfortable.

"You've made yourself a nice place here." Paddy clasped his hands behind his back as he let his gaze wander.

"Paddy, I'm working fourteen hours a day, barely keeping the lights on and the lender off my ass, and the Coast Guard wants to get rid of me." As the only civilian operation in the secure area of Ellington Field just south of Houston, she'd become a thorn in the side of the Homeland Security folks, a tempest stirred up by her neighbor, the Coast Guard's Air Station Houston.

"Your father's daughter." Paddy sounded proud, but not happy. "You'll figure it out—you always do. And the Coast Guard won't evict you. Commander Wilder won't let them." Backlit by the sunlight behind him, his expression was unreadable.

"Wilder! He's leading the charge."

"Don't be too sure."

Sam hated it when her father used that superior tone. "Is that why you came here? To fill my head with ideas that Commander

Wilder is going to be my Galahad? You're wasting your time. Men! They always have an angle. You taught me that."

Her father deflated, a balloon pierced by the sharp point of her cynicism. "Aye. Leavin' your Ma and you—that'll be a sin I carry on my soul. I might not be able to make it up to the Almighty, but I aim to try to fix what's between the three of us."

"I saw what your leaving did to Ma. I'll not be forgivin' you."

"Then that'll be a burden you carry. But don't let my folly ruin your happiness." Paddy turned and grabbed her hands in his, surprising Sam before she could retreat. "I am sorry. I was a fool. Lessons often come too late, but now perhaps it was for the best."

"How can breaking a woman's heart be for the best?" Sam vibrated with anger—this was not the discussion for today, maybe not for any day. She'd shut him out; it was the only way she knew to protect herself. And she'd rather die than see him hurt her mother again.

"Break her heart, perhaps save her life," Paddy murmured, looking pained.

"What?" Sam wrenched her hands from his, then pushed at a lock of curly red hair, tucking it back under her ball cap as she flipped the brim around to the back.

Paddy's expression opened, as if he wanted to explain, reaching for the words before he gave his head a quick shake. "You've got your mother's eyes. So green—a piece of the Emerald Isle."

They were his eyes, not her mother's. Sam had always chaffed under the comparison, but he knew that. She narrowed her eyes as if focus would give her a clue as to the game he was playing. It didn't. It never did.

He dug into his front pocket and pulled out something silver that reflected the light. "Here. Take this." He pressed the object into Sam's hand.

A key.

Small and light—a key to a padlock maybe? "What's this to?"

"The answers, if you ever find yourself lookin' for some." He tried for a smile and then leaned into her. "If something happens, if I don't come back, look where you would expect to find something I hold dear."

A niggle of worry chased a chill down Sam's spine. "Never come back? What are you talking about?"

Patrick drew back, running a hand through his hair, standing it on end. "Phillip has a story. I'm tellin' ya', lass, it's a wild one. Didn't believe him at first. But, they got him spooked for sure."

"Uncle Phil? Spooked?" Sam couldn't imagine what it would take to scare the senior senator from Texas. Worried now, she couldn't keep the sharpness out of her voice. "About what?"

"I can't be tellin' you." His voice shook.

Sam could tell he was afraid. She grabbed his shoulders. "Da? Does this have something to do with your new well? The one you've leveraged your soul to drill?"

"You may be right there, lass."

"You need to tell me."

He shook his head. "Promise me you won't go looking unless I'm not there to give you the answers."

"No."

"Promise. It's bad business." He gave her a slight smile. "Please?"

Her father never asked nicely. "Okay."

"Say it."

"I promise."

"There." He seemed satisfied.

Whirling at the sound of running footsteps echoing off the tarmac, Paddy stiffened. Fear sliced across his face as he pulled away and then stepped back. He relaxed as two figures, one tall and broad, one small and slight, pounded around the corner and through the door.

"Over here." Geraldo motioned. A lean and lanky refugee with shaggy black hair, skin the color of pecan shells, a tentative smile, and a love for anything that flew, the kid had showed up out of the blue one day and stayed, despite Sam's best efforts to run him off.

Commander Wilder, the taller, broader of the two, followed on the boy's heels. Both of them skidded to a stop in front of Sam and Paddy. The boy's eyes, dark with worry, darted between Sam and her father. A look of bemused consternation softened the angled planes of the commander's face. A flush of embarrassment rose. The boy had oversold the danger. The commander should know Sam and her father lived life at the top of their lungs, and, while death might be threatened, they had yet to start shooting at each other.

Sam stashed the key in a pocket then crossed her arms and stepped back. Just like Wilder to dash into her hangar, loaded for bear like...Galahad. She snuck a look at her father. He knew what she was thinking, and he raised an eyebrow to tell her so, which made her smile.

Family.

Suddenly a bit self-conscious, Sam tugged at the damp white tank top that clung to her skin. Not a good choice in hindsight, but it was the coolest thing she had that was clean. Under the intensity of the commander's gaze, she tried not to squirm.

Commander Kellen Wilder. Just his voice warmed her to the core and sent her thoughts tumbling in a direction she didn't want them to go. She'd been fantasizing about him since she'd met him. Tall, broad, and tapered, with blue eyes and dark, almost black hair which he wore a trifle too long to suit his higher-ups, Commander Wilder was a perfect poster boy for the Coast Guard. Whether he intended it or not, his mere presence demanded attention.

Yep, he'd been the stuff of dreams...right up until the Coast Guard focused on getting her operation kicked off the airport. "Can I help you?" Sam kept a mildly interested expression on her face as she met him eye-to-eye. When his gaze shifted over her shoulder to the plane she'd been working on, she allowed herself a moment to appreciate all of Kellen Wilder. She didn't feel bad about that—he invited the attention in the almost-too-tight flight suit, which he wore well, damn him.

The commander looked a bit curious as he glanced between

Sam and her father. "The boy here told me I needed to hurry. Apparently he was worried about a future homicide."

"Homicide?" Sam said as if the idea appealed to her. "None imminent, but my finger is still on the trigger."

Donovan shifted, but he let her do the talking, which put her guard up.

Wilder extended a hand as he clasped the older man's shoulder with the other. "Paddy."

There was warmness between then, and affection, a respect of sorts. "Wilder." The older man gave the commander's hand a solid shake, then stepped back.

To Sam, the fact that her father liked Kellen Wilder was a huge red flag.

Paddy cleared his throat. "I've got to go, Mary—"

Sam silenced him with a shake of her head. Despite the hundreds of times she'd lectured him on the difficulty of being taken seriously as a woman in the man's world of aviation, he refused to understand her adoption of a more gender-neutral moniker.

"Sam," her father quickly corrected. When he said her name, it had a note of finality to it.

She felt a frisson of panic, a need to keep him there, to keep him safe from himself and whomever he was running from this time. "Da?"

"You'll know." He gave her a wink.

With that, he turned and was gone.

Sam stared after him, working to breathe, as if he'd taken all of the air with him.

***

End of Sample
To continue reading, be sure to pick up _Deep Water_ at your favorite retailer.

ALSO BY DEBORAH COONTS

The Lucky O'Toole Vegas Adventure Series

Wanna Get Lucky? (Book 1)

Lucky Stiff (Book 2)

So Damn Lucky (Book 3)

Lucky Bastard (Book 4)

Lucky Catch (Book 5)

Lucky Break (Book 6)

Lucky the Hard Way (Book 7)

Lucky Ride (Book 8)

Lucky Score (Book 9)

Lucky Ce Soir (Book 10)

Lucky Enough (Book 11)

Other Lucky O'Toole Books

The Housewife Assassin Gets Lucky

(Co-written with Josie Brown, author of the Housewife Assassin series)

Lucky O'Toole Original Novellas

Lucky in Love (Novella 1)

Lucky Bang (Novella 2)

Lucky Now and Then (Novella 3)

Lucky Flash (Novella 4)

The Brinda Rose Humorous Mystery Series

90 Days to Score (Book 1)

The Kate Sawyer Medical Thriller Series

After Me (Book 1)

Deadfall (Book 2)

Other Novels

Deep Water (romantic suspense)

Crushed (women's fiction)

Deborah Coonts swears she was switched at birth. Coming from a family of homebodies, Deborah is the odd woman out, happiest with a passport, a high-limit credit card, her computer, and changing scenery outside her window. Goaded by an insatiable curiosity, she flies airplanes, rides motorcycles, travels the world, and pretends to be more of a badass than she probably is. Deborah is the author of the Lucky O'Toole Vegas Adventure series, a romantic mystery romp through Sin City. *Wanna Get Lucky?*, the first in the series, was a *New York Times* Notable Crime Novel and a double RITA™ Award Finalist. She has also penned the Kate Sawyer Medical Thriller series, the Brinda Rose Humorous Mystery series, as well as a couple of standalones. Although often on an adventure, you can always track her down at:

www.deborahcoonts.com
deborah@deborahcoonts.com

facebook.com/deborahcoonts

twitter.com/DeborahCoonts

instagram.com/deborahcoonts

pinterest.com/debcoonts

bookbub.com/authors/deborah-coonts

amazon.com/author/debcoonts

goodreads.com/DeborahCoonts